THE ICARUS GIRL

THE
ICARUS
GIRL

HELEN OYEYEMI

VIKING
CANADA

VIKING CANADA

Published by the Penguin Group

Penguin Group (Canada), 10 Alcorn Avenue, Toronto, Ontario, Canada M4V 3B2
(a division of Pearson Penguin Canada Inc.)
Penguin Group (USA) Inc., 375 Hudson Street, New York, New York 10014, U.S.A.
Penguin Books Ltd, 80 Strand, London WC2R 0RL, England
Penguin Ireland, 25 St Stephen's Green, Dublin 2, Ireland (a division of Penguin Books Ltd)
Penguin Group (Australia), 250 Camberwell Road, Camberwell, Victoria 3124, Australia
(a division of Pearson Australia Group Pty Ltd)
Penguin Books India Pvt Ltd, 11 Community Centre, Panchsheel Park, New Delhi –
110 017, India
Penguin Group (NZ), cnr Airborne and Rosedale Roads, Albany, Auckland 1310,
New Zealand (a division of Pearson New Zealand Ltd)
Penguin Books (South Africa) (Pty) Ltd, 24 Sturdee Avenue, Rosebank, Johannesburg 2196,
South Africa

Penguin Books Ltd, Registered Offices: 80 Strand, London WC2R 0RL, England

First published in Canada by Penguin Group (Canada), a division of Pearson Penguin Canada
Inc., 2005. Simultaneously published in the United States by NAN A. TALESE, an imprint
of DOUBLEDAY, a division of Random House, Inc.
First published in Great Britain by Bloomsbury Publishing.

1 2 3 4 5 6 7 8 9 10

Copyright © Helen Oyeyemi, 2005

*Publisher's note: This book is a work of fiction. Names, characters, places and incidents either are the
product of the author's imagination or are used fictitiously, and any resemblance to actual persons living
or dead, events, or locales is entirely coincidental.*

Book design by Gretchen Achilles

Manufactured in the United States.

LIBRARY AND ARCHIVES CANADA CATALOGUING IN PUBLICATION

Oyeyemi, Helen
    The Icarus girl / Helen Oyeyemi.

ISBN 0-670-04534-9

    I. Title.

PR6115.Y49I23 2005   823'.92   C2004-905403-1

British Library Cataloguing in Publication Data available
American Library of Congress Cataloguing in Publication Data available

Visit the Penguin Group (Canada) website at **www.penguin.ca**

This is all for

Mary Oyeyemi

(Sorry about that time I pretended to be the Angel of Death.)

'Tony

and the other 'Tony, from before.

Alone I cannot be—
For Hosts—do visit me—
Recordless Company . . .

—EMILY DICKINSON,
The Complete Poems of Emily Dickinson

I

ONE

———

"Jess?"

Her mother's voice sounded through the hallway, mixing with the mustiness around her so well that the sound almost had a smell. To Jess, sitting in the cupboard, the sound of her name was strange, wobbly, misformed, as if she were inside a bottle, or a glass cube, maybe, and Mum was outside it, tapping.

I must have been in here too long—

"Jessamy!" Her mother's voice was stern.

Jessamy Harrison did not reply.

She was sitting inside the cupboard on the landing, where the towels and other linen were kept, saying quietly to herself, *I am in the cupboard.*

She felt that she needed to be saying this so that it would be real. It was similar to her waking up and saying to herself, *My name is Jessamy. I am eight years old.*

If she reminded herself that she was in the cupboard, she would know exactly where she was, something that was increasingly difficult each day. Jess found it easier not to remember, for example, that the cupboard she had hidden in was inside a detached house on Langtree Avenue.

It was a small house. Her cousin Dulcie's house was quite a lot bigger, and so was Tunde Coker's. The house had three bedrooms, but the smallest one had been taken over and cheerily cluttered with books, paper and broken pens by Jess's mum. There were small patches of front and back garden which Jess's parents, who cited lack of time to tend them and lack of funds to get a gardener, both readily referred to as "appalling." Jess preferred cupboards and enclosed spaces to gardens, but she liked the clumpy lengths of brownish grass that sometimes hid earthworms when it was wet, and she liked the mysterious plants (weeds, according to her father) that bent and straggled around the inside of the fence.

Both the cupboard and the house were in Crankbrook, not too far from Dulcie's house in Bromley. In Jess's opinion, this proximity was unfortunate. Dulcie put Jess in mind of a bad elf—all sharp chin and silver-blonde hair, with chill blue-green lakes for eyes. Even when Dulcie didn't have the specific intention of smashing a hole through Jess's fragile peace, she did anyway. In general, Jess didn't like life outside the cupboard.

Outside the cupboard, Jess felt as if she was in a place where everything moved past too fast, all colours, all people talking and wanting her to say things. So she kept her eyes on the ground, which pretty much stayed the same.

Then the grown-up would say, "What's the matter, Jess? Why are you sad?" And she'd have to explain that she wasn't sad, just tired, though how she could be so tired in the middle of the day with the sun shining and everything, she didn't know. It made her feel ashamed.

"JESSAMY!"

"I am in the cupboard," she whispered, moving backwards

and stretching her arms out, feeling her elbows pillowed by thick, soft masses of towel. She felt as if she were in bed.

A slit of light grew as the cupboard door opened and her mother looked in at her. Jess could already smell the stain of thick, wrong-flowing biro ink, the way it smelt when the pen went all leaky. She couldn't see her mum's fingers yet, but she knew that they would be blue with the ink, and probably the sleeves of the long yellow T-shirt she was wearing as well. Jess felt like laughing because she could see only half of her mum's face, and it was like one of those *Where's Spot?* books. Lift the flap to find the rest. But she didn't laugh, because her mum looked sort of cross. She pushed the door wider open.

"You were in here all this time?" Sarah Harrison asked, her lips pursed.

Jess sat up, trying to gauge the situation. She was getting good at this.

"Yeah," she said hesitantly.

"Then why didn't you answer?"

"Sorry, Mummy."

Her mother waited, and Jessamy's brow wrinkled as she scanned her face, perplexed. An explanation was somehow still required.

"I was thinking about something," she said, after another moment.

Her mum leaned on the cupboard door, trying to peer into the cupboard, trying, Jess realised, to see her face.

"Didn't you play out with the others today?" she asked.

"Yeah," Jessamy lied. She had just caught sight of the clock. It was nearly six now, and she had hidden herself in the landing cupboard after lunch.

She saw her mum's shoulders relax and wondered why she got so anxious about things like this. She'd heard her say lots of times, in lowered tones, that maybe it wasn't right for Jessamy to play by herself so much, that it wasn't right that she seemed to have nothing to say for herself. In Nigeria, her mother had said, children were always getting themselves into mischief, and surely that was better than sitting inside reading and staring into space all day. But her father, who was English and insisted that things were different here, said it was more or less normal behaviour and that she'd grow out of it. Jess didn't know who was right; she certainly didn't feel as if she was about to run off and get herself into mischief, and she wasn't sure whether she should hope to or not.

Her mother held out a hand, and grasping it, Jess reluctantly left her towel pillows and stepped out on to the landing. They stood there for a second, looking at each other, then her mother crouched and took Jessamy's face in her hands, examining her. Jess held still, tried to assume an expression that would satisfy whatever her mother was looking for, although she could not know what this was.

Then her mum said quietly, "I didn't hear the back door all day."

Jessamy started a little.

"What?"

Her mum let go of her, shook her head, laughed. Then she said, "How would you like for us to go to Nigeria?"

Jess, still distracted, found herself asking, "Who?"

Sarah laughed.

"Us! You, me and Daddy!"

Jess felt stupid.

"Ohhhhh," she said. "In an aeroplane?"

Her mum, who was convinced that this was the thing to bring Jessamy out of herself, smiled.

"Yes! In an aeroplane! Would you like that?"

Jess began to feel excited. To Nigeria! In an aeroplane! She tried to imagine Nigeria, but couldn't. Hot. It would be hot.

"Yeah," she said, and smiled.

But if she had known the trouble it would cause, she would have shouted "No!" at the top of her voice and run back into the cupboard. Because it all STARTED in Nigeria, where it was hot, and, although she didn't realise this until much later, the way she felt might have been only a phase, and she might have got better if only

(oh, if only if only if ONLY, Mummy)

she hadn't gone.

Jess liked haiku.

She thought they were incredible and really sort of terrible. She felt, when reading over the ones she'd written herself, as if she were being punched very hard, just once, with each haiku.

One day, Jess spent six hours spread untidily across her bedroom floor, chin in hand, motionless except for the movement of her other hand going back and forth across the page. She was writing, crossing out, rewriting, fighting with words and punctuation to mould her sentiment into the perfect form. She continued in the dark without getting up to switch on a light, but eventually she sank and sank until her head was on the paper and her neck was stretching slightly painfully so that she could watch her hand forming letters with the pencil. She didn't sharpen the pencil, but switched to different colours instead, languidly patting her hand out in front of her to pick up a pencil that had rolled into her path. Her parents, looking in on her and seeing her with her cheek pressed against the floor, thought that she had fallen asleep, and her father tiptoed into the room to lift her into bed, only to be disconcerted by the gleam of her wide-open eyes over the top of her arm. She gave no resistance to his putting her into bed and tucking her in, but when her father checked on her again after three hours or so, he found that she had noiselessly relocated herself back on the floor, writing in the dark. The haiku phase lasted a week before she fell ill with the same quietness that she had pursued her interest.

When she got better, she realised she didn't like haiku anymore.

In the departure lounge at the airport, Jess sat staring at her shoes and the way they sat quietly beside each other, occasionally clicking their heels together or putting right heel to left toe.

Did they do that by themselves?

She tried to not think about clicking her heels together, then watched her feet to see if the heels clicked independently. They did. Then she realised that she had been thinking about it.

When she looked about her, she noticed that everything was too quiet. Virtually no one was talking. Some of the people she looked at stared blankly back at her, and she quickly swivelled in her seat and turned her attention on to her father. He was reading a broadsheet, chin in hand as his eyes, narrowed with concentration behind the spectacle lenses, scanned the page. He looked slightly awkward as he attempted to make room for the paper across his knees; his elbows created a dimple in the paper every time he adjusted his position. When he became aware of her gaze, he gave her a quick glance, smiled, nudged her, then returned to his reverie. On the bench opposite her sat an immense woman wearing the most fantastical traditional dress she had ever seen. Yellow snakes, coiled up like golden orange peel, sprang from the beaks of the vivid red birds with outstretched wings which soared across the royal blue background of the woman's clothing. Jess called it *eero ahty booby* whenever she tried to imitate her mum's pronunciation of it. Sometimes, when her mum was having some of her friends around, she would dress up in traditional costume, tying the thick cloth with riotous patterns around her head like a turban, looping it over her ears. She would put on the knee-length shirt with the embroidered scoop neck, and let Jess run her fingers over the beautiful stitching, often gold, silver or a tinselly green. Then her mum would run her fingers over the elaborate embroidery herself, and smile, turning her head from side to side as she regarded her reflection in the bedroom mirror. *Iro ati buba*, she would say, lapsing from her English accent into the broad, almost lilting Yoruba one. *This is iro ati buba*. Then she would wrap the longest, widest sheet of dyed cloth around her waist, over the bottom half of the scoop-necked top, and fold it over once, twice, three times, her fingers moving across the material with the loving carelessness of one who could dress this way in the dark. Her mum, standing smiling in the bedroom, her costume so bright it seemed to stretch the space between the walls.

The thought made Jess smile as she sat waiting with everyone else, looking at this woman, who stared back at her, her small eyes squinting out from their folds of flesh, the fluorescent lighting giving her skin an odd, flat finish, as if the dark brown was catching light and not throwing it out again. Jess kept her eyes fixed on the woman, caught by her gaze, gradually growing frightened, as if somehow she could not look away or let this woman out of her sight. Would that be dangerous, to *not* look while being looked at?

On the plane, Jess threw a tantrum.

It was Nigeria. That was the problem.

Nigeria felt ugly.

Nye. Jeer. Reeee. Ah.

It was looming out from across all the water and land that they had to cross in the aeroplane, reaching out for her with spindly arms made of dry, crackling grass like straw, wanting to pull her down against its beating heart, to the centre of the heat, so she would pop and crackle like marshmallow. She had been reading about Nigeria for the past month, and her excitement had grown so much that she had nearly succumbed to that peculiar febrile illness of hers again, but recovered just in time for the yellow fever and hepatitis C injections that she needed. The anti-malaria tablets were disgusting, coating her tongue like thick, sickly chalk.

It was the combination of the two white pills and the leering idea of her mother's country that made her begin to struggle and thrash, screaming, half dangling headfirst out of the seat, nearly choking on her seat belt, fighting off her mother's hands as she snaked herself away from the little chalk circles. Inside her head, she could hear her skin blistering, could almost feel it, and she tried to outscream the sound. She could hear herself. She felt other people looking, heard people stirring, muttering, and felt good to be making this sharp, screeching, hurting noise. Yet some part of her was sitting hunched up small, far away, thinking scared thoughts, surprised at what was happening, although this was not new. She panted as she shook off her father's restricting hands. Sweat was beading on her forehead and her eyelids, and she felt the prickly feeling at the back of her eyelids and that familiar sensation of her eyes almost involuntarily rolling up wards onto her head. It was a kind of peace.

Then her mother, who for a while now had been speaking in a pleading monotone, said something with a sharp buzz, something that she didn't quite catch, and slapped her hard. It was oddly like a cooling wind on her skin, the sting that remained when her mother's hand had left her, and she stopped struggling and hung limp from the side of her seat, her mouth a small, open O, until her father, murmuring reproachfully, settled her properly into the aeroplane seat.

He looked at her, dabbed at her cheek with his handkerchief. "Never mind about the pills for today," he said quietly and put them back into her pillbox.

After a while the minutes sank into each other, and Jess sat still, her eyes following the two air hostesses up and down the aisles. Beside her, she felt her father's heavy, musky-smelling presence, the weight of his arm pressing along hers, heard his shallow breathing as he slept. An air hostess whose name badge said "Karen" smiled quickly at Jessamy, and sleepy as she was, Jess somehow understood that this woman, her jaunty red cap perched atop a black bun of hair, was not smiling at her in particular, but at a child, at the idea of a child. Because she was an air hostess. Smiling at a child. That was what she was supposed to do. Jess gave a drowsy smile in return.

Jess fell asleep slowly, her hand reaching for her dad's. She closed her eyes completely, and the darkness was warm and quiet, like a bubble lifting her higher even than the aeroplane.

Her father reached out and enfolded her hand in his far bigger one. She turned her head a fraction in his direction, opening her eyes into slits. His dishevelled, sandy hair obscured his forehead, and his greeny-blue eyes were half open; they looked darker with the overhead light switched off. He had taken off his glasses, and she could just about make out the two small indents they had left on the bridge of his nose. He gave her a disorientated, inquisitive smile. *Are you okay, Jessamy? Really okay? I'm worried*. But she was too tired to move her face, and, letting her eyes linger on his face for a few seconds longer, to acknowledge the smile, she closed her eyes again and slept, and dreamed a confusing dream that had people and animals and dancing coloured shapes moving in and out of it.

TWO

———

Jess had not expected Nigeria to be this hot.

She stood at the luggage carousel, holding her mum's hand, trying to ignore the stickiness of her orange-and-white button-up top. She could feel the sweat collecting into a big drop in the hollow of her back, and wriggled her shoulders a little, wondering if it would drop and splash the floor like water from a bucket.

The heat was emptying her out already.

Two thin, tall men in khaki shorts were helping people to load their luggage off the carousel. Luggage was moving past her in a disorderly line, some of it big, bulgy plastic bags, striped red-and-white, some suitcases and trunks. The men were laughing and calling out to each other in Yoruba, flashing white smiles at each other, sometimes staggering with the force of their laughter.

Her father was standing near the carousel, his hands in his pockets, watching out for their luggage. Another thing she had not expected: she hadn't expected him to seem so . . . well, out of place. His face was wet with perspiration and flushed pink, and even the way that he stood marked him out as different. The people milling around him all glanced pointedly at him as they passed; their glances were slightly longer than usual, but not out-right stares—more the kind of look that Jess herself gave when passing a statue or a painting. The acknowledgement of an oddity. She looked at him, willing him, at least, to look at her.

He didn't.

Her mum smiled at her. There was something in the smile that Jess could only vaguely describe as *careful*.

It was the same smile that she had worn when they had been going through customs. The official behind the desk had a neat moustache and goatee beard, and his expression had been polite; in fact, overpolite. So solicitous that his face was immobile, and Jess, looking at him from a short distance beneath the counter, thought that he was somehow making fun of her mother. The man had flicked his gaze over her with the same small smile on his face.

Had he been thinking, *Who is this woman who has a Nigerian maiden name in a British passport, who stands here wearing denim shorts and a strappy yellow top, with a white man and a half-and-half child?* Had her mother also put herself in his place, looked at herself from his side of the counter and found herself odd and wanting?

Maybe that had been the carefulness in her smile.

All that the eight-year-old Jess knew was that the smile wasn't a particularly happy one, and that her mother hadn't smiled like that in England.

She felt herself, also, growing careful.

Her mum tugged at her hand, and Jessamy saw a real smile spread across her mother's face, as if she had just remembered sunshine.

"We're going to see Grandpa and your cousins!"

Jess nodded and gave a half-hearted, placebo smile while she thought about this. When she thought of her Nigerian grandfather and cousins, she saw a bustle of people, a multitude, all of them moving so quickly that she couldn't see their faces, and any one of them could be family. Her grandfather would have a walking stick. Would he have a walking stick? Her mum said that he was very active and strong, and so suspicious of people that he liked to do things for himself to make sure that they were done properly. He would have grey hair, like her English grandfather, but his hair would be springy and less silver, sprouting like steel wool. But his face—there was none. She felt her lungs constrict and turned her head away from her mum for a second, struggling to breathe in the humid air.

If she couldn't see him, then how would he see her?

Once they were outside, which was only fractionally cooler than the inside, her father had no sooner tipped the man who had helped them with the luggage than several people hurried across the white paving from where they had been lounging against their parked cars. The sun struck everything, bouncing ultra-shiny colours into Jessamy's line of vision, and Jessamy, now silently clutching her father's hand, thought she might begin to scream when she saw the men, some in the loose, flapping gowns worn, she would later learn, by Nigerian Muslims, descending upon her father as if they wished to swallow him up.

"Here, sir! I have very nice car for you here, air-conditioned, right size to take your luggage, now," one man was bellowing above the din of the others.

"Only ten thousand naira to Ibadan or Ife, or I go take you to Abuja, where there is a Hilton," pressed another one.

They were surrounded by the folds of clothing, the gesturing hands, the smell of ironed clothes and sweaty bodies. Jess felt as if the heat was intensifying, even though she could only see chinks of sunlight through the gaps in the milling gathering around them. She clutched her father's fingers for dear life, her hands alternately sticking and sliding as the pads of her fingers caught his fingernails.

Her father, standing defensively by his suitcase, darted a confused look at her mother, who quite suddenly took charge and began to outshout them all, speaking rapidly in a mixture of Yoruba and broken English.

"*Wetin* you be wanting, now? You no go want us to chop? . . . Ten thousand naira, *sae* everything is okay, or *ori e ti darun?*"

Both her mother and the people surrounding her began to laugh—mysterious laughter, like a liquid, bubbling wall, leaving Jess and her father drenched with it, but still outside. Jess rubbed her forehead with her free hand and squinted at her mother, who seemed to be transformed by her bargaining, bantering tone, then up at her father, who shrugged, putting his own hand to his face to adjust his glasses, which were slipping down the bridge of his nose.

Minutes later, her mother had selected a driver, and the other hopefuls scattered, grumbling good-naturedly. "Daniel, could you help the driver?" she said, abruptly slipping back into her smooth English accent as she took Jess's hand again and led her to the long, egg-brown sedan that would take them to Ibadan.

Seeing her mother get into the front seat of the car and slip her sunglasses on, Jess sat in the backseat of the car. She turned her face upwards so the air-conditioning cooled her skin, and opened her mouth and gulped loudly, imagining that she was filling up with cold air like a balloon. Then she looked out of the side window, straight at a man who was leaning against his car, his jaw working as he chewed gum. He was almost impossibly tall and wearing a rough cotton shirt and a pair of long shorts that reached down to his calves. The light colours contrasted with his skin, and he stood out in gaunt relief against his cream-coloured car, like a paper cutout. He was looking at her, but in a distracted manner, as if she was something to look at while he waited for something else.

The car rocked downwards as her father loaded his suitcase into the back, and she heard his shoes clicking on the white pavement as he began to walk around the car. She carried on looking at the man who had laughed. She even pressed her fingers against the dusty window and brought her face closer to it, peering at him. He watched her laconically, slapping flies away as he chewed. Her father, puffing slightly, opened the car door and threw himself down onto the seat beside her. "All right, Jessamy?" he asked, cheerfully, and although she didn't turn from the window, she felt cooler, as if a lone scrap of home had just blown into the car. England, where people who stared at you would shift their eyes away with an embarrassed, smiling gesture if you stared back. England, where people didn't see you, where it was almost rude to, wrong to.

Would her cousins be like this? Would they look at her, then see her, and just not really . . . well, *care*? See her, and leave her looking, trying to see something?

Then, as the driver got into the seat beside her mother and started up the car, chattering in Yoruba, the man suddenly widened his eyes so that the whites seemed enormous and luminous, and gave a short laugh again as she drew away from the window, startled.

Her father fanned himself with a copy of a Nigerian newspaper that he'd bought as they were leaving the airport. The car began to move away. The man in cream mouthed something.

"Mummy," she said, finally, when the man who had laughed was out of sight and they were moving down a seemingly interminable length of road.

Her mum paused in her conversation with the cabdriver.

"Jess?"

"What does oh-yee-bo mean?"

Her mum twisted around in her seat, looking puzzled.

"What?"

"A man just said it to me."

The cabdriver looked into the rearview mirror and laughed.

"He probably meant *oyinbo*. It means somebody who has come from so far away that they are a stranger!"

Jess settled back against the leather seat, fiddled with her seat belt.

"Oh."

Her father looked up distractedly from a column he was reading about the Nigerian president.

"That's a bit of a shabby thing to say . . ."

He looked at Jess and winked, and she smiled at him.

The driver said something in Yoruba.

Her mother, who had pushed her sunglasses onto the top of her head so that they settled on her thick, slightly frizzy hair, seemed restive. When the driver spoke, she looked at him and said, in a slightly sharper tone than usual, "I think we should speak in English, so everyone can understand."

Mr. Harrison stamped his feet to applaud his wife's sense of fair play.

"Bravo, Sarah!"

He beamed at her, his hair standing on end as usual, and Jessamy smiled too, in preparation for the unifying smile, the smile that they would all be smiling because it was important that they could all understand and share this country too.

It didn't come.

Her mother turned back in her seat and began a discussion with the driver about several places that she used to know in the Lagos area.

In English.

THREE

When they arrived at the Bodija house, Jess's grandfather calmly greeted her mother as if all the things that Jess's mum had told her had happened weren't true, as if it had been just yesterday that he had sent her to England to go to university, not fifteen years ago, a period of time in which she, Sarah, had properly grown up, and her mother, his wife, had died. As if it didn't matter that she had stayed away for so long.

Gbenga Oyegbebi's stillness contrasted greatly with the constant movement of Jessamy's two aunts and her uncle. Aunty Biola had been looking out for the car, and called Uncle Kunle to help her open the main gate (Gateman was eating a late lunch), and Jess immediately saw the three figures jumping up and down at the gate, waving with barely controlled excitement before the car had even drawn close.

Jessamy's cousins had been slightly more reserved. The five older than her, Aunty Funke's and Uncle Kunle's children, greeted her with tentative but almost patronising smiles; the two youngest, Aunty Biola's children, stood as if in awe of her, surveying her clothes, her hair, her entire self with raised eyebrows, twisting their hands together.

She was surprised by her disappointment that none of her cousins was the right age to show an interest in her as a companion, although she had already had their names and ages recited to her by her mother, who had named them off by heart, repeating them as if by rote. Uncle Adekunle's children: Akinola, fourteen; Bisola, twelve; Ebun, eleven. Aunty Funke's children: Oluwatope, eleven; Taiye, ten. Aunty Biola's children: Oluwabose, five; Oluwafemi, four. There they all stood, an uncertain circle, and then her grandfather came forward, greeted her mother, shook hands with her father. Although he seemed mellower and smaller than the picture that her mother had painted for her over the years, Jess had a sudden and irrational fear that he might start shouting at her.

He looked at her, put his hands on his hips in mock consternation, and her cousins and her mother laughed. Her father, standing slightly outside the circle, smiled encouragingly at her. Her grandfather held out a hand. His hands were big and square, spadelike, the palms deeply etched and callused. She took a step towards him, smiling a wobbly, nervous smile that she could not feel on her face.

She did not know what was expected of her.

She had nearly reached him when suddenly, on an outward gust of air, he half said, half announced a name.

"Wuraola."

Who?

She froze, not knowing what to say or do.

Of course, she knew that Wuraola was her Yoruba name, the name that her grandfather had asked in a letter for her to be called when her mother had held her Nigerian naming ceremony. Wuraola means gold.

She *knew* all this . . .

But nobody had ever called her Wuraola, not even her mother, whom she could now see from the corner of her eye making anxious, silent gestures for her to go to her grandfather.

Here, in this stone-walled corridor where the sunlight came in through enormous, stiff mosquito screens over every window and her clothes clung to her like another skin, Wuraola sounded like another person. Not her at all.

Should she answer to this name, and by doing so steal the identity of someone who belonged here?

Should she . . . *become* Wuraola?

But how?

She could not make herself move forward, so she stayed where she was, avoided his touch, looked up into her grandfather's face, smiled and said quietly, but firmly, in her most polite voice "Hello, grandfather."

After they had taken baths, and Jess had been made to eat a little, her mother disappeared with her youngest sister, Aunty Biola, and her father befriended Uncle Kunle, who was clearly as newspaper-minded as he was, and wanted to talk about politics. Swiftly dropping a kiss onto her forehead, her father released her into her grandfather's clutches before mounting the stairs that led up to the roof balcony of the house, gesticulating wildly as he spoke, clutching a bottle of Guinness with his free hand. Her uncle followed closely behind, pointing downwards as if at some artefact that would prove him right beyond doubt, and saying emphatically, "No, no, it's quite clear to me and to everyone that the reason why they don't want Abiola for president is because he's a Yoruba man!"

So her grandfather did have a face. It was a broad, lined face;

the smile and frown lines ran deep into his skin, his eyes made smaller by the loosened flesh around them. He had the same wide, strong jawline with the determined set as her mother, and the same prominent cheekbones, although Jess could see that his were made angular more through the emaciation of age than anything else. He was quite short and moved about very quickly. He didn't have a walking stick.

As Jess sat in the parlour, keeping very still so that she wouldn't take up much space on the brown-and-white sofa, she allowed herself to stare openly and seriously at her grandfather, and he did the same. She felt as if she were a little piece of him that had crumbled off maybe, which he was examining for flaws and broken bits before deciding whether it was worth taking it to be reattached. It was impossible to tell what he thought of her.

She sat at a right angle from him, breathing out silence. He sat very upright (like her, she noted, with surprise), his hands on his knees, the crisp lines of his white shirt almost moulding him, fixing him still in her sight. They were both waiting, supposedly for her Aunty Funke to bring them some soft drinks (her grandfather had called them "minerals"), but really Jessamy sensed that they were waiting to see if they would like each other or not. She stared at him wide-eyed, unaware that she looked overly anxious with her bottom lip jutting out slightly below the top one. She sensed herself on the edge of a screaming fit, already beginning to hear her breath coming faster than usual, feel the flat tightening at the bottom of her stomach. She tried desperately to quash it. She couldn't, wouldn't, mustn't, start screaming at her grandfather. He was not like her English granddad at all. He was . . . someone, something, else, more hidden.

Finally, he smiled, and although his smile was bumpy because some of his teeth were jagged and broken, it was a warming, infectious smile that was reflected in his eyes. It made her smile widely in return. She felt as if the room had been lit up. He held out his arms, and she went across the room to him, almost running. She buried her face in his shirt, her nose wrinkling up as the scent of his cologne mixed with the nutty, sourish smell of camphor that filled the room. He put his arms around her, but gently, so that there was space between his forearms and her back, holding her as if she was too fragile to hug properly. Awkwardly, he patted her light, bushy aureole of dark brown hair, repeating, "Good girl. Fine daughter."

Her grandfather's words had a lyrical quality to them, and she felt lulled, as if she really could be Wuraola, this good girl, this fine daughter. She wondered, briefly, why her mum allowed some people to call her Sarah, and others to call her Adebisi.

Aunty Funke entered the room with a swish of cloth that smelt of Sunlight soap. Jess already knew her smell, but didn't look up from the starched white before her eyes. She heard the clink of the glass bottles being placed on the round table in the centre of the parlour, heard Aunty Funke speaking rapidly in rough, cascading Yoruba. Her grandfather replied quietly, moved a hand to beckon at Aunty Funke to open a bottle.

"What do you want to drink, Wuraola?"

Hearing his words rumble through his chest, she lifted her head and looked at bottles placed on the oval tray. Aunty Funke stood smiling indulgently at her, the bottle opener in one hand, the other hand paused to seize a bottle from the selection. Jess pointed at the Coke.

She looked into her grandfather's face again as they both waited for the hissing sound of gas escaping the bottle, and they both flinched a little from the sheer nakedness of contact between eye and eye. It wasn't unpleasant flinching, but the surprised movement of two who are accustomed to looking closely at other people, but unaccustomed to being seen.

She noticed that her drink tasted stronger, richer, more Coke-y than the cola at home, and she gulped the sweet liquid down eagerly, the taste becoming intermingled somehow with the framed map of Africa on the painted but peeling wall opposite her, the lion-shaped bronze clock, the shapes chasing each other around the neck and sleeves of Aunty Funke's well-fitting *boubou*. She could faintly hear the sound of her cousins playing out front, the younger ones shrieking over the sound of a ball going *smack smack smack* against the concrete of the floor. Her aunt took a seat and began asking her questions, but as usual she was too overwhelmed by taste and colour to speak properly. She could not say very much about herself and whether or not she liked Nigeria so far, because as yet, she knew nothing about anything. Her embarrassed silence spread out like a little pool towards her aunt, and soon her aunt rose and bustled out of the room, making some excuse in Yoruba to her grandfather.

Left alone again, Jessamy and her grandfather sat quietly, her arms now flung around his neck as she marvelled at how at ease she had begun to feel with him. Then, remembering her grandparents in England, she shuddered slightly, wondering if this grandfather would understand that sometimes people needed to have lights on.

"Wuraola, can it be that you are cold?"

Her grandfather sounded amused.

Jess shook her head vigorously, laughing as she did so. Cold! Here?

She looked to the doorway, over which was hung a cascade of vertically arranged brown-and-cream sandalwood beads. They were still swinging from the impact of her Aunty Funke's passing through, and you could see chinks of the landing through them. She could see patches of something else, too. Three of her cousins—she couldn't see clearly which ones, or even if they were boys or girls—stood there, peering curiously through at her, as she sat on their grandfather's lap.

Were they even really there?

She thought she sensed something like resentment in their expressions.

FOUR

"Do you know what your mother did?" Jess's grandfather said to her the next evening. They were in the parlour again. It was nearly dusk; orange light and growing shadows played on the walls. Jess was sitting at his feet, gingerly licking at a round, hard ball of nutty *adun*. He was wearing traditional costume, and she stared at the finely stitched blue-and-silver embroidered waves that ran around the bottoms of his trousers. She wanted to touch them to see if they really did stand out all bumpy. From the corner of her eye she could see her mother, who was curled up on the sofa opposite, engrossed in low-pitched conversation with Aunty Funke. Her mother had stopped speaking, and was gazing at Jess's grandfather with pursed lips. Running her tongue over her *adun* with a slurp, Jess decided to hold out on answering her grandfather for as long as possible. Her instinct that the conversation wouldn't be a good idea was confirmed when Aunty Funke stood and began clearing away, muttering that it was about time that she cleaned the kitchen. The meal had been finished for half an hour.

Jess's mum began helping Aunty Funke to clear away. It

looked strange, seeing her mum, dressed in a shapeless black vest and denim shorts, helping Aunty Funke, who was wearing a yellow *boubou* with green leaves on it. Even though the sleeves on Aunty Funke's *boubou* were rolled up in a businesslike manner so that they bulged just below her shoulders, Jess's mum still looked like the household help.

Jess licked her *adun* ball, and said nothing.

"Wait a minute," her grandfather said, dipping his fingers into the big plastic bowl filled with water. Aunty Funke, who had bent over the table to take the bowl, froze where she was, waiting patiently for him to finish. Using his other hand, her grandfather unhurriedly paddled the water and dribbled it over his fingers, working at his fingernails to remove leftover bits of *amala*. Bits of speckled green okra were swirling around in the water as well. When he removed his hands from the bowl, he shook them a little, dropping water onto the rug. He made a vague, impatient gesture to the general atmosphere, and Aunty Biola came in from outside, as if on cue, holding out a rough green hand towel. He grunted, dried his hands and thrust the towel back at her before silently accepting the toothpick that Aunty Funke offered him and reclining in his seat once more. Aunty Funke left with the plates, but Jess's mother hovered on the other side of the beaded door curtain.

"Wuraola."

Jess jumped when he brought his hand down on her shoulder. She looked up at him, licking the corners of her mouth.

"Mmmm?"

"I said to you: 'Do you know what your mother did?' and you say, 'Mmmm.' Is that respect?"

She squeezed one eye shut and peered at him with mock incredulity, and he laughed.

"I was saying 'mmmm' because you called me," she protested.

"Even then, it's yes, 'grandfather' . . . I mean, what is this 'mmmm'?"

Jess gave up.

"I don't know what my mother did."

(You're going to tell me and she's going to get angry. I can see it already because she's all nervous.)

Jess wasn't sure whose side she was supposed to be on if her grandfather told her something really bad and secret about her mother.

When her grandfather snapped his toothpick and didn't say anything else, she prompted him.

"Was it something really bad?"

"It was just something that she did."

"Yeah?"

(Good or bad?)

He spread his hands. "This is how your mother really is. Sometimes I think that she doesn't know what she's doing at all, at all, but she follows some other person inside her that tells her to do things that make no sense. There is no other way that someone could be so very stubborn, and not pay."

Not daring to look up, Jess reached out on impulse and touched part of the trouser embroidery.

"I sent her to learn medicine in England," her grandfather told her, his voice a mix of amusement and irritation. "Listen, this is what your mother is like. She hadn't even been there six months when she writes me a letter, telling me that she is now studying English. English literature! What job do you find in Nigeria that requires the knowledge of all these useless words? Different words for hot, for cold! Words describing white people, white things, every single story spun out in some place where WE don't exist! It has no value; in my eyes, it is to confuse . . ."

"Confuse, dissemble, obfuscate," Jess whispered.

"What?"

"Dissemble and obfuscate—they're two different words, same meaning: 'to confuse.'"

Silence. Jess heard her mother snort with laughter, then retreat, choking, down the corridor to the kitchen. She looked at her grandfather, whose lips were pinched so tightly together that they looked as if they had been sewn at the corners.

"Hmmm," he said. "Hmmm. I see you are the same."

They both laughed. It wasn't true, of course.

"Anyway, listen. It made me . . . I couldn't . . ." Her grandfather pounded his chest and let out a loud sigh that sounded the twisting of his heart.

"But didn't you want her to be happy?"

Her grandfather didn't answer her question, but arranged the splinters of toothpick on the table. Jess presumed that one or other of her aunts would soon appear to clear them up.

"Wuraola, your mother had no job, she was living far from home, and she was writing and saying that she would find some work and pay for her studies! Such nonsense! I can tell you that I was afraid of witchcraft. I was frightened that some enemy had laid a curse on her head so powerful that it had stolen every single bit of sense from her head."

"It couldn't have been that bad," Jess ventured.

Her grandfather exploded.

"She left her home, and she went to England, and studied English stories, and gave up her own, and gave up all her talk of healing people, and married some *omugo oyinbo* man who knows nothing, nothing at all—" His words slowed and he heaved a deep, snuffling sigh when he saw that Jess had dropped her *adun* ball on the floor and was staring at him wide-eyed, her mouth half open.

"What does *omugo* mean? Is it bad? Was that a bad thing you said about my dad?" Jess questioned, sternly. It sounded bad.

Her grandfather shook his head slowly as Aunty Funke reentered and swept up the toothpick shards.

"Just forget. Forget I said that. I mean . . . that I don't know who your father is; I don't know his people, I don't know what his *name* means and where it comes from. Harrison—what does that mean, Harry's son? Harris's son? Now take Oyegbebi—it means 'kingship lives here.'" He tapped his breastbone. "Here. Here is where kingship lives. I am a princely man, and my children therefore should be proud and strong. Everyone who hears my name and knows my people should know that. I don't know your father, I don't know his father, or what his people have done. It is something about your mother that made her do this, marry a man that she didn't know."

Jess made no reply. It was so breathtakingly obvious that knowing someone's name didn't mean that you knew them that she didn't even attempt to protest. He thought her name was Wuraola, but he was wrong.

"She didn't just take her body away from this place—she took everything. Nothing of her is left here," Jess's grandfather said, sounding more ruminative than upset. "But I must be vain. She dedicates two books to me, and I forgive her."

Jess laughed, then stopped when she realised that her grandfather wasn't laughing with her. He closed his eyes for a few moments and his mouth slackened.

"You are a fine daughter," he said, helping her up from the floor.

"That thing is not in you," he said, as they wandered outside.

One afternoon, Aunty Funke took Jess, Bose and Femi to the zoo.

"It's sponsored by the University of Ibadan, so most people just call it the UI zoo," Jess's mum explained to her at breakfast.

Her grandfather's driver was Gateman's brother, and Jess was finding it difficult to tell the difference between them. She sat in the back of the car, carefully keeping her knees from touching Bose's, and stared at the driver's face in the mirror, trying to differentiate him from his brother. She was also, of course, keeping an eye on Bose, who was speaking in a low voice to her little brother. Femi was tiny, the tiniest four-year-old that Jess had ever seen. He sat in the car in his khaki-coloured shirt and shorts, clutching a round, sweet, yeasty bun left over from breakfast, not eating it. He stared at her more than Bose did.

She focused once more on the driver, whose name she did not know. If his brother was generally known as Gateman, should he then be known as Driver? He was light-skinned and had a long nose. A thin slit of tribal marking crossed each of his cheeks, and as he drove, he spoke cheerfully to Aunty Funke, one hand occasionally coming up from the steering wheel to tug at his earlobe, rub the side of his nose. He was wearing the same squarish upright hat as Gateman; only his was dark brown to match his pressed trousers, whereas Gateman's was green. She nodded once or twice to acknowledge this, because it seemed to her important that there be a difference between a person and their sibling.

At the zoo, she wandered listlessly around, clutching a Gala roll her aunt had purchased from a street vendor on the way. She held it when they passed through the turnstiles and Aunty Funke paid their entry fees, explaining to the woman behind the glass screen that her niece from England was visiting. The woman smiled down at her and asked her how she was finding Nigeria. Yet again, Jess hadn't known what to say.

She still hadn't unwrapped her Gala. It was supposed to be "just like a sausage roll," but she couldn't simply unwrap it and eat it as if it really was a sausage roll when there were all these people milling around her, looking at her so deliberately that she was forced to lower her head and look at the shapes her feet were leaving in the sandy-coloured gravel that lined the paths. She could barely even acknowledge the animals. Some monkeys were climbing around each other in a cage; she could hear them but felt a heaviness, as if she couldn't lift her head under some burden. Here she was, half a world away, still feeling alien, still watching the ground.

Perspiration formed on her cheeks and she put the Gala in the pocket of her three-quarter-length trousers so that she could wipe her face with her hands, momentarily hiding herself to feel cooler.

The only thing that she really *looked* at was the enormous snake in the clear, reinforced glass box. It was dapple patterned, green and black, twined lethargically around a vast wooden branch, the forked ends pointing outwards to form a V independent of its thick, sinuous shape. Bose and Femi pressed their faces and fingers up against the glass, and Aunty Funke laughed at Jess, who stood as far back from the thing as she could. It was dark in the display room, and there was a smell of wet leaves and something tangier, more animal. She couldn't take her eyes off the snake. She found her lips moving, she was praying, but not in English, or even Yoruba, but in some loose, gabbling language that was born from her fear. She just knew that the snake was going to form itself into a whip, launch through the glass, sending sharp, brittle pieces flying everywhere to get them all and make them pay for putting it in a place where it was the focus. Weren't there supposed to be jungles in Africa?

Aunty Funke looked at her and gave a surprised, concerned half laugh. She seized Jessamy's hand and clasped it in her own for a few seconds, then gave the smaller, milky-coffee-coloured hand a pat before announcing that they were leaving.

It was falling to dusk by the time they returned, approaching the main house, in which her grandfather reigned from around the back of the compound where Driver had parked. It was sort of, but not quite like, an old-style compound, the kind that Jess had read about in the bustling, preparing month of suitcases and anti-mosquito cream, the month before they had left. The old-style compounds were supposed to be groups of buildings that housed related relatives of male lineage. Her grandfather's was organised this way, but built differently—his three-storey house, in which everyone congregated during the day, was in the middle, with Uncle Kunle's smaller bungalow directly in front of it, the single-storey house where Aunty Funke and her husband lived to the right, and Aunty Biola's to the left. The other houses stopped the light from reaching the centre, forcing it to push through at angles and in chinks, which was why the inside of her grandfather's house was often so dim and in shadow, except for the top floor and the balcony roof, which during the day were bathed constantly in waterfalls of gold. From where they were, Jess could see the railings running around the top of the roof balcony, and remembered the previous night when she had sat there alone, knees pulled up to her chin, seeing, properly seeing the stars for the first time, open-mouthed with wonder.

Aunty Funke explained that the compound had been this way since the 1870s, when her great-grandfather, who had died years before Jessamy was born, had had it built to house himself and his three wives, who each had children by him. Her grandfather had lived there in one of the bungalows right up until his father had died and he, as the eldest son, had inherited the compound. His brothers, sisters, half brothers and half sisters had all scattered across Nigeria, some as far as Minna and Abuja, others to Benin, Ife, Port Harcourt.

Aunty Funke and Jess were walking around a big grey building that was roughly the same size as the central one. The windows were coated with fine layers of dust, and the outside walls were streaked with fading white, as if the very stone was beginning to crumble away. Jess stared up and up, conscious of her hand caught in Bose's sweaty grip, and even of Femi holding Bose's hand on the other side. Aunty Funke flicked a brief glance upwards, too.

"This is the Boys' Quarters," she told Jess with a smile.

Jess was confused; her expression said it all.

Aunty Funke laughed.

"That doesn't mean that only boys can go in there, it's just that your great-grandfather had it built for his servants, a place for them to sleep and get their three square meals. He needed a whole troop of boys to keep the main house going, and to get water for the individual houses. It hasn't been used for years, because your grandfather hasn't needed servants—he gets us to do all the running around instead! To tell you the truth, because it's old, it's all faulty inside. Certainly not fit for anybody to live in!"

"Oh."

Aunty Funke had passed the edge of the house and walked out into its long shadow towards Jess's grandfather's house. Jess followed, her feet sinking into the gravel as the tender lump of a mosquito bite from a few days ago itched on her ankle. She considered bending to scratch it, but that would have meant letting go of Bose's hand, so she ignored it as she looked up at the points of lantern light that were already blazing from some windows in her grandfather's house. NEPA had already cut off the electricity.

When they had reached the back veranda, something, some feeling of additional heat on the skin at the base of Jess's neck perhaps, made her turn and look at the house that they had just left behind.

Something glittered from the still, solid darkness, something warm, alive.

There were three big windows at the top of the old building, and in the centre one she saw, quite clearly, shadows dancing in a corner just beneath the windowpane, as shadows tend to do when light shifts around its source.

There was lantern light in the window of the Boys' Quarters.

FIVE

———

That night was a virtually sleepless one. After seeing the light in the Boys' Quarters, Jess was unable to stop thinking about it. She lay in bed among her tumbled sheets, gaping without really being aware of it as she considered possibilities. For the first time in her life, she was at an imaginative loss. She couldn't think who could possibly live in that building without her grandfather's knowledge.

As soon as she was certain that everyone was asleep, Jess slipped out of bed and crept out of the room, quailing at first as she stood in the pitch-dark corridor, then relaxing as her eyes adjusted to the alarming shapes and objects that confronted her. Climbing the stairs to the roof balcony, she kept watch, listening to the sounds around her, jumping slightly every now and then when she looked over her shoulder at the looming darkness at the mouth of the staircase below. But no light burned in any of the windows of the empty building that night, and she strained her eyes so much with peering that for a few seconds she confused the clean, steady, white light of the stars with the orange radiance that she had glimpsed before, and her heart nearly stalled on her as she sat breathless, waiting for—

What?

In any case, nothing happened. She had to brave the staircase again and go back to bed as the sun was creeping over the rim of the horizon.

The next morning at breakfast Jess dipped her spoon into her Quaker Oats, then watched the porridge dribble back into the bowl and spatter against the rim as it rejoined the yellowing sugar that sat on top of it.

She pulled a face at it.

Her mum was sitting across from her, a lined notepad on the table in front of her, leaning with one elbow on the table mat, her face half cupped in her other hand, biro to her mouth as she looked into the space above, around, behind her daughter. When Jess played with her porridge, she blinked a little, but kept her gaze vague.

Jess spattered her porridge again.

"Do you not want that?"

"Nope."

"Do you want something else?"

"I don't know. What else is there?"

Sarah Harrison shrugged, her movements slow, unhurried. Jess, aware that there was something about the warm morning air that made you feel unbothered about anything much, eyed her mother attentively. She had only written about three lines on the pad in front of her. "I'm going to write AT LEAST four sides a day," Sarah had said to Jess, her captive audience in the sitting room since she had roped her into helping sit on the suitcases.

Four sides was an infinitesimal amount in comparison with the pages of her novel that remained to be written, and she couldn't even do that.

Deciding not to say anything that would put her mother into a bad mood, Jess waited.

"What else is there?" she repeated eventually.

Her mother scribbled a few more words on to the page before her. "Go and ask Aunty Funke," she said distractedly.

Jess wriggled off her chair and went down the hallway, past Aunty Anike, Uncle Kunle's wife, who was standing barefoot in a wrinkled sleeveless vest with a green-and-blue wrapper tied about her waist, busy ironing a pile of her grandfather's shirts and trousers. She smiled her good morning and continued to the landing, where the staircase went upwards to the roof and the corridor swerved right toward the kitchen. The crackling, static sound of the Radio OYO jingle filled the entire landing:

It's the nation's station!
Oh-why-oh!
It's a happy station!
Oh-why-oh!
It's your favourite station!
Oh-why-oh!
It's Radio Oh-why-oh!

Aunty Anike was singing out of sync with the radio so it sounded like an echo was in the house with them. Jess had to shuffle past her eleven-year-old cousins, Ebun and Tope, and her Aunty Biola, who were sitting on small, three-legged wooden stools with newspaper spread out before them, grating wet, peeled knobs of cassava into bowls. She held her breath so she didn't have to cope with the pungent, almost rotting smell.

They were making *gari*, and Jess, who had eaten *gari* with beans plenty of times, had not known that it was such a long and complicated process. Aunty Funke had explained it to her. The cassava had been left to soak the night before, so that the tough skins would be easier to peel, and when they had been peeled, they would be very finely grated and, once grated, sundried, and once sundried, fried in a sort of cauldron so that the little cassava shavings would crackle and puff up, and then they would be dried again so that they became hard and chewy. All that just to make it not taste like cassava! Jess thought it hardly worth the trouble.

Her father was sitting on a stool beside Aunty Biola, clumsily attempting to peel a cassava with a sharp flick-knife like the ones that the others were using. He wasn't making a very good job of it, as he struggled to keep a grip on the slippery cassava with one hand and make the rapid peeling motions with the other. "Oi, I'm an accountant, not a . . . a . . . well, a cassava peeler, you know!" he protested, as Ebun, Tope and Biola giggled at his attempts. Aunty Biola, her long, glossy weave pulled away from her face with a large silk scarf, took the knife from him and showed him how to peel the cassava. Her smile as she did so made Jess think that this probably wasn't the first time; probably not the second either. Or the third.

Her father smiled gratefully at Aunty Biola, then said "Right," several times, rolling up his sleeves and pushing up his glasses with an air of determination. Then he looked around and saw Jess backed up against the wall in the corner, nearly faint with suppressed laughter.

"That's it! I have to be a role model to my daughter! She can't see me fail, and that's why . . ." He let out a defeated puff of air, blowing his blondy-brown fringe upwards as he did so. "I give up."

He was greeted by derisive laughter, and got up and wandered off in a pretend huff. Jess continued into the kitchen. Aunty Funke was washing dishes at the sink, up to her elbows in frothy white. She turned her head as Jess entered with the bowl full of porridge, and laughed.

"Ehhh-ehhhh! Madam is too good for oats!"

Jess felt herself redden even though she knew that Aunty Funke was joking.

"I don't really like them," she said, shyly proffering the bowl.

Aunty Funke dried her hands and took the bowl from her, put it on the table.

"So what do you want to eat instead? Shall I make you some buns?"

Jess shook her head.

"Don't worry, Aunty. I'm not that hungry."

She turned towards the door and the cassava smell, but was nudged aside by her cousin Bisola, who burst in looking flustered, her hand on Bose's shoulder to stop her from wriggling away. Bose's hair had been combed out of her thick cornrows, and stood out around her head like a dark, springy bush, glistening with hair food and health. Jess smiled at her, and Bose smiled back, before complaining that she wanted Tope to do her hair, not Bisola, because Bisola pulled too hard and nearly broke her head open.

Bisola, looking peeved, cut across her cousin's protestations.

"Mama, I'm about to start braiding Bose's hair for her and I need a candle to burn the ends! Where have you moved them now?"

Aunty Funke yelped with surprise, making Jess jump. "Ah-ah! What do you mean by that? Your aunty Biola just bought another box of candles yesterday! Did you look in the supply room, or are you wasting my time, you this girl?"

was as if the dust that coated everything was muting even the rays of the sun. Everything was a still, uniform grey. Clearly, Aunty Funke was right: no one had bothered to come in here for years.

There was a rickety wooden table up against the wall that looked as if part of one of its legs had been eaten away by wood lice. It was an old-fashioned writing desk with an inkwell set in the corner. Its surface was covered with the film of dust that obscured everything else.

As she examined the tabletop a cockroach suddenly scuttled across it, and she jumped back.

After her pulse had stilled again, she turned and walked towards the end of the corridor, stepping carefully so that she didn't trip over anything. She touched the bluish walls as she did so, to remind herself that she really was there. She could hear and feel her nails scratching against the walls as she passed her hands over them. When she reached the end of the corridor, she stopped, disappointed, expecting there to be a staircase as there was in her grandfather's house. A staircase running straight through the house, leading ultimately to the balcony on the roof. There wasn't one, just a blank wall.

The staircase must, then, be at the other end of the corridor. She walked back, passing the old table.

Then her eye caught on something and she backed up, all thoughts of staircases and balconies and upstairs rooms completely forgotten.

On the surface of the tabletop, someone had disturbed the dust. Scrawled in the centre in lopsided lettering were the words

HEllO JEssY

She stared in silence for a few moments longer, and then turned and ran straight out of the door, running so hard that she couldn't see properly and the rush of air going past her brought tears to her eyes.

Bisola raised her hands in a gesture that was at once defensive and defiant.

"I checked, oh! They weren't there! So you haven't moved them?"

Aunty Funke turned back to the sink and began washing the dishes with a sort of controlled violence, slapping soapy water on them with both hands.

"What do you mean? Of course I haven't . . . Those candles haven't been moved at all, at all. You this girl! I just don't know! You are so LAZY that you don't want to help Bose to do her hair! Well, you still have to do the hair—you can just do plaiting for her until we find the candles, because they are in this house!"

Bisola retreated from the doorway, dragging Bose with her, muttering under her breath, shaking her cousin with a baleful glare when Bose made a final attempt to free herself at the staircase.

"I can't believe it! You ask her to do just one thing and it is too much for her." Her aunt railed after her, "Well, let me tell you something, fine young lady, if I should find those candles, you will be sorry for yourself, that is all I can say!"

Jess fled the kitchen and wandered back past the cassava graters, who were working in concentrated silence, and passed through the clinking curtain of beads at the parlour door. Should she go to the Boys' Quarters and find out if someone was living there?

Should she?

Or was she going to anyway, whether she should or not?

"Hello?"

Jess paused in the middle of the corridor, peering about her. It was so dim in here, despite the windows pouring in sunlight. It

She stopped when she had run all the way around the front of her grandfather's house, heading towards where she heard bantering shouts—noise, normal happy noise—and stood, hunched over, desperately dragging in breath, in the expanse of concrete laid out before the gates. She looked up from the sweat dripping over her brow when she noticed that all the noise had stopped, and saw that Taiye and Akinola, her two older boy cousins, were looking at her with a mixture of concern and amusement. Akin stood in an attitude of boyish enquiry, his nose wrinkled up as he squinted against the sun, holding a basketball loosely in his two hands, and Taiye's hands hung limply by his sides as if he had just dropped them from a raised position, marking Akin.

She wanted to tell them what had just happened to her, and that it meant something more scary than snake-scary. Snake-scary she could scream about and push away from her, but this! Someone was living in a place where no one lived, lighting things in the dark, had been watching her, had *seen* her, and knew her name. She couldn't help but think that this was a very bad thing.

But she couldn't tell them.

Because they were boys, because they were her cousins, because they belonged here and she didn't?

She didn't know.

"Sorry," she managed to whisper, then turned and ran back along the side of the house.

She ran into her father, who was emerging with her grandfather from his study at the end of the corridor. He swept her up into a bear hug, lifting her off the ground as he anxiously examined her face. She twisted her face away, burying her head into his T-shirt.

"Daddy, let's go home now!"

"Ah-ah!"

She heard the now familiar accent of alarm in her grandfather's voice, felt the air shift as he drew closer to her. She clung harder to her father.

"Is somebody doing something to my child that I can't know about? What is happening? Why can't you be happy in my house? Tell me and I will make it right, now!"

To that there was, could be, no reply. She gave a long, shuddering sob, almost a howl, and didn't lift her head.

"Jess," her father said quietly. "Jess, little girl!"

She sniffled, shifted her head and wriggled a little so that her wet cheek was up against his dry one. He smelt of aftershave.

HEllo JEssY.

Jessy?

The second time. This was the second time that someone had called her something that she had never been called by anyone before. First Wuraola, now Jessy. She'd always been *Jess* or *Jessamy*, never a halfway thing like Jessy.

Who was there, hiding in the Boys' Quarters, who called her halfway Jessamy?

She sighed, a faint, snuffling sound, the sound she always made when calming down, drifting off into the reverie that inevitably followed her panics. Her father was still there, and he still held her. She wondered if he wanted to ask her what was the matter. He probably didn't; he probably wanted her to tell him.

Be my daughter, Jessamy. Tell me.

He carried her into the parlour, closely followed by her grandfather, who was making distressed clucking sounds with his tongue. He set her down on the sofa then sat beside her, allowing her to crawl onto his lap and curl up against him. She closed her eyes for a second to draw more breath, still trying to think about the matter in hand without actually, really thinking about it.

She gave up.

In the darkness behind her eyelids, she could still see those words drawn by the unknown finger, drawn when her back had been turned, done noiselessly and quickly. Someone had been there, in the corridor, looking at her, knowing her name, writing her name. Then they had gone.

SIX

Jess was lying on the concrete floor at the bottom of the staircase that ran through the centre house, but she didn't look up at the sky because she was concentrating on the patches of warmth that were playing along her face. She could feel her eyelashes trembling slightly. She felt the fuzzy light disappear as if someone had stepped in the way, felt a hand brush against her cheek and then withdraw. She mumbled an incoherent protest and prised her eyes open.

A girl was standing silently above her, looking down at her with narrow, dark eyes, so dark that, to Jess, lying on the ground, they seemed pupil-less. There was something about her that was out of proportion. Was she too tall and yet too . . . small at the same time? Was her neck too long? Her fingers?

Jess hauled herself up, her hands dragging across the rough concrete, and shielded her eyes, squinting at the girl.

The girl had stepped back as if alarmed, although her face was calm. Her head was tipped to one side and she stood, thin legs apart, like a bird poised for flight; observing a dangerous animal that was about to lash out.

With the shade of her hand over her sun-dazed eyes, Jess realised that this was just an ordinary girl around her own age. She
gave a huge, gusty sigh, feeling her shoulders moving back with
the force of it.

"Hello, Jessy," said the girl. Her voice was heavily accented.

Jess started, then scrambled to her feet.

"Y-you?" she managed to say.

The girl repeated, "Hello, Jessy."

As if it was all that she knew how to say.

Jess looked at the girl carefully. She was slight, and her bushy
hair was tied into two big, round, springy puffs, one behind each
ear, with what looked like trailing, dirty white string. She
was barefoot, and her toes and feet were whitened with gravel
scratches and sand, and, Jess was sure, dust. Her dress was slightly
too big for her and looked uncomfortable, the button-up collar
tight around her neck but the brown-and-white, checked cloth
hanging off her narrow shoulders and ballooning out around her
until it trailed off just below her knees. The skin on her knees
and elbows was ashen and greyish in patches.

The girl stared at her and did not smile.

Neither did Jess, but she felt a smile coming as her relief grew.
So this was the person who knew her name, who had written it
on the table, then sped shyly away on her small, light feet when
she had seen her coming. The girl had probably heard Jess's parents calling to her while she had been exploring the compound
on her own. She smiled, finally, as the last piece of understanding fell into place. She took a few steps closer to the girl, to make
herself better heard.

"Do you live in the Boys' Quarters?"

The girl hesitated, as if listening for something, then said,
very quickly, in an exact match of Jess's voice, "D'you live in the
Boys' Quarters?"

She waited, eyeing Jess apprehensively, her mouth half open, breathing through her nostrils as if she had just made a great exertion. Jess laughed aloud with surprise, giggling into her hand as she took this in.

The girl continued to contemplate her seriously, standing still with her hands by her sides, although as Jess made the involuntary movement that accompanied her laughter, she saw the girl's hand move slightly, as if she, too, wanted to put a hand to her mouth.

"D'you speak English?" Jess asked, as the thought suddenly occurred to her.

"D'you speak English?" the girl said, perfectly naturally, as if she was the one who had thought to say it first.

The feeling clung to Jess that *she* was being asked the questions, and that there was perhaps something more to them, that she was actually being asked something else entirely. Yet the girl's face betrayed no flicker of understanding. Jess began to feel bewildered.

She swayed a little on her feet, tired from the sun, and sat down on the bottom step, looking thoughtfully at the girl. Clearly she had to ask something that would make her give an answer instead of another question.

"Where Do you live?" she asked, on impulse.

"Where Do you live?" It was said almost blithely, with a not-quite grin. A veritable Jessamy-echo.

Jess laughingly threw her hands up towards the sky. "What's your name?"

Again, that listening pause, as if someone was saying something to her, someone speaking on a frequency just higher (or lower?) than Jess could hear, and Jess wondered if the girl had some kind of hearing difficulty. There had been a girl in her class who was partially deaf and had that same concentration and focus when listening to someone speak.

Then the girl spoke, almost without moving her mouth, as if reluctantly: "My name is Titiola."

She shifted from foot to foot, then finally shone a smile as beautiful and fleeting as it was sudden. If Jess hadn't kept her eyes fixed on her she would certainly have missed it, because that glow wasn't waiting for anybody and had vanished in a millisecond, leaving the sober, solemn expression behind. Jess felt as if she was finally getting somewhere. She couldn't help but smile in return as a sort of offering in homage to that now-absent radiance of the girl's.

"Titi . . . sorry, I don't want to say it; I'll say it wrong, and I know your name means something. Um. What's your surname?"

Silence.

Jess spoke awkwardly now, feeling as if she wasn't being understood. "I mean . . . you know! My surname's Harrison. And yours?"

Silence.

Except that this time the girl spread her hands in a strange gesture, her palms turned upwards, her hands stretched out flat. She didn't look at Jessamy, but at her hands. Jess laughed because she didn't know what else to do.

"Um. OK. I don't know what to call you. Titiola?"

She pronounced it *Tee-tee-yo-la*, wincing as she said it, knowing that it sounded all wrong in her mouth, jarring.

The girl's head snapped up, her eyes widening.

"Titiola," she said sharply.

Jess could see that this wasn't going very well. The girl didn't seem to like her, and for some reason it was important to have her liking.

"How about," she said, almost desperately, one hand rubbing against her leg, seeking out the drying mosquito bite, "I call you Tilly?"

The girl withdrew her palms and folded her thin arms, seemed to consider.

"Well, Titi doesn't sound that much like Tilly. Tilly has all L's and not enough T's . . ."

The girl watched her, the corners of her eyes wrinkled up as if she was about to smile again.

"TillyTilly? Can I call you that? TillyTilly, I mean? It has two T's . . . and I don't want to get your real name wrong, and anyway, you call me Jessy when I'm actually Jessamy or just Jess, so Jessy isn't really my real name either . . ."

She trailed off as she realised that the girl was laughing. She didn't laugh like the other kids in Jessamy's class; her laugh was a dry, raspy chuckle that sounded like wheezing. Jess found that she liked it.

Jess laughed too, glad that the two of them were there, one standing, one sitting, in the sunshine, glad that she had been so eager to be friends with somebody for once. It was a peering through good and pretty coloured glass, this gladness, this feeling that someone had been around the compound, knowing who she was, and wanting to talk to her. She had never been sought out this way before. It was funny and pleasing, like a bubbling fizz growing in her stomach.

The girl paused in her laughter, and then looked over her shoulder. Curious, Jess looked too, but couldn't see anything except the Boys' Quarters, which stood tall and grey and empty. Beyond that, she supposed, was only the car park and the back road that led to the rest of the houses in Bodija.

"I need to go," the girl said, saying "go" on a winding-down breath, as if she were about to say something else, say what she had to go and do, but she didn't.

Jess leapt up from the staircase and was surprised to see the girl shrink as if expecting a blow. She began to back away, moving faster with each step.

"Wait! Um. Wouldyouliketobefriends?" Jess asked, anxiously.

The girl stopped stock-still for a few moments, then spoke softly and almost as quickly as Jessamy had.

"Yes."

Another swift, illuminating smile, then she added hastily, "Watch for a light tonight."

She turned and hurtled away from where Jess stood, moving past the Boys' Quarters and around the back of the car park in what felt to Jess, who could hardly follow her figure for the sheets of sunlight wobbling down, like seconds.

Jess thoughtfully climbed the steps up to the middle floor. The air smelt like a mixture of toast and baking bread. Aunty Funke was supervising Tope, and Akin was grunting as he poured cassava from one huge pot into another; they were at the final stage of the *gari* making in the kitchen, and steam billowed from the open kitchen door. Her mother had gone shopping with a carload of old friends. She had tried to persuade Jessamy to come along, but Jess, who had been to the amusement park with her mother, father and these same friends the day before, demurred. It had been almost, but not quite, as bad as the zoo.

In the parlour, she could hear Aunty Biola attempting to teach her father Yoruba, collapsing into helpless giggles whenever he mispronounced his vowels, giving them the flat English sound instead of lifting them upwards with the slight outward puff of breath that was required. Jess couldn't speak Yoruba to save her life, but she somehow had an ear for it, and could hear when it was spoken properly, even catch a little meaning in it. She crept closer to the beads that formed the door curtain and peeped through them.

"*Orúkọ mi ni . . .*" her father began, then stopped, confused when Aunty Biola fell about laughing again. He had said *orúkọ,* "my name," through his nose, as if it was a weird kind of sneezing sound.

"*Orúkọ,*" she stressed gently as soon as she had recovered.

Her father shrugged, grinning.

"That's what I said!"

Aunty Biola slapped her hands together in the typical Nigerian gesture for helplessness, exclaiming, "What am I going to do with this man?!" Then she fell back onto the the sofa as another fit of laughter overtook her.

Jess watched her father fan the two of them with a copy of *Tell* magazine, then she continued down the corridor. She paused outside the closed door at the end, her grandfather's study. Ebun had told her, in the quiet of the night, lying in their beds, when the two of them had begun to speak as they did when they couldn't see each other properly, that the door was always kept shut and locked—ever since the time that Bose, with her hands coated with spicy *adun,* had nearly destroyed the wine-coloured leather bindings of his specially commissioned copies of *Things Fall Apart* and *A Dance of the Forests.*

She hovered outside the door, longing to enter, just to glimpse just once, the rows of shelves Ebun had described to her, and the desk with the official-looking seal on it and to see her grandfather. Since the day she had gone into the entrance of the Boys' Quarters, he was always wanting to know if she was happy, always wanting to make her happy, not in the anxious way of her English grandparents, who kindly, unintentionally made her feel abnormal, like a freak, but in a powerful, questing way that seemed to put her melancholy under a microscope and make her fears appear groundless. And so she quietly seated herself cross-legged on the clean, shiny squares of the floor outside the study, her back against the wall.

Jess closed her eyes and thought about TillyTilly, glad that she hadn't gone shopping with her mother. Should she ask Ebun about her? But she didn't want to, she didn't want to ask anyone, she wanted to keep TillyTilly. TillyTilly was nothing like Dulcie or anyone in Jess's class; TillyTilly was barefoot and strange, and wanted to be friends.

Jess could hear Aunty Funke's laughter ringing down the corridor above the sound of popping, puffing cassava pieces in the black iron cauldron that sat on a big gas ring in the kitchen. Her father was in the kitchen, teasing Aunty Funke. No, Aunty Biola was there too; both of them were laughing at something her father had said in an excited tone of voice.

Aunty Funke called her.

Jess did not reply, didn't even move. She only stirred and opened her eyes when she realised that her grandfather was emerging from the study. She scrambled up and threw her arms around his waist as he emerged, his slippers shuffling out of the carpeted room and onto the linoleum, where she had been sitting. He laughed with surprise and, dropping the key into his pocket, passed his hand over her hair, which was now neatly cornrowed, thanks to the efforts of Bisola.

"So you were waiting for Baba Gbenga! Will you drink with me, madam?"

She nodded furiously, and he laughed again, beginning to move towards the kitchen although she didn't release him. Her mother or father would have detached her, her father gently, her mother with an exclamation of mild annoyance, but her grandfather struggled good-naturedly into the kitchen and ordered Aunty Biola to bring him a Powermalt and a Fanta from the cold crate.

"My granddaughter and I are going to drink our health," he said.

That night, something woke Jessamy. She wasn't sure whether it was a sound or a smell or an abrupt sight in one of her various dreams that made her suddenly open her eyes and stare around. For the first time since arriving in Nigeria, she felt a gaping disorientation; for a split second she couldn't even remember where she was, and everything was dim and out of focus.

Then clear images came tumbling back into her vision and she looked to where Ebun lay, breathing shallowly.

Then she remembered.

TillyTilly.

Was she too late?

She glanced at the window—it was still dark. She sat up as quietly as she could in the bed, then slipped out of the room. As she ran to the staircase leading to the balcony to watch for the light in the window of the deserted house, she heard a sound in the shadow behind her.

Not a voice.

She looked back down the corridor, saw nothing but doors and squares of floor stretching out before her.

There it was again.

A creaking noise.

Like . . . a door.

The noise stopped just as suddenly as it had started, and Jess walked down the corridor, hurrying slightly now, checking each room. She could hear the creaking sound in her head now; it didn't need to be real.

The parlour door—shut.

Her mum's and dad's door—shut.

The storeroom door—shut.

Her grandfather's door—shut.

The study door—partially open, a little space between door and doorpost exposing only more darkness.

What?

Breathless, she gave it a push, just a little push, with the tip of her finger, and slowly, impossibly, the door opened. She felt a thickness in the back of her head somewhere. Her tongue? Her *brain*? How could this door be open?

A face appeared around the edge, and Jess smiled with a deep, wondering joy.

It was TillyTilly, who had broken into her grandfather's study.

"Come in," whispered TillyTilly. Jess could hardly hear her over the other sounds of the night. She saw Tilly's eyes shining.

"It's dark in there, TillyTilly," Jess whispered back, still unable to stop herself from smiling. They both knew they couldn't put a light on in there. In case someone saw, and wondered.

"Don't worry," Tilly whispered, and held out her hand. Jess took it, feeling Tilly's cool fingers link with her own, and then Tilly drew her into the darkness, and she wasn't at all afraid because someone was holding her hand.

SEVEN

———

"Wait a minute."

TillyTilly let go of Jess's hand and Jess heard a thin, scratching sound, then saw a flare of light go up. A little flame danced atop a candle in a saucer in Tilly's hand.

Jess gasped quietly.

"You're the candle thief!"

The two of them smiled conspiratorially at each other in the candlelight, Jess noticing how the flame held up to Tilly's lean face highlighted the triangles of shadow, the hollows of her cheekbones. Her eyes seemed even darker.

Tilly smiled.

"Let's look around," she said.

She took Jess's hand and guided her slowly past each shelf. She passed the candle over the rows of leather-bound and hardback books, bringing the flame so close to some that Jess's breath caught in her throat with amazement at her daring.

"You might set them on fire," she warned, and Tilly looked at her seriously, the ends of the string in her hair bobbing as she nodded.

"I know!"

Jess carefully took some books down from the shelf, thick tomes of poetry by Samuel Taylor Coleridge that sounded exciting, especially in the dark, with bookshelves and a window lit with faint moonlight.

" '*And all should cry, Beware! Beware! / His flashing eyes, his floating hair! / Weave a circle round him thrice, / And close your eyes with holy dread, / For he on honeydew hath fed, / And drunk the milk of Paradise,*' " she whispered to Tilly, who obligingly held the candle so that words were discernible but no wax would drip onto it.

TillyTilly nodded sagely.

"It's a good poem," she said, with a knowledgeable air. "Ancestral voices, and all that."

She actually said *and all that*, with the unconcerned tone of an English person. Jess's expression grew more incredulous when she remembered the first thing she had said, in that pure Nigerian accent: *Hello Jessy.* The girl was a mystery.

TillyTilly smiled almost wickedly, as if she knew what Jess was thinking, but persisted in her line of discussion.

"D'you like it? The poem, I mean? It's called 'Kubla Khan.' "

Jess nodded.

"I like it a lot," she said awkwardly. Tilly had knelt on the floor and begun examining some books at ground level. Jess couldn't remember the last time she'd told anyone what she thought about a poem, or a book, or anything much really. "It makes me think of . . . you know, when something's so different and weird that when it touches other people it makes them different and weird too . . . It's like what my mum told me about Sir Galahad, and how he was the perfect knight, but when he saw into the Holy Grail, he couldn't do anything else but die, really, because of, well, holy dread."

She stood still, upright, her cheeks flushed, deliberately not looking down at Tilly but concentrating on a book in front of her until the gold lettering of the title had blurred. She didn't want Tilly to laugh or make fun or anything; she didn't think she could bear it.

She heard Tilly turn a few pages, then say excitedly, "I know exactly what you mean. Look, it's like here, in Isaiah, where he's made all clean when one of the angels touches his lips with the hot coal."

She had an enormous, expensive-looking edition of the Bible in her arms and was jabbing at a section with her finger. Jess sat down cross-legged on the floor beside Tilly, and they spent a few minutes going through other books that Tilly knew, looking for examples of "holy dread."

"TillyTilly," said Jess, after a while.

"Mmmmmm."

"How come you've read all these books and I haven't?"

Then Tilly said something odd, like: "*I haven't read them, I just know what's in them.*"

Jess looked at her, wondering whether or not to believe her. Then, just to be on the safe side, in case she'd heard wrong, she said, "What?"

TillyTilly didn't look up from her book, but smiled.

"I said I've had a lot of time to get to know what's in them. Also, I'm much cleverer than you."

"Oh."

Jess thought of something else.

"So you sneak in here a lot? How do you do it?"

Tilly shrugged.

"The window."

"The *window*? But my grandfather keeps the key in his pocket and . . ."

Tilly put a dismissive hand up, turned a page, apparently absorbed.

Jess tried again.

"Unless there's another key . . . ?"

A slight nod, but Tilly refused to add anything further. Instead she jumped up and ran over to Jess's grandfather's swivel chair, springing on to it with an expression of glee.

Jess heard it skid backwards on its wheels and put out her hands in a cautionary gesture.

"Shhhhh!"

TillyTilly laughed quietly.

"Push me around the room on this and then I'll push you," she offered, whirling around in the chair, her voice sounding slightly garbled as she spun.

"OK!" Jess eagerly scrambled up, then bent and gathered the books that had been left scattered on the floor a little distance away from the still-burning candle. She slid them back into place, trying to remember which gaps in the bookcase she and Tilly had taken them from. She suddenly grew apprehensive and began to think of explanations should her grandfather awake, and draw his key out from amongst his nightclothes, perhaps, and put the key in the lock . . .

Even as she thought about this, she heard the smooth, metallic sound of key being turned in lock, and an expression of utter panic crossed her face.

Then she heard Tilly laugh. She spun around to find Tilly leaning from the chair so that one of her hands was splayed out against the surface of the floor; she was in a sort of half handstand. As Jess stared at her, she slowly rotated the chair so that it made the soft clicking sound that she had heard before.

"Oh my God!" Jess stumbled backwards, her fingers allowing

her nightie to flow back out around her, her hand moving to press her chest in an attempt to help along the stilling of her heart. "Don't do that ever again!"

Tilly rose from her half handstand so that she sat upright in the chair again.

"Well, I don't think we'll be back in here . . . It's sort of boring, don't you think? All that anticipation!"

Somehow, Jess realised, Tilly had known how much she had wanted to enter this room.

When Jess woke for the second time, she turned over and lay on her back, basking in the morning sunlight that was pouring into the room. She only became aware after a few seconds that she was smiling from ear to ear.

She looked to her side, noting that Ebun had already left her bed, her sheets rumpled and tossed. She could hear bustling activity on the kitchen floor and smell cooking; it smelt like her Aunty Funke's speciality of smoked fish, palm oil and spinach stew. Then she remembered that it was Sunday, and that it was her grandfather's turn to host his Baptist prayer group. Her grandfather was a proud member of the Oritamefa Baptist Church.

She stretched her arms out to either side of her, kicking the covers off her body and pedalling her legs in the air while she thought about getting up. For the past two Sundays, her grandfather had dressed up in white-and-gold *agbada*, traditional costume, with a white embroidered cube-shaped hat on his head and the tail of his costume draped over his right arm, his left hand clutching a slim wooden cane which was purely an accessory, since he walked perfectly well without aid. Aunty Funke would hand Driver the Bible that Jessamy's grandfather needed for his part of the discussion and prayer, and her grandfather would climb into the backseat of the car, careful of his clothes. Then her mother, or Aunty Funke, or Aunty Biola, would close the door for him, and the car would pull out around the back of the house and through the gates hastily pulled open just in time by Uncle Kunle and Gateman. Gbenga Oyegbebi's head would always be held high so that he looked glittering and regal through the shiny windows of the car.

When he was gone, the rush to get ready for church ensued. Her grandmother had been an Anglican and had managed to convert all of her children to Anglican practices, so they were used to seeing their father off first so as not to incur his wrath at their "not praying together as a family." Jess, her mother and her father were the only ones who weren't involved in the scramble to prepare for the eleven o'clock service, since her mother had quietly "given up on organised religion" a few years after her arrival in England, a fact that she refused to discuss with Jessamy's grandfather. She wouldn't allow Jess to be taken to the service either, insisting that she was a gloomy enough child already without the Nigerian warnings of hellfire making things worse. Jessamy's father had obligingly attended the Baptist service with her grandfather the first Sunday and had come back looking wilted, saying simply that the five-hour prayer session had been "tiring."

But this week, her grandfather had left for the service early and was going to return with his friends for scriptural discussion, and these friends, Aunty Funke had warned, would need to eat and drink. Ebun had complained in a matter-of-fact whisper the night before, when they had been drifting off to sleep, that prayer meetings at the house always meant that she and Tope had to get up earlier to go and fetch water for their grandfather to wash with and for Aunty Funke to cook with.

Jess hesitated to get up because she wasn't sure if getting up meant committing herself to meeting these prayer people.

When she heard the resounding *hissssssssssss* of puff-puff batter being dropped into Aunty Funke's big, dented red frying pan,
she nearly fell out of bed and onto the floor in her haste to get
up, then noticed something had fallen from the bed with her.

She smiled silently and with puzzlement as she picked up the
battered copy of *Little Women*, turning it over in her hands. Could
it have come from her grandfather's study? She didn't recall having seen any children's books there, but then again, neither did
she recall any children's books at all in the house, other than the
ones in the box that she'd taken from her suitcase and slipped under her bed.

She got underneath her bed and rummaged in her book box,
just in case. It was darker here, but she could see her own copy
of the book, which was hardback and in pristine condition—the
way she kept all her books, except for the parts of the text that
had been lightly scribbled and replaced with pencilled additions,
some one-sentence long, some as long as a paragraph. Jess made
a habit of amending books that hurt her in some way—some
books had bad things happening to characters in what she felt was
a completely unnecessary and extremely painful way, especially
considering that the situations weren't even in real life, so she had
taken to scratching some of the printed text out and adding hap-
pier things. So far, *Little Women* and Frances Hodgson Burnett's
A Little Princess were her most heavily annotated books.

One day, her mother had caught her and had asked in tones
of mixed disbelief and amusement, "What makes you think that
you know how to tell a story better than Louisa May Alcott
does?"

Jess had not known exactly what to say when it was put that
way, and had found herself replying defiantly, "Well it's not a
proper story if everyone's miserable. It's not fair to make us watch
people be sick, and be poor, and lose everything, and die, and

Beth's so nice you'd think Louisa May Alcott would have treated her better!"

Thinking about this, Jess put her own copy back into her book box and crawled out from under the bed. She opened up the tattered copy that she still clutched, and read, with some surprise, the name

Bisi Oyegbebi

written in neat, small black lettering on the flyleaf.

Her mother's copy?

And beneath her mother's name was her own full name, written in the same wobbly, lopsided letters as the *"HEllO JEssY"* that had been in the Boys' Quarters.

JessaMY WuRaOla HaRRISOn—

SaTuRDaY August 27Th 1994

She closed the book and gave a sudden laugh.

TillyTilly had given her a gift!

She lifted the book to her nose, and smelt the black ink of her grandfather's red-barrelled ink pen. She remembered now having seen the pen there, on top of a stack of papers on her grandfather's writing desk, as TillyTilly had spun her around the room until all the colours had whirled together and both of them had had to stop for a few seconds with their hands pressed over their mouths to stifle their giggles.

Jess quickly crawled back under the bed and placed this new, old book on top of the other books in her box. Then she bounced out of the room to try and persuade her aunt to let her have some puff-puff before she had brushed her teeth instead of afterwards.

EIGHT

————

"Jessy," Tilly hissed, from somewhere in Jess's immediate vicinity. "Psst! Jessy!"

Jess had been sitting on the front veranda of the Boys' Quarters, looking around for her friend. In the central house, behind her, she could hear voices uplifted in prayer and song, Ebun accompanying on tambourine, a bell ringing at intervals. The confusion of sounds meant that she couldn't see where the voice was coming from, but she replied immediately.

"Yeah? Hey, TillyTilly, where are you?"

The bushes near the back gate of the compound rustled, and Jess watched as a noticeable ripple ran through the leaves. She heard Tilly laugh softly.

Jess laughed herself, and jumped up.

"Hey, TillyTilly, that's not fair! Come out!"

Tilly laughed again.

"All right, all right," she said, her voice muffled.

She stepped out of the bushes in a completely different area, to the far right of where the rustling had been. Jess made an astonished whistling sound through her teeth. She had been practising it all morning with Uncle Wole, who had made a similar sound when he had seen the amount of *fufu* that her aunt was preparing to go with her smoked-fish stew.

"Are you sure that you're not preparing for a modern-day Feeding of the Five Thousand?" he had asked in a dubious tone of voice. "You're only cooking for twenty people, you know!"

He had been about to expand on this even further when Jess had begun pestering him to show her the whistling sound again.

Now that Jess *really* had something to whistle about, she made a point of utilising the sound as much as she could. She looked at Tilly and back at the bushes, making the *whsssssst* sound again.

"You run fast," she said admiringly.

Tilly fidgeted, eyed the veranda that Jess had just stepped down from.

"Yeah," she said.

Jess noticed that Tilly had changed her odd outfit from the day before for another one. This time she was wearing what looked like a dim white net curtain that had been bunched and gathered at the arms and neck to make sleeves and a scoop neck. This dress was even longer than before and trailed nearly to the dusty ground.

Jess decided to look at something else in case Tilly noticed that she was staring and got annoyed. She would be annoyed herself if she'd had to wear something like that and someone stared at her, even if it was a friend.

"Thanks for the book," she said finally.

TillyTilly smiled, shrugged.

"It's OK."

Jess put her hands into the pockets of her shorts, then looked around, feeling a little bit awkward.

Tilly appeared to be looking very hard at the floor, her brow

creased with thought, as if she was pondering something difficult.

She lifted her head.

"Would you like," she asked, suddenly breathless, "to go to
the amusement park?"

Jess thought for a moment about the time she'd been there
with her mum and her mum's old school friends. With TillyTilly,
she was certain, it would be different. But—

"TillyTilly, it's Sunday!" she exclaimed. "I don't think it'll be
open!"

TillyTilly folded her arms and gave Jess a scornful stare. Jess
felt the blood rushing to her cheeks.

"Was your grandfather's study open?" Tilly demanded. Jess
slowly shook her head, then nodded it, unsure whether Tilly
meant before or after Tilly had broken in. "Come on!"

TillyTilly started to walk, and Jess stood still for a couple of
seconds, then, laughing, caught up with her.

Even before they arrived at the gates of the amusement park, Jess
was utterly exhausted, and her brown sandals were caked with
dust. The walk from Bodija to central Ibadan, where the amusement park was, was so tiring that Jess started to feel oddly, as if
she was walking uphill and, her vision swimming with her weari-
ness, had more than once suggested to TillyTilly that they turn
back and sit in the parlour with some minerals.

"I'd just need to explain who you were and then we
could—" she began, but TillyTilly interrupted her.

"You can't tell anyone about me, Jessy! Can't you tell that I'm
not supposed to *be* there?"

Jessamy felt as if she were finally getting somewhere.

"So you *do* live in the Boys' Quarters?" she pressed.

TillyTilly just trudged along silently, the back of her dress trailing on the ground. Jess watched the bit of material get steadily dirtier and dirtier.

Finally, Tilly stopped walking and shot her a sideways glance. "I do. Sometimes."

She gave a loud sigh, an irritated sigh,

(look what you've done, Jessy, you've made me cross with your questions)

and shaking her head slightly, continued walking.

Jess wanted to ask if she lived there with her parents, but it was clear from the set of her friend's shoulders that any further questioning would not be welcome. Maybe Tilly was like Sara Crewe and both her parents were dead; that must be why she hid in the Boys' Quarters and was so adept at stealing candles—maybe it was the only way that she could survive.

Maybe.

"TillyTilly, are you angry with me?" Jess cried, hurrying after her friend.

Tilly shot her an unreadable glance.

"No."

Jess felt uncomfortable, as if she should apologise anyway.

"I'm sorry," she offered.

Tilly trudged on, but the fact that she was now swinging her arms slightly indicated that she was in a better mood.

"It's all right, Jessy. I wasn't mad at you."

Liar, thought Jess, *you were. You're a liar.*

She blinked, surprised at this traitorous thought. What could have made her suddenly feel so hostile towards Tilly, who was mysterious and almost magical, opening doors that were locked, living in a deserted building next to a whole family of people without their noticing!

"Just don't ask me any more questions. It's not fair. I don't ask YOU any questions," Tilly pointed out.

67

"Except for when you first came up to me, and you were copying me," Jess reminded her.

TillyTilly suddenly looked confused, passing a hand over her forehead in a distracted manner.

"What?" she snapped. "Shut up!"

Jess's mouth clamped shut. Now TillyTilly was sounding just like the other children at school. She wanted to turn back on her own, but she was scared because she didn't know the way. She decided that she was going to keep on following Tilly, but she was going to let her know that she wasn't happy about it.

"You're being really mean, Titiola," she said firmly, not caring that she had pronounced it in an overly English way. Two could be mean.

Instead of wincing, or getting angrier, Tilly looked at her thoughtfully.

"Sorry," she said abruptly.

Jess revised her opinion all over again. TillyTilly had apologised, and had regained her place as the most interesting person that Jess knew.

"It's all right," she said happily, and they linked arms and walked on.

At the padlocked gates, the words AMUSE YOURSELVES were picked out in yellow-, red- and green-painted bubble letters above them.

TillyTilly surveyed the gates.

"Do you think you can climb over?" she asked.

The gates loomed impossibly high.

"No way!"

She waited.

Tilly cocked her head and looked at Jess consideringly.

"Are you sure? I think you could. *I* could."

Jess shook her head emphatically.

"I couldn't, TillyTilly!"

"All right," said Tilly, and, leaning on the bars of the iron amusement-park gates, stretched her arms out and pushed them open.

The gates went backwards with a gust of warm air, and the padlocks fell to the ground, their chains loosened, sunken in the sand. Jess stared at the enormous padlock at her feet, then up at the gates, then at TillyTilly, then around.

No one was about. She was grateful for that.

"TillyTilly," she said. "What did you—?"

Tilly grabbed her by the wrist and pulled her along. They ran into the park, which was empty of people, but full of swinging movement and the dusky brown of settling sand and dust. Jess whooped and jumped around Tilly in a circle, almost inaudible below the music from the bumper-car dome and the whirring of various machineries. The Ferris wheel, which stood a little distance from the slides, flashed bright neon red and green. Tilly and Jess slapped hands and bumped hips, laughing in disbelieving exhilaration. Jess ran over to the big yellow inflatable slide, and climbed to the top of it. Arms stretched up to the sky, her mouth ready to shout with elation, she launched herself downwards, slipping and skidding and bumping down to make it last longer.

It was as if the amusement park was *alive*. The bumper cars were whirling about, dots of colour playing over the roof of the glass dome that they were housed in, and Jess could imagine ghostly passengers swerving crazily over the tracks on the floor.

Jess climbed to the top of the slide again, and watched the Ferris wheel turn slowly at first and then faster, until it was a steadily rotating wheel of light. She stared around, gaping as she realised that all of this was really happening, and suddenly sat down.

"TillyTilly," she began to say, then the sound became a squeal as she found that she was freefalling down the slide again.

When she reached the bottom, she caught her breath and then ran around to where TillyTilly was jumping up and down by the bumper-car dome.

"Come on!" Tilly said and leapt into a moving car.

Jess hesitated, afraid of jumping for a seat and missing, but TillyTilly waved at her impatiently with one hand, already steering herself away from the other cars that were randomly colliding with the one she had selected.

"What are you doing just standing there?" Tilly demanded, standing up in her seat, turning the wheel so far to the right that she nearly veered into the wall.

Jess laughed and ran for a bumper car, which swerved out of her way. She managed to skip out of the way of another, which had been heading for the back of her legs. She could hear Tilly laughing and calling out, and began to feel flustered.

"You can do it, Jess! You can get one! Just jump!"

Jess grabbed at the very next bumper car that came her way, throwing herself at it and clambering up into the seat, scratching her shin on the chrome as she did so.

Tilly immediately drove at her, ramming into Jess's car before she got a chance to handle the steering wheel properly. The jolt shuddered through her body, making her teeth chatter, and Tilly threw her head back and laughed, moving away to bump an empty car. Jess, gritting her teeth, intent on revenge, managed to dodge Tilly's bumper car, positioning herself so that she could slam into her with maximum impact.

She did, and Tilly's mouth opened up into a pinky brown cavern with sharp white teeth as she gave a little scream of surprise, then called out, "Brilliant!"

Later, when they had been on everything and the electricity from the control box had run out (NEPA), the amusement park was still again.

That was when Jess looked around and realised that the sun had set.

"Oh my God, TillyTilly! We're . . . I'm going to be in BIG trouble!"

Just the thought of what her mum was going to say to her made her feel queasy.

Tilly didn't look all that concerned.

"Then we'd better go home now," she said, leading the way out of the park.

"Are we . . . you going to leave the gates open?" Jess asked, trotting after her as she started down the road.

"I'm too tired to pull them shut," Tilly flung out over her shoulder.

"I could help," Jess offered.

Tilly stopped, reached out and hugged Jess. As Jess awkwardly hugged her back, unused to having her arms around a body smaller and skinnier than her own, Tilly suddenly whispered into the air between them, her breath tickling the curling tendrils of Jessamy's hair.

"Thank you for wanting to help," she said, "but you need to get home now. Don't worry about it."

She left Jess at the back gate of the compound and scurried away, not looking back.

The cars that had been parked outside the compound when Tilly and Jess had left that morning were all gone. Only her grandfather's car remained, the dark blue of it making a mere outline in the dark.

As Jess edged carefully past it, her mother and Driver sprang out of the car. Jess jumped back, a little whimper escaping her as the faceless pair advanced. Then, when they drew closer, she saw her mother's tight expression of anger, and saw her crumple into tears.

"Oh my God, Jessamy! You are so selfish! Where on earth have you been?"

"I'm sorry, Mummy," she said, falling forward and burying her face in her mother's long T-shirt. But for some reason that she couldn't have explained even to herself, once her mother could no longer see her face, Jess's expression of remorse shifted into an empty reflex expression, the corners of her mouth tugging up into a smile.

NINE

Jess was alone downstairs, the top three buttons of her gingham checked dress undone as she steadily bounced a tennis ball off the wall of the centre house. She was pretending not to know that her parents were watching her from the top window, probably talking worriedly about her. Lips pursed now, her brow furrowed in concentration again as the *thwacking* sound of ball against brick became intermittent with the muffled drop of the ball hitting the ground.

A few minutes later, as Jess was reaching into the dust for the ball which she had just dropped, she looked up. She had heard someone moving, coming around the corner of the house.

Was it her mother?

Her mother had made her stay up nearly the whole night being talked at about how she should never, ever, try to run away, especially since this wasn't like England where police would actually stand a chance of being able to find her if she had been hurt somewhere. Sobbing, her mother had told her how scared she had been, had told her about ritual murders. Jess had watched

73

impassively, some part of her shocked and embarrassed at her own lack of emotion, wishing that she could feel something and be truly sorry.

If she saw her mother turning the corner, she would run around the other side of the house, she decided.

Enough was, after all, enough.

A face appeared around the corner, grinning mischievously. It wasn't her mother; it was TillyTilly.

Relieved, she turned to her friend, who was wearing the same dim white costume as the day before. The beautiful, dark puffs of her hair sprang out from above the bits of string that dangled down below her ears, and she had the sleeves of the dress rolled up to the elbows.

"Did you get into much trouble?" Tilly asked, catching the ball as Jess threw it at the wall.

"Not really," Jess said, after some consideration of the admonishments and "Praise Gods" that had heralded her arrival in the house. Her father and her grandfather had returned shortly after her, having been searching the immediate area.

"All right. Good."

Tilly bounced the ball against the ground. Jess leaned against the wall and watched her.

"Did you say anything about me?"

Jess shook her head.

She expected Tilly to smile, but she didn't; the expression on her lean, thoughtful face remained the same.

"You're leaving soon."

It was not a question, and Jess remembered with a shock that this was so. Her mother had told her to begin packing a few days ago, and when she hadn't, had dragged Jess's suitcase into the bedroom shared by Jess's parents and begun packing it herself, marching into Jess's room to fetch her book box, armfuls of clothes and underwear, shoes.

There was some languidness latent in the Nigerian atmosphere that made her forget the meaning of time passing—she could hardly even begin to understand that she'd been in Nigeria for nearly a month.

"Yeah," she said, finally. "Tomorrow, actually," she added, a note of astonishment in her voice.

Tilly laughed, a breathy laugh that was like her usual, wheezing laugh, but shorter.

"Will you forget all about me, Jessy?" she asked.

Jess stared incredulously at Tilly.

"What? Never!" Blushing, she added, in an undertone, "You're amazing, TillyTilly."

TillyTilly gave a full laugh, a gasping, delighted sound.

"You are, too," she said, her tone sober.

Jessamy's blush deepened. She put her hands behind her back and blew outwards.

There was a brief silence, in which Tilly's nose wrinkled up as she thought silently. She looked sideways at Jess.

"Would you like to be like me? Like, be able to do the things I do, I mean?"

Jess nodded so hard she felt as if her brains were bouncing about inside her head.

Tilly nodded too, and Jess briefly got that odd feeling again that her actions were being mirrored.

"I'll write to you," Jess offered, adding, lamely, "if you give me your address."

And your surname, she thought, surprised at how much she didn't know about the girl.

TillyTilly threw the ball at the wall, caught it, turned it over in her hand, staring at it. "Don't worry about it," she said. "You'll see me again."

Jess believed Tilly; how could she not? And she had discovered that she liked surprises.

When she looked up, she saw the trailing tail of Tilly's dress disappear around the corner and realised that TillyTilly had just said goodbye. She felt oddly disappointed.

Wasn't there supposed to be more to a "goodbye" than that?

She clutched her chest, almost crying in her panic. How could she stay? How could she make Tilly stay, the being-friends stay?

O God, please help me to stay friends with TillyTilly, please, please, please. Let me keep her. She is my only friend; I have had no one else. She gave me a book, my mother's book. I have had no one else.

Unable to bear her own thoughts any longer, she ran around the back of the house and towards the Boys' Quarters, almost flying. She could hear her teeth chattering, as if she were cold, could feel a scream building up. She hesitated on the veranda, then resolutely putting her smaller fears aside, charged in, past the table with its fresh layer of brown dust. She turned left and ran down the corridor, dimly hearing her feet pounding on the ground.

"TillyTilly," she said aloud, almost cried out.

Silence. Dust settling, floating through the air.

She reached the staircase.

Unlike her grandfather's stone staircase, this staircase was wooden. It looked as if it was rotting, crumbling away.

How could anyone live here?

She was scared. Those steps wouldn't hold her weight, there was no way that they were going to—

With a leap, she was on the bottom step. She wobbled, held her balance, ran up the stairs, trying to keep her feet from breaking through the softened wood.

Her foot jabbed through the wood on the top step, and she clutched at the banister as she fell to her knees, thrashing as she struggled to free herself. What if there were splinters? God, what if an enormous splinter of old wood just punched right through her foot, through the skin, through the bone?

"TILLY!" she screamed.

Silence.

She freed her foot by relaxing and wiggling it gently, gently out.

Her sandal had fallen through.

She was afraid to put her bare foot down on the floor; who knew what could be stepped on in this old place

(there might be fragments of bone, maybe people had died in here)

and so she hopped along on one foot, peering around her.

The top floor was completely unlike the bottom one, which was similar in structure to her grandfather's. The top floor looked like an attic. The roof sloped into an odd-shaped peak over her head, a feature of the house that she was pretty certain was not discernible from the outside. The slope of the roof made her feel dizzy, spun thin, as if there were no sky, just grey stone above, and dust below. A row of closed doors spread out before her, and enormous cobwebs covered some of the old, heavy wooden doors.

But there were no spiders.

Unnerved, she stood as still as she could on one foot, listening for a sound, any sound that would indicate that her friend was here.

"TillyTilly," she called, softly. "TillyTilly, I came to see you."

Her voice sank into the silence like a heavy stone in water, but without ripples. The silence was stifling, stealing her words and making nothing from them.

The doors lay dimly before her.

She really, really, really didn't want to open one.

What was TillyTilly playing at? If she were here, friends or not, Jess was going to get angry with her about this.

A thought struck her. Maybe Tilly's *parents* were here, hiding because they thought that someone who lived in her grandfather's house had found out about them and wanted to kick them out!

She would have to open the doors, but slowly and quietly, so that if they were in there, in one of the rooms, she wouldn't alarm them. Gingerly, she touched the handle of the first door in the row, then drew back her hand. The handle was strangely cold.

It's made out of metal, stupid girl.

She forced herself to grip the handle again. She pushed the door open, her breath coming fast and then slow as she prepared herself to see two people huddled in a corner, glaring with hostility.

But dust floated in this room too, and the window was coated with it. It was a wonder that she had been able to see any light that night. In fact, had she really seen a light? Standing up here, she began to doubt it.

She hopped to the next door, feeling more confident. She would be all right. When she turned the handle, she found this room the same as the last. She started to feel as if she was in some sort of game show where she won whatever she found behind the doors. So far she had won nothing at all.

Behind the third door was some sort of display, or maybe a shrine.

As she stared at it, standing just outside the doorway, she felt the hairs on the back of her neck prickle. It was a picture, drawn in black charcoal on a tall wooden board that had been propped against the far wall of the room. The picture was a rough drawing, done in thick, sweeping strokes, a sketch of a black woman with thick, glossy hair that had been coloured in with the charcoal in a scribblelike intensity. Her expression was unsmiling but serene, the eyes wide and dark, seeming almost to see Jess where she stood, wavering on one foot, peeping around the corner of the door. And the charcoal woman's arms—her arms were grotesque. Surely nobody could have arms that long! They were completely out of proportion to her body, long and thin, tentaclelike, stretching to her ankles. She had been drawn wearing a *boubou* with odd, swirling patterns that Jess had never seen the like of before.

And in front of the wooden board with the charcoal woman was a whole array of candles, some tealights, some big candles in empty, battered cans of Milo, some smaller ones arranged on a saucer. There were lots and lots of candles. None of them were lit, but she could see that they had all been burning at some point. They looked burnt down, their wicks black.

She felt that she should shut the door and leave this room.

"You shouldn't have come in here," TillyTilly spat.

Jess jumped as if she had been slapped, feeling a guilty tingle on the back of her neck. She spun around.

"Tilly!"

Tilly did not reply. She moved into the room, stepping over some candles, nimbly skirting others. She stepped in front of the board and spread her arms out so that Jess could no longer see the charcoal woman properly. In a sense, Jess was relieved, but she was also alarmed by the cold manner in which Tilly eyed her. She desperately wanted to ask what this was all about.

She didn't ask.

Instead, she apologised.

"I'm sorry," she said, for the second time in two days. Maybe she just wasn't good at the whole being a friend, having a friend thing. Maybe it was something that needed practice. Which would explain why she was so bad at it. She stared at her bare foot, noticing how naked it looked beside her sandalled one.

Tilly sighed.

It was a forgiving sort of sigh, and Jess looked up hopefully.

Tilly was now at the doorway, although Jess had not sensed any movement within the room. The slope of the roof was definitely messing her up.

"Never mind," Tilly said, stepping out into the corridor with her and closing the door.

Tilly guided her down the stairs, showing her the safe places to step on. Jess explained about her shoe falling through the staircase, and Tilly laughed. Jess laughed too, having overcome the panic she felt at the time, secretly feeling sorry for TillyTilly that she had to live in an old, dusty, odd house like this one.

Something occurred to her.

"Were you in there when I first came in?" she asked.

They had reached the veranda, and Jess had jumped off it and turned around to look at Tilly, who was still standing up on it.

Tilly snorted.

"Of course not."

"Oh," said Jess. "OK."

TillyTilly gave her a considering glance, a shake of the head.

"Go home now," she said, and Jess could tell by the way she said it that she didn't just mean "go back to your grandfather's house" but also "go back to England."

" 'Bye, TillyTilly," Jess said.

TillyTilly gave her that fantastic, brilliant, but brief smile.

"See you later, Jessy," she said, and went back into the house.

II

ONE

It was Jess's "settling in" time at school. She needed this to be, well, settling in. Whatever that was.

It had been just over half a school term since they'd returned from Nigeria, but Jess still hadn't "settled." Before and after her return to England, and school, Jess had been frenzied in her activity, and then she had been ill, and her father didn't think that she was ready for school again. Her mother insisted that Jess had to go; nothing was wrong with her, she could use the first few days to "settle in" again. Then her father had asked Jess what she thought about it. Did she want to go to school tomorrow?

Jess had raised her eyebrows at him in surprise.

What a silly question. As if she ever wanted to go to school.

And now they were asking her, giving her a choice: School, yes or no? Yet she felt confused, because she somehow knew by the way that her father was looking at her, his eyes cautious behind his spectacles, that although he had been arguing with her mother about whether she should go to school or not, he would like her to be brave, to be completely recovered, to be a normal child who wanted to see her friends at school. And her mother wanted her to go, simply, Jess supposed, for the sake of going, and rules, and being there if the school was open and nothing was wrong with you.

They were offering her a choice, a chance to say "no," when if she did, one would be angry and the other disappointed. Was it really, actually, a choice?

With a small, almost unnoticeable movement, her eyes flicked helplessly from one face to the other.

"Yeah," she said finally, and was rewarded with smiles from both.

Ever since they had returned to England, Jess had been looking out of windows for extended periods of time, sailing eagerly towards the front door whenever there was a knock or the doorbell rang. She spent hours painstakingly braiding a special friendship bracelet for TillyTilly in the tiniest sections possible, then unpicked it and began again because the colours were all wrong. The atmosphere of tense, coiled-up waiting in her had confused her parents, whom she had caught several times gazing bemusedly at each other.

Then, after this period of absorption (with . . . what, exactly? friendship bracelets? expectancy? impossible to tell) came the inevitable fever, the whites of her eyes tinged pink, her head lolling dejectedly on her pillow, her fingers limp as if the bones in them had evaporated. She mumbled, made small sounds, like singing noises, broken songs, because when she was ill she could never speak properly.

Jess's parents had, thankfully in her opinion, given up carrying Jess to the GP whenever she ran such a high temperature. Her GP, Dr. Collins, was as baffled as they were. Jess had already undergone extensive tests: for allergies and anaemia, of all things. They all proved inconclusive because nothing, he explained looking at this little girl who was pulling weakly at her clothes because she was hot, and trembling violently because she was cold, was physically wrong with her.

Jess invariably got over it. Her mother made her eat *pepe* soup with digestible specks of ground beef in it, and her English grandmother insisted she sup chicken soup with barley, and she began to sleep properly again and totter about to get things she wanted when her mother, absorbed at the computer in her study a few doors away, didn't immediately answer her calls. She would sway when she got out of her bed, fizzing, coloured dots dancing before her eyes as she wobbled across the floor, zigagging like a baby learning to toddle.

Then she recovered (and still no TillyTilly!) only two days before school started again.

When she finally arrived in the classroom, the rest of Year Five was listening to Miss Patel reading a passage about Sir Francis Drake's travels from a thin hardback book with a bright picture of his ship, the *Golden Hind*, on the front. Colleen McLain and Andrea Carney looked at her and whispered behind their hands to each other. Colleen McLain was very clever; she always finished her work faster than everyone else and would sit straight in her chair, her arm waving rhythmically in the air: "*Miiiiiiiiiiiiss. Miiiiiiiiiiss.*"

She had reddish brown hair in a long bob, and often, when strands of her hair came loose from where she had tucked them behind her ears (she never wore her hair in a ponytail or braid), instead of pushing them back, she would chew the ends, leaving the strands darker, wet and coated with pale globules of saliva.

Jess thought it was disgusting.

Colleen thought Jess was disgusting, although it was never clear why. It was a different thing every day. Mostly, when Jess didn't want to talk about her ideas in class, Colleen thought that Jess was showing off, making sure that she would be coaxed and pleaded with, but how could Jess have explained in a coherent way that she was scared? Once you let people know anything about what you think, that's it, you're dead. Then they'll be jumping about in your mind, taking things out, holding them up to the light and killing them, yes, killing them, because thoughts are supposed to stay and grow in quiet, dark places, like butterflies in cocoons.

There was no way that anyone was ever going to get into her mind. Not ever. Fine, she'd do the work, yes, fine. Fine, she'd sit with a straight back and crossed legs, smiling so hard her cheeks hurt: *Who can sit up the straightest? Me, me, me!* Yes, she could do all that, but after that, something in her said: *They should leave* me *alone and let* me *read my books, let* me *think my thoughts.* If they pushed her too far with their requests for her to open up, interact more, make friends, she would scream. They knew it. She'd done it before.

Despite the
(disgusting)
chewed hair, Colleen was friends with everyone in the class, even though some would quarrel with her when she got too bossy, which was often. She wouldn't get bossy in an outright way, but she would force people to see things from her perspective through a simple tool: scorn.

"Oh my Lord," she'd say, looking to heaven as if God was nodding in silent agreement with her, "you're not *really* going to do that, are you?"

And Andrea Carney would titter disdainfully somewhere behind Colleen's left shoulder, or maybe, for variety, her right.

If some hapless child organised the class at playtime for a game of Bulldog on the rare occasion the biggest playing space in the

Juniors' playground could be wrested from the Year Six basketball boys, they would look at her in alarm. If Colleen didn't play, then Andrea wouldn't play, and if Andrea didn't play, then Sonia, who was Andrea's cousin, wouldn't play, and if Sonia wouldn't play, then Alison Carr, the prettiest girl in the class, wouldn't play . . . and so on. Tunde Coker and Samantha Robinson, two people who always tried to get the class together and make peace between warring factions, were the ones who most often fell victim to Colleen McLain's sarcasm.

Sometimes they would rebel—Samantha had pulled Colleen's hair after school one day and scratched Andrea when she had tried to come to her best friend's defence—but mostly they would sigh and give in, because "Colleen's all right really."

Jess, who saw everything but participated in nothing, observed Colleen's little attacks to secure her permanent leadership, and felt most sorry for Tunde Coker. He actually made an effort to talk to Jess whenever he saw her, bravely struggling to revive a conversation that died almost before it started. Jess would feel like turning away in despair, unable to explain that she just couldn't say anything worthwhile when other people were talking to her, but also unable to say anything friendly to dispel the feeling Tunde jokingly expressed that she "didn't like him much."

Jess liked Tunde Coker quite a lot—the habit he had of digging his hands so deep into the pockets of his tracksuit trousers that it looked as if he had two hand-sized bumps growing out of the sides of his legs; the long, slow, lopsided smile that he smiled when someone said or did something funny. He rarely laughed, but he also never seemed to take conversation seriously, was constantly smiling as if words washed over him like an impure tide of meaning, searching instead the face of the person he was talking to with his eyes. Yes, she really did like him quite a lot, although she knew that he, much like any other boy in their class, would do anything the blond, dimpled Alison Carr asked.

Not that she disliked Alison Carr, either . . . Everyone in their class, except for Colleen McLain, was OK. Even Andrea Carney was OK—she had taken Jess to the school nurse once when Nam Hong had tripped her up in the playground and she had cut her knee badly. That was the problem—everyone was just OK.

Jess sat down, keeping her back straight, as if someone had attached a hook and string to her skull and was yanking the string taut so that her head went up, as she strove to ignore Colleen and Andrea's glances prickling on her back.

I have a friend an amazing friend who's coming to see me soon and she's better than the two of you put together and she listens to me I talked about a poem with her and I don't care if you don't like me and and and . . .

"OK, Year Five, settle down, SETTLE DOWN! Get to the tables—we're going to make some information booklets about Sir Francis Drake now—"

But Miss Patel didn't get a chance to finish, because just at that moment, Jess bent double and, putting her hands over her eyes, began to scream and scream and scream.

TWO

"Jessamy?"

Jess raised her head from her knees and looked around blearily, her eyes still smarting from her tears. She stared at Mr. Heinz, the headmaster. She recognised him from assembly. His dark brown hair was sprinkled with grey, and his tie stood out from his sleek navy-blue suit because it was red with yellow smiley faces on it.

Mr. Heinz drew a chair out from beneath the clean white nurse's desk, and sat down. He clasped his hands in his lap, then lifted them, linked them together, pushed the lattice made by his joined fingers outwards. Jess silently watched his hands, her own hands creeping to her face to rub at her eyes. It was quiet.

Say something.

He didn't.

She lost patience.

"Yes, Mr. Heinz?" she asked, wanting him to say whatever it was that he was here to say, show his concern, his dismay, and then go away so that she could be by herself.

"Jessamy," he began again. "I wanted to ask you—are you

happy in your new class? I mean, obviously, I know that some-times it all gets a little bit stressful and you, you know, erm, vent your feelings and so on, but in general, is it all right there?"

Jess had calculated one weekend that on average she had at least one serious tantrum in school per week. She had laughed with a kind of embarrassment, thinking *No wonder my class thinks I'm weird.* Was it getting boring?

She remembered how, one day, Colleen McLain had said something pretty horrible. Colleen had been with Andrea and Andrea's cousin Sonia, and she had said loudly, with several glances to make sure Jessamy was listening, "Maybe Jessamy has all these 'attacks' because she can't make up her mind whether she's black or white!"

Jess hadn't known what to think about what Colleen had just said,

(I mean, is it true?)

but she knew that her mum would have gone mentalist.

So she hadn't told her.

"Sir," Jess said finally, in a small, polite voice, "I hate being in that class, but I have to go to school, so I might as well not com-plain."

He did not seem surprised by what she said; if he had, she would have thought him an idiot—after all, he must have at least discussed her with Miss Patel, if not noticed all the times that she'd had to go home after a particularly bad tantrum when they couldn't get her to settle.

Jess realised another thing.

She hated the word "settle."

Mr. Heinz cleared his throat.

"You could always go back to Year Four," he said.

Jess almost laughed at him outright, hysteria bubbling in her throat as she remembered his visit to her house to speak to her parents about moving her up to Year Five. Her mother had looked long at her, an assessing sort of look, as if she wasn't sure whether to object or to be proud that her daughter was going to be advanced "a whole class," as she put it—as if someone could be moved up by half a class. Offering the plate of biscuits to Mr. Heinz, she had said in a matter-of-fact, somewhat Nigerian manner, that she had no objection to Jessamy's being moved up a year. After all, it wasn't irrevocable, was it, and there would be a trial period first. Mr. Heinz had taken a biscuit. Yes, Jessamy would think later, laughing, that her mother had been very Nigerian about it, had hidden her pride. Give her any scenario, and that calm acceptance that Nigerian children might be singled out for anything would emerge: *What is that I hear you say? You have randomly and spontaneously decided to elect my daughter as Prime Minister? Well, all I can say is: good choice.*

But her father—Jess had watched him turn the lenses of his glasses towards him and stare at them as if they were another pair of eyes looking back. He looked around the living room before speaking, and Jess followed his gaze: he seemed to be taking in the dark-red sofa and chairs, the plum-coloured light filtering out from the lampshade. He fiddled with his glasses again and seemed to be hesitating.

"It's, erm, not Jess keeping up that I worry about," he had said, his usually buoyant voice sounding almost muffled. Jess, her mother and Mr. Heinz waited to see what exactly he *had* been worrying about.

"Erm, well, I just thought maybe she might not actually, you know, like it."

Sarah Harrison laughed, and so did Mr. Heinz. Jessamy had heard and was glad to hear that her father worried about these things; she was starting to think that no one did. She took a small bite of her bourbon biscuit.

"Well, we did say that nothing's definite until Jessamy's tried it out," Mr. Heinz said. Jess looked at him guardedly—he laughed with his mouth open too wide.

The confidence in Mr. Heinz's voice seemed to make Daniel Harrison shrink somehow, but Jess, watching from beneath her eyelashes, could not see exactly how or what the change was. Daniel looked at Sarah, who gave him a slight shrug (*They want to make our daughter special; what can we do?*), then he looked at Jessamy. Jessamy took another self-conscious nibble at the biscuit. She did not like to, could not, eat very much in front of strangers.

Then her father looked at Mr. Heinz.

"Let's try it," he said, his tone suddenly cheerful. "Where's the harm? If you don't like it, you'll tell us, won't you, Jess?" he added.

Another one of those choiceless, spiral questions. She had to think carefully, clutching the biscuit in her palm as a talisman against the three faces looking at her. They had suddenly become a *group*.

What could she do?

Thinking of this, now, Jess put her head down and cried quietly, miserably.

After a few minutes, when Jess had composed herself, the nurse returned her to her class, where she spent the rest of the day going through the motions of being a Year Five pupil, hunched over a stack of coloured paper with scissors, glue, a copy of the book that Miss Patel had been reading from, and some coloured pencils. She vaguely noted that there were three other people at the table with her, but said hardly anything to them, not even when Jonathan Carroll and Nam Hong's wet-tissue fight ended up hitting her in the face. She gave a nod in acceptance of their apologies and continued snipping and colouring, placing things against the page, making sure that the only thing that she had any control over would look just right. She talked to Tunde Coker, who was also at her table, even less than usual, and steadfastly refused to look at Colleen McLain, who as always finished making her Sir Francis Drake booklet before anyone else.

"Bit slow, aren't you, Jessamy?" Colleen called out loudly, and Jess pretended not to hear, in fact, did *not* hear, made it her business only to hear the small clicking sound of Tunde's pencil breaking as he pressed too hard, and the scratchy, grating sound as he sharpened it up again.

THREE

At home after school, Jess settled herself cross-legged on the tall
kitchen chair, drinking her chocolate milk and eating a makeshift
cheese, peanut butter and chocolate-spread sandwich. The food
wasn't exactly making her memory of the afternoon go away, but
it was helping. As Jess chewed, she ran her eyes over the green-
and-white tiles running around the kitchen walls, particularly the
area where the tiles ran behind the fridge and out the other side
again, like a length of ribbon. Sometimes she left incriminating
chocolatey hand marks on the white tiles.

A rap at the back door.

She glanced at the kitchen clock; it was only four o'clock and
her dad didn't usually finish work until five.

Jess jumped up and pulled the back door open.

"Hi," TillyTilly said.

Tilly seemed different, just a little different. She stood just
outside the door, one hand on the doorpost, almost exactly the
same height as Jess, just as before, but— She was wearing shiny
black buckled shoes, and kneesocks like the white, crocheted
ones that Jess herself was wearing, and a checked green dress.

Her face seemed fuller, her arms firmer, as if she had put on some healthy weight, and her hair! Her hair was completely different.

When Jess had thought about TillyTilly, she'd pictured her two enormous puffs of hair bound with thin, trailing string. But now the two puffs had been braided into thick, stubby plaits, the end of each plait brushing a shoulder.

"I like your hair," Jess said, a hand flying up to her own single plait. She felt shy and embarrassed all of a sudden, as if things were too different.

Then TillyTilly smiled, and everything was all right again. Jess felt warmed. She smiled back, stepped aside for TillyTilly to come in.

"Me and my parents have just moved into the area," Tilly said.

"Oh," Jess said, trying to suppress her excitement.

TillyTilly had done it again! She'd done the impossible! Tilly might even go to her school! Why not? Jess had no doubt that Tilly would soon get herself moved to Year Five as well, but until then they could eat lunch together and maybe even play clapping games in the playground like the other girls did, and with Tilly there, she would be able to ignore Colleen McLain completely, as if she didn't even exist, and—

"So, d'you want to do something?" TillyTilly asked, laughing a little.

FOUR

"Let's go upstairs," said TillyTilly.

Jess hesitated in front of her mum's closed study door, not knowing whether she was supposed to make some kind of introduction. She hadn't had anyone whose parents her mum didn't know to play before.

TillyTilly pulled at her hand.

"Come on!"

Jess's room was gloomy because the curtains were drawn. The smell of lavender, her mother's latest scent craze, hung in the air, and Jess was suddenly extremely aware of the way that her room looked.

It looked too full. There were too many big, chunky things robbing space, air. The shelves . . . did they really need to be there, so wide and wooden, only half full with slim, gaudy paperbacks, the shelf sections opening into gaping squares of the blue-painted wall behind them? And her bed in the corner beneath the window, the patchwork quilt sprawled over it seeming to swell with a greedy fatness of colour! She was almost alarmed. She looked sidelong at TillyTilly, a quick, embarrassed glance, then went in through the doorway, feeling her toes squishing into the clumpy tufts of spotty rug. They gravitated towards Jess's desk, looking at the pictures and postcards on the wall above it.

"Hmmm," TillyTilly said, staring around. "There doesn't seem to be very much we can do here." She turned her gaze on to Jess. "D'you have any games?"

Jess shook her head. TillyTilly stood silent, her head tipped to one side, her eyes darting around the room. Her nose wrinkled up as she thought. Jess began nervously clicking her desk lamp on and off. She saw TillyTilly's eyes flick across towards the lamp, then away again, as if the sound, the constant shift between circle-light and square-darkness bothered her. Soon, Tilly's eyes did not shift from the lamp anymore but remained on Jess's hand, Jess's hand clicking the lamp on and off.

Jess frowned and stopped fiddling with the desk lamp.

"Games . . . D'you mean like Connect 4 and snakes and ladders?" she asked. When TillyTilly, head still cocked, didn't reply, Jess continued: "I don't really have games like that . . . My mum doesn't like playing them all that much, and my dad's usually doing something else . . ."

TillyTilly stood on one leg and rubbed the sole of her foot against the kneesocked length of her other leg. It was distracting, and Jess's words slowed down, and then died.

"Haven't you got any brothers or sisters?" TillyTilly asked, switching feet. She had her arms out as if she was going to launch into the air any minute and just fly away. Jess perched herself on the edge of her desk.

"No," she said. "You would've seen my brother or sister in Ibadan if I had one."

TillyTilly dropped her arms to her sides. She looked at Jess, her gaze ruler-straight, intent.

"But . . ." she said softly, "I thought . . ."

Jess waited, feeling a little sick. There was a key in her chest that was being tightly wound until it hurt.

TillyTilly twiddled the end of one of her pigtails and smiled.

"D'you know a girl called Colleen McLain?" she asked.

Jess jumped, just a little surprised at this new line of conversation.

"Yeah," she said. "She's horrible. She thinks she's amazing, and she chews her hair, and she hates me."

TillyTilly looked suitably impressed by the gravity of all this, her eyebrows raised in what Jess fancied to be a mix of disapproval at Colleen's behaviour and amazement that she could dislike Jess.

"And I hate her too," Jess added, after a split-second reflection.

TillyTilly had begun to move around the room, picking up one and then another of Jess's tiny painted china horses, examining the bright, thick crayons lined up in her wooden crayon box.

"I know Colleen as well," she said, shaking her head slightly, as if amazed at the girl's unlikeability. "She's just as horrible to me as she is to you, you know. She's out of order."

"Yeah," Jess affirmed, nodding vigorously, bemused but glad to have some support.

TillyTilly lowered her voice into a conspiratorial whisper, leaning closer to Jess as she did so, even though it was only the two of them in the room.

"We should *get* her."

Jess stared into TillyTilly's eyes, fascinated by their sleek shine. She felt disoriented, as if she was about to fall off the floor and land on the ceiling. The other objects in her cluttered room seemed smaller, lighter, blurry.

"Get her?" she echoed.

TillyTilly gave a solemn nod.

"As in . . . beat her up or something?"

Jess wanted to draw back so that she could touch something and be sure that her room wasn't really escaping her, but instead she found herself inching closer to Tilly.

TillyTilly gave an impatient toss of the head.

"No, not beat her up. *Get her.*" TillyTilly stared at her, one eye narrowing almost to the point of being closed in a wink, then suddenly burst out laughing.

Jess stepped back, shaking.

"Jessy, you idiot. I was only joking," TillyTilly said. "Come on, let's play outside."

"All right," said Jess. "Just let me tell my mum."

Her mum, cast in profile by the light, was typing furiously in her study, her body swaying backwards and forwards slightly, as if she was dancing her ideas. The curtains were wide open, and the rich orangey sunset drowned everything in evening colour. She waited. After a few seconds, her mum stopped typing.

"D'you want dinner or somesuch? Is something the matter?"

She was smiling; she was pleased; her eyes were far away and things were happening before them, behind them.

"Um . . . can I play out?"

Her mother raised an eyebrow.

"*May* I . . ."

Jess rolled her eyes at her mother's fussiness, and Sarah Harrison laughed aloud.

"With whom? And for how long?"

"With my friend Titiola. And for about half an hour." Even though Jess had pronounced the name wrong, she knew better than to say "TillyTilly." She could just envision her mother asking: *What kind of a name is that?*

"Titiola?" her mother said with interest, pronouncing the name properly. "A Yoruba girl, then? Who are her parents?"

Jess shrugged.

"I dunno! They just moved in around here! I *dunno!*" she repeated, a little excitedly. *Are you going to let me play out or not?*

"All right . . . fine . . . but can I meet her?"

"Dunno . . . she's shy."

"What? Well, you can play out with her today . . . and maybe you should have this Titiola over one of these days so that I can meet her . . ."

Jess ran into her bedroom and grabbed TillyTilly by the arm. They passed the study door in a blur of green and white and giggles, clattering down the stairs and then outside.

"Let's go to Colleen's house," TillyTilly said once they had reached the front gate of Jess's garden. Jess opened her mouth to protest, but TillyTilly had already darted away, and Jess, afraid to lose her, sped along behind.

Colleen McLain's kitchen was much, much neater than Jessamy's.

If Mummy saw this, Jess thought, awestruck, *she'd go mad and make Daddy help more.*

She stood open-mouthed, looking around at the yellow-and-pink transfers on the kitchen tiles, the transfers that exactly matched the linoleum on which she and Tilly stood. Tilly nudged her and pointed, laughing, at the spotless white surface of the fridge, the Post-it Notes pinned to it with bright plastic fridge magnets. Even the handwriting was neat, evenly formed: *Elaine, we've run out of milk* and *Don't forget Colleen's dental appointment on Saturday.* The room was filled with a light steam, which was emerging from the pot bubbling out stewy smells on the cooker. Meat, potatoes and some kind of green vegetable, maybe. It was the bubbling pot, the fact that Mrs. McLain was actually in the process of making dinner and would probably return to the kitchen any minute, that alarmed Jess.

"We're going to get caught, TillyTilly!" she whispered. She ignored TillyTilly's snort of derision as her eyes began surveying the room for places to hide.

Both Jess and Tilly froze as the sound of a woman yelling floated in through the doorway. From upstairs?

". . . can't believe you! This is too much for me! What exactly is the *matter* with you?"

There was no response other than the snuffling sound that accompanied weeping.

The woman's voice grew even louder, if this was possible.

"Ohhh! Jesus God!" the woman snarled.

Then came a quick, staccato whacking sound, followed by another, and another. Loud. Jess flinched.

"Get out of my sight!"

"TillyTilly, we weren't asked here . . . I should go home before my mum kills me," Jess said urgently. Her voice seemed to boom into the long quiet that followed those hard whacking sounds. *Before my mum kills me.* How could she have said that? Suppose it had happened, right here, and someone's mum had killed them?

"It's not even as if she's a nice girl anyway. And no one ever died from a slap, Jessy," TillyTilly said, her hands in the pockets of the green-and-white-checked dress. "Besides," she continued after a short pause during which Jess reflected that none of this made her feel any more comfortable, "she was probably hitting a table or a wall with something. White people do that, I think."

Jess laughed aloud, then clapped her hand over her mouth to stifle the sound. TillyTilly began pulling her towards the kitchen doorway. Jess bent her knees to make herself heavier, but it didn't work. Tilly continued to drag her, and she began to panic.

"What's *wrong* with you? What are you *doing*?" she hissed, trying to free her arm from Tilly's bony but surprisingly strong grip.

"Well, we have to see what all this is about."

"No, we don't!"

"We DO," TillyTilly insisted. "I'm not having you going home and thinking something's happened to Colleen McLain."

They were tussling in the passage now. Jess managed to snatch her arm back.

"I'm not coming. It isn't fair," she snapped, not sure what, exactly, it was that was supposed to be fair.

Then Mrs. McLain came down the staircase, swinging down the passageway towards the kitchen, a laundry basket filled with crumpled clothes tucked under her arm.

(Oh no!)

Jess seized her friend's arm, realising that she and TillyTilly were standing directly in Mrs. McLain's path, that they couldn't just run away without making things look worse than they were—

But Mrs. McLain wasn't looking at them.

Her eyes seemed to slide over them as if they were part of the pristine, stripy wallpaper that covered the passage walls.

How could she have missed them?

Mrs. McLain swept into the kitchen, and they heard the laundry basket being placed on the floor, the clatter of the pot lid as it was lifted, the slam as it was replaced.

What had just happened?

Jess turned to TillyTilly to see if the enormity of Mrs. McLain's somehow not seeing them had sunk in with her as well. TillyTilly shrugged, then began to laugh her gasping laugh. Jess let go of Tilly's arm and looked behind her at Mrs. McLain, who was on her knees loading clothes into the washing machine.

"Shhhh, TillyTilly, oh, don't laugh, you're making me laugh as well," she pleaded.

TillyTilly sighed, chuckled a little more, then came to an abrupt stop.

"Let's have a look around," she suggested.

"Wait!" said Jess.

TillyTilly, who had by now already reached the entrance of the sitting room, turned.

"What?"

"How come Mrs. McLain couldn't see us?"

TillyTilly looked at her without smiling or saying anything. It was a patient look,

(come on, Jessy, think about it)

and Jess suddenly found herself thinking of the big, grey amusement-park padlock at her feet, pushing into the sand.

"We're invisible," she said hesitantly, then, at TillyTilly's nod, more boldly: "We're invisible!"

"And she can't hear us, either, so I don't know why you were making such a fuss about me laughing," TillyTilly added.

Somewhat experimentally, but trusting in Tilly, Jess threw her head back and laughed, then looked quickly at Mrs. McLain, who was now measuring out washing powder Mrs. McLain didn't turn, made no indication of hearing.

"You're . . . magic, aren't you?" she asked TillyTilly, anxious not to sound silly, but also anxious for confirmation.

TillyTilly smiled. "Nope."

"Then . . . what? How can you do these things? I mean . . ." Jess began, then remembered that TillyTilly got cross when asked questions.

"Never mind," said Tilly hastily. "Let's go and bother Colleen's mum!"

They ran into the kitchen and danced around Mrs. McLain, who was compiling a shopping list. The washing machine hummed and spun.

"Hello, Colleen's mum . . . Did you know . . . your daughter's really ugly?" TillyTilly bellowed, waggling her head from side to side in an alarming manner. She had taken a stick of spaghetti from a jar on the counter and was holding it above her upper lip like a moustache.

"Hmmm . . . olive oil," Mrs. McLain muttered, biting the end of her pencil.

TillyTilly poked Jess. "You do something too!"

Jess looked around wildly, then had an idea. She ran over to the sink and put the plug in, then turned on both taps so that both hot and cold water came gushing out with a sudden hiss. TillyTilly, jumping up and down with delight, her plaits bobbing, started throwing fistfuls of sugar into the whirling pool of water that was building up. Not wanting to be outdone, Jess picked up the salt container and began pouring a thin stream of salt grains in as well.

(I cannot believe I'm doing this.)

"I think you'd better add sugar and salt to your list, Colleen's mum!" TillyTilly shouted above the sound of the water.

Mrs. McLain did not, at first, notice what was going on. She was kneeling by a floor-level cupboard, rummaging through it, but she emerged when the water over-reached the edge of the sink and began trickling down the side of the unit. She looked up and saw both taps on, the salt container rolling on the floor. One hand went over her mouth, and she said, "Jesus," long and loud.

Next, Jess and TillyTilly were in the sitting room, jumping up and down all over her puffy cushions. Jess felt oddly as if she were swimming, buoyed up not only by her own will but by something behind, in front and all around her until she didn't know whether she was in this mad, happy frenzy because she wanted to be or because the situation had propelled her. They scrambled off the sofa when they heard Mrs. McLain shout, "COLLEEN! You get down here right now! I'm doing the washing!"

They raced to the doorway, hearing Colleen thump her way down the stairs.

"I don't want Colleen to get into trouble because of us," Jess whispered to TillyTilly, as Colleen passed them without a glance, clutching a small bundle in her hands. Colleen's eyes were red, and she was sniffling, although the usual strand of hair was tucked into her mouth and she was chewing it nervously.

"Why not?" Tilly asked, looking surprised.

"It's not fair . . ." Jess began, then changed her mind. "Actually, I think I do want her to get into trouble, but I didn't want to say so because it's bad of me to think that, especially after she already got into trouble." She frowned at TillyTilly, awaiting her verdict.

TillyTilly gave a characteristic shrug, the shrug of one with an untroubled conscience.

"I don't think it's bad of you at all. Colleen's a pain in the bum."

Jess began to speak but was silenced by TillyTilly, who held up a hand and pointed in the direction of the kitchen. They both leaned out of the doorway in time to see Mrs. McLain snatch the bundle from Colleen and shake it out. Knickers. A whole bunch of different coloured knickers, some of which fell to the floor as Mrs. McLain shook them out. She ignored the knickers that had fallen to the floor, and with a jerky, stabbing gesture mashed the pair she held into Colleen's face. They could only see Colleen's back, but Jess felt sorry for her when she sprang backwards yelping, her shoulders hunched as if she was trying to make herself disappear.

"Don't you ever hide your wet knickers again, do you hear me?" Mrs. McLain shouted as she bent to scoop up the fallen knickers, pinching the material between her fingers and holding it away from her with an expression of distaste. "Your room *stinks*! If you're so ashamed of wetting yourself, then why don't you just *stop*! You're eight years old, for Christ's sake! And you're wetting yourself *every day*! Well, you can bloody well think again if you think I'm going to allow you to shame me by taking you to some kind of doctor like your class teacher suggested!"

Colleen began to cry and protest at the same time, her hands over her face. Jess couldn't properly hear what she was saying. She turned to Tilly to ask if they should go, only to find that TillyTilly was now lying on the sofa kicking her legs in the air, her body twisted with silent laughter.

"Oh my God," Tilly managed to gasp when she saw Jess looking at her in surprise and dismay. "Isn't it hilarious? Colleen McLain wets herself!"

FIVE

It was that night that Jess first began having the dreams about the woman with the long arms.

After her mother had read her some of the new book that she was writing and had tucked her in, Jess still did not feel sleepy, so she sat up and tried to read the copy of *Little Women* that TillyTilly had given her, thinking that a familiar story would make her feel drowsy. It did, but not because it was familiar. The story line was subtly different somehow, although she couldn't be absolutely sure what the difference was, or whether it was just the shadows creeping along the pages.

It seemed that Beth, who was far and away her favourite character in the book, was now   kind of mean. She stayed in the house all the time and she didn't like anybody, and she was always hiding from people and watching them and feeling jealous because they were healthy and she wasn't. But this was all wrong. Beth was the one whose words and character Jess held closest to herself, the one who broke Jess's heart by dying as bravely as Jo had lived. Jess began to think that maybe she wasn't reading *Little Women* but another story altogether and it wasn't a very good story, and . . .

She felt as if she were moving, maybe in a bus or an aeroplane, and all sorts of objects were rushing past her with incredible speed, although not one thing touched her. It was quite dark—she could see, but she didn't know what she was seeing. There was a full-grown man trapped inside a glass bottle, pounding helplessly on the sloping sides, mouthing words of entreaty as the air inside the bottle slowly ran out. He stared at her and stopped beating the glass; she stared at him. She couldn't understand this. She did not know who the man was. It was a glass Fanta bottle, like the ones in Nigeria. The bottle went spinning away from her. There was no wind. Jess realised that it was a tunnel that she was in, a kind of tunnel. A tunnel that turned and turned and sucked things through it. But she was not moving, she wasn't flying away, she was standing still while the tunnel moved. And then the woman came to her, the woman that she had seen drawn in the Boys' Quarters. She was flying alongside a stream of debris and paper, and the first thing Jess saw coming out of the darkness was her arms. They were like dancing pieces of string, although thicker, and Jess thought at first that she would be afraid. But she wasn't. The woman landed and her legs cycled as if she was pedalling air, trying to stay on the ground and not move. She looked at Jess and smiled, her arms waving from side to side, elbowless, jointless. Her boubou *was floating. But there was no wind. The woman was still smiling when the tunnel took her flying again, and Jess smiled too. "We are the same," said the long-armed woman, as she flew away. She wasn't speaking in English, and it wasn't Yoruba either.*

"Yes," said Jessamy. "Yes."

On Friday, the school nurse told her that she could eat her lunch in the school office as usual, but then she had to go to the playground.

Jess glared at the nurse; she must have got it wrong. She never went to the playground at playtime.

The nurse was unmoved. Mr. Heinz had said he didn't think it was necessary for Jess to stay alone in the nurse's office for the whole of lunchtime. "Take your time over your lunch, though, pet," she said, pretending to be sympathetic.

Fine. I'll make my food last for the whole of lunchtime.

"Mr. Heinz says he'd like you to be in the playground by one o'clock," the nurse said as she left.

One o'clock!

Jess almost growled with her discontent, wishing that Tilly Tilly had come to school with her so that the playground would be bearable. But she would probably see her after school. She brightened at this thought, and unwrapped her sandwich, then groaned. It was tuna and sweet corn. Inside the sandwich bag was a typed note from her mother: *We've run out of mushrooms.*

Bad day. Bad, bad day.

Later, in the playground, Jess was sitting on one of the green benches that formed a row until they reached the far wall. The teacher on duty stood across the playground, eyeing her. She didn't want the teacher to come over and ask her if she was all right, so she bent her head and carried on reading. She'd abandoned *The Lord of the Rings* for now and was concentrating on *Little Women* instead. Now that it was daytime, she was surprised that she had thought the story different. It was exactly the same. Even now, her fingers were itching for a pencil to "correct" with, to draw over the offending lines so you couldn't even make out the shapes of the letters. She smoothed her ponytail, twisting some of the hair around her finger, and turned the page. Year Five boys began running in circles around her bench, throwing handfuls of leaves at her, but soon went away when they realised that she wasn't taking any notice of them.

When she next looked up, the teacher was trying to stop a fight that had developed in a corner of the playground between two Year Six boys. It looked as if they were fighting over who got to kick a penalty. From the corner of her eye, she could see Colleen McLain and Andrea and Sonia Carney coming towards her. They were all smiling, nudging each other, arms linked. They were a *group*. Jess began to feel dread dripping slowly like water in her stomach. She shifted and cleared her throat, telling herself not to worry, not to be surprised.

What can they do to you anyway? They'll only say stuff.

She should have expected this, should have known that no matter what she knew about Colleen McLain, it didn't make Colleen the sort of person who wouldn't pick on other people. True, Colleen's mum pushed her daughter's knickers into her face and made her cry, but Colleen was also clever and a leader and she didn't like Jessamy. This confused Jess so much that she sighed deeply. She had a headache.

The *group* stopped in front of her. "Oh, is it a new girl?" they asked each other, expressions of mock wonderment on their faces, thoughtful fingers placed beside mouths. Colleen, clearly enjoying herself, even stroked her chin.

"I think it is," one of them said.

Jess refused to look up from her book and couldn't tell whether it was Andrea or Sonia. Although they looked nothing alike, they both had a high, nasal quality to their voices, as if they couldn't breathe properly.

"It looks like Jessamy," said Colleen.

"It can't be!" said one of the others. "Jessamy never comes to the playground. She's always off having a fit in the nurse's room."

"Yeah," said Andrea/Sonia. "And she's got no mates, either, so why would she come to the playground?"

Jess gritted her teeth.

"But she looks just like Jessamy," Colleen said loudly, leaning closer to Jess. Jess thought that she could smell the saliva on her hair.

Oh, the disgusting, disgusting saliva and this *group* not liking her; it took all the nerve she had not to let herself fall backwards off the bench and carry on screaming long after she'd hit the ground.

Then Colleen McLain poked her in the forehead, which shouldn't have happened.

Jess lashed out and hit Colleen square in the face so that she staggered back, holding her cheek and shouting. She couldn't stop there; she ran at the other two, needing to scatter them so that they wouldn't be a group anymore. Andrea Carney pushed her and she grabbed Andrea's struggling arm and stuffed four fingers into her mouth and

BIT her, and bit and bit, and even chomped *(tried to eat her up)*, snarling, clawing at Andrea's shocked face with her other hand until Colleen pulled her off by her ponytail, and the teacher on duty came running over, all jangling keys, blowing her whistle as if that was going to help, and Andrea was crying and nursing her hand, and Sonia was saying "Oh my God . . . she's mad," and Colleen was trying to tell the teacher that Jessamy started it.

The teacher on duty stared at Jessamy. It was always the quiet ones that suddenly lost it. Jess sat back down on the bench, clutching her copy of *Little Women*, staring at Andrea, who was being taken to the nurse by Sonia. "I'm gonna kill you," shouted Sonia, crying herself. Jess was watching them both crying and did not really know what to think. She felt bad about biting Andrea: after all, it wasn't Andrea's fault; Andrea had taken her to the school nurse's office once. It was Colleen McLain who was the problem and the puzzle. It was her.

"You," said the teacher on duty. Jess looked at her. The teacher was pointing at her. "You're on the wall for the rest of lunchtime play! And I'm putting you in the Incident Book as well! There might be a letter home about this!"

Jess got up and went across the playground to sit on the low wall that all the playtime offenders had to sit on. They weren't allowed to get up without permission until the bell went. Nam Hong was on the wall as well, and Samantha Robinson. She didn't know why, she didn't ask.

"What are you doing here?" Nam asked. He was chewing bubble gum. Maybe that was why he was on the wall in the first place; it was just like him to reoffend whilst being punished.

"Had a fight." Jess wanted to keep the conversation as brief as possible. She twisted her hands together, avoiding eye contact with the other two.

Sam Robinson leaned over.

"I saw! Wow, that was madness!" she said admiringly. "Sonia Carney's gonna kill you, though. Her big brother's at secondary school, you know."

Jess shrugged, wondering if TillyTilly would be able to fight Sonia Carney's big brother. She also wondered, briefly, what TillyTilly would say about what had just happened. She thought it might be something like, *"Brilliant! They're all out of order anyways."* She hoped it would be something like that.

Then Colleen McLain came over.

Again.

What now?

"Don't you ever touch me again," Colleen shouted, jabbing a finger at Jess.

Sam and Nam looked at each other, almost rubbing their hands with anticipation. Jess didn't respond.

"Did you hear me? You stupid freak show! Everyone thinks you're mad, you know! You do all these . . . STUPID things and I bet you think they're amazing but no one likes you because of them! You're one of these people who'll never be normal! You'll probably end up in a *mental hospital* or something! You're just lucky the teacher came before I belted you one!" Colleen's face was red and although she stood some distance away from the wall, Jess could see that she was shaking with anger. Jess opened up the book to the page that she had last been reading. "Don't you DARE ignore me!" Colleen raged. "You better apologise to me! APOLOGISE! Before I beat you up! My mum says it's not your fault you're mad, she says it's the way you've been brought up. Your family is *weird*, didn't you know?"

Nam gave a half laugh, half gasp. "Oh NO! Jess, are you going to have that? You should knock her out!"

Jess focused on the words and on making them not dance about on the page. She had to ignore Colleen, had to.

"You think you're the cleverest girl in the school, don't you?" Colleen shouted at the top of her voice, then reached over and knocked *Little Women*, Jess's book, Jess's mother's book, out of her hand.

They both stared at it as it lay on the ground. Then Colleen stamped on it, and the paperback cover crushed and crinkled beneath her Caterpillar boot. Jess watched Colleen's boot messing up her mother's book. She shouldn't have brought it into school.

Sam Robinson jumped in the air with astonishment and excitement before remembering that she wasn't supposed to stand up while on the wall. She sat down again.

Jess didn't move but began to speak in a low voice, so low that Sam and Nam had to come close to hear what she was saying. So did Colleen.

"I don't think I'm the cleverest girl in the school, and I don't think I'm amazing, and I'm not mad and you don't know anything about me so you'd better shut up before you say anything else because I might hit you again and then my parents will be angry because I'll be in the Incident Book twice."

She paused, then looked up at Colleen McLain with an

expression that made the girl draw back. Jess's usually hazel brown irises seemed darker.

Jess's voice grew in volume as more people from their class gathered, trying to see what was going on. She caught sight of Tunde Coker making signals to her, mouthing *Are you OK?*, but she ignored him. She continued speaking in a monotone, conscious of the fact that now that she was humiliating Colleen McLain she should be feeling happy, or remorseful but glad, or at least something:

"And my family is not *weird*. Or, if they are *weird*, they're not as *weird* as your family. There must be something *weird* about your family, Colleen, to make you wet yourself every day, and there must be something *weird* about your mum that makes her go berserk about it and push your wet knickers in your face. If I'm *weird*, you're *weirder*, so shut your big, fat, ugly, baby mouth."

There was a burst of laughter from all around. Tunde Coker smiled.

Nam Hong stood up on the wall, pretending to hold a microphone to his lips.

"Is it true, Colleen?" he asked, holding his microphone fist out to Colleen.

Colleen McLain's mouth opened and closed in shock.

"It's not true!" she said, finally, ignoring Nam's "microphone" and speaking to the others from their class. Her cheeks were even redder than before. "She's lying!"

Sam Robinson gave a guffaw of laughter. "We know it's not true, Colleen. But it IS a pretty wicked thing to make up when you're having an argument with someone!" She looked at Jess, who was picking up her book, with growing respect. "I never thought you'd *say* something like that!"

"Look," said Nam, "Colleen's gone off into the girls' toilets!" And it was true. Colleen had fled sobbing across the playground, her hair bobbing frantically as she ran. Alison Carr volunteered to go after her, but to everyone's surprise, Jess stood up from the wall.

"I'll go," she said.

Sam looked doubtful.

"You're not allowed, you're on the wall," she said. Then: "Besides, it's better not to have another fight in the toilets."

"Yeah, also, I don't think she's, like, speaking to you," Alison chimed in, to laughter from the others.

Jess shook all these objections off. She had begun to feel as if she had done something very bad and only had a few minutes to make amends before she was punished. There would be . . . consequences if she didn't make an effort to sort it out. It didn't matter if Colleen told Miss Patel or the teacher on duty, or even Mr. Heinz; the worry was vague and distant, but still there. She shouldn't have said that in front of everyone, even if Colleen had stamped on her book. She didn't think TillyTilly would think much of it, but she was going to apologise to Colleen.

Colleen was absolutely silent in the cubicle. If Jess hadn't peered beneath the closed door and seen her feet in their Caterpillar boots, she would have thought that Colleen wasn't there. She stood at one of the sinks, staring at herself in the mirror, shaking her ponytail from side to side, watching the fluffy hair bounce. It would be easier to talk to her own face, maybe.

"Colleen?"

Silence.

"Um, Colleen?"

"What. Do. You. Want."

"I'm sorry."

Silence.

Then the cubicle door opened with a grating sound as Colleen unlocked it, and Jess could see her leaning against the now open door, her face flushed, her eyes gleaming, angry. She had pushed all her hair behind her ears for once, and a tuft of it was sticking up on the top of her head. She looked around to see if Jess had brought anyone with her.

"So, what do you want me to do: apologise for stamping on your stupid book? Because I'm not sorry. I'm glad I did it."

Surprised, Jess turned from the mirror to face Colleen. She hadn't expected an apology from Colleen McLain; nobody got apologies from Colleen.

"I don't want you to apologise. It wouldn't help me anyway." More silence.

"Well, if you're feeling better, I'm going to go now," Jess said, feeling stupid.

But Colleen stopped her. "How did you know?" she demanded, flushing a deeper red and staring at the floor.

Jess grimaced. How *had* she and TillyTilly been able to do the things that they had done yesterday? Because now there was no question that it had really happened; Colleen had just indirectly admitted some of it herself. Jess had tried to push these sort of ideas away when she was with her friend, but now, seeing what her knowledge had done, knowing that for once she had actually hit someone with what she knew, she felt sort of
(uneasy)
about it.

Colleen was still looking at the floor.

"I heard Miss Patel talking to the school nurse about it one lunchtime," Jess said, finally. She wanted to forget the stupid knickers. "I'll say I was lying," she offered.

Colleen glared at her, then stepped out of the cubicle and pushed her way past Jess.

"I already said that."

SIX

It was Jess's dad's day off, and he picked her up from the school playground, taking hold of her hand but saying little as they crossed the road and began to walk through the park. She wasn't sure whether a teacher had already phoned home about today, so she kept quiet too, swinging her book bag in little arcs through the air with her free hand.

"Daddy."

"That's me," he replied, smiling.

Jess smiled too before her expression became serious again.

"Are you all right?" she asked.

Her father swung their joined hands.

"I'm fine, Jess."

She was half running along beside him to catch up with his strides.

"Daddy."

"Me again!"

Jess looked down at the ground. It was moving past quite fast because she was scurrying now, almost tripping over her book bag.

"Something happened at school today." She waited for him to interrupt, to ask *Did you have* another *tantrum?*, but he said nothing. "I got in trouble. I hit Colleen McLain and I . . . Andrea Carney was in the fight as well. They started it! And I had to sit on the wall, and I got put in the Incident Book. And they didn't! It's not fair."

She bit her lip, waiting for him to let go of her hand and make her walk on her own so that she could "think about what she had done."

"Dulcie's going through a fighting period at school as well," her father muttered. Jess couldn't think what this had to do with her.

"Look, you know that it's just not on for you to go around hitting people, even if they DID start it," he began sternly. "I mean, what do you think the world would be like if we all went around hitting each other when we were cross?"

Jess blinked a few times, trying to imagine this.

"It'd be madness," she offered.

"Exactly! So don't you start! This is not going to happen again, is it?"

She looked at him, blinking, surprised and dismayed. He wanted her to say that it wouldn't happen again, but she didn't know, she couldn't say; she hadn't even known that the fight was going to happen in the first place. It was like saying: *What a surprise! It's raining! I don't like rain, so it won't happen again, will it?*

"It won't happen again?" her father insisted.

Hmmm. Jess could now see that she was agreeing to too many things. Perhaps now it was time to make a stand, time to—

"No, it won't," she muttered. Next time, next time would be make-a-stand time.

When they got home, her mother was in the hallway speaking on the phone, the cord twisting around her wrist, her other

hand to her forehead. She gave them a look as they passed, pointing a finger at Jess to make sure she stayed where she was. Jess
and her dad looked at each other somewhat guiltily.

"Oh no," said Jess's dad. "That must be the school on the
phone."

"Mmmm, yes, I see," her mum said quietly. Then: "Right.
Well, I'm sorry about all that. I'll make sure she understands that
it's *shocking* behaviour."

She directed the words "shocking behaviour" at Jess, raising
her eyebrows with an angry sarcasm. Jess held on even more
tightly to her dad's hand.

When Sarah Harrison came off the phone, she beckoned Jess
into the sitting room. Jess followed, half pulling her father along
by the hand, but her mother said, "Daniel, let her go. She's got to
learn that she can't keep on doing this, and you're not helping."

Jess's father let go of her hand, but argued, "You're saying she
can't 'keep on,' but this is the first time she's actually hit anybody.
I've spoken to her, and it won't happen again."

Her mum didn't reply, but jerked her thumb in the direction
of the sitting room again, and Jess bolted in, cringing past her
mother for fear of getting one of the rogue slaps to the side of
the head that Sarah would sometimes give if she thought Jess had
behaved badly. Her mother shut the door.

"D'you see what I mean?" Jess heard her father say. "She's
scared you're going to hit her. This isn't the way to make her behave herself, you know. It doesn't matter whether you were
brought up that way or not —"

"You can criticise my upbringing later, if you like. Right
now, I'm trying to discipline my daughter. Did you know that
she BIT someone? It's bloody embarrassing, Daniel! Where on
earth would she get that idea from?"

Jess sat on the very edge of a chair, craning to hear where her mother's voice was coming from. The muffled quality of it suggested that she had her head in a kitchen cupboard. So it would be the tins. She heard her father clattering up the stairs, removing himself from the situation.

Her mother reentered the sitting room, and Jess flinched almost without realising what she was doing. Her mother, bearing an enormous tin of pineapple chunks in each hand, looked puzzled.

"For God's sake! Nobody's going to smack you, child," she snapped.

Jess couldn't hear her properly over the *thwack thwack thwack* sound that she had heard in Colleen McLain's house, the sound that was replaying in her head over and over.

She wanted to put her hands over her ears, but her mum would lose it—Nigerian parents, her mother had once explained, could actually kill a child over disrespect. It had been known to happen.

Her mother thrust the pineapple tins at her, making her hold one in each hand. She felt the fleshy parts between her fingers stretching with the weight of them, felt the hard metal push into her palms. They were too heavy to hold. She wouldn't last.

"See, I know for a fact that talking to you won't help, but I just don't know what to do with you anymore. So whenever you feel like hitting or, for God's sake, BITING someone—like some kind of animal!—whether this is at school, or *anywhere*, you just remember these tins and how heavy they were to hold up for a whole half an hour."

Jess didn't look up at her mother's face, but saw her hand point to the far corner of the sitting room. She walked over, turned to face the wall, and put the tins down for a few seconds so that she could find a comfortable kneeling position.

"And no resting on your bum! If you do, I really will smack

you! I'll be checking on you: you do not move, or put those tins down!"

Jess could already feel the prickling behind her eyes. She knew that she was going to cry because it was stupid and embarrassing to be kneeling here facing the wall holding two tins above her head, and because her hands would hurt for ages afterwards, and also because she would be terrified for the whole half hour that if her hands just couldn't take it anymore and she let a tin drop, it would crack her skull open. If she died, it would be her mother's fault, and she would come back as a ghost and let everyone know.

"Hate you," she mouthed. "I hate you, hate you, hate you." Her arms were wobbling already, there was no way she would be able to hold them straight up, the weight of the tins would break her hands.

Her mum was still in the room. "I'm not going to do the whole 'it's for your own good' thing," she said, in a gentler tone of voice, "but if you do this for half an hour, I'll come and get you and then you can have Jesstime and we'll say no more about it. I'll consider it a lesson learnt. OK?"

Jess did not reply. She closed her eyes and concentrated on making her arms towers, strong towers that could hold up these stupid measly tins and even crush them and make them not exist. A half-hour tower, that's what her arms would be.

"OK?" her mother repeated.

Jess could picture her standing in the doorway, her arms folded. *Stupid, horrible woman.*

"OK," she managed to say, although it sounded more like a whine—*Ohkaaaaaaaaay*—because it was mixed in with a repressed sob and the strangled, snuffling sound of trying to draw in breath through a nose blocked with mucus: *uh-uh-uhhhh, uh-hhh, uhhhhhh.*

She would never eat tinned pineapples again, not ever, she vowed, knowing even as she promised herself this that she would probably eat some later. Yes, that was what she could do, she could think about how, in half an hour, this would not be happening anymore, and although she would never forgive her mother, things would be back to normal.

Why couldn't things stop changing around so that she wouldn't feel as if she should love her mother one minute and hate her the next? It was too confusing. Sweat was forming on her forehead and she could feel beads of it on her upper lip.

"Hate you," she whispered, filled with an anger that she could barely believe. She wanted to be swept up by it and throw the tins away from her, maybe break the television, some ornaments. "*Ohhhh . . .* hate you."

"Who, me?" she heard TillyTilly say.

TillyTilly?

She opened her eyes, feeling the tears that she had squeezed up behind her eyelids spill out, and peered around the room.

TillyTilly was a little distance away from her, looking inquisitive.

She looked exactly the same as she had the day before, the end of one of her pigtails sweeping her shoulder, her head tipped a little to the side in her customary gesture, a small puzzled smile creasing the corners of her eyes.

Jess stared at her, open-mouthed, then twisted around slightly, listening for her mother. She couldn't hear her, so her mother must have gone upstairs. Jess lowered her arms, but still did not risk letting go of the tins.

"My mum didn't let you in, did she," Jess said. It wasn't a question.

TillyTilly shook her head, looking pleased with herself, then she gestured at the tins.

"What's all this fuss about? Just because of the fight?"

Jess was unsurprised that TillyTilly already knew.

"Yeah. The school phoned."

TillyTilly shrugged, as if to say, *What can you do?*

"TillyTilly," said Jess, after a little while. "TillyTilly, when are you going to show me how to be like you?"

TillyTilly began making her fingers walk on their points over the top of the tins.

"I never said I'd do that," she said, looking at Jess out of the corner of her eye.

Jess sighed impatiently.

"Stop messing about! You said you would at Bodija—"

TillyTilly interrupted her. "No, I didn't. I asked you if you'd like to do the things I can do, and you said 'Yeah,' and that was it. So there. I don't see why you should start getting angry with me just because your mum's punishing you with pineapple tins." She tittered in a mocking way that Jess didn't like, and Jess felt little ice-cold stabbings behind her eyeballs. Tilly stopped laughing when she saw the corners of Jess's mouth turn downwards.

"Sorry," she said gruffly. "Don't be a crybaby about it, though."

"Please, please make me be like you, TillyTilly. Come on. Please!"

TillyTilly adjusted her body so that she was sitting cross-legged.

"Yeah, yeah, I will," she said. "Later. Not now. You don't like school very much, do you, Jessy?"

Jess shook her head vigorously.

"I bet I'd like school if you came. Why don't you come to my school?"

TillyTilly nibbled her fingernail, looking distracted.

"I can't. I'm older than you lot."

Jess was astonished. She hadn't thought about that.

"You don't *look* older than me," she said, in a doubtful tone, adding in alarm: "What, even older than the Year Six girls?"

TillyTilly nodded, just once, then said, glancing at the ceiling, "Your mum's coming."

Tilly approached Jess and wrapped her thin arms around her shoulders. They rocked quietly back and forth and Jess felt her breathing slow, the heaving movements of her chest growing still as her friend's cool hands and the smell of some sort of light, leafy pomade in Tilly's hair comforted her. She closed her eyes. It was the embrace of someone who could protect her. Then the smell of fading greenery escaped on a waft of air as, eyes still closed, she heard Tilly's light feet pattering across the sitting-room floor.

Jess expelled air, an unconsciously blissful smile on her face, then, hastily balancing a tin on each palm, raised herself up on her knees and extended her arms again. This time, she did not close her eyes; even the sharp pain of the tins' hard roundedness on her skin seemed to recede. She was wondering, as she stared at the wall, why Tilly had left, especially since she could be invisible. Unless her mum was magic too, and would be able to see her and would ask all sorts of questions. And Jess knew Tilly didn't like questions. Or maybe Tilly could do these things for one day only and then they ran out. Maybe she had run out of invisibility. She heard her mother at the door.

"Oh, Jess! You're still here, I'd forgotten. All right," Sarah said, "get up and give me the tins. On Monday we can talk about maybe having your new friend over, hmmm?"

Jess turned, her knees grazing painfully against the carpet as she swivelled her body around on her knees.

"Has half an hour gone?" she asked incredulously.

What *was* it about time and TillyTilly?

SEVEN

It was Sunday afternoon, and Jess's parents were going to take her to Dr. McKenzie's house, "just for a visit." Dr. McKenzie was a psychologist, which mainly meant that he was supposed to know a little bit about what was happening inside her head, and be able to make her feel better by talking to her. This was scary. They were in the park, and Jess was winded from playing an energetic game of chase with Tilly, when Tilly, who was not at all out of breath, suddenly said "McKenzie" in a musing sort of way, as if the thought had just come to her on the air. Jess stretched her legs out across the bench and fanned herself with her hands, even though it was cold weather now and she had already undone the zip of her green puffer jacket.

"Oh yeah . . . he's a psychologist. Psychologists—"

"Jessy, I know what a psychologist is!"

"Sorry. Um. They're taking me to see him, Dr. McKenzie. Just for a visit, and if he thinks he can help, then I'm supposed to see him quite a lot."

Tilly, chewing on a thumbnail, didn't respond immediately,

and Jess, gazing at her lying on the frosty grass in her school dress, couldn't keep the amazement off her face.

"Aren't you even a diddy-bit cold, TillyTilly?"

Tilly rolled over onto her back and kicked her legs in the air before sitting up and jabbing a finger at Jess, her mouth turned down in a frown.

"Don't go and see that man," she commanded. Her finger was trembling as she pointed, and Jess, who had never seen Tilly scared, was surprised and a little scared herself.

She began zipping her jacket up, looking away from Tilly.

"I've got to go," she mumbled. "My mum's making me."

TillyTilly, who was no longer in sight, snorted from somewhere, and Jess felt a little more courageous now that those accusing eyes weren't on her.

"And . . . I sort of want to go anyway, y'know," she added, very quickly and in a low voice, in case she needed to take it back.

TillyTilly rematerialised on the bench beside her, crossly pushing Jess's legs aside to make more room.

"Why d'you want to go? What do you need help for?" she demanded, without moving her face.

Jess grimaced; she hated it when Tilly did that—it was like talking to some sentient statue.

"Don't do that, TillyTilly," she pleaded.

Tilly didn't respond, but kept her keen eyes fixed on her.

"I s'pose . . . I want to go because I'm not very . . . um, well, I'm not like Dulcie, or Tunde, or even Ebun. I'm just not—"

"What?" Tilly cried. "So now you WANT to be like those silly people? You want *him* to make you like *them*?"

Jess wondered why Tilly was getting so agitated, as if *she* were the one who was being made to see this psychologist. Maybe she was worried that Dr. McKenzie would say that she was made up.

"I won't tell him about you, TillyTilly," Jess reassured her hastily, but Tilly folded her arms and glared off into the distance. "TillyTilly, there's something about Dulcie and Tunde and even the others, even Colleen, that's *too* different from me. It makes me . . . weird. I don't want to be weird and always thinking weird things and being scared, and I don't want to have something missing from me, and—"

"Shut up!" Tilly leapt up from the bench and paced up and down in front of Jess. "You're shabby! You keep saying something's missing when nothing is! So you're still going to see him!"

"I've GOT TO, though, TillyTilly! My mum—"

"He won't help you, Jessy. There'll only be trouble," Tilly said darkly. Then she stalked away, leaving Jess alone on the bench surrounded by icy bushes.

Dr. McKenzie lived in Bromley, not that far from Dulcie. The bus went past the train station, and once they had passed it, the downslope of the road was familiar to Jess. The streets, and the area around the Baker's Oven beside the train station, seemed at first teeming with people, but as Jess watched, she realised that it was the reflection of the glass in the shop window mixing in with the reflections of people standing in the bus behind her. Her eyes had gone out of focus without her noticing it.

"Jess, say hello to Dr. McKenzie," Sarah urged as they arrived, thrusting the reluctant Jess forward a little. The doctor laughingly insisted that they call him Colin. Jess gaped up at him, managing a squeaky "Hello." She hadn't expected him to be so tall and so . . . red. Dr. McKenzie was very thin, maybe even almost as thin as TillyTilly, and the long hands clasping Jess's own were smooth, pale and slim-fingered, their length broken only by the clean encirclement of a white-gold band on his wedding finger. He looked young, younger than Jess's father, and his face was slightly gaunt although his cheeks were ruddy. Even if his mouth wasn't smiling, his faded blue eyes and the crinkling of the skin around them reassured her that he was friendly. But—his eyebrows were red! His eyebrows *and* his tousled, slightly up-standing hair—the most peculiar sort of red that Jess had ever seen, like orange paint, although the eyebrows were darker. Oh, she mustn't stare, she had to *not* stare at Dr. McKenzie's hair, but he caught her awestruck gaze and ruefully ran a hand through the tuft, saying, "Curse of the McKenzies."

Dr. McKenzie's sitting room was bigger than theirs, and it had stranger pictures on the walls: fierce, clashing daubs and waves of colour trapped behind glass. The walls were painted lilac instead of wallpapered, leaving still, bare expanses between the framed pictures. This way, you could see the corners of the room sharply: it was like being in a carpeted box, but it wasn't cold. If anything, it was slightly too warm in the room, but neither was it claustrophobic—perhaps because of the enormous, south-facing windows. Jess teetered apprehensively on the edge of the cushioned bamboo-cane chair, feeling as if her hair had been combed and brushed too flat and close to her head. She wondered when Dr. McKenzie would start trying to work out what she was thinking; at the moment he appeared to be doing a lot of inconsequential talking with her parents, about the holiday in Nigeria and so on. He kept looking at her as if she was supposed to be talking too, but Jess remained resolutely detached.

They met Mrs. McKenzie, who was small and curly blond in much the same way as Dr. McKenzie was tall and red. She was filled with a sort of smiling energy that made her seem constantly in transit, whether she was bustling about with tea and biscuits, or even sitting and talking, her foot tapping.

Jess was nibbling on a biscuit forced upon her by Mrs. McKenzie and looking at a picture to the left of the doctor's head. It wasn't a painting, it was a large black-and-silver framed photograph of, as he explained when he saw her looking at it, his daughter when she was five. Jess couldn't help smiling a little at the chubby, freckled-limbed five-year-old kneeling in a blue swimsuit by an attempted sand castle, wielding her red plastic spade before the wet heap of sand and squinting irritably into the camera, visibly outraged at being interrupted. Her hair was a wild bundle of auburn almost as curly as Jess's own, only short. She had obviously been touched by the "curse of the McKenzies" too.

"That's just one aspect of Siobhan's character," Dr. McKenzie told Jess with a wry smile before directing her attention to Siobhan's most recent school picture, propped up against the wall on a low shelf filled with knick-knacks. To Jess's surprise, the nine-year-old Siobhan still wasn't smiling. Jess, who had an automatic camera smile, thought that you weren't really allowed not to smile for school pictures. Siobhan looked attentive but a little surprised, her grey eyes gazing, it seemed, at the top of the photographer's head, a black barrette pulling her hair back in bright waves around her round, freckled face.

Then a soft impatient "Oi!" and Jess shot a startled glance at the doorway to find the girl herself, or at least the tip of her pointy nose, a length of black legging and the swoosh of green skirt over it. Jess glanced at her father and Dr. McKenzie, who were still deep in quiet conversation now that Jess's mum had gone off somewhere with Mrs. McKenzie, then she looked back at the sitting-room door, where half of Siobhan McKenzie was now in view—she was crouching in the hallway, holding on to the door-post with one hand. At first glance, it looked as if her stomach was a distended, square shape until Jess realised that she had something shoved underneath her green T-shirt. She beckoned to Jess, then abruptly disappeared. Jess didn't know what to do about this and she sat, half poised to rise from the chair, for another second or so before Siobhan's tousled head snaked around the doorpost again and she gestured frantically for Jess to come.

"The bag!" she hissed.

Jess, bewildered, picked up her rucksack, which had *The Lord of the Rings* in it, which she'd brought in case she got bored, and scurried over to Siobhan, who promptly took it from her, pulled a box of Milk Tray from underneath her T-shirt and shoved it in. She thrust the bag back at Jess and beckoned her upstairs.

"Come on. You can have some," she promised, as they started climbing the stairs.

Mrs. McKenzie called out from the kitchen. "Shivs?"

Siobhan paused with one hand on the banister and smiled apologetically at Jess.

"Yeah?"

"Just checking you're back in, love. How's Katrina?"

"She's all right—her piggy bank broke, though, and she's had to put it all in a jam jar."

"Aww! We can get her another one for her birthday."

"Yeah . . ."

Siobhan showed Jessamy into her room, which was a sky-lighted, rainbow-wallpapered heap of clothes, shoes, papers and cuddly toys, and kicked the door shut. She took the bag from Jess and dumped herself on her bed, ripping the cellophane off the chocolate box with her teeth and spitting bits onto the floor. When she had the box open, she stared at Jess, who was sniffing at the faint scent of bubble gum in the air, with open curiosity.

"You can sit down if you want."

Jess took a seat on the edge of Siobhan's bed and indicated the row of pristine-looking Barbie dolls ranged against the far wall.

"Wow! You must have nearly all of them!"

Siobhan grinned widely and tossed a chocolate into her mouth, then offered the box to Jess, who gingerly picked one out at random. It turned out to be a praline—yuck.

"Yeah, they're not all mine," Siobhan said, waving at the Barbies. "Some are Katrina's, but it's my week to have 'em." She rattled the chocolate box at Jess, who refused with a shake of her head.

"My mum won't let me have Barbies. She thinks they're evil. She says they, um, can't be a role model for real women because they represent this white idea of beauty."

Siobhan considered this in silence, her brow wrinkled as she bit into another chocolate, holding the other half, oozing caramel, in her hand.

"Yeah, but there's, like . . . black ones, too," she offered.

Jess shrugged.

"My mum says . . . they look just like the white ones, only with a different skin colour."

Siobhan finished her chocolate and put the box down on the bed between them before asking, "Yeah? What d'you think?"

"I don't know . . . They're only dolls, I s'pose. I wouldn't mind one."

Siobhan scratched her head bemusedly. "Yeah," she said, half-heartedly, then seemed to make up her mind about something and opened her mouth to show Jess her asymmetrically chipped front tooth. It had happened when she'd been playing a strange variation of blindman's buff with "some idiot called Anna," who had tied a belt over her eyes, told her to go forward, forward, forward, in pursuit of a special stone, effectively instructing Shivs to walk into a wall. Before Jess, amazed, could respond to this, Siobhan tapped the chocolate box between them and airily embarked upon another subject.

131

"These are from Katrina. She lives two doors down," she explained. "It's my birthday tomorrow, but my mum's really weird about me having chocolate, so she'd probably take them away—that's why I had to sneak them in."

"Happy birthday for tomorrow—"

They found themselves sniggering conspiratorially, then Siobhan rolled off the bed and tugged at the leg of Jess's jeans. "What's your name?"

"Jess—well, Jessamy, really."

"I'm Siobhan, but I HATE being called Ginger, so don't! Call me Shivs, all right?"

A nod from Jess, then a pause in which Shivs ate some more chocolate.

"I'm supposed to be talking about psychology with your dad today," Jess finally confided.

"Oh. Are you feeling really sad or something?" Shivs eyed Jess gravely and gave her knee a solicitous pat, which set Jess off laughing again. She didn't think she knew anyone as . . . solid, as *there,* as this girl. She wondered for a moment if TillyTilly would like Shivs. She, Jess, certainly did.

"I s'pose I'm sad sometimes, but not right now," she assured Shivs. "I get scared of stuff."

"Scared? What of?"

Jess shrugged, unable to put it into words and unwilling to try.

"Hah! Well, you should hang around with me then, 'cause I'm not scared of anything! Not a single thing," Shivs told her, laughing.

Looking at her stretched languidly out on the floor amongst her scattered belongings, Jess believed her. She began to reply, then stopped short as she caught sight of a copy of *Hamlet* by her foot and picked it up.

"This yours?"

Shivs was playing with a small pink teddy bear, making it dance. She flicked a glance at the book Jess was holding and nodded briefly.

"Wow," Jess said, excitedly. "Are you reading it? D'you think it's good? My mum's just started reading it to me and I think it's—"

Shivs threw the bear at Jess with a loud guffaw of laughter. "Jess, it's not REALLY mine, it's my dad's! I borrowed it one time to trace that man on the front."

"Oh."

Shivs turned onto her stomach and looked consideringly at Jess.

"You can understand all that boring Shakespeare stuff? You must be really clever then." She sounded impressed—impressed and something else that Jess couldn't quite identify. Suddenly tongue-tied, Jess shook her head and tried to say that her mum had to explain quite a lot of it to her, but Shivs cut her off. "Maybe that's why you get so sad," she said, "because you're clever."

Jess thought about that, but before she could respond, Shivs asked, "D'you know your phone number?" Jess shook her head and Shivs laughed. "Me neither, you know! But I have to learn it next year, just in case."

"Yeah," Jess said quickly, but was unable to stop herself asking: "Just in case what?"

"Dunno" Shivs began, then suddenly catlike, she sprang forward and knocked the box of Milk Tray off the bed so that it rolled underneath it, chocolates spilling everywhere. Before Jess could ask her what was going on, Mrs. McKenzie opened the door and smiled at her.

"There you are, love . . . So you and Shivs are getting on. Good . . . But d'you want to come and talk to Colin now?"

No.

"Yeah," Jess said, getting up and slinging her rucksack across her shoulder as she looked nervously at Shivs, who gave her a confident thumbs-up.

" 'Bye, Shivs."

"Jess, I'm going to call you tonight," Shivs said, following Jess to the door. Jess nodded, trying to appear nonchalant, but feeling embarrassingly warm. "On the phone, all right?"

Talking to Colin about psychology wasn't as scary as Jess had thought it would be. She quite liked him. They were just sitting in the kitchen by themselves drinking hot chocolate with marshmallows floating in it; she felt embarrassed drinking in front of him so she had to put her other hand over her top lip whenever she sipped. He asked her what she thought of school, and if she'd liked it in Nigeria. Sometimes she felt a little bit uncomfortable, because the minute she'd answered a question he seemed to have another related one ready to follow it up straightaway, and some of the questions were quite hard, like, "How do you know that that teacher thinks you're weird in a bad way?" But he didn't really ask the questions as if he was demanding an answer, but more as if he didn't need to know but would quite like to. She liked that. And she found that whenever the conversation got too tiring, she could just say, "I don't know, I don't know," in an anxious way, and he would stop and start talking about something else.

He told her about how, when he was a little boy, he had nearly drowned, and he told her how scary it was with all the water churning and filling him up. It surprised her a lot that this had happened to him, and she'd had to ask him how he'd felt when he was safe again, because she couldn't imagine a great tall person like him drowning.

"Well, I'll tell you something, Jess—I very quickly began to feel as if it had never really happened, as if it had actually happened to someone else," he replied.

She thought for a minute that he was going to ask her if she'd ever felt like that (she didn't think she ever had), but he didn't. She had also sort of expected him to be writing things down, like a report, but he didn't do that either.

There were other times during that conversation that Colin McKenzie really surprised her. The first was when he asked her what it felt like when she was screaming. She stared blankly at him, nonplussed even when he said that she could write it down if she wanted to. And she didn't even know *why* the question caught her so off balance—maybe it was because he had assumed that there *was* something for her to feel when she had a tantrum.

The second time was when he asked her to say the first word that came into her head in response to the words that he was going to say to her—she was too startled, too unprepared by this proposal. She wanted to bite back every word she said, or substitute it with another, but Dr. McKenzie, steadily stirring his hot chocolate with his spoon, went on inexorably churning out words.

"Mummy."

"Um. Big. No——"

"Daddy."

"Small. Smaller, I mean, than——"

"School."

"Nobody."

"Jess."

"Gone?"

"Where have you gone, Jess?"

She had no idea.

That was surprising, too.

EIGHT

———

The next time Jess saw TillyTilly, it was a Saturday morning. It was a warm day, almost stickily warm. Jess was lying on her bedroom floor with a ream of blank paper and her crayons and paint box beside her. Her mother's copy of *Little Women*, the cover Sellotaped onto the rest of the book, also lay beside her. Every now and then the telephone would ring, and her mother would run to it from the kitchen, shouting "I'll get it, I'll get it!" even though only Jess and she were at home. There was going to be a party tonight, held by a friend of Jess's father's family, and Aunt Lucy and Uncle Adam were going, and so were her father and her mother. Jess's mum was frantically telephoning every babysitter that had ever been recommended to her, hoping that one would be able to babysit on such short notice: "Today! This evening!"

Jess's dad had said reprovingly, "You shouldn't have left it so late, you know. Lucy offered, but you were so concerned that she'd find a babysitter that would only suit Dulcie and not Jessamy . . ."

Jess's mum had simply looked up from her diary of telephone

numbers and growled in a threatening manner, the sound rumbling deep in her throat. Jess's dad had remembered something terribly important that he needed to do, and went away.

Jess herself had been offended by the concept of the babysitter.

"I'm not a baby," she had insisted over breakfast as she carefully nibbled at the brown crust of her toast before starting on the real stuff.

Jess's dad had patted her cheek and then tweaked her nose in a comforting manner.

"I know. You're enormous, an enormous huge girl."

"What?!" Jess stuck out her tongue.

Her dad stuck out his tongue too.

Her mum joined in.

They all waggled their tongues at each other, then carried on eating. After a few seconds of companionable munching, Jess pursued her theme.

"Can't me and Dulcie just stay here by ourselves? We'd behave! You'd just need to leave some food, and we'd tuck ourselves in and everything."

Her mum laughed so hard she nearly choked on her toast. She kicked Jess's dad under the table, and he laughed a little too then explained, "The thing is, Jess, little girl, you and Dulcie have this thing where sometimes you fight. Imagine if we left you by yourselves —it'd be mayhem. Also, it wouldn't be safe because you wouldn't know what to do if something happened."

"Something like what?"

"Well, like intruders or something. People coming into the house uninvited."

Jess thought of TillyTilly.

"What's wrong with that?"

Jess's mum sipped at her orange juice.

"Jesus on toast, Jess, we're not leaving you and Dulcie alone and that's that."

"But do we have to have a *baby*sitter?" Jess wailed. "Couldn't you just drop me and Dulcie off at Grandma and Grandpa's?"

"Thing is, Jess, old man," her father said, drumming a little tattoo on the table with his butter knife, "they're going to the party as well."

"You just can't win. Sorry," her mum added.

At that point, Jess had rolled her eyes and, taking another bite of her peanut butter on toast, had resigned herself to the indignity of the as yet nameless babysitter.

As she lay surrounded by paper and scattered crayons, her head resting on her outstretched arm, Jess began thinking about one of the dreams that she had the previous night. She wanted to remember it—it had been nice—but it was too vague. The woman with the long arms had been smiling, flying through her dreams again, and Jess thought the woman might have been hugging her, the arms looping around and around Jess's body, holding her, the skin smooth like a velveteen rope. Jess didn't know how she could have thought that she was scary before. Or maybe it had been the drawing that was scary, the black squiggles, and the actual woman was lovely. The arms took some getting used to, though. She tried to draw the long-armed woman, her crayon skimming over the smooth paper, but the browns that she used were all wrong, either too light or too dark.

She glanced up from the paper when TillyTilly ran into her room and jogged up and down on the spot, then skipped, then hopped, clapping all the while, as if she was doing some elaborate form of exercise.

"Hello, Jessy," she puffed, still bobbing. It sounded rhythmical: *Heh-low (clap) Jeh-see (clap)*, it could be a song.

Jess laboriously coloured in the woman's *boubou*, then pushed her papers away and stood up. She, too, began jumping up and down, clapping, concentrating on not hitting the floor so hard that her mum would shout, "Are you having a one-woman wrestling match in there?"

"What *(clap)* are *(clap)* we *(clap)* do *(clap)* ing *(clap),*" she said, after a little while. TillyTilly shrugged and carried on jumping. She was moving around the room in a circle now, and Jess followed. Downstairs, her mother was interviewing someone on the telephone, "Do you have experience with . . . well, sensitive kids? My daughter's easy enough to please in terms of feeding and entertainment and for the most part, behaviour . . . What? Yes, of course, but the thing is, she has this enormous imagination and . . . yes, mmmm, exactly, you know what I'm talking about! That's it! She gets so absorbed, so caught up in things! And then she *upsets herself.*" The rest was muffled. Jess tried not to strain her ears so that she could listen better, but it was always fascinating for her when she heard herself being talked about, described.

But TillyTilly called her attention back to the room. She had crouched down in the area that Jess had just vacated and was systematically crumpling up sheet after sheet of the long-armed-woman drawings that Jess had begun and abandoned.

Now she was even tearing them, her eyes narrowed in an expression of if not quiet anger, then at the very least intense concentration.

Rip, rip, rip, scrunch.

Somehow, Jess did not dare to stop her.

Downstairs, her mother continued speaking.

"Oh, the other girl, my niece? She's fine. You should have absolutely no problems with her . . ."

When Tilly had finished ripping up the pictures, even the one that Jess had been doing when she came in, she scattered the handfuls of ripped paper on the floor, laughing a little bit, a raspy chuckle. She looked completely absorbed, as if Jess wasn't even there.

Jess stepped forward, a little nervously. Her voice wobbled as she spoke.

"Why did you do that, TillyTilly? I was only trying to . . ."

She paused because she had been expecting Tilly to interrupt her, but the girl rose slowly from her crouch and simply gazed at her, unblinking, her head turned slightly away from Jess. There was definite hostility there. Jess began to feel a little resentment herself. This was the second time that TillyTilly had acted strangely over the woman with the long arms. Could it be that Tilly didn't want to . . . well, *share* her?

"You spied," TillyTilly said in a low voice. She stood very still and continued to stare at Jess. "You shouldn't have gone in there."

Jess folded her arms. "I apologised already," she said firmly.

TillyTilly smiled.

"Yeah," she said, as if only just remembering. "You did."

"Well then," said Jess, refusing to smile herself.

TillyTilly sank back down to the floor and grabbed a light-brown crayon.

"Come on, let's do some drawing," she said, smoothing a piece of paper out before her. She grabbed some brown and green crayons and a bit of black charcoal, and began to draw.

Jess stayed where she was, reluctant to give in just like that. But curiosity got the better of her, and she sidled over to see what TillyTilly was drawing. It was a girl with her hair in two pigtails, wearing a green-and-white-checked dress; Tilly was drawing herself. For someone who was supposed to be even older than the Year Six girls, it was a bit rubbish. It made Jess feel dizzy to look at it, and she'd seen plenty of people drawings done by other kids in her class. The arms and legs were sticklike, and the torso was too rounded, like a dumpling. The checked squares on the dress were gaping, irregular holes of white surrounded by green, and the pigtails were scribbles of charcoal, looking like flaps of tangled hair sprouting from an otherwise bald brown scalp. The eyes were far too big, taking up half the face, and were too round. Jess was tempted to laugh, partly because she didn't know what else she could do at such a drawing, but knew she couldn't do much better herself. The weirdness of the drawing might have had something to do with the way in which Tilly was clutching the crayon. Instead of holding it like a pencil, she was holding it as one would a thick stick, or a baton: all her fingers curling around it. The lines that she drew were identical in their thickness and straightness, and when she tried to round them into more anthropomorphic shapes, they went haywire.

Jess raised her eyebrows in wonder,

(I don't think you are older than Year Six, TillyTilly)

then quietly sat down and began her own drawing. She was drawing a rainbow arching over a house. She was quite good at houses and rainbows, and trees as well, but avoided drawing people because she was bad at people. Also, she didn't want to embarrass TillyTilly, because as bad as she was at drawing people, she was almost certain that her people drawings were better than Tilly's.

She stuck her tongue out a little with the exertion of colouring the windows in blue, even right up to the very corners for a perfect picture, and when she looked up, she saw that across from her, TillyTilly had her tongue stuck out a little too as her eyes scanned Jess's face. Jess smiled uncertainly. *What is she doing?* TillyTilly smiled her rapid and fast-disappearing smile, then closed her mouth again and carried on drawing.

When Tilly had gone, Jess spent the rest of the afternoon lying on her bed, drowsing. Her head had begun to ache again, and she wondered if she shouldn't go and get something from her mum for it, then decided that she couldn't really be bothered to get up. Also, her mum would probably think that it was all a trick so that she'd have to stay and take care of Jess. Soon, the heat of the day outside began to annoy her, and she tugged her curtains closed. There would probably be a storm tonight, she thought feebly, curling up with one arm draped across her forehead to block out the light.

Jess had just opened her eyes after another short, confused nap in which she had been unsure if she was awake or asleep, when she perceived, out of the corner of her eye, that there was someone staring at her from outside her room, virtually filling the passageway with their presence, which sounded like a continuous buzzing, clicking hum. It was like *hmmmzzzmmmzzzh-mmm,* over and over. It felt as if it had been staring at her for a very long time, with the biggest eyes she had ever seen, only she hadn't noticed. It was very, very tall yet didn't seem to have a body, but appeared to be made of a sort of vibrating blackness. Blackness like the darkest jelly. *Hmmzzzmmm.* It looked as if the tall thing wasn't going to come in, but it certainly wasn't about to let her out either. She felt light-headed and not at all concerned about it, although if she had been well, she might have been worried. She could hear herself humming a wordless song, as she did when she was feeling poorly. Oh, she was definitely quite ill.

Finally, she mustered enough concern to look directly at the person, and then discovered that it wasn't actually there, and that she had been the one making the humming, clicking sound herself, with her teeth and tongue.

So that was all right then.

She fell asleep properly.

She was feeling much better in the evening, when her mum, wafting scent all over the place, hugged and kissed her good night.

Her father kissed her on the forehead.

"See you later, enormous girl," he said.

Jess gave him a grudging smile. She sat herself on the bottom step of the staircase and watched as they went through the door, leaving it open for Aunt Lucy, who was struggling to free herself from Dulcie. Uncle Adam was already in the car; he was driving them over.

"Don't goooooooo, Mummy, it'll be a rubbish old party any-way," Dulcie entreated, holding on to Aunt Lucy's leg for dear life.

"Come on, Dulcie, you're being silly," Aunt Lucy said. She sounded as if she was beginning to get very annoyed.

The babysitter, who was standing by the staircase, her arm resting on the banister, observed the situation and sprang into ac-tion. Jess watched. Her name was Lidia, and she was at university, far older than Year Six. She was studying something long and boring-sounding that began with a B. Jess wished she could re-member what it was, but it had been said too fast. She had thought that Lidia would look boring as well, because you had to be boring to spend your time babysitting, but she wasn't; she just looked like a normal person, only wearing dangly wooden ear-rings. She had the nicest hair, too, long and thick and dark. Plus, she had brought a whole bag full of good stuff with her: puzzles and food and things. She was from Madeira. Jess hadn't said a word to her yet, because she was going to look up Madeira and then say something interesting about it in front of Lidia (and Dul-cie) so that Lidia would think she knew all about it. *So . . . why don't you have bells in your hair in the usual Madeiran tradition?* she'd say, and Lidia (and Dulcie) would look at her and realise that she was not to be messed with, nor, more importantly, a baby.

"Dulcie," Lidia said, walking towards Dulcie and Aunt Lucy, "guess what? I've got some ice cream! I bet you like chocolate ice cream."

Dulcie hesitated, and then let her mother go.

"Yeah, I like chocolate ice cream," she admitted, as her mother gave Lidia a grateful smile and, dropping a kiss on Dulcie's forehead, left. "But you didn't need to say it like that, as if I'm an idiot or something: *nyehnyehnyeh . . . do you like ice cream? Nyeh.*"

Lidia laughed. "All right, sorry."

Dulcie glared at Jess and tossed her blond hair around.

"What are you looking at?"

Jess did not deign to reply. She knew what the tossing of the hair meant; it was a demand for admiration. Everyone always went mad over Dulcie's long blond hair—it was just like Alison Carr's. In fact, it was possible that if Dulcie Fitzpatrick had lived in Jess's area and gone to Jess's school, Alison Carr would have had some serious competition. There'd have been rival factions, Dulcians and Alisonites, and Jess would have claimed the friendship of the others as the cousin of The Dulcie. Hmmm. Jess looked at Lidia, waiting for her to say, *Wow, Dulcie, your hair is so nice. Such a pretty girl,* but Lidia didn't say that. She looked at the two of them and said, "So, do you want ice cream or not?"

Jess got up and followed Dulcie and Lidia into the kitchen. Dulcie was already holding Lidia's hand, and she didn't even know her! What a suck-up.

Dulcie pulled out a chair at the kitchen table and waited while Lidia started scooping out the ice cream. It was softening already, dripping down the edges of the scoop as Lidia began squishing it into the bowl. Jess remained standing, eyeing Lidia suspiciously. Dulcie gave her a smug glance, basking in the knowledge that she was bound to be Lidia's favourite. Lidia was humming as she began spooning ice cream into a third bowl, and Dulcie's preening was cut short by Lidia turning around and handing her the ice cream and a spoon. Jess stifled a laugh at Dulcie's angelic expression as she said, syrup-sweet, "Thank you, Lidia."

Lidia looked unconvinced. "Hmmm," she said.

She turned to Jess.

"Aren't you going to sit down? This is your house, after all!"

Jess took a seat around the table from where Dulcie and Lidia sat. There was silence as they all ate the ice cream. Jess could see Dulcie's eyes moving back and forth. She was probably trying to think of something engaging to say or do.

After a few seconds, Dulcie put her elbows on the table and wiped her mouth.

"So, when are you going to beat us?" she asked.

Lidia looked startled.

"What?"

Dulcie eyed the babysitter apprehensively.

"You know . . . that's what babysitters do . . . They beat people when their parents are gone." She looked at Jess for confirmation, but Jess just ducked her head with an embarrassed laugh and went on with the slightly less complicated business of eating the ice cream. It was quite difficult with Lidia and Dulcie across the table from her. She put one hand over her mouth so that they didn't see her eating.

Without answering Dulcie, Lidia picked up her bowl and announced that she'd brought some videos, or they could play with the Connect 4 that Aunt Lucy had brought and left at Jess's house.

"Which d'you want to do first?" she asked.

Dulcie, looking disappointed that she hadn't managed either to frighten Lidia with her knowingness or annoy her with her annoyingness, nudged Jess.

"Oi. What shall we do?"

Jess shrugged and squashed ice cream beneath her spoon.

Lidia looked at them both and shook her head, smiling a little bit. Her earrings swung.

"Well," she said. "Let's go into the sitting room!"

As they passed the staircase, Jess looked longingly upstairs. She wanted to go and read up on Madeira in the world encyclopaedia that she'd taken up to her bedroom in preparation as soon as she'd been briefed on Lidia by her mum. She knew that Dulcie would have made fun of her if she'd started reading the encyclopaedia in the sitting room, and it also wouldn't have been a surprise for the babysitter. Lidia put a hand on her shoulder and guided her into the sitting room. Jess remembered the telephone conversation she had overheard and realised that it might be difficult to get away from Lidia this evening, seeing as she had been identified as the problematic child.

They settled down cosily, with Dulcie cuddling up to Lidia on the sofa and Jess sitting cross-legged in front of the television as they watched some taped back-to-back episodes of *SuperTed* and *Teenage Mutant Ninja Turtles*. They had seen one episode of each programme when the telephone rang. Jess looked around at the other two.

"It's *your* house," said Dulcie, taking her thumb out of her mouth. "You can't expect Lidia to get the phone just because she's old."

Jess sighed and began to get up, but Lidia got there first.

"Hello?"

Jess and Dulcie watched as Lidia flushed bright red and shot them an embarrassed glance before she continued speaking in a lower voice.

"Oh my God, Paul, how did you get this number? You're not supposed to call me when I'm babysitting!"

Dulcie bounced up and down on the sofa cushions. "Ahahahahaha! Lidia's got a boyfriend! Kissy kissy!" She pouted and smacked her lips several times while Jess watched open-mouthed as Lidia went even redder and then laughed.

"Oh, that's Dulcie, one of the girls I'm looking after tonight," Lidia said, her colour going down. She raised her voice so that they could hear her properly and stuck her tongue out at Dulcie, who laughed delightedly, hiding her face in her hands and falling back onto the cushions. Jess turned back to the television. SuperTed and Spotty were arguing.

"Yeah . . . she's already asked me when I'm going to beat her . . ." Lidia laughed again. "Yup, I'll see you tonight." A pause. "Yeah, ten, maybe ten thirty. Okay, buh-bye." Another pause, then Lidia smiled, flushing again, and said, "Yeah, me too."

"I love yooo, I miss yooo," Dulcie sang in a falsetto, her arms flung out wide. "Kissy kissy," she added, blowing her hair out of her face. She squealed in mock-terror and scrambled off the sofa, running around it as Lidia tried to catch her and tickle her. Jess could feel the vibrations of Dulcie's feet pounding on the floor. Then Dulcie stamped in her ice-cream bowl by accident. "Oh!" she squeaked. "It's cold, it's COLD!" She began hopping around, waving a foot in the air. Lidia collapsed in laughter.

Then there was a sound from somewhere above their heads. It was unmistakably a clicking, maybe of a door or window opening and closing again. Then there was another louder, heavier sound, like something falling over. Jess imagined feet walking upstairs, someone looking in the rooms.

The three of them froze. Jess looked outside into the passage, where it was dark. The kitchen was opposite the sitting room, separated from it by the staircase that led to Jess's mum's study and the bedrooms. She was wondering if this was a situation like her dad had been talking about, an intruder situation. It hadn't sounded so bad at breakfast, but now Jess realised that she didn't like uninvited people. They all waited tensely for another sound, but there was nothing.

The house had become a shadowy, empty space where people could come in and out if they wanted to, touch things, take things, lurk.

"What's going on? Did you turn the passage light off?" Dulcie demanded of Lidia.

Her voice was even more raucous than usual. Lidia put a hand to her forehead as she tried to remember. Jess tried to remember too.

"It doesn't matter whether I turned off the passage light anyway, because the . . . the . . . sound was from upstairs," Lidia said, standing up. "Probably something just fell over by itself, but I think I'd better have a look," she added uncertainly.

"No, don't, you silly person," Dulcie said, holding on to Lidia's arm. "We should call the police. We were watching this programme, and there were robbers, but the man said he was going to go and see what was happening, and the robbers bashed him over the head and took his computer, and Mummy said, 'See, he should have called the police!' "

Lidia strode across the room, Dulcie holding on to her arm and wailing "No, no," Jess quietly following. Lidia pressed the switch for the passage light, and the lightbulb flickered. A sputter, a flare of illuminating light, then it died. They peered about in the darkness, and Lidia groaned.

"The lightbulb had to go just now, didn't it," she sighed. "Well, all right, fine." She and Dulcie darted across the passage and into the kitchen, where the light was still working. Jess stood in the sitting room, straining to see what they were doing. She was badly frightened, and her fear was a numb chill that held her rigid in the certainty that, if she moved too suddenly, everything in sight was going to fall on top of her. She focused on the lighted kitchen. Dulcie was sitting with her legs dangling over the side of the sink unit, singing quietly and off-key about beating up robbers, and Lidia had found a heavy stainless steel frying pan. She held it up, swung it a little bit. "All right," Jess heard her say. Lidia took Dulcie's hand in her free one, and they came back to the passage. The hand that held the pan was shaking, and she kept taking deep breaths. All three of them stood listening again, and there was still no sound. But Jess couldn't stop thinking about the first clicking sound, as if someone had actually *come in*. But how would they have come in from upstairs? There were no windows open.

Lidia mounted the staircase, telling Dulcie to wait at the bottom with Jess, and as they both peered upwards, their arms around each other in the goose-bumped solidarity of unease, Jess and Dulcie saw her turn the bend in the staircase that took her out of sight. There was a few moments' tense quiet in which they heard her switching lights on and off in the different rooms, then Lidia returned, the frying pan dangling limply from her hand, a smile on her face.

"I don't know what we heard, but there's no one upstairs and all the windows are closed, so *that's* all right."

As Lidia spoke, Jess was staring behind her with her mouth open. For just a second, she had very indistinctly seen a large corner of checked cloth peeping out from round the bend of the staircase, then it had dragged upwards. As Lidia came down the stairs, Jess ran up, her heart thumping.

"Jessamy, can you come here, please!"

TillyTilly was curled up in a sort of ball on the very top step, her bony knees drawn to her chin, her face in the shadows. Jess couldn't see her expression.

"TillyTilly! What are you doing here?" she whispered, her heart rising up and up until she thought it might burst right out of her mouth. She wanted to touch her friend, at first to see if she was really there, but then, quite suddenly, she crossed into fury. She wanted to pinch Tilly, and scratch her. But she didn't quite dare. Cautiously, Jess took another step upwards, then when she could see Tilly's face properly, she stood a few steps down and folded her arms.

"You really scared us, you know!"

Tilly didn't reply. She wasn't looking at Jess, but somewhere to the left of her. Her gaze was preoccupied, her thin cheeks sucked inwards as she frowned deeply.

"Jessamy! What are you doing! Don't make me come up there and get you!" Jess heard Lidia threaten.

"I'm coming. I'm just getting something from upstairs," she called.

"Well, hurry up," Lidia said.

Jess looked back at TillyTilly, who was now, suddenly, looking at her, and she became worried for a few seconds that maybe this wasn't TillyTilly at all, but someone else altogether.

"She's a Portuguese," TillyTilly said angrily. She nearly spat the word "Portuguese" out, her accent becoming somewhat Yoruba as she did so.

Jess was puzzled.

"I'm glad I scared her. I should have *got* her," TillyTilly muttered, pressing her face against her knees then shaking her head as if to clear it.

Jess sat on the step that she had been standing on.

"Why? She's quite nice, actually."

TillyTilly glared.

Jess was tempted to take back what she had said, then decided not to.

"She *is*," she insisted, then added, "and anyway, she's not from Portugal, she's from Madeira. It's different, isn't it?"

"Portuguese," TillyTilly maintained, shaking her head emphatically and pointing at the ground in a short, sharp gesture that Jess recognised as her uncle Kunle's favourite "earth be my witness" one.

Jess was quiet for a few seconds, thinking this over.

"Did you do that thing with the passage light?" she asked finally.

TillyTilly rocked backwards and forwards a little and said nothing.

"Jessamy! What are you doing?" Lidia called.

"She's going to come and get me in a minute, and I haven't even looked anything up about Madeira," Jess said in tones of resignation.

TillyTilly uncurled her body and grabbed Jess by the arm.

"Do you want to give Lidia a proper fright?" When she saw Jess's expression of doubt, she persisted. "It'll be fun, I promise!"

Jess looked consideringly at TillyTilly, then smiled.

They stood up and held hands, Jess's face turned towards TillyTilly's for a moment before Tilly moved behind her. Jess could hear her breathing and her small, ticklish laugh as Lidia came upstairs.

"The light's working again!" Lidia said, switching it on. "Jessamy!"

Her feet on the stairs sounded thunderous to Jess; giant's feet coming up a mountain, displacing bits of rock and moss.

Everything seemed to *sloooooooow dooooooooooown*.

As the light flooded the stairway, and as Lidia and Dulcie's heads came poking around the staircase bend, Jess saw Lidia's mouth open to address her, then both Lidia's and Dulcie's mouths stretched wider in amazement and shock as TillyTilly's arms enfolded her from behind and pulled her

d

o

w

n

and *through* the staircase, the carpet and the actual stair falling away beneath her feet as if she and Tilly were going underground in a lift that would never stop descending. The scene changed to a sort of blanketing brown darkness, hollow and moist, and Jess's head was spinning and she was laughing and screaming at the same time, like the slide, like the slide, only more . . .

TillyTilly was silent, so quiet that Jess thought that she wasn't there, and had to waste a moment of the glorious free fall to twist her head, gasping in, the air jetting madly through her nostrils and lungs, to look at Tilly, whose cheek was now pressed against hers, her mouth open in a silent laugh. Jess's hair was blowing into Tilly's face, and she couldn't think that this was really happening, couldn't *believe it* until they crashed.

"No," she heard TillyTilly rasp as they began to dip and plummet, "no, we're not supposed to—"

They smashed against the ground so hard that Jess felt broken and winded, her face pressed against the ground, the weight of TillyTilly lying half across her back. The insides of her mouth hurt from where she had inadvertently bitten herself. She could taste blood on her tongue.

Ohhhhhhhh. It hurts.

Tilly's head had banged hard against the back of Jess's head, and she felt as if a bump might be growing there. TillyTilly rolled slowly away from her, then they both lay still. Jess began to feel claustrophobic when she realised that, wherever they were, there was no room to sit up. There was a thick layer of the brown darkness above, and she was lying on some more of it. She crumbled the stuff between her fingers and realised, with wonder and alarm, that it was earth, the stuff the daffodils in the playground were planted in in the spring. It was earth, but it was dry, so dry, and hard. She and TillyTilly had been falling through earth as if it was air!

And now they were stuck.

She began to find it harder to breathe the more she looked upwards to the compacted earth that lay only a few centimetres away from her nose. Suppose it all came falling down? They must have fallen quite a way. She wondered what Lidia was doing, and that made her laugh a little bit. What would Dulcie be saying? Would Dulcie be in awe of her now, and think that she was magic? She was beginning to feel drowsier and drowsier the less that she was able to breathe. And it was dark down here.

She turned her head and fixed her eyes on the outline of her friend, who was lying very still. From where Jess was lying, Tilly's eyes appeared to be closed. She was breathing evenly, so she was probably awake. Maybe thinking.

"TillyTilly," she whispered. "What happened? Why did we crash? Are you going to get us up again?"

TillyTilly opened her eyes. They were almost luminous.

"We fell. I don't know why. It's all right. I can get us up again."

She sounded defeated, unhappy.

"It was a good trick, though, TillyTilly," Jess said encouragingly. "Dulcie's and Lidia's faces! Did you see them? It was so funny! And it was fun when we were falling, although I suppose we couldn't have expected to keep on falling forever—"

TillyTilly might have smiled, but Jess couldn't see properly. Jess coughed weakly.

"I can't really breathe properly anymore; it's like . . . there's no room . . ."

TillyTilly made a sort of clucking sound in the back of her throat, then she reached out, feeling for Jess's hand. Jess met her halfway, and Tilly squeezed her hand reassuringly. Then TillyTilly simply stood up, pulling Jess, who struggled and kicked a little, bracing herself for suffocation, upwards with her.

Jess felt earth push into her face and her mouth, and she *drank* it, as a vast amount of air whistled past her ears, and TillyTilly's hand fell away from hers, and she was standing, spitting out the dank taste of the soil, on the staircase, alone. Dulcie and Lidia were now at the top of the steps; they looked as if they had just been searching for her in the bedrooms.

"Oh my GOD! There you are! What . . . what did you do? Where did you go to?" Dulcie screeched, before Lidia could say anything. "I'm telling your mum!" she added, in tones of high indignation. She hopped up and down on the top step, jabbing her finger at Jess. "You are SO WEIRD! You weren't like this before you went abroad! What's HAPPENED to you?"

Jess knew she wasn't helping matters by giving vent to hysterical laughter. She was numb.

Lidia, spotting a wrongness in her, came forward and cupped Jess's face in her hands, her own hands shaking. She cleared her throat.

"You just . . . ran away and hid, didn't you?" she asked, nodding her head slightly to give Jess a lead to follow.

Jess began to shake her head, then looked at Lidia properly. She could see that Lidia was frightened, really quite badly frightened. Obediently, Jess nodded.

Lidia gave a trembling sigh, and let Jess go.

"Don't do that again," she said sternly. Then: "Tell you what, why don't we all play snakes and ladders?"

NINE

The next day was Sunday. Jess was tired and feeling unwell again, but she got up early to say goodbye to Dulcie, who was being picked up by her parents. Dulcie had been asking her questions for ages the night before.

"Where did you go when you vanished?"

"Through the stairs," Jess had replied sleepily, one side of her face pressed into the pillow. The insides of her mouth still hurt. That was how she knew the whole thing, or at least the end of the fall, had been real.

"Where after that?" Dulcie persisted.

"Just down."

"Down *where*, Jessamy?"

"Just *down!*"

Jess hadn't told Dulcie about TillyTilly because she didn't think TillyTilly would like it.

All through breakfast, Dulcie eyed Jess suspiciously, then finally asked her aunt why her daughter was so weird.

"What?" her mum said, laughing.

"She disappeared yesterday, you know!" Dulcie said, widening her blue eyes for effect. She moved her toast to illustrate what had happened. "She just vanished! And she says she fell through the staircase. Maybe the staircase isn't safe, Aunt Sarah. You probably need to get that staircase fixed, Aunt Sarah."

Jess squirmed as her parents glanced at each other, then looked at her in puzzlement, waiting for her to say something.

"I was only joking about falling through the staircase, you idiot." Jess scowled. It was appalling that she and Dulcie were wearing matching My Little Pony pyjamas. It made them somehow the same. Dulcie's were purple, and Jess's were pink. The gaudy, raised ponies lined up on the front were staring at her with fake-gentle eyes. Jess hoped her ponies were staring at Dulcie the same way.

Jess's dad tutted. "Jessamy, don't call your cousin an idiot."

Jess spattered her cereal, pretending that she didn't know her mum was eyeing her. She felt a quiet surprise at herself for having spoken up and called Dulcie an idiot in the first place. Ever since she had come back from Nigeria, she felt as if she was becoming different, becoming stronger, becoming more like Tilly.

"Sorry," she said, in as low a voice as she could manage.

As soon as her dad had returned to his Sunday newspaper, she glared at Dulcie and mouthed, *Idiot.*

Dulcie grinned and put down her toast. "Ohhhhhhhh, Uncle Daniel—!"

Uncle Adam and Aunt Lucy arrived to pick up Dulcie and take her to Mass. Dulcie threw her arms around her mother's waist. Jess noticed that her mum and dad looked embarrassed, as if Aunt Lucy was making them feel uncomfortable.

Aunt Lucy waited. Jess's dad cleared his throat and looked

around, somewhat nonplussed, then appeared to remember something.

"Ah, Jessamy, guess what?" He beamed. "You're getting another cousin soon!"

Aunt Lucy blushed in a pleased sort of way, and Uncle Adam put his arm around her. They looked like a picture-book family: blond man, blond woman, cute little blond child. Jess hummed to herself under her breath; she did that sometimes when she was confused. She realised that everyone else already knew and they were looking at her as if they were expecting her to *say* something. Her mum was smiling, but her mouth was a little wobbly so it didn't end up looking like a real smile.

"Ummmmmmmm," said Jess. "Yeah, cool. Where am I getting this new cousin from again?"

Uncle Adam laughed and laughed, and so did Aunt Lucy and Jess's parents.

"What your dad meant was that I'm having another baby," Aunt Lucy said, patting her stomach. Jess looked at her with her mouth slightly open, then remembered to smile. Aunt Lucy smiled back.

"That's why she's been getting sort of fat," Dulcie explained, grinning, and her dad and Uncle Adam laughed again, although Aunt Lucy didn't.

"These kids," she said, looking up at the ceiling, "these kids."

Jess wasn't really listening to all this: she had been watching her mum for a few seconds now. What was the *matter* with her? Her mum's laughter was strained, and straightaway she began collecting the dishes from the table. She took them to the sink and began washing up, her elbows jabbing in and out of the space around her as she scrubbed. Jess continued to hum underneath her breath. She heard her father ask Dulcie if she was pleased that she was getting a new brother or sister, but Dulcie said, "No! I don't want a stupid new brother or sister! I hate them already."

Her dad raised his eyebrows and looked at Aunt Lucy and Uncle Adam from beneath his fringe. Now Jess's aunt and uncle looked flustered.

"Well, that's not the way to talk about your new brother or sister," Daniel said.

"I know," said Aunt Lucy, hurriedly helping Dulcie into her coat. "But what can you do?"

"You could take her to church," Jess's mother said from the sink. She suddenly sounded a lot more cheerful. Jess wanted to remind her mum of that complicated thing she had said about giving up on organised religion, but sensed that there could be big trouble if she did.

Aunt Lucy's face was properly flushed now, and she half pushed Dulcie out of the door. Uncle Adam followed, pausing to waggle his ears at Jess. Jess laughed. Uncle Adam was always mucking around when no one was looking, and a lot of the time he'd put sweets and money in her pockets.

Jess's dad looked at her mum, who was still washing up, then he looked at Jessamy.

"Hey, Jess, enormous girl," he said, "d'you want to play out with Tilly, or go and play in your room, or something?" Sarah had told him about Jess's new friend, and he hadn't been able to say "Titiola" properly either.

Jess shrugged. She'd just realised that she didn't know how to find TillyTilly, or whereabouts she lived. It might be near Colleen McLain's house, because she'd known where that was and Jess hadn't.

"I'll go and see if I can find Tilly, I suppose," she said, and got down from her chair.

"Let's go to the park and have a picnic," Jess said, after some thought. She had been standing on the pavement outside her house, looking up and down the street. How was she to find TillyTilly? Then she'd had an idea, and she'd called, at first in a low voice, then in a louder one, "TillyTilly! Oi! TillyTilly!" And before she'd had the chance to feel stupid, Tilly had come down the street, laughing, skipping. Tilly had found a piece of rope from somewhere. Jess didn't want to touch it; it looked dirty. Tilly's green-and-white school dress was as crisp as ever, but the hairbands at the ends of her plaited pigtails were coming loose.

The first thing TillyTilly had said was, "What shall we do?"

So Jess suggested the picnic.

"A picnic?" said TillyTilly. "Good idea!"

Jess smiled, pleased at TillyTilly's approval. Usually Tilly was the one with all the ideas.

"I'll get my mum to pack us some food."

"OK," said TillyTilly. She leaned on Jess's front gate to wait.

Jess ran back into the kitchen. Her mum wasn't there anymore, but her dad was. He was standing by the sink, looking out of the kitchen window as he sipped at a cup of milky coffee. She knew that any minute now there was going to be a cascade of brown liquid when he decided that he'd drunk enough. Her father never finished his coffee.

"Daddy, can we have some food for a picnic?"

Her dad smiled at her.

"Of course you can. What do you want?"

"I don't know! Anything!"

Her dad poured his coffee down the sink, then turned to the fridge.

"I hope your friend Tilly's not fussy!"

For the picnic, Jess's dad gave them some sausage rolls, some mushroom sandwiches, two slices of her grandma's apple pie, and a carton of orange juice with two paper cups and a shopping bag to put all the rubbish in. "Make sure you two don't litter the park," he said. Then he'd asked if he could be introduced.

"Wait a minute," said Jess, clutching the bag full of things. "She's sort of shy, she might not like it."

She poked her head out of the back door to signal to Tilly. Her friend had moved farther down the pavement and was already shaking her head "no."

Jess drew her head back in.

"She's shy," she confirmed, and her dad laughingly threw up his hands.

"OK, fine! Have a good picnic, and say hello to her for me, then!"

Jess nodded and ran out to meet TillyTilly.

"Race you to the park," cried Tilly, dropping her length of rope, and Jess ran the short distance to the park as hard as she could, running so hard that everything—people, shops, houses, Tilly—seemed to blur into each other.

But TillyTilly still got there first.

"It's not fair," Jess complained, bending over to get her breath back.

TillyTilly wasn't even winded; she sat down and, assuming a cross-legged position, started taking things out of the bag.

"Never mind," she said, "at least you came second!" And she nearly bent herself double with her wheezing laugh.

It turned out that TillyTilly wasn't that hungry. She picked at the sausage rolls, shaking her head at them even when Jess explained that they were "just like Gala."

"Gala?" she said, wrinkling her nose.

Jess began to get the feeling that had crept up on her before, that this was either not Tilly or a different TillyTilly from the one that she had first met in Nigeria. But it was only a momentary sensation.

"You know . . . Gala . . ." she pressed.

TillyTilly shrugged her shoulders and began sliding the mushrooms out of the mushroom sandwiches and nibbling them. She wouldn't even touch the apple pie, but she drank some orange juice. Tilly's lack of appetite spoiled Jess's, and they ended up wasting most of the picnic. They had found a nice spot on a bench surrounded by green bushes with the tiniest red berries on them.

Around the corner was the painted wooden-and-steel roundabout, and once they had put the remains of the food in the shopping bag and thrown it away, they took turns pushing each other on it, shrieking with mixed fear and delight as the whole world went flying past and they tried to catch up.

Soon Jess was tired again, and she returned to the bench and lay on it. TillyTilly stretched out on the grass, pulling a tuft of it between her fingers.

"What shall we do now?" Tilly asked, after a few minutes of silence.

Jess had been thinking about things. She turned to look at Tilly.

"What do you want to be when you grow up, TillyTilly?"

TillyTilly looked surprised, then shook her head, laughing.

"I don't know," she said.

She gave Jess an odd look. It was more of a stare, like she couldn't see Jess properly and was trying to get her into focus.

"What about you?"

Jess laughed. "I don't know . . . I'd like to fly."

TillyTilly scratched her head. "You mean, like in an aeroplane?"

Jess shook her head. "No, fly, like when we were falling yesterday, but only, like, upwards."

TillyTilly smiled then, the swift brilliance of her smile lighting her whole face.

"Oh," she said. "I think you'll do that; I think you'll be a flier. I'll be one too."

Jess closed her eyes and beamed with satisfaction. If TillyTilly said so, then it would be true. She would fly.

"Jessy," she heard Tilly say. Jess opened her eyes again. TillyTilly was sitting up now, wriggling and restless. "What shall we do?"

Jess shrugged.

"We should write a poem," said Tilly.

Jess sat up and stared.

"A *poem*? What about?"

"I dunno . . . I came up with the idea; now you do something!"

Jess scratched her knee. "We don't even have a pen or paper."

TillyTilly felt in one of the pockets of her school dress and came up with a blue biro. She smiled again. She had a much crumpled, but blank, sheet of paper, too.

Jess began to laugh.

"What else have you got in your pockets?" she enquired.

TillyTilly tapped the side of her nose.

It took much quiet thought with their heads bent together over the paper, whispering ideas. Jess was sure that writing the poem took a long time, although she wasn't sure how long, because she didn't have a watch and she didn't quite know what it *was* about time and TillyTilly. Halfway through, something was wrong with the pen, and Jess got blue ink all over her hands, but managed to finish writing down the poem. It was disappointingly short for so much effort. TillyTilly took the paper and smoothed it out, then read it aloud, her finger running over the crossings-out and scribblings to get to the actual poem:

"All my thoughts have left, with her.
I thought I'd kept them in my head
But when I tried to find the thoughts
They all told me she was dead.
I asked if I could go to her
To find my thoughts, to think one day,
But they said 'No,' 'cause she'd prefer
To keep me, too, and make me stay."

They sat quiet for a few minutes, arms flung loosely around each other, cheek pressed against cheek, then Jess sighed and shifted, breaking the loop of arms and legs.

"It's a sad poem," she said, "definitely really sad." She felt as if she hadn't written it, and neither had TillyTilly. But they must have, because they'd come up with the rhymes. "What rhymes with 'head'?" she'd asked Tilly, and Tilly had squeezed her eyes shut while thinking, then whispered in her ear so that the word was all tickly, "Dead."

Jess put the poem in her own pocket to copy it at home, but they had to throw the ruined biro away. Then, just as TillyTilly started to say something, Jess heard a clamour of voices.

Trish Anderson from Year Five came careering around the bushes.

"Hello, Jessamy!" she called out.

Jess shrank in her seat and looked at TillyTilly, then realised that she had vanished. The bit of grass that she had pulled up lay on top of the growing grass. Jess stared, frowned, then turned back to Trish, trying to think.

"Whatcha doing here by yourself?" Trish asked. She sat down on the bench next to Jess.

Go away, thought Jess, *oh, just leave me alone.*

She had just realised with stunning clarity that she was the only person who saw TillyTilly. She put a hand to her mouth as she tried to sort this out in her mind. She didn't know why it hadn't occurred to her before. TillyTilly had not met anyone in her family, no one had met her, and she refused to meet anyone. And even when Jess was with TillyTilly, never mind that people couldn't see Jess; the most noticeable thing was that they couldn't see TillyTilly. She suddenly felt very small and a little bit scared.

Is TillyTilly . . . real?

All she knew, as Trish began talking and calling her other Year Five friends over, was that even if TillyTilly wasn't real, if it was a choice between there being just her and Tilly or her and real people, she'd much, much rather have Tilly.

"I wasn't by myself, I was with my friend," she said suddenly, interrupting Trish's flow of speech. Trish had been offering to push her on the swings. Even though she would've liked that, Jess turned her down. It would somehow be disloyal to TillyTilly to hang around with Trish and her friends. Also, she needed to go home and think about all this and, later, copy out the poem.

"I think I'd better go and find her," she added.

Trish shrugged, laughing.

"All right, suit yourself."

Jess didn't remember to show her mum the poem until the next morning, just before school. The day started with a general feeling of discontent. Her mum read the poem at the kitchen table as she ate her bacon sandwich. When she got past the first line, she put down the sandwich. Her lips began moving without any sounds coming out as she read the poem to herself, then she read it again, her eyebrows raised. Jess had written *By Jessamy Harrison and Titiola* at the bottom. Even if TillyTilly wasn't real, she had reminded herself, she still deserved credit for the poem. She would have to discuss the realness thing with TillyTilly today, if she saw her.

She couldn't even begin to think what she meant by "not real."

Jess was tempted to spatter her porridge, but knew it drove her mum mad, and so refrained, hoping to be rewarded with some positive comments about the poem.

"Jess," her mum said, finally, putting the sheet of paper down, "are you sure that you wrote this?"

Jess drank some orange juice before answering, drinking slowly to show how offended she was.

"Yes, me and Tilly did. What's wrong with it?"

Her mum looked at the poem again, shook her head.

"How old is Tilly again?" she asked, suddenly, looking at Jess.

Jess shrugged uncomfortably.

She felt as if she was keeping a terrible secret for her friend: *The thing is, she's not real, but it's a secret.*

Her mum picked her sandwich up again and took a bite, looking reflective. She kept glancing down at the poem.

"Muuuuum," Jess said impatiently.

"Mmmm?"

"What d'you think of it? D'you like it?"

"Jess, if you were unhappy, you'd tell me, wouldn't you, darling?"

Jess was confused. This had nothing to do with anything. She was now being forced to consider her answers so as not to make her mum cross with her, when all she wanted was for her mum to like the poem. Her mum waited without appearing to be waiting, eating her sandwich, checking her watch. They were going to be a little late, as usual.

"Yes," Jess said finally in a very small voice. "Do you like the poem, though, Mummy?"

Her mum stood up and got Jessamy's coat, began helping her into it.

"It's . . . quite mature, Jess. It's a bit of a sad poem, isn't it?"

Don't ask me about it, I'm asking you.

"What were you and Titiola thinking about when you were writing it?" her mother asked when they headed through the park to school. Jess moped. There was something too cheerful about her mother today, something too jaunty in her walk and the questions she asked. Jess could sense it, it was almost tangible; her mother didn't think that TillyTilly was real either. That must be it.

"We were just finding rhymes."

Her mum nodded. "Right. Well, I *do* like it, Jess, it's just . . . well, I think it's . . . I like it, but if you want the truth, it . . . well, sort of confuses me that it was written by you. Do you understand what I'm saying?"

"You think it's too mature."

"Yes."

"But you're the one who reads me Shakespeare and stuff! How do you *want* me to write?"

Her mum ruffled her hair.

"Jesus on toast, Jess, I dunno."

TEN

___

In the sitting room, Jess sat watching her mother dial, calling
Nigeria. Her mum looked up and flashed her a smile in between
punching in the last two numbers, and Jess smiled back, preparing herself for the odd feeling of hearing Bodija over the phone
again. They both waited.

"Hello? *Iya* Jessamy calling from London!" her mum said.

There was a static pause, then Jess could hear a faint, crackling shriek of delight sounding from the other end, then a string
of questions in piercing, fast Yoruba. It sounded like Aunty
Funke, but it could well have been Aunty Biola. Jess watched her
mum throw back her head and laugh, before responding in
equally fast Yoruba. She turned, treading a small half circle on the
carpet, then suddenly looked at Jess. She seemed to catch her
self and winked at Jessamy before questioningly indicating the
phone. Jess nodded.

"Funke, here is your girl, o," she said in English, laughing.
She handed the receiver to Jess and dropped into one of the
sitting-room chairs.

Jess gripped the receiver, pulling the mouthpiece closer to her

167

face. Her hands were slightly sweaty and the phone felt slippery. She licked her lips.

"Hello, Aunty," she said, listening for the audible echo of her voice bouncing down the phone line in a way that it did not when she was speaking to somebody in England.

There was that unnerving split-second delay before Aunty Funke crackled so that it was sharp and shrieking, "Jess! How is everything, eh?"

The question was imbued with unmistakable menace and malice.

Jess was instantaneously miserable and frightened; the way that she always was at first. This fear lasted a few seconds, then, before it was allayed and she could speak to her aunt comfortably, the phone would be taken from her by her mum.

On the telephone to Nigeria, Jess was seized by the fear that it wasn't Aunty Funke she was talking to, but some thin, winding spirit that had intercepted the call, taking on her aunty's accent and tone of voice, turning every sentence into a shrill cleaving of the nerves.

"I'm fine," she whispered, letting the sound be stolen from her as the echo mocked. Now she had said she was fine twice. She almost added "Aunty," but caught herself. This wasn't her aunty Funke who made puff-puff in her lucky pan and sang while washing up at the sink and complained loudly—in English, for Jess's benefit—whenever she was annoyed. The response was again delayed.

"Say what? Ah-ah, you this girl, won't you speak up?" The wicked spirit thief sounded darkly amused, spitting out the question although they both knew that Jess's throat was too dry from this ordeal for her to talk properly.

Every single time, she thought it might be different, but it never was; she never got to speak to her aunty Funke.

"I said . . . I'm fine," she bellowed into the phone. She was suddenly enraged beyond belief, unaware of the fact that she was almost snarling. "How are *you*?" she added, belligerently.

The echoes were louder this time. Her mum took the phone from her, arching her eyebrows in bemusement before speaking to her sister in Yoruba. Jess couldn't understand exactly what her mum was saying, but it sounded apologetic. She wiped her hands on the skirt of her school dress, and the green-and-white check reminded her of Tilly. Without another word, she left the room and went through the kitchen and out of the back door.

But Jess couldn't *find* TillyTilly. She was lost to her, shrunken from her sight.

Jess understood implicitly that this had something to do with her realising that Tilly wasn't real. She wished she hadn't thought it, that her happiness hadn't been stretched and pulled out of shape by that idea. How could she have . . . ?

As she ran through the park, a flurry of arms and legs and dress, searching frantically for her friend, the dread and panic thickened and bloomed in her lungs. She forced herself to stand still on the pavement, made herself draw in deep, deep breaths until she thought that she might suck herself inside out with the force of her breathing. A group of older children chasing each other down the other side of the pavement all stopped to look at her. One of them was a boyish-looking brown-haired girl wearing a baggy off-white T-shirt with *Heartbreak High* written on it in yellow letters. The girl yelled out, "Oi, wassamatter with you, man?"

Jess dropped to her knees and bowed her head, ignoring them. She didn't mind them staring, she was used to it. When she had sufficiently quieted, she lifted her head.

"TillyTilly," she called softly, then waited, listening, looking for TillyTilly to come skipping down the road, or running, maybe, or even to appear silently beside her.

Can't you see I'm sorry—

No Tilly. Jess felt weak and dizzy, but she got home, and went into the kitchen and leaned against the table. She didn't realise how odd she looked until her mother came to find her and gave a little shriek of surprised dismay. Jess heard it only dimly, as if the sound was being filtered through small holes in her hearing, the rest of which was filled with a low, resonant humming.

"Heh! You this girl! You were fine just thirty minutes ago!"

Jess turned her head and gazed at her mum, tottering a little with the effort to keep her neck straight. *How could she have started feeling this ill so fast?*

"It's Tilly," Jess tried to explain. "She's gone away." But it didn't come out properly, because something was the matter with her tongue; it felt far too big for her mouth, and made flaccid, flapping movements against her bottom row of teeth and her lips. She realised that she was making her illness-singing sounds again.

"Jessy," TillyTilly said quietly, insistently, from somewhere in the room. "Jessy, Jessy, Jessy."

Jess, sprawled on the bed with the covers half falling off her achingly hot shoulders, came down from where she was floating in the darkness with the long-armed woman, and rolled over from her stomach onto her back.

"JESSY," Tilly said again, her voice full of impatience.

Jess hesitated; the voice sounded different with her eyes closed; it sounded . . . older, somehow.

"Did you think I would leave you? We're twins!"

Jess heard Tilly's words, but didn't respond. She didn't want to. She was glad that Tilly had come back, but . . . the woman with the long arms was smiling and telling her a story about a boy and a magic bird that spread its wings over the land and made everything green and good . . . The words were making her feel fresher, coating her in dew. TillyTilly was speaking insistently, and her words were layering over and under the storyteller's.

". . . Jessy, you guessed without me explaining that I'm . . . that I'm not really here. I mean, of course I'm really here, just not *really really* here, if you see what I mean . . . Most of the time I'm somewhere else, but I can appear, and you haven't imagined me! Remember Colleen's house? And the amusement park? You know you couldn't have imagined those!"

Jess did not move, but she listened to Tilly and to the soft, accented voice of the long-armed woman saying, ". . . And then the bird brought rain clouds, and its wings were pouring with rain, and the drought was over . . ." She felt TillyTilly's bony hand brush her face and then withdraw, and this made her open her eyes. TillyTilly was nowhere to be seen.

Later, when Jess was caught up in a particularly bad bout of the fever and the room seemed to be *throbbing*, widening and contracting with shimmering heat, Tilly came back, and Jess was scared. Tilly was standing by her bedside, and she was smiling, but she was . . . folding over and crackling and jumping to different parts of the room like a piece of paper blown by a volatile wind. Tilly was paper-thin and peeling around the edges, and just beyond her, a pair of long, dark brown arms was snaking in through the open door, and the hands on the ends of them were trying to hold the smiling, paper-doll Tilly in place. She knew, now, that TillyTilly and the long-armed woman were somehow the same person, like the two sides of a thin coin.

There was no wind.

Jess screamed, and Tilly flew away, and her mum came instead.

Sometime in the night, Jess fell out of bed and lay exhausted on the floor. She made a feeble attempt to grasp the bedcovers with her hands so that she could pull herself back up, but soon abandoned the idea. She lay still, licking her dried-out lips, and tried not to hum or sing; she didn't want her parents to be worried. Her mum had sat with her for the rest of the afternoon after her latest scream, forehead wrinkled as she distractedly scribbled notes for her book on her notepad. Jess, tumbling in and out of sleep, couldn't be sure, but thought that she heard a baby crying. It wasn't like proper crying, the way she'd heard babies on the bus crying—it was a weak sort of snuffling sound, *ehh-hhh-ehhhh*, as if the baby had already cried a lot. She lay still, staring straight up, a frown etched on her face as she tried to discern where the sound was coming from. It sounded quite near. She felt as if, beneath her breastbone, her heart was twisting in time to the feeble cries.

The sound grew louder. Jess paused, and then ducked her head so that she could see beneath her bed. There was a moment of pointillism, her vision swimming out of clarity and into a group of coloured dots, then reforming again. She couldn't . . . There *was* a baby there: a tiny baby, a whole *baby*, naked aside from the dirty white shawl it was wrapped in. A baby. Left there underneath her bed, somehow, how? Jess stared through the gaps between her spread fingers as the baby kicked its legs and coughed out another gasping cry. Under her bed. She couldn't touch the thing, it wouldn't be real, it would get bigger and bigger and heavier and heavier, and kill her, like in the story her mother had told her about the wicked spirit that disguised itself. She couldn't see its face; it was so helpless, it was tiny; the thing was crying, she couldn't touch it, could she?

Almost without realising it, Jess had carefully placed her hands around the baby and brought it out, and settled it awkwardly on her lap so that she could put her finger into its feverishly hot little fist. The child was silent now, staring and solemn.

Oh my God, her skull—

Jess could see places where the top of the baby's head looked scarily soft, and was seized with a fear that she would let the child drop and her head would smash open. Then she checked herself. Why had she supposed that the baby was a girl? There was no way you could tell from the pale, wrinkled-up little face with its luminous eyes filled with brown light. The hair was dark and tightly curled. It was tangled. She tried to draw the finger of her other hand through the baby's hair, and then realised that she wouldn't be able to keep the baby on her lap if she did so.

Whose are you?

Jess sat for a few minutes, her head pressed against the side of the bed to stop it from aching so, her finger caught in the baby's hand, her eyes fixed on the girl—she knew it was a girl. The girl stared at her as well. She waited for the baby to get heavier.

Then there was a rush of air as TillyTilly leant over from Jess's bed and deftly slipped the little girl from Jess's lap. Jess jumped, then managed a small, sleepy noise of relief that someone was here to help her. She climbed onto the bed so that she could watch TillyTilly playing with the baby, bouncing her up and down on the covers, moving her arms and legs through walking motions. When she caught Tilly's eyes, Tilly smiled, but said nothing and continued to dandle the little girl. Jess's head felt worse and she could see spots of heat begin to float before her eyes.

She closed her eyes and when she opened them again she was lying flat, and the air was filled with the sound of the baby's crying. TillyTilly was sitting at the end of the bed, and she spread her arms wide the better to show their emptiness. Jess fought to sit up, but she couldn't; it was as if there were weights on her chest. She quickly became terrified. Why could she only *hear* the baby? She wanted to see her again, play with her.

"TillyTilly! What happened to that baby?"

TillyTilly did not reply.

Tilly was the one making the buzzing, humming noise; Jess knew that now. She was at the door, making the sound without opening her mouth.

"TillyTilly, please don't make that noise. I don't like it, it's making me ill," she protested.

All the noise stopped—the crying, the humming, everything. The silence was thick.

"Where's that baby?" Jess whispered.

TillyTilly executed a twirl in the doorway. "She's dead . . ."

Jess stared at her friend. Her lips trembled as she struggled to speak, to think.

"You—?"

TillyTilly smiled graciously, as if she wasn't really concentrating on the topic at hand, but on something else.

"Don't be silly, Jessy, I couldn't kill anyone. I'm only little." She laughed.

Jess couldn't laugh along; she was afraid again, and knew that something bad had happened to the baby.

"Then how come she's dead?"

TillyTilly folded her arms. "I don't like to say . . . but it's your mother's fault." Then she dropped quite suddenly out of sight. Jess crawled to the edge of her bed and looked down at the floor. TillyTilly was lying flat out, like a starfish, grinning up at her.

"What are you talking about, it's my mum's fault?" Jess demanded. She had a teetering feeling—not as if she was about to scream, but a flatter feeling, as if she was about to fall down very hard and not be able to get up again.

Tilly kicked her legs in the air.

"Ask her—there were two of you born, just like there were two of me. The other one of you died," she said, unbelievably casual, so matter-of-fact that Jess was fine with it until the meaning hit her.

Then, unexpected even to herself, Jess began to cry: hot, dry, racking sobs that robbed her of her breath with every spasm. She buried her face in her pillows. It was . . . too much. The baby had been there, and then it wasn't, and then it was dead, and then it was her sister . . . and she still felt so poorly, so poorly. The humming sound was faint in the air again. She knew it would get louder.

"Stop it, TillyTilly, PLEASE STOP IT!" she shouted, then froze, realising that she had been too loud. She heard the creak of one of her parents stirring in their bed, and the humming noise escalated, but no one came. She turned onto her side away from Tilly, but Tilly was waiting on the other side of the bed.

"I'm not making that noise," TillyTilly explained, baffled, and she climbed into the bed and hugged Jess close. TillyTilly's body was so cold, the chill radiated through her. Jess's heartbeat slowed down and she felt . . . protected. But the humming noise was *so loud* now that TillyTilly was in the bed with her!

It was hurting her ears.

"We're twins to each other now," TillyTilly whispered fiercely, hugging Jess again. She patted Jess's hair, her cheek, her cold fingers chasing Jess's fever away with every touch. "We've got to look after each other. We're twins, best friends."

Jess nodded, unable to speak. She felt like crying again. She didn't understand.

"Her name was Fern," TillyTilly whispered in Jess's ear, as Jess began to fall away from the room, fall into sleep. "Your twin's name was Fern. They didn't get to choose a proper name for her, a Yoruba name, because she was born already dead, just after you were born. You have been so empty, Jessy, without your twin; you have had no one to walk your three worlds with you. I know—I am the same. I have been just like you for such a long time! But now I am Fern, I am your sister, and you are my twin . . . I'll look after you, Jessy . . ."

ELEVEN

The first foggy waking thoughts, emerging through dappled gauze, were of Fern. The memory of the baby girl made Jess big-eyed with wariness at first, then it captivated her. She started off thinking about how tiny Fern had been, how fragile and moon-light pale, and then she realised with a shock that she, too, must once have been like that.

Exactly like that, in fact.

She held her hands up in front of her and tried to imagine them as pudgy little fists; tried to create a continuity between a time when she didn't know herself and now, when she was all too aware of her Jessness.

Had her mother held each of their hands, acted as a link between the child that was feeble and limp, and the one who kicked and screamed?

Had her mother—?

Jess abruptly tried to turn away from thoughts of her mother when she remembered that terrible, dark thing that TillyTilly had said.

It was your mother's fault.

177

Heartless.

Was her mother heartless?

It seemed like it. She laughed and acted as if everything was normal, and surely you had to be sad forever if your baby died, it was such a sad thing.

Instead, Jess tried to imagine what it would have been like to share this room with Fern, her . . . sister.

Jess shifted and felt the sun on her face; someone must have come in and drawn her curtains open while she slept.

Fern would have looked just like her, and the similarity would have given Jess that confidence to connect and *tell* her things . . . confide in her instead of screaming out her fears. Could it be that simple? *I scream because I have no twin.* Jess doubted it, distrusted the way that it came out so smoothly.

Her line of thought was interrupted by her mother coming in.

Her mother was a shadow-lady, strange and dark, grotesque. It was her fault about Fern, and now her voice was too loud, her eyes too dark, as she came towards the bed.

Sarah said, "And how is your body this morning?"

Without consciously knowing what she was doing, Jess flinched in a flurry of bedding, nearly falling from her mattress in her gesture of avoidance. When she realised that she had an arm defensively up over her face, she loosened her body and, shocked at herself, flopped back down among her pillows, raising her eyes apologetically to her mum's face.

Her mum had taken a step back and seemed to have receded, become smaller. Bemused, she had folded her arms across her upper body.

It's Mummy, it's Mummy. She's not going to—she won't.

"I'm feeling a little bit better, but my head still aches and I'm really thirsty," Jess managed to say.

Her mum didn't reply immediately, but looked hard at Jess and then, swiftly, around the room. Finally she nodded.

"If I bring you some orange juice or tea or something, can you see if you can manage to get up and brush your teeth, darling?" She was walking backwards towards the door. Her expression was now determinedly untroubled, and she hadn't touched Jess at all, and Jess was glad. Then she felt bad. She didn't know if TillyTilly was lying. Had Tilly lied before? She couldn't remember. But she needed to know about what had happened to Fern, if Fern was even real.

"Mummy—"

"Jess?"

"Did I have . . . Was there two of me?" At the last minute, Jess realised that she couldn't say "sister"; the word wouldn't fall off her tongue.

Jess looked up at her mother, who stood trembling with her hands clasped together as if in prayer. She had never seen her mother like this; her mother never prayed.

"Yes. There were two of you. Brush your teeth and we'll talk about it when I come back."

With careful movements, she left the room and fell into a jerky stagger, one of her blue slippers falling off as she careered into the toilet.

Not quite knowing what she was doing, Jess noiselessly followed Sarah's path to the door. Sticking her head out of her bedroom door, she saw her father, who was brushing his teeth at the bathroom sink. He put down his toothbrush and pressed both hands on the sink, leaning forward as he listened intently to her mother's stifled sobbing through the wall. Jess, trembling, tensed herself, preparing to duck back into her room.

Jess was crying too, angry with herself, stuffing her fingers into her mouth to keep quiet so that she wasn't heard and blamed. When her father reached out and knocked on the wall between bathroom and toilet, she heard her mother take a shuddering breath.

"Sarah! What's happened? Can I come in?"

"I'll talk to you later."

"Can I come to you?"

"No. I'm all right. I'll tell you later."

"Oi, I'm coming."

Jess retreated into her room, drawing the door carefully behind her so that it didn't slam. She wiped her tear-stained face with the sleeve of her nightie and sank to her knees on her bedroom floor, stretching her arm up uncomfortably to hold the doorknob so that the door was open just wide enough for her to hear. She had to strain and press her ear against the airy gap between door and door frame.

Jess's mum mumbled something that her father didn't catch.

"Whatty whatty?" he asked.

"She knows about it," she said, through the door.

"I don't get this. I'm an idiot. Talk me through this—what's happened? Something's reminded you of . . . it?"

A brief pause, then: "I didn't know I was allowed to remember."

By now, her mum was out on the landing. Jess could feel her footsteps on the floor as she paced up and down by the telephone stand. Her mum was sniffling. She didn't say anything for a minute.

Jess fidgeted as she felt her arm going dead. They couldn't be talking about Fern and calling her "it."

"She knows about her. I don't know how she knows. She's like a witch; she doesn't even look right . . . Her eyes—"

"Look, Jess couldn't possibly know."

"Shut up! You don't know, Daniel! They know! THEY AL-

WAYS KNOW! Twins . . . they always . . . Oh my God . . . she's like a witch."

"Sarah, no. Look, I'll explain to her, I'll talk to her . . ."

Sarah began rambling, her voice trembling.

"Three worlds! Jess lives in three worlds. She lives in this world, and she lives in the spirit world, and she lives in the Bush. She's *abiku*, she always would have known! The spirits tell her things. *Fern* tells her things. We should've . . . we should've d-d-done *ibeji* carving for her! We should've . . . oh, oh . . . Mama! *Mummy-mi*, help me . . ."

TWELVE

———

Jess and her mum were hurrying through the park, nearly late for school again. There was a heaviness and awkwardness in Jess's limbs that made her feel even more aware of her movements, her breathing, than usual. Despite the talk with her parents and the assurances that it was nobody's fault that Fern had died, that Fern was in heaven (she had noted the slight wince that had twisted her mother's mouth when her father had said this), she felt haunted. She wished desperately that TillyTilly had not brought her the baby and had not told her about her sister. She didn't want a dead sister. She was scared that Fern might want her to be dead as well.

. . . *She'd prefer*
to keep me, too, and make me stay.

Out of the corner of her eye, Jess watched the colourful, frayed ends of her mother's headscarf flying out. It was Wednesday, but she was thinking of the old man who always sat on the park bench on Tuesdays. He hadn't been there yesterday, and Jess had been surprised by how strange that felt, walking past the stained brown slats of the bench, her gaze coasting over his absence. He wasn't like TillyTilly or like Fern: she couldn't even visualise him there once he was gone; as if his image and form had been wiped cleanly off the outer surface of the park, leaving an expanse as clear as . . . a whiteboard, or Mrs. McLain's fridge. Yet since Fern everything seemed changed. Maybe he was still there somewhere on the inside, like the darkness left by the rain and food and liquid that discoloured the wood of his bench. What she needed was for the long-armed woman to tell her some simple story that could show her how to know the difference between leaving and being taken away, spell caster or spellbound.

She asked her mother why she didn't tell her fairy tales.

"I do, Jess! I tell you the African ones, don't I?"

This was true.

"Yeah, but what about the ones like, you know . . . 'Sleeping Beauty' and stuff?"

Her mother shrugged dismissively, swiftly lifting her free hand to her throat to rearrange her scarf. "You can read those for yourself. They're simple enough."

Jess waited. She wasn't sure if the "normal" fairy tales that her mother omitted to tell her, the ones that always made her seem stupid when the other kids talked about them and she didn't know them, really were simple. More leaves skittering away underfoot, and her mother was still silent, tugging on Jess's hand as they moved under the trees. When she was sure that no further reply was forthcoming, she asked, "You know in 'Sleeping Beauty,' when she falls asleep?"

"Yeah . . ."

"How come everyone else falls asleep as well?"

They were out of the park gates and about to cross the road now. The lollipop man smiled at Jess, who smiled shyly back. "Late again, eh?" he greeted. Jess watched her mum smile and shrug, somehow making these sheepish gestures seem unapologetic. They were now paced at a half run down the pavement to the school building.

"Everyone fell asleep because of the fairy's spell, doyface," her mother said as they came to a stop at the school gates. Jess pulled a thoughtful face as she gripped the handle of her book bag. Her mother gave her a little push. "Come on, woman!"

"Yeah, but Mummy, why did the fairy make everyone else fall asleep?"

Her mother looked heavenward and gave a little sigh, her hands jammed in the pockets of her faded blue dungarees.

"Ummmm. Because she was a good fairy, and she didn't want the princess to wake up years later surrounded by dead bodies, I suppose!"

Her mother pushed open the gate for her and paused, patting her green-and-blue-checked headscarf into place around the edges. "Anything else?" she asked.

Jess bit her lip and turned as her mother shut the gate. She gripped the black bars and stood on tiptoe so that she was taller.

"Are you sure that's the reason everyone fell asleep when the princess did? Because of the good fairy?"

When her mother stared at her with raised eyebrows and a slight smile, Jess realised that she'd let a thin, fretful tone creep into her voice. She made her heels touch the floor again and, turning her eyes downward, carefully began to untwist the strap of her book bag from around her palm.

Her mother leaned across the gate and touched her wrist. Her voice was kindly.

"Yeah, I'm positive. It was the good fairy, Jess, because she had good intentions. I think I might know what you're worrying about. When I first heard of that story, I used to wonder about what everyone in the castle dreamed about while they were asleep—whether they all dreamed the same thing. What if they were having a nightmare and they couldn't wake up because the spell hadn't been broken yet?"

Jess made no direct response, but looked over her shoulder to indicate that she had to get away because she was probably now officially Late Late.

Her mother nodded.

"You better go."

Jess turned and started running towards the secretary's office, her book bag thumping rhythmically against her knees. She drew to a halt before she reached the glass doors. Her mother was calling her. She turned and looked back towards the gate.

"Yeah?"

Her mother leaned over the gate again. "I just wanted to know," she called out, "if that was the thing that was bothering you? What I said?"

Jess blinked. It was incredible that her mother could really believe that a mother's dreams, a mother's fears, were the same as her child's, as if these things could be passed on in the same way as her frizzy hair had been, or the shape of her nose.

"Yeah," she said, pulling open the door and retreating backwards into the lobby. From behind the glass, she watched her mum nod, smile, wave.

The truth was, Jess didn't know what had frightened her about a whole castleful of people falling asleep just because one girl had. She had no idea, and no wish to explore this fear. But with her mother, it always seemed to be about reasons. Why, why, why? Didn't she know that knowing why didn't make things any less scary?

The ridges in the carpet felt too big, like narrowly spaced islands. Her knees were crushing them, but they were denting her shins in a grotesque kind of revenge.

Jess shifted uncomfortably and licked her lips, then parted them in an O of slowly dawning dismay as her eyes settled fully on the row of books that she had spread out before her, cover touching cover. Shooting a frightened look around her, she dropped the green-and-yellow-handled scissors to the floor and hurriedly began closing the books, smoothing crumpled edges of torn paper back between the covers. She hadn't realised, somehow, what she had been doing. No, that was wrong—she'd known that she'd been cutting the pictures out, but only on a detached level, like someone within a dream. She had gone into the book corner and picked out the books with lots of pictures, her fingers smoothing over the glossy encyclopaedia photograph of the girl with the short blond hair gazing into the mirror at herself. Two girls, two smiles, snub nose pressed to snub nose. It was like twins. She had to show TillyTilly. But she couldn't take the book in her book bag: it was too big, and it was a class book, not a take-home book. Then the scissors, biting the paper into slim pieces—the paper had been stiffer than she'd expected, and she'd had to place a firm hand on the page so that she was able to cut out the girl properly. She had been dimly aware that she was humming under her breath, and the humming lengthened to deep pauses in her breathing as she had found other books with other twins, and soon she was sucking a fleshy paper cut on the pad of her index finger whilst continuing to cut with her other hand.

But now, now she was going to get in trouble. To her left was a small heap of thin paper cutout twins, waiting to be shown to TillyTilly. She glanced at the one on top—an illustration of a pair of woolly-haired black boys in blue shorts playing football—

before she scooped the fragments into her cupped hands and poured them into the green-and-white-checked pocket of her school dress. Then with trembling fingers she quickly began gathering up the incriminating flaps and fringes of paper scattered around her. She was interrupted by Patricia Anderson— *Call me Trish, saves time, hahahaha*—who made her jump.

"Oi," Trish said, momentarily pausing in the noisy chewing of her gum. "What're you doing in here, man? We're gonna watch *Geordie Racer* and that *El Nombre* video in a minute." When Jess, her heart thumping as she crumpled the leftover scraps in her hand, didn't immediately respond, Trish continued, "You know . . . *El Nombre/Writing numbers in the desert sand!*"

A few of the twin pictures fell from Jess's overstuffed pocket as she stood, and, dread leaping in her stomach, she bent and scrabbled for them at the same time as Trish, laughing, bent and picked one up. Trish held it in the air and pulled a face. It was the picture of the boy twins and the football, stark against Trish's hand. Jess stared at it, her mind working furiously, searching for escape routes.

"What's this, anyways?" Trish asked, as if it was something simple that was answerable in a few words, a sentence.

As Jess's palms began to sweat when she realised how peculiar this must look, a cramped thought began to unfold inside her. *Something is really wrong with me.*

Other kids didn't do this sort of stuff, she was sure, even if they were twins.

She moved forward to snatch the picture away from Trish's amused gaze, but Trish had turned it over. There was book print on the back; they both saw it. Jess fled the book corner and pushed past Jamie and Aaron, who were bringing in the TV and video for *El Nombre*.

In trouble again, she just knew it. Twin pictures fluttered out behind her as she raced down the corridors, hearing only her school sandals slapping against the floor and the sound of her laboured breathing as she mumbled almost incoherently, "No, no, no, no . . ." Almost before she realised it, she had flung herself against the gate, her fingers scrabbling at the catch. Someone was coming up behind her, shouting

(roaring),

shouting, "*Jessamy!*"

"No, no, no, no!" She lashed out without turning around, kicking and swinging one arm out behind her. She heard a pained gasp as she made contact with cloth and flesh (an arm, a leg?), and her other arm curled itself tightly around one of the bars. *Trouble.* Oh, she was really in trouble now! It wasn't her fault, it was Fern's. Fern had taken her thoughts, because it wasn't her—

There was a brief struggle as Jess was prised from the gate, still kicking. It was Miss Patel, red-faced, shouting at her.

"Stop this right now! STOP IT!"

The words and the face and Fern and TillyTilly and the pictures and *El Nombre* and the numbers in the desert sand were all hurting her, burning her. They were all tied to her with bruising string, and they would trail her wherever she went, even though she wasn't to blame for any of it.

Jess allowed herself to go limp in Miss Patel's restraining grasp.

Jess's eyes were closed. She was trying to hide in the dark.

Of course, she knew that she was actually in Mr. Heinz's office, but she preferred to pretend that she was somewhere else, somewhere drifting and quiet. She was on a big high chair, and Miss Patel was on the chair beside her. Miss Patel was wearing too much perfume, and both she and Mr. Heinz were waiting for Jess to apologise for her behaviour.

Mr. Heinz's voice broke into Jess's lovely dark.

"Jessamy? We're waiting."

He sounded annoyed. What, Jess wondered, could he have to be annoyed about? Then she remembered the books. She supposed they were sort of his property. Jess kept her eyes closed and tried to think how TillyTilly would sort this out.

"Jessamy, stop this at once," Miss Patel snapped, from somewhere in the drift. "I really don't know how much of your behaviour is precocity and how much of it is plain attention-seeking."

Jess's feet began drumming against the floor: tap, tap, tap.

"It's like you're playing some sort of *game* where you want some kind of control over us. Believe me, I've heard stories about you, young lady. And it's all got to stop. You can't keep disrupting the class this way, it's selfish."

Selfish. She didn't know what she was supposed to think of that.

Jess's eyes opened almost involuntarily, and she stared at Miss Patel's face, at her mouth moving and the fading patches of eye makeup that clung to her skin. The skin beneath Miss Patel's eyes looked fragile and nearly transparent, as if a finger brushing against it could puncture her. She looked, Jess realised, as if she had been crying. For some inexplicable reason, Jess began to feel very cross. No, cross was the wrong word. Cross was just stamping and shouting.

This was a little house, with a ceiling that kept getting higher and higher, a hot place with no windows. This was anger. Defiantly meeting Miss Patel's eyes for the first time, Jess watched their constant, nervous sideways flick; Miss Patel's hands kept twisting themselves in her lap.

Are you scared of me or something? You say you think I'm being attention-seeking, but you really think I'm WEIRD.

Jess turned away and frowned, kicking the leg of Mr. Heinz's desk. She hated Miss Patel. Miss Patel was still talking. Her parents would have to pay for the damage to the books; her parents weren't going to be very pleased with her. She had never liked Miss Patel; Miss Patel had started it—*Having problems with the work already, Jessamy?*—blaming her for being moved up when it wasn't her fault. And now she was trying to get all upset.

Well, if Miss Patel was upset, then good.

And if she thought Jess was weird—fine, OK, good!

She needed to be still, but she couldn't. Mr. Heinz carried on talking; Jess carried on kicking, kicking. TillyTilly was connected with her being in trouble again.

But if it wasn't her fault, was it Tilly's? And if it wasn't Tilly's fault, was it hers? How could she *be* so angry and not burst?

She was hot.

She tugged at the collar of her dress and said suddenly, without looking at anyone or anything in particular, "I'm not going to apologise."

She had cut across Mr. Heinz; he had been saying something about maturity. There was no going back now. She had to continue. She kept her eyes on the middle distance.

"I'm NOT sorry. I don't care. I'm glad I kicked Miss Patel. And I'll kick her again if she doesn't just GO AWAY!"

Then, nothing—except for her relief and the stir in the air caused by Miss Patel abruptly leaving the room with a noise that sounded like a sob. Jess slumped in her chair, kicking against the leg of Miss Patel's vacated chair. She locked eyes with Mr. Heinz, whose mouth was now set in a grim line.

"What am I going to do with you, Jessamy Harrison?" he demanded.

Panic-stricken now, Jess gave the tiniest of shrugs. But there was no time for the question to be addressed, because her mum had arrived, flustered, the trailing end of her headscarf flicking around behind her ears, to take Jessamy home.

"You're telling me that you destroyed school property so that you could show this to your friend Tilly?"

Jess, cross-legged on her bed, stared at her toes, wiggled them, then gazed at the picture flopping forlornly between her mother's fingers. It was the blond girl with the snub nose, the one who was so happy to see her mirror-twin. Jess heaved a sigh.

"Yeah."

The cutout fell to the floor; her mother had discarded it distastefully. Next, she spoke sternly.

"Jessamy. I want to know who Tilly's mother is. I'm going to speak to her so that we can sort this out."

Jess picked at a toenail and sighed. Surely her mother had figured out that TillyTilly wasn't properly real? She was glad that she hadn't let her parents know that it was Tilly who'd told her about Fern.

"I don't know who Tilly's mum is," she said, when she had spun the silence out for as long as she dared.

Her mum clicked her tongue in irritation.

"I thought as much. You don't know anything about this girl."

True.

"Jess, what's the matter? Why did you do that, cut out all these pictures? Is it because of Fern?"

Yes.

"No," Jess whispered. Her head had begun to hurt.

Her mum took a deep breath.

"You scared Miss Patel, you know. Mr. Heinz too. They're being very patient with you . . . it would have scared anyone. Listen . . . do you think you're going to do anything like that again, Jess?"

"I don't know." Now her throat was hurting, a slow ache in rhythmic thuds.

"What do you mean, you don't know?" The irritation in her mum's voice was tangible. "You're the one who chooses what happens, Jessamy! YOU can decide not to do things like that if you don't want to!"

Who'd said that she'd *wanted* to cut out the pictures? Jess clambered in beneath her covers and burrowed. "Like the fairy," she said. It came out muffled.

"The FAIRY?"

"The one that made everyone fall asleep because the princess did. She chose what happened."

Only when Jess peeped out from under the covers did she realise that her mum had left the room. She scurried out of bed and picked up the scrap of paper that had fallen to the floor.

Clutching it in her hand, she waited tensely on the edge of her bed for TillyTilly. She didn't come. It was very quiet downstairs, although both her mother and father were there. So they weren't talking. Jess wasn't quite sure what that meant. Still holding the mirrored blonde girl, she padded down the passage to the bathroom without switching on the light and peered into the mirror, watching herself intently, one hand pressed hard against the rim of the basin. She blinked several times, trying each time to catch her reflection out in the dim light. Then she pressed a finger against the cold glass, joining herself to her reflection, pointing, marking herself. It was something of an accusing gesture. She stood this way for a while, listening to the sounds of the house, narrowing her eyes as she watched her own solemn face, and heard the woman with the long arms begin to sing to her softly, sweetly. She couldn't properly understand how the long-armed woman was supposed to be Tilly. The song was sad, and Tilly never was. There was a story in the song, but she couldn't understand it.

After some time, she started as if she had just woken from a trance, feeling the salty wetness of tears trickling down her face. The mirror had misted up; she couldn't remember whether she had been breathing on it. It was cold. She thought that she could make out that her reflection was smiling.

A trick of sight or of sensation?

Cautiously, Jess wiped at her face, then crumpled the blonde mirror-twins between her fingers and went back to her bedroom.

THIRTEEN

Jess was in pain, worse than she'd ever been before; it was overflowing into miniscule gasping sounds, and it was making her vision, her stomach, her very mind, turn cartwheels amidst splashes
of neon-bright colour. She wished desperately that she would
swoon, like people did in books; she wished that she could. Her
mum had said (jokingly?) that black people couldn't faint, but she
didn't know if that was true, or even if it applied to her. Neither
did she know whether she was awake or asleep, but whichever
she was, she needed to be the other. For a full second, her senses
imploded in a violent jolt, and no part of her could be spared to
wonder if this was a dream. The searingly, impossibly hot coal
that she pressed to her mouth was burning not only her lips and
fingers, but, it seemed, every inch of her by association. She must
be dreaming—where would she have found this thing, and why
would she so doggedly continue to pass it over her lips, bursting
the skin in an agony of heat and blood when the thing that she
most wanted was to drop the coal and make it stop? Her whole
body was quivering with the struggle to take her blistering hand
away from her mouth.

She didn't even know where she was. But it was so dark, what she would normally have called Dark Dark, the only thing glowing the fading embers so firmly enwrapped in her fingers. Yet she must be awake, because there was TillyTilly, who never came into her dreams, jumping up and down excitedly, encouraging her, reminding her that this was what they'd read about in her grandfather's study: how the angel had cleansed Isaiah, telling her that she could do it. Jess had had no idea just how much it actually *hurt* to be purified. She had long forgotten what exactly it was that she was to be cleansed of. Her nostrils flared as she struggled to control her pain, to make it smaller, to pretend that she was not here until it all stopped or she died, or whatever was going to happen happened. She struggled to focus on TillyTilly, looking at her for as long as she could, pleading with her eyes for help. TillyTilly cocked her head to one side and looked as if she was calculating "for" and "against," then she came forward and snatched the coal from Jess's hand, which now fell, limp, to her side. TillyTilly rolled the coal around in her hand, even tossed it in the air a few times, then smiled and shook her head at Jess, as if to say, *What was all that fuss about?* But Jess was too stunned by the sudden absence of pain to be amazed at what Tilly was doing. She careered around in a half circle and then spun to the floor, hands held over her mouth as she struggled not to retch. She had to contain the smarting of the cooling flesh on her fingers.

God, it was so dark. Were they in that place that she and Tilly had fallen to before? Tilly bent over her, gently touching her shoulder. And smelling the cool, leafy scent of Tilly's hair pomade, Jess gazed up at her, gaping a little with the effort of dragging air into her lungs when all she really wanted to do was curl up and not hurt anymore. She couldn't see Tilly properly; her vision was blurring and it was as if she could only receive visual information about Tilly little bits at a time: the blue and turquoise of the friendship bracelet tied to her bony wrist; the green ribbon trailing from the end of each of Tilly's bushy black plaits; Tilly's eyes, widened now with concern.

"Jessy—"

From behind her back TillyTilly now drew out what at first looked to Jess like some model or figurine, but as she brought it closer and Jess could make out the way that Tilly's hand fitted around it, she saw that it was a black cup; some kind of chalice, even. Instinctively, she shrank back, pushing Tilly away from her, although she didn't know why. The pain in Jess's fingertips flared even more violently than before at the simple contact between her hand and Tilly's arm, and she let out a cry and fell onto her side. They were in some sort of open space—it was definitely earth beneath her, but there was no light anywhere.

"Look inside, Jessy," Tilly insisted.

Jess weakly shielded her face with her arm, unable to speak for a few moments.

"Come on, Jessy, look inside! I did!"

"Stop it," Jess managed to croak. And after a while, Tilly did.

When Jess next became aware of herself, the first thing she noticed was that the pain had left her. Her hands flew to her mouth, then she held her fingers up in the half-light to find that the skin was whole and unpuckered. It was still nighttime and she was in bed with the door half open, letting in a slice of light from the passageway. TillyTilly was there, in the room with her, Jess knew, although she seemed to have decided not to show herself.

"TillyTilly?" she whispered.

After a pause as soft as folding cloth, TillyTilly whispered back. The sound seemed to reverberate in the air.

"Jessy?"

"What just happened to me?"

There was no audible reply to Jess's question, but it somehow seemed to Jess that TillyTilly might be laughing silently. She didn't think that the cleansing had been funny.

It wasn't real, anyway, she told herself. If you had been burnt but it didn't show, did that make it real or not?

"Listen," Jess began. "I keep getting into trouble, Tilly." She had decided that maybe Tilly shouldn't tell her things and show her things that she shouldn't know about.

Like Colleen McLain and the knickers. And

(deadbabysister)

Fern.

TillyTilly finally spoke again. "It's my fault."

Jess sat up, looking around for TillyTilly. The last thing that she'd expected was for her friend to sound so miserable.

"Listen, no! It's not *really* your fault. You didn't make me do anything, but—"

Tilly switched on Jess's desk lamp, and Jess could see the outline of her shadow sitting on top of the papers on the desk, hugging her knees. She definitely hadn't been there before. It was almost eerie.

"You keep getting into trouble," Tilly said mournfully. Then she seemed to straighten. "You're right, it's *not* my fault," she said, suddenly cheerful.

Jess sighed, too tired to keep up with Tilly's change of mood.

"Well, all I wanted to ask you was if we could stop—"

Tilly interrupted her, speaking as if Jess hadn't said anything. "It's Miss Patel's fault about you kicking her, you know. She didn't have to be so horrible to you."

Jess thought about that, and she thought of Miss Patel's hands clasped in her lap, then wished she hadn't because it made her angry again just to think about it. Miss Patel crying!

And Miss Patel thought Jess was weird; weird in a bad way. Jess didn't know whether she'd been thinking aloud or not, but Tilly, now at the end of Jess's bed, nodded vigorously.

"She thinks there's something wrong with you," Tilly said with a snort. "Well, there's something wrong with her, more like!"

This made Jess feel better, and she giggled, until she thought of something.

"But I can see you, though, and you're not really here. That's weird, isn't it?"

TillyTilly laughed and wriggled farther up the bed so that she was kneeling directly in front of Jess.

"That's different, duh! We're special! We're twins! Miss Patel's horrible, even more horrible than Colleen McLain, and she got shamed, didn't she!"

Jess had to laugh again at that.

Tilly pulled at the ribbon on the end of the right plait and added, with her short, brilliant, sunrise smile, "Listen, I'm going to *get* Patel, anyway."

Jess frowned and drew back, her heart suddenly thudding behind her rib cage.

"What d'you mean, *get* her?" she whispered fiercely. "I didn't say we could do that!"

TillyTilly laughed scornfully.

"You're such a baby! Trying to take it back 'cause you're scared! Remember, you said it to me three times: '*Get her, get her, get her, TillyTilly!*'"

Jess jumped slightly at hearing Tilly's extremely accurate mimic of her voice, wondering if she could really have been angry enough with Miss Patel to say that. She couldn't remember.

"And then you felt really bad for saying that," Tilly continued, sounding even more disdainful, "so you did that cleansing thing with the coal. Remember now?"

Jess remembered, and as she did, she reached out and plucked at the short sleeve of Tilly's school dress.

"TillyTilly, please don't, please, please, please!"

Tilly removed herself from Jess's grasp and laughed derisively.

"Ah, shut up. You're only saying that because you think you should. But really and truly, I know that you want her *got*."

"I don't!"

"Liar, liar, pants on fire." TillyTilly stuck out her tongue, but Jess refused to smile. She stared at Tilly in horror.

"What are you going to do?"

"None of your business. She won't die or anything, though. Probably."

"PROBABLY? TillyTilly, I'm going to get in trouble again because of you!" Jess realised that she had raised her voice into a wail, and she fell silent, glaring at Tilly, who had moved to the door and had her hand on the doorknob.

"Getting in trouble," Tilly whispered, with her quicksilver smile, "is that all you're bothered about these days? Listen, no one will know you wanted her *got*, only me. It'll be funny, and it'll serve her right, Jessy. You'll see!"

The next morning after breakfast, Jess was sitting on the stairs tying her shoelaces and fretting about Miss Patel, when her mother approached her. A slim white-covered book was under her arm and a cheerful expression fixed on her face. Lowering her head, Jess made out the brightly coloured words *All About Africa* on the front cover of the book and resisted the temptation to roll her eyes at being patronised. She shifted her attention to the laces on her other shoe.

"Do you know what an *ibeji* statue is, Jess?" her mother asked, in a voice that seemed to Jess to be overloud.

She shook her head and waited to be told.

"Move up, woman." Her mum dropped herself down onto the step beside Jess. "In the old days in Nigeria, people were kind of scared of twins—some people still are. Traditionally, twins are supposed to live in, um, three worlds: this one, the spirit world and the Bush, which is a sort of wilderness of the mind."

Jess was intrigued. "For the *mind*? A wilderness for the mind?"

Her mum smiled. "You can think about that in your own time—"

This was clever. Jess had been about to ask her what exactly "the mind" was.

"Anyways, if one twin died in childhood before the other, the family of the twins would make a carving to Ibeji, the god of twins, so that the dead twin would be . . . happy."

"How would that make the dead twin happy? I mean, I don't think I'd be that happy if—"

"Ummmm, that was just the way it was traditionally done, Jess."

Jess fiddled with one of her laces before pointing out: "Doesn't sound very Christian, does it?"

There was a pause, then her mum made an odd choking sound. When Jess slyly peeped at her from under her eyelashes, she found that Sarah was laughing. She made mock-strangling motions towards Jess's neck.

"Do you have to be so precocious ALL the time?" she demanded.

Jess giggled.

"Go on then. Bayjee statues and all that, Mummy."

"B-bayjee!" her mother repeated, sounding as if she was about to collapse into helpless laughter again. Then she sighed, seemed to pull herself together. "The statue would look like the dead twin, only it would look like them when they were grown up. And there were ceremonies and stuff to do with the statues, but you don't really need to know about all that . . . all to make sure that the dead twin was peaceful . . ."

Jess nodded with some disdain at *All About Africa*.

"You can show me the picture now."

Her mother opened the book to just the right page and presented Jess with a large photograph of a wooden *ibeji* statue in some museum.

Jess looked and looked, then pulled the book from her mother's lap into her own, her fingers tracing the features of the statue, her lips moving in silent amazement as she tried to understand. The statue was beautiful, looked about half human height and was intricately carved—the broad lips, the sloping cut of the chin, the stylised markings around the eyes. It was of a boy twin, but despite that, it was familiar. As she moved her fingers over the long, long arms of the statue, she realised that she had already seen one of these; a poorly done one, drawn with charcoal, not carved.

Jess's mum was still talking, but Jess heard her softly spoken words as if from far off: ". . . Thought it might make you feel better about Fern if we had one of these made for her and kept it at Bodija for you . . . Jess, what d'you think?"

FOURTEEN

———

At the sink, washing up for Miss Patel, Jess noticed that stuck on the wall directly in front of her was Colleen McLain's book review of *The Lion, the Witch and the Wardrobe*. As she dropped another glue spreader into the pot designated for the cleaned ones, Jess noted with a certain satisfaction that Colleen's neat, rounded handwriting revealed at least two spelling mistakes, even though Miss Patel had told them all to check their final drafts twice, and to use a dictionary or ask her if they got stuck. *The Witch dicieved Edmund.*

"Listen, Jess," Miss Patel said from beside her, as she lathered her hands and stuck them under the cold running water, "Mr. Heinz spoke to your mother, and she let us know that you've had a bit of a nasty shock from some family news, so it's OK. But if you feel sad or angry or anything again, you can come and tell me."

A few minutes later, Miss Patel was walking around the class handing back projects on the Aztecs. Her hair was pulled back into a ponytail so tight that it made her face look different, narrower and broader at the same time. Jess took her seat beside

Trish with great trepidation, wondering what had happened. She couldn't decide whether she was glad that Tilly hadn't *got*
Miss Patel
(yet?)
or whether she was cross with Tilly for not doing what she'd said she would. But maybe . . . maybe Tilly had just given Miss Patel a fright, like when they'd scared Lidia—

Trish started complaining about her mark.

"Oi, look at this, I drew this wicked Aztec warrior on the front, and she only gave me two merits!"

"Oh," Jess said, looking at her Aztec warrior, which was actually quite good—he was snarling ferociously and holding a huge knife dripping with blood. But Trish had coloured him in wrong—his shading was closer to African than to Aztec.

"Yeah, oh well," Trish said, flicking the cover grumpily. "I'll get, like, five merits when we do the Christopher Columbus one. My granddad's Spanish."

Jess had stopped listening by now; she was watching Miss Patel, who was approaching them with work sheets.

Trish brightened and nudged her.

"Oh yeah! Did you get in trouble for cutting out that stuff from the books? You're a bit mad, really, aren't you?"

Jess eyed Miss Patel nervously as she put a work sheet down on the table. Miss Patel explained that it was mental arithmetic; all important questions about if someone had blah-blah eggs and gave away blah blah of them and found blah-blah more eggs, how many eggs would they have in the end? Trish had gone quiet and was now industriously sharpening her pencil. Miss Patel was about to move on to the next desk when Jess found herself blurting, "Sorry, Miss, about yesterday. I AM really sorry, and I won't be bad again."

Miss Patel looked surprised.

"That's OK, Jessamy. Don't worry about it—" and, turning away, she slapped two sheets down in front of the dismayed Aaron. "One to replace that sheet you 'lost' last mental arithmetic lesson," she told him.

That evening, Jess's mum made her "prawn thing," which was a mixture of spicy prawns and mushrooms, for dinner. Usually, it was Jess's favourite, and even now she wanted to eat it, but couldn't. The bed of rice under the prawns looked too sharp somehow, like lots of little white knives pointing out in every direction. It smelt so nice, but she was scared that it would hurt to swallow. She gave a small, resigned sigh, having found this to be the case with toast, biscuits and even ordinary bread in the past week or so. Surreptitiously, she tried to flatten a few grains of rice with her fork to see if they looked less spiky afterwards, but she stopped when she saw that her mum was looking at her thoughtfully.

The mushrooms were probably the best thing; forget the prawns, she'd choke. The mushrooms were soft and slippery. She picked out a slice of mushroom and chewed it for as long as she could to make sure that it would go down without hurting. It was no good: it still hurt, even after all that chewing. Her throat felt as if something was blocking it, expanding from the inside, and she couldn't breathe properly.

She must have made some sound or betrayed something in her expression, because now both her parents were looking at her; her father still chewing, his fork poised in midair, and her mother with her hands pressed flat on the table as if she was about to rise. Jess carefully placed the other mushroom in her mouth, and everything returned to the way it had been before.

Suddenly the telephone rang. As the shrill sound lasered

through her, Jess drew a choking gasp and jerked backwards, her arms flailing windmill-wise as she fell sideways onto the floor. There was a pause, then a burst of laughter from her parents. Jess buried her face in her hands as mixed horror and glee coursed through her. She knew, she just *knew* that the phone call was something to do with Miss Patel. She'd been *got*, she'd been *got*, she'd been *go* —

"Jess, come on, what're you doing? You've heard the phone ring before." Her father held out his hand, a note of amusement in his voice, and Jess allowed him to help her up, fixing a shaky smile on her face. Her mum had answered the phone: it turned out to be her friend Naomi. Sarah came a little way into the kitchen, holding the phone to her chest.

"Daniel, would you and Jess do the washing up when you're done? I'm going to be talking for a while."

"I was going to wash up anyway . . . I mean, you cooked," Daniel said, mock-indignant. Sarah smiled, then walked backwards into the hallway and settled herself on the staircase with the phone on her lap. Jess drank some more water, avoiding her father's now intent gaze. He seemed determined to ask her something, but she quickly got off her chair again and pushed her still full plate a little towards him.

"Daddy, I'm finished. I'm going upstairs now."

"Jess you only ate the mushrooms!"

"Not hungry." Jess stuck her bottom lip out. Underneath the table, she made a diamond shape with her two index fingers and two thumbs touching and stared through it sulkily.

"The thing is, though, enormous girl, you haven't been hungry for ages. You weren't hungry at breakfast today . . . or, come to think of it, yesterday. And, well, what did you have for lunch?"

"Sandwich." She'd been able to eat only the mushrooms out of that, too.

"Are you sure? I think you should start eating school dinners—"

"DADDY! No, I'm not having school dinners! I'm NOT!" she shouted.

There was a fleeting hush. Her dad blinked behind his glasses, looking surprised.

"Don't shout, Jess. If you feel that strongly about it—"

Her mum seemed to materialise from nowhere with an almighty cuff to the back of her head. Jess yelped, tears forming in her eyes.

"Don't you EVER, and I mean EVER, shout at your father like that, all right? If he says you're having school dinners, then that's what's going to happen. We've been spoiling you."

Jess shrank, her arms raised protectively over her head in anticipation of another blow.

Her dad spoke tentatively from behind her. "Sarah, I was handling that . . ."

"You weren't, though! If that had been *my* father 'handling that,' she would've been flat on the floor with a few teeth missing!"

Jess waited for her dad to retreat—though he'd actually have to pass her mum to leave the kitchen. To her astonishment, he rose and crossed the room, raising his voice.

"Just for saying . . . loudly . . . that she didn't want school dinners?" He adjusted his glasses and put up a hand, cutting off Jess's mum as she began to respond. "Is that the way to handle a situation like this? I don't get you, Sarah—one minute you want to hire a psychologist and the next you want me to beat her senseless. What is it that you actually want?"

"Oh my God! 'Beat her senseless!' I love the way you quote me on something that I didn't even say! And now, now you're implying that my father's some kind of savage! It's just . . . it's just DISCIPLINE! Maybe you just don't understand that! You're turning this into some kind of . . . some kind of European versus African thing that's all in my mind . . ."

As Daniel interrupted her, Jess, cringing, saw her opportunity to slip behind her mother and flee upstairs. Her mother didn't believe in sparing Jess the arguments, saying that arguing about things was a normal part of life—*Nobody can agree all of the time*—and that she wasn't about to hold back her opinions for anybody. But Jess couldn't help thinking that maybe if she, Jess, were more, well . . . normal and got into less trouble and didn't scream and get sick so much, then her mother wouldn't be standing in the kitchen in a state of outrage at Jess's grandfather being indirectly called a savage. Most of the arguments seemed to have something to do with her. And now Jess had Miss Patel to worry about as well as her parents. Just thinking about that teacher made her feel ever so slightly nauseous, as if her very name tainted the air with impending doom. In her bedroom Jess sat down at her desk and swung around on her chair, thinking of TillyTilly and the *ibeji* statue, her mind carefully edging around Fern. She couldn't understand it—if TillyTilly wasn't really really here, then how could Tilly have had a twin who had died? She tried to imagine two TillyTillys, but the mind boggled.

"Hey, shut up," TillyTilly said crossly from Jess's bed.

Jess frowned and started to swing her chair away so that her back was to Tilly, but Tilly jumped up and gaily clapped her hands together before seizing the back of Jess's chair and spinning it.

"Oi, d'you still want to be able to do the things I can?"

Jess planted her feet on the floor so that she stayed still, checking TillyTilly's expression to see if she was serious.

"Yeah," she breathed, trying to work out whether this would mean that she too wasn't going to be really really there anymore. That might not be so good.

"Only for a little, little while," TillyTilly added, seeing Jess's hesitation.

"Will it hurt?"

TillyTilly laughed.

"DUH! Of course not! This is what'll happen: you'll be me for a little bit, Jessy, and I'm going to be you!"

Jess giggled at the idea, wondering if her parents would notice.

"OK!"

TillyTilly crossed to the other side of the room and started jogging up and down on the spot, her plaits bobbing as she chuckled. Jess was overtaken by a wave of mirth, and had to press both hands over her mouth so that she didn't laugh too loudly— her parents were now talking quietly downstairs. Oh, her stomach was hurting, and her eyes were watering; she needed to stop laughing and breathe a little, but she just couldn't. She didn't even know what was so funny.

"TillyTilly—what're you going to do?" she managed to ask, and began to repeat her question when there was no reply, but stopped short when Tilly, still laughing, rippled towards her, her dress, ribbons and hair yanked backwards by some chill tunnel of billowing air.

It happened in the gap between the seconds. Realising that they were about to collide, Jess, mouth open in a silent yell of alarm, tried to step aside. But Tilly had already grabbed her by the wrists, spinning her around in a manic, icy dance, then—

hop,

skip,

jumped inside her,

and Jess, screaming now,

(YOU SAID IT WOULDN'T HURT!)

had changed her mind, and she *didn't* want to be at all like

TillyTilly. It was so cold inside that it was like heat, like the searing of the coal, and there *was* no TillyTilly, just this bursting, bubbling hotness, and, and, she couldn't let this flame stay inside her because *it had to be put out*—

But Jess wasn't *there* anymore.

She was vaguely aware that she was still in the room, but it was now a frightening place: too big and broad a space, too full, sandwiching her between solids and colour. She felt as if she were—*being flung*, scattered in steady handfuls, every part of her literally thrown into things. She could sense the edges, the corners of her desk, the unyielding lines of her wardrobe.

Stunned, she recalled enough of herself to remember that she wanted, needed, to be Jess again. She had to get Tilly to swap back, she had to force herself to concentrate. It was difficult, like squeezing herself into box after brightly coloured box, each one a little smaller, until she was properly *here* and *now*, with Tilly who was now Jess. Jess's mum was in the room now, talking to Tilly-who-was-Jess, saying, *What's the matter, why did you scream?*

She had to concentrate, she was being poured out, like a thin, sweet liquid that stuck to every surface it encountered . . .

Tilly-who-was-Jess was in the bed now, her face turned away from Jess's mum because she was having trouble working Jess's face; it was as if she found Jess's features—her lips, her eyelids—too heavy, and the expressions came out too exaggerated and stiff; one eye seemed set in a permanent wink while the other was opened wide, staring. *Sorry, I was tired and I fell asleep, but I had a bad dream, I'm all right now,* Tilly-who-was-Jess said, in a slow, funny voice. Her eyes flicked upwards, and Jess-who-wasn't-Jess sensed that Tilly had seen her, floating near the ceiling, because then she jerked the covers up over her head and wriggled down deeper in the bed.

(Oh no you don't.)

Jess's mum hesitated in the doorway, a strange expression crossing her face before she shrugged and went back downstairs.

Jess-who-wasn't-Jess sank herself to bed level and pushed hard at the slope of Tilly's shoulder through the covers, falling back stunned at the contact so that she was left bobbing in midair again. Tilly-who-was-Jess *screamed* at her touch, screamed and screamed and screamed as if she couldn't help it. Jess could feel that she was scared, and distantly thought that it was odd for TillyTilly to be scared of her.

Jess-who-wasn't-Jess watched her mother storm up the stairs, fly into the bedroom and drag her daughter right out of the bed. Her father was close behind her; both of them were arguing at the tops of their voices.

Tilly-who-was-Jess was being shaken. She didn't stop screaming, though. It was as if the touch from above had opened a floodgate of sound in her.

Shake, shake, SHAKE.

The little girl's head and legs bobbed alarmingly in every direction, as if she were some squalling rag doll. Tilly-who-was-Jess kept right on shrieking—

"Why are you SCREAMING?"

"Sarah, she's hysterical, for God's sake!" Jess's dad strove to pull his wife away from his daughter, but some kind of last straw seemed to have snapped for Sarah.

"Shut up! Shut up! SHUT UP!" she snarled.

It was difficult to tell who she was shouting at; Jess-who-wasn't-Jess assumed that it must be the other Jess, but Sarah's eyes were on Daniel. He flinched at the rawness of the sound, and in that second, Sarah began pulling the still-screaming Jessamy downstairs to the basement. They did not notice that Jess-who-wasn't-Jess was desperately trying to wedge herself between them and into her mother's arms.

"So you want to scream! Good, fine! Scream in there!" Sarah banged hard on the locked basement door in response to the frequent thumping and kicking noises coming from inside. Tilly-who-was-Jess was still screeching at the top of her voice.

"Oh, shit, shit, SHIT!" Sarah's voice cracked as she cradled her wrist, which she had knocked whilst slamming the door. Jess-who-wasn't-Jess slithered like a whisper over her skin, but she didn't notice. Jess's father, who was sitting on the bare steps leading down to the basement with his head in his hands, looked up distractedly.

(See me? Can you?)

Sarah was shaking her wrist out, her teeth gritted.

Jess felt the hairs on the back of Daniel's neck rise as, from inside the basement, Tilly-who-was-Jess whispered, *"Daddy."* His brow knitted in surprise, and they both heard.

"Sarah, let her out. You've made your point."

"Dadddyyyy!" Tilly-who-was-Jess was screaming now. *"Daddy Daddy Daddy Daddy!"*

Sarah looked at him coolly.

"She hasn't finished her tantrum," she said. Then she leant against the wall and burst into tears, putting her hands over her face just a second after Jess and her father saw it crumple.

Daniel took off his glasses and fiddled with them awkwardly. He heaved a sigh and tipped his head back to stare at the bit of ceiling above him—Jess was weaving smoke patterns on it—that was actually the sitting-room floor, as if it would yield him a solution. From the basement, Tilly-who-was-Jess screamed on.

After a little while, Sarah rubbed at her face with both hands and looked at him. "I can't do it," she said, calmer now. "I can't mother this girl. I try, but . . . I'm scared of her."

Daniel held back his fringe so that he could better resettle his glasses, and raised his eyebrows at her.

211

Sarah gave a half laugh, exhaling hard.

"And then, and then I get angry with myself for being scared of her, and then I get angry with her for making me scared."

She looked at him again, this time, it seemed, uncertainly.

Jess was inside the basement now, whirling around Tilly-who-was-Jess, threatening her with a touch.

(you will do more, more, more than scream, if I touch you just once)

and Tilly-who-was-Jess was prostrate on the floor with her hands over her head, her hands flopping at the wrists, her fingers splayed as she pawed at the dusty rug that was speckled with chipped plaster from the ceiling. Unsatisfied, but unsure how to approach her body when it looked so ugly and weak, Jess carefully gathered herself and settled in a mass on top of her old yellow high chair, by the box with silvered barbecue equipment peeking out of it.

Outside the basement, she heard her father ask, "What are you actually scared of?"

Jess knew when Sarah had dropped to her knees on the floor, pressing her ear to the basement door. She knew when Sarah turned to face Daniel again, leaning her back against the door. Jess knew everything. Everything was tearing her apart.

"I don't *know* what I'm scared of! That's why it doesn't make sense, it's stupid! I . . . I just feel like . . . like I should know her, but I don't know anything. She's not like me at all. I don't think she's like you, either. I can't even tell who this girl is—"

"So you lock her in the basement."

Sarah stood and folded her arms across her chest in a defensive gesture, but her next words were gentle. "Look, I don't want to fight about this anymore."

Daniel nodded. His tiredness was tangible to Jess. It tasted . . . brown.

Jess-who-wasn't-Jess realised that something had changed. Tilly-who-was-Jess had gone quiet. She wobbled across the basement, walking so exaggeratedly that she touched her heel to the floor before putting her foot down, and with excruciating concentration on her face, began to snatch at the wisps of Jess-who-wasn't-Jess.

The monstrosity of a pink T-shirt and jeans on a thin little body that wasn't working properly. A spatula with a wooden handle fell out of the barbecue box as Tilly-who-was-Jess's heavy hand disturbed it. She was *swiping* as if at a fly, and it was clear that she couldn't actually see. She was looking, but she couldn't see. She didn't seem to care; her gaze was fixed and serene as she alternately shuffled and tiptoed along the room as if compelled by some dragging magnet. Tilly was going to touch Jess.

Despite her most tearing, pulling effort, Jess couldn't help but gather up like a ball of wool into Tilly's arms.

Tilly-who-was-Jess looked blindly around the room with Jess's eyes, and smiled.

(I'll swap back now. I'm sorry.)

But all Jess could do once she was herself again, and in one place, and whole, was scream. It wasn't proper screaming, but the result of a kind of pressure on her lungs so that she made a piercing noise like steam whistling out.

She felt bruised all over, but, steadily, she rubbed her hands together, wishing that she could get them so soft with sweat that the skin would come away all by itself, in gentle blood, the way tissue paper split and sagged in water.

(Dear God, please take my skin, take my feet, and my hips, because she's been in them and spoiled them and made them not work.)

Then she knelt down and prayed to be free from TillyTilly.

When Jess came out of the basement, she didn't cry. She had no tear marks on her face, and was completely dry-eyed. She was all right. When she looked up at Sarah, she felt slightly bemused, without knowing why. It was a feeling of using borrowed eyes that she would soon have to return—her mother looked prettier, and more distinct. There was beauty in the unravelling wool coming from the shoulder of her grey jumper. She tried to step back and look some more, but Sarah immediately caught her up in a hug.

"Are you OK, Jess? Yeah? I'm sorry that I had to do that."

Jess stood stiffly for a few moments in Sarah's embrace, then her arms timidly crept around her mother. She was looking at her father over Sarah's shoulder, and his encouraging smile in her direction was returned with a solemn one. She had to reassure him, so that he knew the difference between her and Tilly.

Later in the evening, when Jess and her father were sprawled on the sofa in the flickering darkness of the living room watching one of Jess's *SuperTed* tapes, Jess poked at her pink fluffy slippers with her toes, then looked up at her father.

"Daddy?"

She'd thought, when they'd heard Tilly screaming it in the basement, that maybe he'd flinch or stir uneasily the next time she said it to him, but to her relief he smiled and flicked her nose affectionately.

"That's meee . . ."

"I don't want to be in Year Five."

She was greatly surprised by her father's response. He pulled her, elbows and all, into a hug, and whispered into her hair, "I know."

FIFTEEN

"Jess, tell me a secret," Colin McKenzie cajoled.

Sitting on the low, red-cushioned chair opposite him, Jess tried hard to think of a secret that wasn't TillyTilly. She thoughtfully cast her eyes over the low table scattered with papers that stood a little away from them, then at the tiny, silver-framed and blue-tinted landscapes ranged across the cream wallpaper of his office. Her mother, sitting beside her, was not as overly attentive as she had been on the first session. She was scribbling away on her notepad, maybe even sneaking a glance at her watch every now and again.

"I get scared a lot," Jess said, finally. She wasn't sure whether that counted as a secret, but she hadn't really mentioned it yet.

"A lot?" Dr. McKenzie probed, offering her a Jelly Baby with a slight smile, as if they both knew that it was also an excuse for him to have another one. It made sense: Shivs must have inherited her sweet tooth from someone. Jess shook her head, then drew in a breath and peered sideways at her mother, who was still writing industriously, apparently absorbed. It made her feel better that her mother was trying her best to make her feel that she could talk.

"I'm scared of everything—well, most things, I think. I'm always scared, for no reason. Sometimes I forget about it, but it's still there, because then something happens and I remember."

Sarah suddenly seemed to be paying attention. Though she hadn't looked up from the pad, her pen had stopped moving, and there was a new stillness about her.

Dr. McKenzie waited until Jess had recovered eye contact with him before asking, "What about Fern? Are you scared of her?"

Jess unclenched her hands when she realised that her fingernails were spearing her palms.

"Of course I am! But I try not to think about it. I think she's going to—like, *get* me."

She gulped, frightened at the meaning, but happy that she'd said it now. The words made it sound lesser.

Good.

Dr. McKenzie was looking attentively at her mother; Jess didn't dare look at her. Then his pale eyes turned to her.

"Why do you think Fern would get you?"

Duh, that was easy.

"Because I'm the one who's alive. She might be angry or something. Because it's not fair."

Dr. McKenzie regarded her gravely. She wondered whether he was laughing at her on the inside: *I thought she was supposed to be clever.*

"Fern was a baby when she died, Jess. She's not going to grow up and get angry in the same way that you or I can. Or . . . do you think that babies can get angry that way?"

Jess knew what was supposed to be the right answer. She mutely shook her head in response to his question, since there was no point explaining that she just *knew.*

Dr. McKenzie said, "Hmmm."

What does that mean?

"Jess, what do you think Fern would have been like if she were your age?"

Slightly panicked, Jess stared at the table again, drumming her fingers on her lap. Her mother's waiting silence was oppressive.

"I don't know! I don't want to talk about her anymore, please."

Dr. McKenzie waited, then asked, "What does it feel like when you remember that you're scared?"

She knew better now than to be surprised by this. She tried to sort it into words. "I feel as if that fairy cast a spell on me, only she's a bad one—"

On viewing his inquisitive expression she added, "The fairy, in 'Sleeping Beauty'? The one who cast the spell so everyone fell asleep?"

"Ah, yes. I remember." He nodded, slowly. "So you feel as if everything's been changed, just by your being scared? Tell me if I'm getting it wrong, OK? So instead of falling asleep, you . . ."

"Scream," Jess finished, in a low voice, so determined now not to look at her mother that she was terrified her eyes would swivel in her head of their own accord. All she could do was hold on tightly to her seat and look at Dr. McKenzie, who was now gently asking her to close her eyes.

"Just close them tight. Don't worry. No one's coming near you. I just want to see something."

Puzzled, Jess obediently clamped her eyes tight shut and waited in that familiar, smooth dark that was at first punctured with impressions of the colours that she'd seen when her eyes had been open. There was a still quiet, and no one said anything. Then, from nowhere, Jess's stomach tightened as she began to feel frightened.

What had happened to the other two?

The hush was like an isolating sheet of glass, slicing her away from Dr. McKenzie and her mother so that she was adrift and alone; the surrounding darkness was no longer a refuge now that she had no one to hide from.

Her eyelids twitched furiously as the rational part of her mind told her that of course they were still here, they were just being quiet. But she needed to *see*, if only to make sure that her surroundings had not grown solitary and strange.

She knew that if they had been taken away, it would be TillyTilly who had done it.

"Jess," Dr. McKenzie said, and she quivered at his voice, because it sounded so different. She hadn't realised how important it was for her to be able to see someone in order to hear them properly. She decided, for some reason, not to answer; he was somewhere on the outside of her eyelids and he could see everything while she saw nothing.

"Jess. Are you scared now?"

A brief nod. Oh, she wanted to open her eyes but she didn't want to. She was already forgetting what it had all been like before she'd closed them.

Dr. McKenzie spoke again.

"Jess, this is your safe place. You can't be truly scared in your safe place. When your eyes are closed, you're inside yourself, and no one can get you there."

Jess's lips trembled, and she finally opened her eyes and stared at him. Did he really believe that? And how could he know for sure?

"Why can't someone get me inside?" she asked.

He shook his head at her as if she was silly for not knowing. "Because it's OK," he said softly. "Whatever you feel in there is OK. It's not bad or wrong. You're scared, and that's all right. You can just *be* scared and then stop. Nothing happens in between."

But what about a twin, a twin who knew everything because she was another you? Could *she* do something in that time in between?

"Promise?" she asked.

He smiled soberly. "That's for you to promise yourself, Jess."

It was OK to be scared. What a bizarre idea.

One day, a girl forgot the sun.
Her song had fled, so softly fled,
Thus, she lay down in darkling sleep
To follow, blinded, where it led.

The ibeji *woman came to Jess in her sleep and drowned her in a blue blanket that had sorrow in every fold. She said to stop being scared about the swap, and that she should dream instead, dream in the swim of things.*

Forget, forget, forget . . .

"But, TillyTilly," Jess said, "you shouldn't have done it: it scared me, it's not . . . it's not like sisters." And the ibeji *woman, this could-have-been-would-have-been Tilly, swam out of sight in billowing blue, asking, "What is like sisters, then?" But Jess was sliding breathlessly down into the waiting sky, so she couldn't find the words to tell TillyTilly that sisters was something about being held without hands, and the skin-flinch of seeing and simultaneously being seen. But in falling, Jess herself knew that she needed to understand the precious danger of these things, and what they meant, or she would never be happy.*

When Jess awoke, she felt tingly and refreshed, and her fingers found the skin of her cheek as soft as if light silken cobwebs lay over her face. By midmorning, when Trish grabbed her in the corridor and told her that Miss Patel wasn't going to be in for ages, so Year Five had an "easy peasy" substitute teacher called Mr. Munroe, the silk had disintegrated, and Jess felt brittle and breakable.

"What happened to Miss Patel?" she asked nervously, unsure if she really wanted to know.

Trish shrugged and popped her bubble gum, golden in the knowledge that her mornings and afternoons would now chiefly consist of tormenting Mr. Munroe.

"Well, Mr. Heinz said she had a family emergency, but Jamie's brother's in, like, secondary school and he told Jamie one time that sometimes when they say that it means the teacher's gone a bit mental."

Jess stared at her, feeling as if she should burst into tears but unable to muster the energy.

"Haha," Trish prompted her, chewing hard.

"Haha," Jess said, after a second's delay.

SIXTEEN

When Jess and her parents got back, two days before New Year's
Eve, from the week they'd spent at Jess's grandparents' house in
Faversham, there was a message on the answerphone for Jess—a
first. It was from Shivs, who had honoured their six o'clock calling protocol. Listening to Shivs on the answering machine was
weird—she kept leaving breathy pauses so that it felt as if this
wasn't a recorded message, but her talking in real time.

"Errrr . . . hello, Jess . . . oi, call me back . . . I've got SOME-
THING TO TELL YOU! Yeah . . . Merry Christmas . . . yeah,
BYE."

Jess dumped her rucksack in the hallway, ignoring the fact
that a leg of her pyjamas was falling out from the top where she
hadn't zipped it up properly. She glanced at her mother for permission before running upstairs to fetch the purple address book
with the pink hearts that only had one phone number in it. Jess
carefully punched in the numbers that she knew by heart, a small
crease of concentration in her forehead as she double-checked
the book so as not to get it wrong.

She was relieved when Mrs. McKenzie picked up.

"Good evening! I'd like to speak to Siobhan, please," she said, trying to be as polite as possible.

"Is that you, Jessamy? How are you? How was Christmas?"

"I'm fine, thanks . . ."

Jess didn't know what else she was supposed to say, and so she waited patiently for Shivs to come to the phone.

"It must've been you who's been quoting *Hamlet* to Shivs—she's utterly impossible now—keeps running around the house saying that we shouldn't mind if she puts on 'an antic disposition.'" Mrs. McKenzie laughed, and Jess found a laugh had been surprised out of her too.

"Anyway, here's Shivs—say hello to your parents for me, will you?"

"Yeah, I will."

There was some rustling, and then the sound of Siobhan abusing her mother.

"Oh, so NOW you've finished TALKING to her?"

"I was just saying hello—"

"You weren't, though! You were all TALKING and stuff. Listen, she called for me, all right, not for you."

"She's holding on for you, you dozy mare. Take it."

"Hello?" (From Siobhan.)

"Hi," Jess said, smiling, both at being here, speaking to Siobhan, and at the conversation that she'd just overheard.

"Oi, Jessamy, where were you, man?"

"Went to my grandma and grandpa's. They've got no Tescos where they live or anything."

"Is it? Do they have Goo?"

Jess rolled her eyes; she'd forgotten Shivs's current obsession with Goo, the blobby stuff that looked like congealed mucus and came in a capsule. You were supposed to collect different colours, both of Goo and capsule, until you had them all.

"Don't think so," she told Shivs.

"Well, it's lucky you went, then, and not me!"

"Yeah . . ."

Jess fiddled with the green-and-white friendship bracelet that was wrapped around her wrist. Siobhan had made it for her in honour of Nigeria.

Behind Jess, something heavy fell over (she suspected that it was the Christmas tree) and her mum said "Figs!" really loudly.

"You know my cousin, Dulcie, the one I told you about?"

"Yeah. She thinks she's amazing."

"Yeah. Well, I taught her the new clap for 'Finger of Fudge' . . . She was sooo annoyed . . . and guess what, she didn't even know 'Milkman, Milkman'!"

Shivs snorted with the full force of a girl who is known in her primary school as the queen of clapping games.

"Not so amazing after all then, is she?"

Jess was about to reply, but Shivs cut her off.

"Guess what . . . You know the other day, when you tripped over that stick thing?"

This turned Jess's attention to one of several new puckered scars covering the areas between her kneecaps and ankles.

"Actually, I didn't trip—you pushed me, and it was this huge branch," Jess corrected her friend.

"Yeah, OK . . . Anyway, guess what happened when I was coming home! I found a GOLDEN GOO, man . . . in a capsule and everything—it was opened a bit, but still . . . I really needed a golden one, so I picked it up, and my dad pretended he didn't notice, cause my mum would KILL ME for picking stuff up from the ground."

That was impressive, but also just Shivs's luck. Most of the boys in Jess's class would kill for a golden Goo. Jess said so.

"Yeah, I know! But then this dog started chasing me and my

dad, dinnit, and it was this big fat dog, and the woman who owned it was like 'Ginger, Ginger,' not really bothering to STOP IT or anything. And the dog was black, anyway, so why call it Ginger? Anyway, so it probably wasn't her dog. So I think the dog thought we were playing a game with it or something . . . and I tripped over, and I hit my face, and I got a great big cut on my knee!"

"Oh. What does it look like?"

"It is going to be a BADMAN scar," Shivs said grandly. "My mum put some stuff on it, but it's going all peely."

"Wicked!"

"I know!"

"Are you going to tell anyone that you ran away from the dog?"

"No way . . . I already told Katrina that I fought it and it bit me, and that I might have RABIES."

"Wicked!"

"I know!"

Jess thought she might be having some trouble with loyalties.

On Saturday morning, she was spread out on her bedroom floor drawing pictures with TillyTilly and trying to think of something to say that didn't have anything to do with Shivs. Tilly always seemed to get cross whenever she talked about her. After a few seconds she still hadn't thought of anything, so she bowed her head and concentrated on the snake that she was drawing. It was a big fat green-and-black python squiggling across the page, and she had to use red to get the forked tongue right. She tried to look over at Tilly's picture when she'd finished her own, but Tilly squirmed away, shielding her piece of paper with her arm. Jess exhaled gustily.

"TillyTilly, are you cross with me?"

TillyTilly looked up and sighed irritably before snatching the piece of paper before her, crumpling it into a ball and stuffing it into the pocket of her school dress.

"You made me spoil it," she complained.

Jess waited patiently before repeating her question.

"I'm not cross with YOU. I just don't like Siobhan. I don't think she's a very good friend, not like I am."

Jess started colouring the white paper behind the snake a light green. She was perplexed. TillyTilly was much cleverer than her and knew nearly everything—so if she said that Shivs was a bad friend, then she must be right. But Shivs was funny, and always thought of fun things to do, and she didn't think Jess was weird. So TillyTilly might have got it wrong this time. Maybe.

"Why don't you think Shivs is a good friend?" she asked, doubt smudging the features of her face.

TillyTilly reached out and pulled angrily at Jess's friendship bracelet until Jess had to drag her arm away in order to save it from being torn apart.

"DON'T!"

"You like her better than me," Tilly said. Her voice was pitched slightly higher, tinged with the dawning of surprise.

Jess issued a swift denial, "I don't, I don't," her chief objective being to get Tilly to stop being cross with her. "Me and you are twins, and Shivs is just my friend—"

But then, feeling as if she had betrayed Shivs, she added, "—and she IS a good friend, and really nice!"

TillyTilly stared at her, unconvinced.

"Don't tell her about me," she warned. Then, with a sly smile creeping over her face: "She'll think you're mad."

Jess felt her skin flush an angry red.

"I know," she muttered, tossing her green pencil back into the pencil box. "She wouldn't understand about . . . all that."

"People who aren't from the same place as us don't understand about all that," Tilly corrected her. "I came to you in Ibadan because you were sad, and all by yourself. And I came to you here because you were sad, and all by yourself. You had no twin anymore. And you wanted me to come," she continued, as a note of reminder.

"I know!" Jess found herself trying not to scowl. What was the matter with her? What Tilly was saying was true. TillyTilly was her best friend, and they'd gone to the amusement park, and Tilly was the only one who understood about Fern, and sometimes she was the long-armed woman who told stories and sang—

"I'm not going to GO AWAY just because you have a new friend!" TillyTilly spoke from the chair now, her arms folded.

"I KNOW," Jess cried, then, realising that the sound was too harsh. "I don't want you to go, anyway!"

"I know!" TillyTilly mimicked Jess's voice uncannily before springing off the chair and turning a perfect cartwheel. "D'you still want to be like me, Jessy?" she said as Jess gazed on in admiration.

Jess thought about it, then realised that she didn't, really. And that she hadn't for some time. For a little while it had seemed to be . . . OK just to be her, Jess. She packed up the rest of the coloured pencils as she racked her brains for a tactful way to say it so that Tilly would be nice again, but when she turned around, TillyTilly had gone.

That evening, Shivs and Dulcie were coming to stay over; Shivs by mutual agreement, Dulcie because . . .

"I'm coming next time that clap-games girl comes around, OK?" (from Dulcie, at Christmas) and: "You can't just FORGET to tell her! That's a little shabby, Jess . . . I'm surprised at you!" (from Jess's mum, the day before yesterday—blah, blah blah)

Jess was unsure how she felt about Dulcie and Shivs meeting *(what if they liked each other better?)* and she was also a little indignant that she was expected to share her friends with Dulcie. When had she ever asked to play with Dulcie's friends?

Shivs phoned at five o'clock to say that she was about to get in the car with her dad to be driven over, and also that she was bringing her special glittery blue cat's cradle string because she'd just remembered that Jess had told her Dulcie was rubbish at cat's cradle. Shortly after this, Dulcie, wearing her show-off jeans with lavender glitter around the pockets and her blond hair in a glossy French plait, was dropped off by Aunt Lucy, who, tired and puffy, had started to look much more pregnant. Dulcie immediately bounded upstairs with Jess to display her new charm bracelet and (out of earshot) to complain about Sarah Harrison's Barbie ban, while downstairs, Lucy's brother tried to persuade her to stay and have a cup of tea "or something," an offer wearily rejected with the assertion that if she didn't head for home now, then she never would.

Upstairs, once Jess had sufficiently admired the star saying "I wish . . ." and the moon saying "I dream . . ." and the heart saying "I love . . ." in tiny letters that hung from Dulcie's silver charm bracelet, Dulcie bounced on the bed and looked in disdain at the two blow-up mattresses that dominated the floor of Jess's bedroom.

"Bags I this bed!"

Jess, taking advantage of the falling dusk to creep to the window and draw the curtains closed, cackled wickedly and elicited a small scream from her cousin.

"Oi, no, the bed's mine. That's the rules!"

Dulcie clambered off the bed and stumbled her way to the light to turn it on.

"No it isn't!"

"It IS, though—"

"I'm telling Aunt Sarah! I'm *not* sleeping on the floor, my mum said she doesn't like it!"

"Ah, shut up! You slept on the floor before! You just don't want to sleep next to Shivs 'cause she'll see you with your mouth all open like *uuuurghh* . . ."

They erupted into a twittering storm of giggles as Dulcie tried to grab Jess's ponytail and chased her around the room as she leapt over the mattresses and scrambled across the bed.

"I give up, stop, stop," Jess panted, collapsing onto one of the floor mattresses, and Dulcie, smiling triumphantly with wisps of hair floating out of her formerly immaculate plait, fell onto Jess's bed.

"You're all different again," Dulcie commented, after a few moments in which Jess had crawled over to her cousin and was laughingly attempting to tuck the escaped hair back into its previous order. "I wish you'd just decide how you were going to be and sort of . . . well, BE it!"

Jess was about to reply when they both leapt up in response to the sound of Colin McKenzie and his daughter being greeted downstairs. Shivs bolted up the stairs with her overnight bag slung across her body, shouting excitedly as Jess and Dulcie sped towards the staircase with Dulcie in the lead, resulting in a Shivs-Dulcie collision in which they both fell down. Jess hung back and let out a shout of delighted laughter as her mum came up the stairs and watched with her lips pursed and her hands on her hips in mock disapproval. Shivs and Dulcie rapidly untangled themselves and rose, each girl's face stained crimson with embarrassment. Shivs looked particularly striking.

"Er . . . sorry," she managed, before tossing one pigtail over her shoulder and brushing past the still "ouch"-ing Dulcie to whisper to Jess, "Look at her hair!"

Sarah had gone back downstairs, calling out to Colin that it was only a minor collision, and Shivs ran back to the top of the stairs to shout out "Bye, Dad!" before he left. Jess had to struggle to maintain a straight face as Dulcie instantly began to ingratiate herself with Siobhan. As soon as Shivs had thrown her overnight bag into the corner of Jess's bedroom—"With stuff for later," she promised with a devilish grin—Dulcie pulled out her hair bands and sat on the bed, running her fingers through her hair so that the plait was loosed and the straight yellow length of it fell down her back.

"My hair got messed up before," she said plaintively. Shivs looked unimpressed, but Dulcie forged ahead: "Could you and Jess do something else with it?"

"Don't mind." Shivs shrugged and looked at Jess. Dulcie, who by now had assessed where the power lay, also looked at Jess. Under the pressure of all this looking, Jess tried to muster some authority.

"OK, we can all have pigtails like Shivs. Shivs, you take that side of her head, and I'll take this one—then you two can do my hair." Accepting a hair band from Shivs, she took a deep breath and eyed both of them as sternly as she could. "Then we're making puff-puff." Shivs pulled a face at Jess, then snorted with laughter, busily smoothing out her half of Dulcie's head of hair with her hands.

"Sorr*ee*, your majes*tee*," Dulcie drawled, then looking upwards at Shivs, demanded: "So do you know any more clap games or what?"

Shivs grinned and started plaiting, ignoring Dulcie's yell of "Argh!" when she pulled too hard. "Too many for you, my little friend."

"Little! How old are you, then?" Dulcie asked, belligerent.

"Nine."

"So'm I! So how am I your 'little' friend, silly!"

"No, *you're* the fool—I meant that," Shivs paused and looked questioningly at Jess, "met-a-for-i-cal-ly." When Jess nodded sagely over Dulcie's head, Shivs looked triumphant, if a little confused, but Dulcie's bewildered silence was enough for Jess to keep her reservations over whether Shivs's statement actually made any sense to herself. She wasn't exactly sure what a metaphor was yet, but they'd found the word in some long review that Jess's mum had been writing about someone else's book.

Later that evening, Jess and Dulcie were in the kitchen with Jess's mum and her friend Bisola Coker, Tunde's mum. They'd just finished making their final batches of puff-puff and were carefully dropping them onto napkin-covered plates. Across the passageway, Shivs, who had gracefully bowed out of the puff-puff making when she'd realised that they weren't just going to be watching Jess's mum cook, was involved in an intense game of marbles (using marbles that, she'd proudly told them earlier, she'd stolen from her cousin Martin) with Jess's dad. From what Jess could tell, Shivs's victory whoops were met only by low groans of defeat from her father, and hardly ever the other way around. Jess was a little bad-tempered herself since both Mrs. Coker *and* her mum had commented that, overall, Dulcie's puff-puff had come out better than hers.

"Maybe you're a bit African by association," Mrs. Coker

teased Dulcie, who nodded before turning to Jess with a superior smile and sticking her tongue out.

"But *I'm* the Nigerian," Jess wailed, flapping a napkin at her mum to get her attention. "You can't SAY that!"

Sarah smiled over at Mrs. Coker, then conceded, "Maybe it's this new puff-puff pan. Maybe because Dulcie used it second, hers were more fluffy. It must be like Aunty Funke's pan . . . the more you use it . . ."

Jess ignored her. Everyone knew that it was all in the batter. She took a big, doughy bite of one of her own puff-puffs and declared that she thought hers were better anyway (and they were!), privately wishing that she and Shivs hadn't agreed to call off the cat's cradle contest. When Shivs followed Jess's dad into the kitchen, cheerfully patting the marbles in her pockets and demanding "one of those puffy things," Dulcie and Jess both rushed forward with their plates, covertly elbowing each other out of the way as Shivs looked from one plate to the other. Jess's heart sank as she sniffed appreciatively at the air above Dulcie's plate and said to her, "Yours are all nice and fluffy," before she picked up one of Jess's flatter, darker ones with a chipped toothed grin. Her sleeve was rolled up from her marbles match, and a bit of the blue-and-white friendship bracelet that Jess had made her was showing.

"Ohhhh," Dulcie had just begun to complain when Jess's dad leaned forward and scooped up one of hers, saying with a wink, "Sorry, Jess, but I just can't resist Dulcie's."

That night, Jess wrapped the covers around herself on the floor mattress farthest from the bed, Dulcie having after all bagged her bed and Siobhan the mattress in between. They had just finished a box of Cadbury's Roses and a bumper bag of salt-and-vinegar crisps smuggled in by Shivs, whose skill for procuring chocolate seemed to grow in direct proportion to the severity with which she was forbidden it. Dulcie, having been, to Jess's great satisfaction, knocked out of the clapping-game competition, had adjudicated the outcome of the final round: two-person Hanky Panky, Shivs versus Jess, which Shivs won. Dulcie was now complaining in the dark, a sleepy monotone diatribe. Shivs was fast asleep with her face turned into the pillow. Jess, too, was on the edge of sleep, Dulcie's voice swimming in her ears.

As Jess's eyes flickered shut for longer and longer periods of time, she began to hear an underworld of sound beneath the normal one of Shivs's regular breathing and the thin whine that she always heard in her ears when she concentrated too hard on hearing. There was something else: faint at first, but stronger and stranger the more she listened for it. It was some sound stuck between the echo of bongo drums and the sound of something (a stone?) rattling inside an empty space, a hollow space, throbbing and clicking until she feared that it would shake the ground. Fighting the paralysis of sleep, she struggled to sit up, but when she did the sound chased itself away into the dark, leaving only a profound silence, like being under water. Jess stared around the room, watching the shapes of things in the shadows, then lay back down again, only to spring up, terrified, when Dulcie raised her head and gave a sharp scream from her bed.

"TILLYTILLY," Jess shouted before she could stop herself, scrambling up and jumping forward onto the bed.

Dulcie was quivering under the covers, but she was alone, and all right. She seemed to be all right. Jess's mum appeared at the door and put the light on.

"What happened?"

Dulcie, wide-eyed and pale-faced, looked into Jess's pleading eyes, gulped hard then looked away and gave a shaky laugh followed by a more genuine, rueful one.

"Nothing, Aunt Sarah. I'm sorry. I just thought something touched me."

When Jess's mum had gone, Dulcie sat bolt upright in the bed and asked in a dramatic stage whisper, "All right, so which one of you crawled over and pinched my foot?"

Silence.

Jess and Shivs looked at each other in the dark, Jess's heart pounding so hard that she thought she might be sick.

Oh, TillyTilly, leave her alone, please, please.

"Come on, just tell me! Whichever one of you it was, your hand was SO cold! I thought it was a dead person or something—" Dulcie's voice had grown tentative, and she was now kneeling up on the bed, peering at them.

Shivs started giggling helplessly. "It was me," she spluttered. "I was only pretending to be asleep! Sorry, Dulcie, but your foot! It was just THERE, waiting to be pinched!"

The wave of relief that washed over Jess had such force she was dizzied and nearly rolled off her mattress.

"You two are SUCH scaredy-cats! Your faces!" Shivs continued, as Jess plucked helplessly at her covers, trying to rein in her laughter as she sent a mental apology to TillyTilly.

"Well, ha ha," Dulcie said crossly, and lay back down.

"Jess." Shivs flicked Jess's face. "Your cousin's all right, you know."

SEVENTEEN

On Sunday morning, a while after Shivs and Dulcie had left, Jess was sitting on the kitchen floor listening to the strong, riotous rhythms of Ebenezer Obey and His International Brothers as they leapt through "Bisi Cash Madam." The singing, which was in Yoruba anyway and so incomprehensible to Jess, was nowhere near as good as the actual music, which was dancing in Jess's head and making her want to get up and run up and down the room. It was like a beat jumping inside her, telling her something fun, but she couldn't get up because her mum, smelling of the palm oil that they'd eaten with yam that morning, was cornrowing her hair in preparation for school tomorrow. She wriggled impatiently, wishing she'd never asked for cornrows now, as her mum's fingers raked globules of hair food through her hair before plaiting it firmly and a little painfully to her scalp. Her mum tapped her on the shoulder with the comb that she held between her teeth, and Jess knew that that meant to keep still. She groaned and resisted the temptation to put her hand up to her head to feel the amount of unplaited hair left—it would only end up feeling as if there were still loads and loads left to do. Her father wasn't even there to amuse her by reading aloud unusual stories from *The Observer*. He was still in bed, pleading exhaustion. This had gone uncommented on by Sarah, who was in a good mood anyway and had started playing one of King Sunny Ade's albums on the cassette player as soon as she'd woken up. Jess and her father could only conclude that all was well with the book.

Sarah cheered a particularly good stretch of uninterrupted music—the high, plucking sound of the electric guitar weaved in with steady keyboard and drum notes—then she puffed her cheeks out in mild exasperation as the comb dropped out of her mouth.

Jess picked it up, but instead of taking it back, her mum kept plaiting and said, over the music, "Tell me something interesting about school."

"School? Um."

"What?"

Jess decided what to say and raised her voice so that Sarah could hear her properly.

"Ummmm. Well, at singing assembly there was this song about everyone being the same, and I can't remember all of it, but some of it went. 'Whether black or white skin / With a frown or a grin, / Well, the Lord loves us all just the same . . .'"

"Hmmm," said her mum. "The Lord, hey?"

Jess giggled. "Mummy, why don't you like the Lord?"

Sarah began another plait

"It's not that I don't *like* him, Jess. It's just— hmmm. Was there a picture of the Lord on the song-slide? Was he by any chance a white hippie?"

Jess shrugged as carefully as she could so as not to disturb her mother's busy hands.

"There wasn't a picture of the Lord, actually. There was this picture of a black boy, and he was frowning, then there was a smiling white girl, and Nam Hong put his hand up and said, 'Miss, that's shabby, because it's saying all black people are moany and all white people are happy.' "

She listened, smiling, as her mum made her strange, suppressed laughing sound. After a little while, partly to take her mind off the smarting of her scalp, Jess asked, "Why does it matter if Jesus was a white hippie?"

Her mum stopped plaiting and wiped her hands down on her jeans.

"Sometimes it can be hard to really love someone or something when you can't see anything of yourself in them," she said, turning Jess to face her. She lightly touched Jess's mouth. "Jesus doesn't have lips as big as yours, and his skin is fair. How can you ever be as good as him on the outside when there's nothing of him in your face?"

"Because it doesn't matter about faces?" Jess offered.

Her mother shook her head just once, looking a little bit sad for a moment.

"Peace to those who are far away, and peace to those who are near at hand," she murmured.

Jess was confused.

"What?"

Sarah turned her daughter back around. "Nothing, Jess."

Jess became worried, and decided to abandon the line of thought. "If there was a black Jesus, he'd have to look like Grandfather," she decided aloud instead, ignoring her mother's shout of laughter.

When her father woke up, Jess joined him and her mother in the sitting room and lay on the floor in front of the television, trying to read *Little Women*. But she fell to thinking about Tilly. It seemed that the better friends Jess became with Shivs, the more questions she had about TillyTilly. Although she was used to Tilly's disappearing and reappearing, her apparent knowledge of everything, and her ability to do anything she wanted, even make Jess invisible, Jess now wanted to know exactly what it meant for TillyTilly to be not "really really" there. And where her friend went to when she disappeared. These were all questions that she wouldn't dare to ask TillyTilly.

Jess couldn't exactly picture TillyTilly flying all the way over to Ibadan and back to the lonely Boys' Quarters, although she supposed that she could if she wanted to. This led her, unexpectedly, to think of the base sound that she'd heard hidden beneath all the other ones last night, and how scared she'd been. She closed the book and laid her cheek against the tattered cover.

The phone rang, and Jess jumped up when her mum shouted from the hallway, "It's for you, Jess!" She took the receiver and put *Little Women* down on the telephone table, on top of the Yellow Pages.

"Oi," Shivs said, "we were supposed to tell scary stories last night, you know! I just found the torch in my bag."

"Yeah, well, I don't know any scary stories anyways—"

"I bet you do! You read all those books!"

"Not scary ones."

"Well, I know loads! OK, here's one: There was this boy called Johnny, right—"

"Shiiiiivs!"

"And Johnny's mum sent him to the market to buy a chicken leg—"

"Shhhhhh."

Jess caught a movement from the corner of her eye and looked to see TillyTilly sitting on the bottom step of the staircase. Her hair appeared to have unravelled from her thick plaits and rose up in two puffs, just like before, in Nigeria. Jess waved at TillyTilly as Shivs kept talking, and Tilly gave Jess a quick smile before Jess turned back towards the telephone table and pleaded, "Shivs, you know I don't like those stories!"

"All right, sorry," Shivs said contritely, then: "Guess what! Martin went to Cornwall, and he saw a ghost!"

Jess was about to reply when what felt like a damp white sheet flew over her. Taking a few steps backwards, she flapped at the covering with one arm, floundering until she came to a standstill.

"Oi, Jess, I have to go in a minute," Shivs was saying, and Jess was trying to speak into the phone but her fingers kept slipping *through* it until the curve of the receiver was suddenly solid again in her hand and the sheet had sucked into her skin so that she felt cold and taut. As if through rippling sheets of cloth, Jess heard herself sneering, "Don't phone me again with your stupid stories, white girl."

Shivs laughed. "Oi, Jess, you're rude, y'know," she said, then waited for Jess's answering giggle.

She waited and waited while Jess's lips moved silently, struggling to take back those TillyTilly-words. But before she could say Jess-words, Shivs had said stiffly, "Fine then," and hung up.

The minute that she did, TillyTilly darted out from behind Jess and up the stairs in a gleeful streak of green-and-white school check. Jess, drained of energy and weak with fury, gripped the edge of the telephone table and listened for the sound of Tilly's footsteps overhead before she scrambled after her up the stairs.

Jess was LARGE with her anger, gasping aloud as she stomped into the bathroom then kicked at the toilet door, looking for Tilly. She found her in her mum's study, sitting on the chair before the switched-off computer.

"Get away from there," Jess told her in a loud whisper. "My mum's work's on that!"

TillyTilly shrugged and stayed where she was.

"Why are you all angry?" she asked innocently, before Jess could get her words out properly. Why was she ANGRY?

"You—you upset Shivs! And she thinks it was ME!"

"It *was* you. You said it, didn't you?" TillyTilly stuck out her tongue.

"How did you do that?" Jess cried, no longer making the effort to keep quiet.

TillyTilly only smiled.

Drawing closer, Jess jabbed a finger at her.

"Who ARE you, TillyTilly?"

"Your sister—" The corners of Tilly's mouth had turned down now.

"What about before that?"

TillyTilly moved across the room so that she was standing almost nose to nose with Jess.

"You like HER better than me," she glared, "or you wouldn't be making such a stupid fuss."

Jess completely lost her head at that, lost it like she never had before. Baring her teeth in a snarl, she pushed TillyTilly away from her so hard that she staggered.

"I DO like her better than you! So what! You're mean, TillyTilly— so, so mean, even if you are clever! And you try to make me mean as well! It's more like sisters with Shivs than it is with you—" She advanced on TillyTilly, who was now retreating backwards towards the computer, cowering somewhat. "And with Shivs, it's safer!"

Tilly stiffened and stood still.

"Safer! So Shivs is your sister! So you're scared of me!" she blazed.

Jess halted, uncertain whether or not to retract, and whether she should draw closer. She didn't want to. Something was happening to the air around TillyTilly; there was some sort of breeze sticking to her outline, as if she was drawing it in.

"I'm going to phone Shivs back," Jess faltered, "and I'm going to—"

"Tell her it was me!" TillyTilly screeched, running at Jess with a whoosh, ribbons trailing. Jess, frightened, backed up quickly, but Tilly stopped short a few centimetres away and
pushed
at the space between them with her fingers until Jess felt it actually cave in.

TillyTilly smiled grimly when the screen of Sarah Harrison's computer monitor was slashed across as parts of it fell out with a soft cracking sound. The air filled with sickly wisps of smoke, and Jess could see an orange fizzle starting somewhere near the back of the computer. She let out a soft whimper
(Oh, trouble, I'm in trouble again)
and TillyTilly said to her from somewhere amidst the thickening grey, "You're scared of me . . . good!"

When all the fuss had calmed down, Jess, unwilling to take the blame for breaking the computer, told her mum that it was TillyTilly who'd done it. Sarah groaned, but she was not as angry as she could have been, since her files were all backed up on a series of neatly labelled disks, but she was extremely annoyed at the expense of having to buy a new computer.

"I thought I heard running around upstairs! Well, what on earth did she DO to it? I don't think it can be repaired."

Jess looked down at her shoes, shamefaced. She had no reply to all this.

Her mother frowned and said, "You're NOT to let your friends go into my study, and in fact, once you've found out

Tilly's mum's name or her telephone number, you're not to have Tilly over here, all right?"

Jess, nodding glumly, was inwardly appalled. How was she supposed to *stop* TillyTilly when she could do anything that she wanted?

It was nearing the end of Monday afternoon, and Jess was sitting in the very middle of the sofa watching the last few minutes of *Count Quackula*. Her mother was upstairs in her study installing the new computer that she'd marched out and bought that day, and Jess had already finished her jam-and-cheddar sandwich. She clutched the cushions on either side of her in preparation for the end music, which she always found scary, even though she knew it was silly to. It was the lightning splintering the skies above the silhouette of the castle, and the eerie, insane cackle that did it. Controlling her desire to whip around and check behind the sofa (just in case), she began laughing quietly to console herself, an edge of terror in her laugh as the credits for the cartoon rolled. Then she jumped as light flooded the room. It was her father, whom she had not heard come into the house, and as he sat down beside her with a knowing smile, his arm stretched out along the back of the sofa as if he'd been there all day, he said, "Worrying yourself with Count Quackula. Again . . ."

Jess buried her face into a cushion and groaned. "Dad-dyyyyy—"

She stopped as her ears were flooded with the familiar buzzing sound

(hmmmmmmmmmzzzz)

and got onto her knees on the sofa, peering over it until she could see—at first blurrily but then in sharp relief—TillyTilly stretched out on the floor, halfway into the sitting room and half out into the passageway. She looked as if she had fallen there, silently.

Her head was flopping listlessly to one side and her limbs were spread limply, looking more as if they surrounded her than belonged to her. Jess, embarrassed, tried not to look at her pink knickers. After the initial throb of panic at seeing Tilly, Jess stared for a second longer when Tilly didn't get up but continued to gaze impassively at the ceiling. Looking up at the ceiling herself, only to find nothing there, Jess began to feel afraid for her friend. What was the matter with her? And how could she be getting poorly in the same way that Jess did?

Knightmare was on now, and as Jess glanced at her father to see if he had noticed anything, she found that he was staring vacantly at the television with his mouth half open in an oddly unfinished expression. Torn between wondering what was the matter with him and what was the matter with Tilly, she looked back at Tilly, willing her to get up. Finally she could wait no longer and scrambled over the sofa. She crawled cautiously towards the still figure spread out in front of her, but when she reached TillyTilly her eyes were closed, and Jess had to bend close to her face in order to hear the halting cycle of her breath. Jess briefly thought of things like hospitals or the GP before dismissing them. Instead, she enfolded the other girl in her arms and pulled her upright, into a sitting position. TillyTilly was *light*—so light it was like holding cotton wool. Or nothing at all. But Jess was still scared of her: scared of the ice that lingered in the touching, and of the glint in her hidden eyes. Nevertheless, she pulled TillyTilly closer to her, thinking that somehow her own warmth might make her better. Cradling the back of Tilly's head with one hand, her fingers brushed one of Tilly's spongy puffs of hair as she whispered, "TillyTilly, what's the matter? How comes you're all poorly?"

TillyTilly didn't reply, but shifted a little and squeezed her lips together as if trying to suck in the very air.

"I didn't mean it when I said you were mean," Jess said tremulously. No, she couldn't be a baby about it; she had to think of something. Think! She was struck by an idea. "Are you pretending, to scare me? Because of the fight?" she asked, moving back so that she could watch Tilly's face. No, her skin was too ashen, almost as if smeared with dark grey face paint. Suddenly distracted, Jess gazed curiously for a moment at the back of her father's motionless, blondy-brown head. The flickering of the TV screen seemed slowed down, or speeded up, or both, since she couldn't make any sense of the dialogue, or even of the image. Jess was suddenly aware of a distortion of time, a twisting that alarmed her because Tilly had never done this so obviously before. It was unnerving.

She turned back to TillyTilly, whom she had inadvertently let flop back down to the carpet. She tightened her grip. What would happen without TillyTilly, and where, now, would Jess see something of herself? No, she couldn't think about herself right now, Tilly was ill —

(Oh, she's mean, oh, she's my sister, oh TillyTilly don't go . . . don't GO, don't be sick like this, you're not supposed to hurt.)

Could a person survive losing *two* twins?

It was too, too miserable being a child and not being able to know these things or believe in a future change. So strange, being powerless to do anything for her own happiness.

Now they were both crying, and Jess was startled because she had thought at first that it was only her. She wanted to wipe her face so that her tears didn't drop onto her and Tilly's clothes the way that they were. Tilly's eyes were still closed, but she was sobbing so hard that her body was shaking in Jess's arms. Then Tilly drew a great sigh and fell quiet, breathing almost noiselessly. She opened her eyes and motioned to Jess to let her go, and eased herself backwards on her hands.

"I don't want to be like this," she told Jess, letting her hands fall into her lap. Her head was drooping distressingly, as if she couldn't hold it up.

Jess sniffled and wiped at her eyes.

"It's my fault, isn't it? Because I've been a bad sister."

TillyTilly smiled, and there was a bewildering moment of blur between her and would-have-been-could-have-been Tilly, the wise-eyed *ibeji* woman, who wasn't actually there, couldn't be there at the same time as TillyTilly.

"No, not that. It's like . . . You know when we fell?"

Jess remembered the flying-sinking feeling and nodded.

"It's like that," Tilly whispered, smoothing out her skirt with her trembling hands. Big tears were falling from her eyes again.

"It's not what's supposed to happen. Something's wrong. I can't—"

Jess watched as Tilly's lips moved noiselessly for a few moments, as if she had forgotten how to speak, or what the words were. With effort, she met Jess's eyes and said, "If only you could speak Yoruba. Or understand it."

Jess reached out and timidly touched Tilly's hand. "I'm sorry that I can't, TillyTilly. Can't you teach me?"

She wanted to be a better sister, too, but she didn't think she could ask Tilly about that.

"Jess!"

Astonished, Jess gazed upwards to find that she was kneeling teary-eyed in the living-room doorway, at her mother's slippered feet.

"What's the matter?" Sarah asked, equally surprised.

Jess opened and closed her mouth, then gave a little laugh and moved aside so that her father, sock-footed and carrying a plate with a sandwich on it, could reenter the sitting room. Both her parents looked at her expectantly. With growing disbelief, Jess yet again felt herself slipping into the gap—that gap of perception between what is really happening to a person and what others think is happening. She stood up and said, lamely, "I hurt myself."

"Where? Shall I take a look at it?" Her mum maintained steady eye contact with her, and Jess, disturbed, wondered if the gap was not as wide as she had thought it was. She couldn't bear a halfway gap; it had to be a chasm or not there at all—fitting pieces together would be dangerous and doomed to misunderstanding.

"No, I only stubbed my toe, it's all right now," she said, quickly.

"Jess, d'you want some of this?" Daniel interrupted from the sofa, apparently under the impression that Jess wanted to eat something as boring as ham and cheese in a sandwich.

Jess was relieved when Sarah's eyes slid off her towards him.

"I like the way you're eating ham now when I'm doing a ham thing for dinner," Sarah admonished.

As her father replied, Jess tried to creep past her mother. She was stopped by a tug at the beaded end of one of her cornrows.

"Hey, you. It's nearly half past six, and you haven't asked to phone Shivs yet! You two arguing or something?"

Jess hesitated, then shook her head. She still had to sort that out.

"Actually . . . can I use the phone?"

Her mum nodded, and Jess bolted up the stairs to her bedroom to find the purple address book.

Shivs was a long time coming to the telephone, and when she finally took the call, her voice was gruff.

"What?"

"Shivs, I'm really sorry about yesterday."

"So?"

"So I'm sorry! You should accept my apology. Jesus, what d'you want from me?"

"Don't take the Lord's name in vain," Shivs said automatically, as Jess had known she would, then they both collapsed into laughter. Finally, Shivs drew a breath and then asked, "What happened, anyway?"

Jess bit her lip. "Umm . . . well, I was just joking. I didn't even mean it! I was about to say 'jokes,' but then my dad's friend Jonathan made me jump and I dropped the phone, and when I'd picked it up you'd gone."

Shivs gasped, apparently at the audacity of the lie. "Ohhhh, what's WRONG with you, Jessamy Harrison! The truth shall set you free—I heard you breathing!"

"What's all this Bible stuff, anyways?" Jess asked, buying time. What on earth was she supposed to say now? And she was already so worried about TillyTilly, who was not supposed to be sick.

"My mum made me go to church on Sunday. Dry as a bone. Jesus was some boring man, but still, I DID hear you breathing— it was like *huhhh, huhhhh, huuuuh*—"

Jess, having swiftly made up her mind, interrupted her. "All right, listen, I'll tell you about it one day. All I can say about it now is that I'm really sorry and I didn't mean it."

"Yeah? Tell me one day like when?"

"Like . . . not now."

"Oh, fine then, if you want to be all mysterious," Shivs said, then: "Me and Katrina are best friends again—we made up today." They'd had a fight over one of Katrina's Barbie dolls, which was now missing a pink-plastic high heel, an occurrence that

Shivs swore *(wet and dry, stick a needle in her eye, if this turns out to be a lie)* wasn't her fault.

"Oh."

"But me and you are still best friends. It's just Katrina's my school best friend, OK?"

"OK!" Jess didn't complain, even though she didn't have a school best friend herself.

"I've got to go and eat my dinner now," Shivs said.

Jess could faintly hear Mrs. McKenzie calling in the background.

"All right. Bye."

"Bye," Shivs said cheerily. "I'm glad we made up. I didn't take the friendship bracelet off, not even in the bath! And it took AGES making yours."

After Jess had finished using the phone, her mum called Nigeria and spoke to Jess's grandfather. Jess, sitting patiently on the steps waiting for her turn and bracing herself for the usual fear-provoking sound-echo on the line, pricked her ears up when she heard her mother mention the word *ibeji*, then look at her and turn away slightly before continuing in rapid Yoruba. She hadn't talked with her mum about the issue of the *ibeji* statue for Fern again, preferring to keep it quietly in her mind for now while she worked out exactly how it was supposed to make Fern happy. When her mother finally stopped speaking and passed the phone to her saying, "There's only a few minutes left on the card," Jess spoke eagerly into the receiver.

"Hello, Grandfather!"

"My Wura! How are you, how is everything?"

She grimaced at the echo.

"I'm all right!"

"Good girl! Fine daughter!"

Jess smiled at a man who would say that she was a fine daughter just for being all right. Her grandfather's next words made her heart stand still.

"Eh-heh, and also, have you heard from your friend?"

Jess's eyes widened and she sank down on the bottom step of the staircase and looked through into the kitchen at her mother, who was slicing onions at the chopping board.

"Friend? Which friend? I mean . . . um. I do have friends, but which one . . . ?"

"Ha! You this girl! Have you forgotten already? That thief friend of yours who was stealing my candles and taking them to my own Boys' Quarters," her grandfather said equably.

Jess was silent, and the muteness wasn't just inside her, but everywhere at once.

"Akin said that you came out of the Boys' Quarters that day when you wanted to go home. *Sae* you remember?"

"Yes," Jess whispered.

"I told him to check the place, but that foolish boy just went to the front steps and came back to tell me it was nothing. I checked the whole place myself a few days ago."

"I didn't have a friend there," Jess said weakly.

"Eh-heh now, so you didn't have a friend there! You were crying to go home and then afterwards you didn't want to leave. You *oyinbo* are strange," he teased.

Jess put a hand over her mouth so that he didn't hear her laborious breathing. Had he found the board with the *ibeji* woman on it? He couldn't have. He would have said something. But if Tilly had taken it away, then where was it?

"Wuraola." Her grandfather's voice was serious now.

"Mmmm?"

"Two hungry people should never make friends. If they do, they eat each other up. It is the same with one person who is hungry and another who is full: they cannot be real, real friends because the hungry one will eat the full one. You understand?"

"Yes, grandfather." She was scared now, because she knew he wasn't talking about food-hungry. She almost understood what he was saying; she was sure of it.

"Only two people who are full up can be friends. They don't want anything from each other except friendship . . ."

Jess sprang up from the step, eying the darkened staircase as her grandfather's voice was cut off with a loud series of beeps. Then, seeing nothing, she relaxed and gave a relieved laugh as she realised that it was only the lack of money on the phone card that had divided her grandfather and her into separate spaces again.

"Jess," her mother called from the kitchen, "you hungry?"

Jess, who had dropped the phone with a clatter, calmed herself and replaced it carefully.

"Not really," she said, chewing on her bottom lip.

"Pssst!"

Jess, who had run up the stairs ahead of her mother to prepare herself for the first two fits of *The Hunting of the Snark* read out in a Yoruba accent, stopped short before entering her darkened bedroom. The sound didn't come from there.

"Jessy—"

Jess looked to her right and to her left, then moved cautiously down towards the bathroom and pushed the door open. The bathroom was cold, but the square, white-framed mirror above the sink was coated with what looked like condensing steam. She took a couple of steps inside, wondering what TillyTilly was doing, then she tried to step back out again, not liking the indistinct way her outline loomed as she approached the mirror. But, with a rattling sound, the bathroom door slammed shut, as if pushed. When she touched the handle, it was so cold that she jumped away lest her hand stick to it.

"TillyTilly," Jess whispered, and her voice sounded so, so small that she almost didn't realise that she'd said it aloud. "I don't like this. I don't like it," she said, trying to sound firm and assertive. Tilly had to stop it now.

No sound, no movement. It was dark in the bathroom, but Jess somehow knew better than to make a move towards the light switch. The tiles had a pale white glow of their own. Shivering, Jess rubbed her arms and moved forward to the mirror, as she knew Tilly wanted her to. With one hand, she tremblingly rubbed away a corner of the mist, only to see her own eye peering back at her.

"Jess?" her mother said, sounding as if she was at the other end of a long, hollow tunnel, rather than just outside the door. "You all right?"

"Yeah," Jess murmured, now smudging mist away with her fist. Then, louder: "Yeah. I'm just brushing my teeth."

"New habit?" her mother asked, with a smile in her voice. When there was no reply, she said, "Well, I'll be in your bedroom, all right?"

"Mmmm."

Jess had now cleared a rough little patch of mirror, but was bewildered to find that she was only looking at herself. What exactly had TillyTilly wanted her to see? It was Jess, just herself, her hazel eyes darting bemusedly around the mirror, her pale brown oval face framed with the beginnings of the thick cornrows that swung to her shoulders and ended with the brightly coloured bustle of wooden beads. She leaned closer, squinting, then gasped aloud as her reflection spoke to her.

"I want to swap places, Jessy."

It was Tilly's voice, but Jess's mirrored mouth moving.

"Sw-swap?" Jess stammered, touching her face even as she tried to discover how this could be. Her reflected eyes narrowed and passed over her coolly, and the cheeks were sucked in thoughtfully before Tilly said, "Yes. I've decided that it's about time."

Jess, moving rapidly towards the bathroom door again, was trying to reconcile this Tilly with Tilly-who-was-ill. She'd changed again: two Tillys, nice Tilly, nasty Tilly, TillyTilly. She disagreed with Tilly's last statement with a frantic shake of her head. "I'll scream again," she warned.

TillyTilly chuckled indulgently, but remained standing still in the mirror-world she inhabited, even as Jess was moving, trying to force the bathroom door handle down despite the cold.

"All right then, scream. They'll only put you in the basement again, and we'll swap places there. People don't care when you scream, Jessy, because—" from the inside of the mirror, she leaned closer to the surface and it seemed to bulge and stretch as if she would tumble out, "—because it's really annoying."

Jess put a hand to her mouth, trying not to let her heart feel too full that TillyTilly, who was supposed to understand, was saying these things to her. She also began to feel the stirrings of anger amidst her fear.

"I'm not swapping," she warned, but her voice came out thin and squeaky—a frightened voice. Oh, she was scared again. She'd never been *more* scared.

"Yes you ARE."

TillyTilly sounded frustrated. As she spoke, all four taps, the two for the sink and the two for the bath, turned on with a single sharp *hissssss*. The plugs were already in place.

"Next the water pipes," TillyTilly warned, as Jess stared uncomprehendingly at the gushing water. Some of it leapt impossibly and splashed Jess where she stood. All of it was cold.

"A person could drown in here," TillyTilly added, from the mirror. "The water would have to rise fast though . . ."

"Never, never, never," Jess whispered to herself, unsure what she meant, and she closed her eyes tight and hid from TillyTilly, even though her hands and feet were numbing with cold. She could hear the rushing water drumming away in the bathtub.

"I'm not full, but you're the hungry one," Jess said between clenched teeth, as a cold hand

(was it within or without?)

touched her.

She was scared! She was so scared it was in her eyes and her hands and her bones and hair and teeth—

It was OK.

It

was

OK—

Then, without opening her eyes, she was caught in the crisp outward shattering of glass as *the mirror crack'd from side to side*, flying out of its frame. At the centre of it all was TillyTilly, manically screaming, "Seven years' bad luck! Seven years' bad luck! SEVEN YEARS' BAD LUCK!"

"What are you?" Jess cried out from her safe place.

Tilly's reply: "I don't KNOW! You know! YOU know!"

Sarah heard the sound of loud breakage in the bathroom, and was there half an instant after Daniel, who had flung himself against the door and forced it open. There was a thin layer of cold water on the floor—it was from the overflowing bathtub. Water was also pouring gradually from the edge of the washbasin as well, since all the taps were on. And Jess, sitting near the middle of the room, small and inscrutable in her blue T-shirt, was surrounded by a myriad of glittering mirror pieces. Inexplicably, the white mirror frame was empty on the wall above the sink, rocked slightly to one side. In the middle of all this sat Jess, silently clutching her purple toothbrush, holding it out as if it were an offering. It had bits of glass in the bristles; she'd been incredibly lucky not to be blinded or hurt. Glass was everywhere—Jess blinked and shook her head; pieces of mirror were in her hair and scattered on her clothes and the floor. It broke the spell.

At the light clinking sound, Jess's mum stepped gingerly into the room, moving quickly over to Jess and brushing her down with a towel as Jess's dad turned off the taps.

Jess was *light, light light-headed* with tear.

"Mummy," she said, impatiently shrugging off Sarah's attentions with the towel as she was led out of the bathroom, "You have to believe me! I didn't do it! It was TillyTilly—"

Then she stopped, confused, and said nothing more.

Her mother's eyes grew wide and fast-blinking, the lashes trembling.

"So TillyTilly came here tonight and decided to break something again, hey?"

Sarah handed the towel to Daniel and started down the stairs to fetch the dustpan and brush. She needed to change from slippers into shoes as well.

Jess's dad now took his turn. "Jess—"

Jess wriggled away from him and started back to the bathroom.

Despair. Despair. It was as if they were all on Tilly's side, determined that Jess be blamed for something that she didn't even know she'd done. She could see Tilly's plan, and she could see that it was going to be one long line of TROUBLE until she didn't want to be Jess anymore.

Desperately she said, "You don't believe me! Well, OK, I'll clear it up. It's my fault, anyway—I made all this mess!"

Restraining her, Daniel tugged Jess out of the way as Sarah, looking clownlike in a pair of his black boots, reentered the bathroom, clicking her tongue at the extent of the sprayed glass. Jess kicked hysterically, hearing the rasping sound beginning in the back of her throat, the one that preceded a screaming fit.

Jess's father picked her right up, and both of them saw a nerve tighten near Sarah's jaw. But she bent over and steadily began to sweep the shards of glass into the dustpan, shaking the brush every now and again to dislodge shining specks.

Jess made one last blind swipe at the bathroom floor, her arms spinning around in an attempt to break free from her father's hold, then she yelped as glass spiked the top of her palm, and a bead of blood sprang from an area on her palm just below her middle finger. She stopped struggling and stared at it, fascinated.

"Oh God, Jess!" Her father sat her on the top step of the staircase and took her hand, inspecting it, but Jess snatched it back and held her hand up before her face, gazing absorbedly at the cut.

So now she bled, when the skin wouldn't lift from her hands before.

She let out a low whine and rocked back and forth, and her father

(*go away, GO AWAY*)

tried to take her hand back in his.

Sarah had dropped her dustpan and brush and was repeating, "Daniel, you'll need to get some disinfectant and some cotton wool—"

Jess looked up from the cut, and stopped them both in their tracks.

There must have been something in her gaze that held them both so stiff, but she didn't care.

Sarah shrank back, murmuring, "Jess, what is it?"

"Shut up!" Jess fired back, cradling her hand at her chest. "Shut up! It's all your stupid fault anyway. You don't believe me, just when I need you to—"

"Daniel, get the disinfectant," Sarah said steadily. She and Jess were staring at each other.

Jess couldn't stop spitting out words, because they were words like blades to hurt, and if she swallowed them, she'd be scraped hollow. She didn't like saying these things, but she didn't know how to stop.

She wanted to stop.

Her mother was holding on to the top of the banister as if preparing to flee, only not yet.

"You hate me, anyway! You want to hit me when I scream just because YOU got hit! She wouldn't BE here if it wasn't for YOU—"

Daniel stayed stock-still, his eyes fixed. Jess was spilling over, spewing out words.

(Daddy daddy daddy daddy daddy)

"And it's all YOUR FAULT about Fern! You think it's your fault, and it is, it is, it is!"

Jess's voice had escalated to some peak of dark satisfaction, and Sarah winced and closed her own eyes with a slight shaky nod of something like acceptance. But it was Jessamy's eyes, like cold hard stones, like the girl that Fern would have been, that made Daniel start forward, carpet slipping under his feet, and wildly strike out almost before he knew what he was doing, hitting his daughter with such force that she jerked backwards with a whole-body snap.

"DON'T talk to your mother like that," he yelled, looking neither at Sarah nor at Jess. His voice wobbled on the last few words.

Her mother put her arms around Jess and gently touched her cheek, rubbing the spot that hurt.

"Disinfectant," Daniel said, slowly heading down the stairs.

Jess stared, bewildered, after him, feeling tides turning in her stomach. Everything, everything had crossed over in the spin of a second.

EIGHTEEN

———

Jess went to sleep nursing the cut on her hand. She kept thinking about the peculiar
(whiteblanket)
feeling that had overwhelmed her when she screamed at her
mother. Had TillyTilly been the glass that cut her? Not only that,
but the way her father had looked at her: horrified, repulsed, she
could see it over and over again.

So now they both hated her, they were a *group* of two. Well,
fine, she hated them too. But she couldn't help weeping a little
when she remembered that now she didn't even have TillyTilly
anymore.

She fell asleep for a little while, but woke up when TillyTilly
appeared.

"Oh, Jess," TillyTilly laughed, spinning in circles, her arms
out. She was hiccupping and giggling, then suddenly suppressing
tears, the dimensions of her face stretching impossibly so that her
eyes were like long, pale, luminous slits in the night. "You're
afraid of me! It's changing us! Stop . . ." She gave a raucous
whoop.

The air was condensing; it was the only way to describe what was happening—there was a sort of mist, a palpability, an elusive smell like madness. Jess knew with all the certainty of childhood that her bed was a haven from which she must not stray. She must beware, because *TillyTilly was no longer safe.*

Had she ever been?

The very fabric of TillyTilly was stretching, pulling apart, a brown cycle of skin and eyes and voice whipping around Jess and the bed in ever-decreasing circles.

Jess dropped onto her hands and knees, curling herself up closer to the bedclothes. It was dark with her eyes open, dark with them closed. She could smell Tilly's skin. The leafy pomade had intensified into a wet, rotting vegetation smell. Could she call for her mother, who was a wall's thickness away? Candles burned, and on the outside of Tilly's circle of tea lights, Jess knew that the terrible, beautiful, long-armed woman would be there, setting the air humming with her presence, looking on.

"Ohhhh," Jess whispered. She could feel shadows falling, cold across her. "Ohhh . . . please, please, don't let this be happening. I want this not to be real. I want this not to be . . ."

TillyTilly laughed then, and the room (and the bed) seemed to Jess to tilt sickeningly from side to side.

Tilly is trying to shake me off the bed.

Clutching the sides of her bed so hard that one of her nails bent inwards over itself, Jess gave a sharp cry and forced herself to open her eyes, blinking away the wetness that filled them. The room was dim and still, filled with a bitter smoky smell, but no one was there.

The door . . . but the door was too far away.

too . . .

far . . .

away . . .

"I'm only little, Jessy." The voice came from above her, a high, lilting, singsong voice that sounded younger than TillyTilly's normal voice. "Just a little girl. Nothing more. Do you find it hard to believe? I thought you wanted to be like me? That's your problem! You always want to know where you belong, but you don't need to belong. Do you? DO YOU?"

Jess did not look up or give any indication that she had heard, even though her stomach was heaving and she could taste the bitter bile juice at the back of her mouth.

"You really need to hate people," TillyTilly continued.

Pause.

"You deserve to."

Then something began to drip slowly onto Jess's back, so slowly that she almost didn't feel it until she felt the cloth of her pyjamas cling and stick to her back. She nearly put her fingers to the wet patch, but, with enormous effort, lay still, her eyes wide and watchful. She felt as if her mind was slipping away from her, soaring so high that she would not be able to reclaim it. If only the liquid, whatever it was, wasn't so very hot, so hot that it numbed her skin and felt freezing cold.

How can this not be over?

TillyTilly was still speaking, and Jess, unmoving, allowed the words to drift in and out of the air around her. Whatever happened, she would not leave this bed.

"Go on, Jessy, hate everyone, anyone, and I'll *get* them for you," TillyTilly screeched. "The whole world. We're twins, both of us, twins. Doesn't that mean something?" Then, more hesitantly: "Jess. Help me. I don't even know what I'm doing. I'm scared."

But Jess didn't respond. TillyTilly was a liar. She said it didn't matter about belonging, but it did.

"Land chopped in little pieces, and—ideas! These ideas! Disgusting . . . shame, shame, shame. It's all been lost. Ashes. Nothing, now, there is no one. You understand?"

TillyTilly's voice, changing in timbre, beginning to sound like an adult woman's now, carried on unstoppably: "There is no homeland."

"I don't understand what you're saying, TillyTilly," Jess whispered. But there was no pause in the rant, and by now the dripping had increased in flow to a thin yet steady torrent. Jess did not, could not and would not look up. She must be spared, she must not be touched.

"Do you suffer through making your own suffer?" Tilly raged. "And then our blood . . . spilt like water . . . like water for the drinking, for the washing . . . our blood . . . I'm a WITNESS. Twins should know what each other suffer!"

The flow seemed to have stopped. Hardly knowing what she was doing, Jess turned her head to the side, and then looked upwards, slowly, slowly, holding her breath, already crying because now she knew that she didn't want to close this gap between seeing and being seen—

"There is no homeland—there is nowhere where there are people who will not *get* you."

Something hanging upside down from the ceiling; face dangling a few centimetres away from hers; those pupils, dilated until there was no white; those enormous, swollen lips, almost cartoonish except that they were deepest black, encrusted with dead, dry skin, coated here and there with chunks of

(I don't know, I don't want to know, please don't let me ever know, even guess)

something moist and pinky-white . . .

The lips, which had paused, continued to move. Transfixed,

she caught a glimpse as they moved over a small, mauve stump; the remains of a *tongue*.

"Stop looking to belong, half-and-half child. Stop. There is nothing; there is only me, and I have caught you."

And it was only at this point that Jess began to scream, long and loud, as the silent, never-ending torrent of reddish black erupted from that awful mouth, and engulfed her, baptising her in its madness.

The worst thing was that it was all really happening.

NINETEEN

———

"Two of me. No, *us*. TillyTilly, JessJess, FernFern, but that's three. TillyTilly and JessFern? Or FernJess?" Jess, sitting upright, was mumbling questions to herself in the streaming daylight from her window. She was perched on the end of her bed, pushing her book bag across the floor with her foot. "Who are you, TillyTilly? You know, you know." She had a dry feeling at the back of her throat from being hungry and thirsty and not quite daring to go down to breakfast despite repeated irritated calls from her mother. Before this she had washed quickly, expecting the silent, silvery taps to jet forth sprays of water, but they hadn't. She'd brushed her teeth and put on her school dress and cardigan before carefully reaffixing her hair beads all by herself. She hadn't had the bathroom mirror to do it in and had had to use the little swing mirror on her desk to do the beads. And now her thoughts turned to TillyTilly, who was fragmenting and becoming double, and how she, Jess, was to keep herself safe from everyone.

There was a knock on her closed bedroom door.

"Jess, can I come in?" her father said from outside.

Jess leant from the bed and scooped up her book bag, clutching it to her before saying, "Yeah."

Daniel, dressed for work in suit and tie, put his head around the door. He looked surprised. Jess aimed a kick in his direction. Had he expected her to be lying in bed poorly, her laboured breathing and pink-tinged eyes an indication in themselves that she would be unable to go to school that day?

Instead Jess was vertical and fully dressed, quiet, with her chin resting on her chest as she stared absently at the floor, swinging her legs, which were in high white socks and ended in black lace-up shoes for the cold weather.

"Listen, Jess. Yesterday, you behaved appallingly towards your mother."

No response visible or audible from her.

"True or false?"

Finally: "True."

"Right. You behaved badly, but I didn't mean to hit you as hard as I did, or even hit you. You know that."

(Yeah, right.)

"Your mother's forgotten all about it, and I want to as well. Can't we make up?"

Jess nodded because she knew she had to, and grudgingly offered her father a handshake, which he somehow turned into a swift hug. As she wrinkled her nose at his change of aftershave, she also became aware of how glad she was that it was morning. She didn't think that she could bear another night of Tilly-tricks all alone.

"Should I say sorry to Mummy?" she asked into her dad's shoulder.

Daniel let Jess go and chucked her under the chin. He smiled.

"Probably."

Jess was forced out of her safe place by the shock of Colleen McLain's voice. And when she looked at Colleen, who was viewing her with a mixture of concern and glee, she also saw TillyTilly, who was really, impossibly, here in the classroom, sitting opposite her at the table.

"Hello again," TillyTilly said in a conversational tone once Jess had allowed herself one frightened glance in that direction. "I really *am* sorry about before, and I'll make it up to you! I don't even want to swap places anymore, honest!"

Jess twisted away in her seat and looked instead at Colleen.

"What?" Colleen half stretched out a hand with a small, confused intake of breath, and Jess was disgusted to find that her eyes were filled with tears from being so frightened of Tilly. She rubbed at her eyes hard with her knuckles, and Colleen chewed disgustingly on her hair and stared at her with those narrowed brown eyes before asking, "So, what, shall I get Miss or not?"

"Don't," Jess told her hastily, as across from her TillyTilly said, "I understand, you know, why you hate him worse than her now. It's worse when they're always nice and then they change like that."

"Shut up, shut up, shut up," Jess hissed, hands to her ears again, then let out a little sob before she realised that Colleen hadn't gone away, but was still hovering.

Colleen paused, then pulled out the chair beside TillyTilly, shielding Jess from the view of Sam Robinson and company, who were now beginning to look over.

"Look. What are you telling me to shut up for? I wasn't even being nasty," Colleen began heatedly; then, when Jessamy didn't reply, she locked her fingers together and lowered her voice.

"Why are you crying? Jessamy, you shouldn't cry in front of people, seriously."

TillyTilly had stopped talking and was now staring at the oblivious Colleen, a poisonous smile hovering on her lips. Their elbows were almost touching. Jess drummed her feet harder on the floor and tried to ignore all of this, but Colleen scraped her hair back behind her ears with her fingers and leaned across the table, still talking earnestly.

"You've got to tell Mr. Munroe, and he'll let you go to the toilet or something. I'll come with you if you want. Just stop crying, OK?"

"Help me," Jess said faintly, sliding off her chair and under the table. Both TillyTilly and Colleen were gazing at her in consternation now, their expressions momentarily identical. They blurred; she didn't know which she was supposed to be scared of now. And the classroom: the classroom was an elastic cube and it was twanging, throwing her with it from side to side as it grew bigger and smaller, bigger and smaller, pulsating like a brightly lit heart with book reviews and timetables on its secret, inside walls.

"Help you? What? Oi, Jessamy—" Colleen crawled under the table, but Jessamy didn't reply, because it turned out that half-black people could faint after all.

It was proving awkward, this after-school session with Dr. McKenzie. She didn't want to answer any of his questions, because they were so difficult. She almost wished that she had agreed to have the appointment on another day as her mother had suggested when she picked her up from the nurse's office at school.

She felt so sleepy.

But she daren't stop concentrating because that would leave a crease in her vision for TillyTilly to slide gaily on in.

Jess reminded herself again that she mustn't believe that Tilly really wanted things to be the way they were before; she had to remember that there were two Tillys. It was difficult because she wanted the nice one back, the one who had said she would take care of her and had brought the *ibeji* woman.

Jess realised that she had to be careful not to blurt out "TillyTilly" in every sentence. The two Tillys filled her thoughts to bursting.

Now Dr. McKenzie was asking her about yesterday; her mum had told him all about it. Why? She couldn't remember. She hadn't screamed—but she had been mean, and her dad had hit her for the first time. Her father . . . a thought niggled at her: something else had happened about him. What? Any coherent thought was lost in the swim.

"You said that a friend of yours broke the mirror," Dr. McKenzie began.

Jess looked at her mother before replying, "Yeah." There was a moment's silence before she shook herself and remembered to say, "But it was me. I was lying 'cause I thought I'd get in trouble."

Dr. McKenzie nodded understandingly, then said casually, "And were you lying about who broke the computer as well?"

Jess wasn't stupid. "No."

"This friend . . . Tilly. She lives around your area?"

(Nooooooo, don't ask about HER now.)

"Yeah."

"And you two go around together quite a lot?"

"Um . . . I s'pose so."

"Sarah, have *you* met Tilly?"

Jess's mum shook her head.

"Not from lack of trying. Apparently she's shy. Good at breaking things, though, judging by my computer."

Sinking farther down into her chair, Jess adopted a resigned expression as she began to recognise that Sarah probably didn't believe her about the computer either.

"How would I have broken your computer, Mummy?"
(Did you not see how badly that computer was broken? Mummy, I am eight years old, and I am not very strong.)

"How would TILLY have broken it?" her mother countered.

Jess shrugged despondently, lifting her hands before dropping them hopelessly. Dr. McKenzie watched her for a few seconds before offering her a Jelly Baby. She took one, but didn't eat it, pressing at it with her fingers instead.

"Jess," Colin said at length, "it seems as if it's more important to you that your mum believes that Tilly broke her computer than the mirror in the bathroom. Why do you think that is?"

Surprised, Jess realised that she hadn't thought about it in that way.

"I don't know."

"Is it because you knew the computer was more important to me, because it had all my work on it?" Sarah asked gently.

Jess gave a disgusted shrug.

"I don't know! You don't believe me, anyway. You want me to tell you things, then when I do, you don't believe me. What's the point?"

"I believe you, Jess," Dr. McKenzie said quietly, leaning over and tapping Jess's wrist to get her attention. "I know that things can be real in different ways."

Jess ignored him. Now he was trying to say that TillyTilly was imaginary.

"Like . . . say I have an idea of . . . a mermaid, the mermaid is real, but not real in the same way as this table is," he said, knocking the table in question.

Glaring at him, Jess said, "That's nice." He didn't understand at all. An idea of a stupid mermaid couldn't come to you and scare you; an idea of a mermaid couldn't *get* your Year Five teacher so she never came back. Jess finally popped the flattened Jelly Baby into her mouth for comfort.

And now Dr. McKenzie leaned back in his chair again and asked, "Why are you angry?"

And Jess said, "Because I'm tired and you're confusing me."

Then Dr. McKenzie said, "Jessamy, are you scared of your mum?"

Just like that.

Jess, now feeling wide awake, peered at Dr. McKenzie then at her mum, who was looking equally surprised.

"I don't know," she said finally, being as honest as she could be, because he'd told her that if she wasn't honest then she wouldn't feel better. The words came out in a rush. "Sometimes I feel like she wants me to . . . I don't know. She wants me to be Nigerian or something. And I don't want to be changed that way; I can't be. It might hurt."

"Hurt?" said Dr. McKenzie.

"Yeah, like . . . being stretched."

"Jess, it's not a matter of my wanting you to be Nigerian— you are, you just are!" her mother said. When Jess looked at her, she continued, "You're English too, duh. And it's OK."

It wasn't. She just didn't know; if she could decide which one to be, maybe she would be able to get rid of TillyTilly, who was angry with her for worrying about it. Ashes and witnesses, homelands chopped into little pieces—she'd be English. No— she couldn't, though. She'd be Nigerian. No—

"Jessamy, you're a very articulate child, and your ideas are sometimes . . . surprising. Did you know that?"

A shrug from Jessamy. What did he want her to say?

Dr. McKenzie leaned forward again. "Have you not thought that sometimes your mum might find *that* a little bit scary as well? I know I would."

Jess shook her head and frowned seriously at him.

"I'm not scary."

"Hardly anyone thinks of themselves as a scary person, Jess."

"Is this your last appointment for today?" Jess asked, after a moment's consideration. The doctor looked intrigued, but nodded her a yes. "Can I go back with you to see Siobhan for a few minutes? I just remembered that I've got to tell her something really important." She glanced at her mother, who had started to object.

"Sarah, you can come too, if you want," said Dr. McKenzie. He appeared to ponder for a moment, chewing his lip, then nodded affably and checked his watch before popping another Jelly Baby into his mouth. "We still have some time left, though . . ."

When Jess had, in a halting fashion, told Shivs as much about TillyTilly as she could, leaving out the events of the night before so as not to scare her, Shivs nodded her head serenely.

"That's a bit cool, you know," she said thoughtfully, before tiptoeing to the bedroom door and putting her ear against it to make sure that they weren't being listened to. "So she only talks to you when no one else is there?"

Jess, sitting cross-legged on Shivs's neatly made bed (the only tidy thing in the room), gazed at her best friend in fixed astonishment.

"You don't think I've gone mad?"

Shivs shook her head and yawned, running her hand through the curly tangles of her hair until she inadvertently made them stand upright like a brush. Jess stifled a giggle and decided to leave her that way.

"Nah . . . you're not mad, and you're not one of those stupid kids who have imaginary friends just for something to do. This girl called Gemma . . . in my class . . . she used to have some imaginary friend called Katy. Katy, y'know! Not even something like TillyTilly and all the time she was like 'You can't sit there . . . Katy's sitting there,' but sometimes she'd forget Katy was supposed to be there and sit there herself, the plum!" She laughed, and Jess, astounded to hear this brief account of something so far from her own experience, fell back on to the bed laughing herself. Shivs came over and dropped onto her knees at the bedside, settling herself before saying, "And Gemma wasn't scared of Katy."

Jess sat up, her face serious now. "I didn't say I was scared of Tilly!" (She was.)

Shivs lay flat on her back, then sprang up, hands out, eyes wild as she imitated Jess on the night when Shivs and Dulcie had slept over, shouting out "TILLYTILLY!" in the dark. Then she fell back on to the floor, laughing, but Jess couldn't join in. She hadn't known that she'd looked like that. She was embarrassedly gulping back tears again, and Shivs sprang up again and climbed onto the bed, putting an arm around her shoulder, pressing her cheek to Jess's.

"Oi, if I had a friend who kept appearing and disappearing and *got* my teacher, I'd be a little bit scared that they'd *get* me, too! So listen, what *is* TillyTilly? I mean, is she dead or something?"

Alarmed, Jess stared upwards at the skylight before replying, almost as if she'd expected TillyTilly to be there, her thin limbs and body pressed flat against the glass, her face a squashed smudge with malevolent eyes, mouth moving in promises to *get* them. Shivs, laughing, glanced up too, and they looked at each other, smiling, while Jess spoke, Shivs pretending to wipe sweat off her forehead.

"I don't know what she is . . . she said that I do know! But I think she's wrong, because I have no idea."

"Maybe she's your sister, the one who died." Shivs thoughtfully blew the hair out of her eyes.

"No . . . I don't think so somehow. I mean, why would she be at my grandfather's house? I don't know, actually."

"Or maybe your mum had a twin that died?"

Jess looked doubtful.

Shivs shook her head in wonder. "I can't believe that was her on the phone!"

"You think I'm lying about that?"

"No, but . . . well, it didn't sound any different from you, not even a very little bit."

"That's because she kind of made me say it—"

"Yeah? How?"

"I don't know . . ."

Shivs grimaced. "Do you still want to hang around with her, this girl?"

Jess didn't have a chance to reply because Mrs. McKenzie knocked on the door and put her head around it, speaking urgently. "Jessamy, you have to go home now."

Jess couldn't understand the note of worry in her voice, but she got up quickly, saying to Shivs, "Don't tell anyone—"

"I promise!" Shivs licked her finger. "See this wet, see this dry, man!"

Jess's mum was outside the door with Mrs. McKenzie. As soon as Jess came out, she put a hand on her shoulder and began guiding her hurriedly down the stairs, calling out goodbye and

"We'll let ourselves out" to Mrs. McKenzie. She was breathing hard in a fast, flustered way, and Jess looked up at her before seizing her hand and squeezing it for reassurance.

"Mummy, what's the matter?"

Her mother looked at her with a look of trying to place her in context, as if she'd only just remembered that Jess was there, and now who she was.

"Daddy's ill. He's in hospital, Jess. We're going to get a taxi to go and see him."

That was when Jess remembered, too too late, that TillyTilly had said she was going to *get* Daniel Harrison. She didn't want this to be her fault, but she knew that it was—

(TillyTilly, don't make my dad die for being scared of me.)

"Ill? Ill how?"

Alarmed by her daughter's trembling, Sarah reached out from amidst her own shock and squeezed both of her daughter's hands to calm her. She hoped that Jess wasn't going to faint again; her lips seemed drained of colour.

"I don't know yet, Jess. Apparently he collapsed at work."

Jess knew that if she could picture her father, she could hold him in her mind and make him be alive and make him be all right, but everything about him had dissipated—once he had fallen out of the line of her sight, she couldn't properly remember what it was like when he had been there.

TWENTY

They didn't know what had happened to Jess's father, and they didn't know exactly what was wrong, but he had been "well" enough to be discharged from his overnight observational stay that morning.

Yet as soon as Jess got home from school, even before, she knew what was the matter with him. it was TillyTilly, Tilly's verdant, earthy smell clung to him in clumps, but instead of making him light and fast-moving like she was, it dragged Daniel's arms, legs and head down so that he moved more slowly and deliberately than he had before, as if everything lay just out of his reach. He looked up infrequently, lethargically pushing at his glasses when they started slipping down his nose instead of just raising his head. He kept saying that he was tired, so tired, but his voice was so uninflected that it seemed that he didn't even mean it. It was difficult to tell what he was thinking, or whether he was too tired to think at all.

Jess's mum had told her on the way home from school that the first thing her father had done when he returned from the hospital was to go to bed, leaving her to call his work, Aunt Lucy and Jess's grandparents to let them know that he was back home. He hadn't got up since then, and Sarah was worried that they might have given him some drug at the hospital that was having an adverse side effect. This probably meant that Jess's grandma would be over later that evening with some chicken-and-barley soup. The phone was ringing as they came through the door; Jess dropped her book bag, kicked off her shoes without undoing the laces and ran upstairs, glad that her mother was too busy answering the phone to tell her not to bother her father, or to follow her upstairs. She had wondered if she would find TillyTilly there, had braced herself for Tilly to be guarding the door to the bedroom, but she wasn't, she wasn't there at all. It seemed she'd known that this time Jess would demand an answer . . . and a remedy.

Her father lay as immobile as a column beneath the covers, which he had pulled up over his head. His back was to the door, and his oblong-framed, steel-rimmed glasses were on the bedside table beside the lamp.

Jess crept closer and touched the glasses for reassurance before she gingerly put a hand on his shoulder. "Daddy?"

"Mmmm." He didn't turn over. She moved around to the other side of the bed so that she could see his half-open eyes looking over and past her, towards the window. Could he SEE her?

"Daddy." She tugged fearfully at his hand, feeling the ice of Tilly's skin as his fingers didn't curl around hers in return. Instead, leaving his hand to her

(a gift—yours if you want it)

he closed his eyes fully, as if she had said nothing at all.

Jess moved nearer to his face and touched his slackened skin with her other hand; she wasn't ready to let go of his hand yet. In contrast to the rest of his face, his closed eyelids were stretched in a swollen tautness. What was happening to his features? He breathed as if he were sleeping, but there was a wakeful fever-sickness in the occasional, involuntary-seeming twitch of his mouth.

Suddenly, he sighed gustily, sending her heart into a startled convulsion.

"Jess, I'm sorry."

She let his fingers slip out of her grasp and said, overloudly, "Sorry?"

Slowly, slowly, his hand went to his forehead, but he missed his face and his fingers brushed jerkily against the headboard as if the limb had fallen out of control.

Jess watched in horror: no one could tell her that it was going to be OK—this wasn't her father at all, it was a thing, slurred of speech, emptied, inside out, outside in, by two girls, one of whom could bring seven years' bad luck in a razor-edged shatter of a looking glass. Had Tilly *taken* something from him that made him forget where and who he was and put him in some other place, alone?

"Daddy! What happened to you?"

"So tired."

"Daddy—"

"Fell. Down far . . ."

Her skin tingled at his words; he sounded younger than she did.

"Far?" she whispered.

"Tired. Sorry, Jess. Be better later."

Jess wanted to touch his hand again, but she didn't dare—there was no reassurance there, the hand wasn't his. Moving away now and crossing the room to leave, she could almost hear TillyTilly whispering to her

(he'll never hit you again, Jessy)

and in despair, she wished aloud, past caring whether he heard, that she'd got angry at her mum instead. Why hadn't she got angry with her before? Because she was scared of her? But couldn't you be angry with people that you were scared of? No, it was her dad's fault: he shouldn't have changed the way he had, he shouldn't have looked at her like that—

"Put on the lights," her father said from the bed, his voice suddenly alert. The childish note of command in his voice made her jump to the light switch faster than his normal, gentle request would have. But—

"No, not those lights," he whispered, in his own voice now.

"Oh."

Jess turned the light off again and slunk away to her own room, wanting to disappear.

TWENTY-ONE

Jess had expected TillyTilly to come again in the night, and so approached sleep as an extension of the concentration that she put into going into her safe place. Although sleeping, always she was aware of sound and movement, so when she felt TillyTilly in the room, knocking on her dreams, she stayed still.

When TillyTilly said and did nothing, she cracked open one eye to find that circles of orange light were flickering in the corner of her room by the window, and TillyTilly was sitting cross-legged in the middle of them with her head bowed and her back to Jess. Rows of candles, her mother's tea lights. Jess's breath caught in her throat and she almost sat up, fearing that her curtains would be set alight, but then she saw, facing her, the charcoal-on-board drawing from the Boys' Quarters, lit up by the stolen fire. She hadn't seen it for so long, and it still scared her; it wasn't like the *ibeji* woman at all. The picture really was badly drawn: childishly drawn, in fact, unnerving and somehow vital in the thick and careless sweeping of black. It was wrong, all wrong, and wild. TillyTilly had drawn it herself, *for herself*, and Jess's mind reeled at this, tried to reject it, then could only cry out, "TillyTilly!"

(I'm so sorry, sorry for you, TillyTilly, you really are alone.)
But as soon as she spoke, the candles were gone and so was the board, and so was TillyTilly.

"You're dead," Jess said to the empty, lightless corner, "aren't you?"

Saturday morning. "TillyTilly," Jess said to the air in her bedroom. She was half in and half out of the room, just about to leave it as she looped one end of her skipping rope around her arm. "Shivs is coming over . . ."

After a brief pause, TillyTilly said, "Yeah? Well, I hope you have fun."

Jess looked around, waiting for Tilly to materialise, and when she didn't, said, "Just don't DO anything, OK?"

"I won't."

There had been a truce between them for the past few days; partly because Jess realised that she couldn't make TillyTilly go away no matter how hard she tried, and partly because of Tilly and the candles. *Getting* people for Jess was supposed to be how TillyTilly stopped herself from being alone, but she didn't seem to understand the irrevocability of the *getting*. Jess's father hadn't shown much improvement or been able to go to work for the past week, and Jess had been certain that someone would turn to her and ask her what she had done—Tilly's mark on him was so obvious to her. Instead, the word "depression" had frequently been said in low tones when her mother and Aunt Lucy thought that Jess was out of earshot, and her father's mantra seemed to have become, "So tired. Be better later." All he did was sleep, and sometimes sit in the sitting room for an hour or so, unspeaking, watching television with an empty expression before going back to bed. And he was eating hardly anything.

How could this have anything to do with something normal? Only Tilly could do it, and it seemed that Tilly didn't know how to make it better. "I'm sorry, Jess," she had said, over and over, hugging her, when Jess had come upstairs with the report that her mother was asleep on the sofa with her mouth half open and a pen slipping slowly out of her fingers. Tilly didn't need to remind Jess that she only *got* people on Jess's instruction, and Jess knew that the fact she could never remember being angry enough for that meant only that she didn't want to remember.

Shivs didn't understand when she said that her father's being ill was her fault.

"It's not," she said confidently, her curls flying as she skipped on the spot with her neon-pink rope. "When you said that before, I asked my dad what was wrong with your dad, and he said it's something that he can . . . thingie—overcome."

Jess had purposely guided Shivs away from the empty bench that was her and Tilly's favourite, leading her instead to the swings. "That depression thing?" she asked.

Shivs shook her head impatiently and caught her breath.

"Dunno. Listen, how silly is it that you think you did it? Think about it . . . duh!"

Jess dropped her skipping rope and tried to think how to tell Shivs that it was TillyTilly without saying it aloud.

"Ummm, Shivs?"

Her friend had just counted twelve uninterrupted skips and now stopped, beaming.

"What?"

"Actually, nothing."

Walking around to the back of Jess's swing snickering, Shivs gave her a hard push, and Jess gasped laughingly as she rocked upwards.

"You know your friend TillyTilly?" Shivs asked, when Jess's swing had slowed.

"Yeah . . ."

"Does she still hang around with you?"

"Yeah."

"Does she still scare you?"

That was a little bit more difficult. In some ways it was an enormous yes, in others, no.

Shivs breezed on despite Jess's lack of reply.

"Anyways, I was wondering if I could meet her. But then I remembered you said she only comes in the room when it's just you two—"

"She's started coming in when other people are there too, like once with my dad and once in my classroom," Jess interjected quickly. Why had she said that? Did she really think that she could risk TillyTilly meeting Shivs? She supposed she was curious.

"So, what . . . d'you think you can get her to come in the room when I'm there?" Shivs casually rippled the end of her skipping rope across the grass, as if playing a one-woman game of Colours.

Jess already knew the answer to that. She dragged her feet across the ground as she pushed the swing backwards.

"She'll come only if she wants to." Then: "Is this because you don't believe me about TillyTilly?"

Shivs got on to the swing beside Jess.

"Nooo," she said slowly. "It's just I was thinking about her a lot, and I was wondering if she was, you know . . . nice."

"She can be! Nice people aren't nice all the time!"

"Yeah, but, you know . . ." Shivs trailed off, unable to put into words what she was thinking.

After they'd foraged for their own lunch in the kitchen, Jess looked in the sitting room to see if either her mother or father was down there. Her father was a slumped figure on the sofa, his hand on top of the remote but not pressing any buttons as advertisements reeled across the television screen. Shivs stayed politely outside the door while Jess bolted in to pick up the cold cup of coffee that she knew would be at his feet. There was a delicate, shrivelled skin over the top of it that Jess broke with the spoon, trying to estimate how much he'd drunk this time. Darkly dried coffee circles told her that he'd had maybe two, three sips. He didn't look at her, didn't seem aware that his daughter was there, standing in front of him.

"Daddy, shall I pour the rest away for you?" Jess was trying to reassure herself with the fact that her dad never finished his coffee, anyway—if she didn't pour this cold brown liquid down the drain, then he would do it, standing over the kitchen sink watching it swirl hotly away. She waited for him to speak.

He still didn't look at her, but when the advert for Coco Pops had finished, he nodded. "Thank you."

Carrying the cup carefully in her hands, Jess passed Shivs and poured the coffee down the kitchen sink. Shivs, who followed her, watched in silence. Jess put the cup down in the sink, then changed her mind and washed it, dried it, put it back with the other coffee cups so it wouldn't be lonely.

"Where's your mum?" Shivs asked.

Jess dried her hands on a napkin and beckoned Shivs upstairs. "She's probably in her study." She was writing far, far more than she used to, and was crabbier about being interrupted.

Jess's dad had apparently decided to go back to bed again and was shuffling dreamily up the stairs ahead of them. They couldn't overtake him: the staircase wasn't wide enough. Jess was embarrassed and shot an apologetic sideways look at Shivs, but Shivs only grinned at her before grabbing her arm and starting to give her a Chinese burn that meant they had to stop on the stairs for a few seconds anyway, involved in a hushed, giggling scuffle. When they finally made it to Jess's bedroom, Shivs swung the door shut as if it was her own, kicked her buckle shoes off under Jess's desk with a whoop and took a running leap at Jess's bed, only landing by luck. Jess cringed and, more sedately, sat on the chair at her desk, pausing to reach underneath and put Shivs's shoes neatly side by side so that she wouldn't have to scrabble to find them. Shivs picked up *The Complete Works of Lewis Carroll* from Jess's bedside and flicked through it, finding the place where *The Hunting of the Snark* had been bookmarked.

"Hmmm. A snark, hey," she said before dumping the book on Jess's pillow and bouncing excitedly up and down. "So, let me see TillyTilly!"

"She's not seeing me," TillyTilly warned, from outside the bedroom door.

Jess jumped and looked at Shivs, who was repeating her earlier demand and didn't seem to have heard anything. Jess went to the door and leaned against it, murmuring pleadingly to the girl that she knew was on the other side.

"Please, TillyTilly, just for a minute," she begged.

"Is that her?" Shivs toppled off the bed and started coming towards Jess, but was waved back.

TillyTilly gave a sigh.

"Fine. Just for a minute, but she can't look at me, she has to turn around."

"No, don't do it, then," said Jess, "if you're not going to do it properly. What's the point of that? How's she even going to know you're there?"

"She'll know."

"How?"

TillyTilly said nothing.

Jess chewed on her lip, agitating over how this would work

out, then spun around to face Shivs, who was now sitting at the foot of the bed in hushed, expectant silence.

"Listen," she began, "TillyTilly's being all shy for some reason, so she doesn't want you to look at her. So, um, could you close your eyes and put your hands over them?"

Shivs looked surprised, but obliged. "Is she ugly or something?" she enquired, wriggling in her place.

"No! I don't know why she's—"

TillyTilly opened the door and came in, closing the door behind her again. She looked at Shivs, then looked at Jess giving a wide-armed shrug. Shivs was now completely still.

"That wasn't you opening and shutting the door, was it, Jess?" Shivs said in a low voice.

Jess shook her head no, then remembered that Shivs couldn't see her.

"It wasn't me, it was TillyTilly," she explained.

"Come here and put your hand on my head," Shivs ordered.

Jess moved across and placed her hand on Shiv's tumbled head of hair.

"All right, now tell TillyTilly to do it again. Open and close the door, I mean."

TillyTilly shook her head belligerently, and made an exaggerated bored expression, but went back over to the door when Jess looked at her pleadingly and nodded her on. She opened the door and slammed it shut.

"Oh," Shivs said wonderingly. "Oh."

"You two better stop slamming that door," Jess's mum shouted from next door.

Shivs giggled at that. "You three, more like," she said.

Jess took her hand away from Siobhan's head and moved back again.

"Can I talk to her?" Shivs asked.

TillyTilly shook her head at Jess, waving her hands violently to indicate that she would not be persuaded on this one.

"She doesn't want to talk," Jess told Shivs. How rubbish was this?

"Oh," Shivs said, sounding crestfallen before coming up with another idea. "Will she come and sit beside me?"

Jess looked at TillyTilly, who held up a finger to her to indicate that she shouldn't say anything, then began walking in a wide circle around Shivs, noiselessly climbing up onto the bed and jumping down again when she had to walk behind her. She was looking at Shivs carefully, unsmiling, almost grim-faced. Jess, watching, was briefly worried that TillyTilly might break her promise and do something, but she showed no sign of any such intention.

Siobhan was struck by how cold she felt, but it was a constantly moving coldness, sometimes giving way to normal air, as if it was expanding all around her. She feared that it might tighten, and she longed to rub her arms, but didn't dare drop them in case she saw TillyTilly. She didn't want to see her at all: from the moment that Tilly had come into the room, Shivs had felt a . . . *badness*. It was the only way to describe it: it was like being sick and hearing rattling in your ears that wasn't really there; it was slow, bottomless, soundless, creeping . . . and it wasn't just inside her stomach, but inside her head as well, slowly building in pressure. She'd had to make sure that she wasn't imagining it, she'd needed the security of Jess's touch to ensure that she wasn't alone in the room with this . . . thing. This was not another girl. This was not the kind of imaginary friend that you'd mistakenly sit on. She was a cycle of glacial ice.

"She's walking around me in a circle," Shivs whispered slowly, trying not to let her arms tremble. She heard Jess let out a little cry of amazement and was seized with a sudden, irrational fear that this thing would stop moving and dart out a sly, fleeting touch that would take her away forever and ever.

She almost shouted out, almost. But she didn't—she was tougher than that, and anyway, she realised with a breathtaking suddenness, this was not her fear to hold but Jess's. This thing meant to harm Jess, punish her in a bad way, the worst way, maybe. Siobhan was scared that Jess was going to die. She had to tell her.

"Jess, this—"

Jess moved forward towards Siobhan, who was fighting the quivering of her own lips to speak. She wanted to touch her, but TillyTilly, still unsmiling, put up a cautionary finger indicating that she should go no nearer. She had now stopped directly in front of Shivs, close enough to touch her. Shivs stammered senselessly for another half second as Jess watched, baffled and uneasy.

"This. It's not . . . good. SHE'S . . . not good. You need to—"

Glancing quickly at TillyTilly, who was by now backing away towards the door, looking as bewildered as Jess, Jess approached Siobhan and hugged her, listening for the almost inaudible words that she was whispering, "This is so, so bad. She doesn't have to be here, Jess. You don't have to see her. You know that, don't you?"

"I—"

TillyTilly had gone. It felt as if she had fled.

And half an hour later, Shivs had fled too; everyone was fleeing away from her. Shivs had called her father to come and pick her up to take her home.

"It's my fault, isn't it?" Jess cried, following Shivs down the stairs and outside to the waiting car. Shivs was pale, why was she so pale? Why was she so scared of TillyTilly when she wasn't the one who'd been caught in the glass, and she wasn't the one who'd lain whimpering in the dark with an unknown wetness dripping on her back? Shivs wasn't supposed to be scared.

"It's not your fault, duh," Shivs said, lightheartedly. It was almost convincing, but only almost. She waved at her dad, and climbed into the backseat of the car, busily doing up her seat belt.

Jess leaned in and peered at Siobhan.

"What was so scary?"

Shivs glowered at her when Dr. McKenzie turned around and asked, "What was so scary about what?"

"Nothing," they both said hastily, and he laughed.

"Well, I'm sorry I'm so nosy, then! Shivs, ready to go?"

Shivs nodded, and Jess leaned back out of the car and slammed the door shut.

"Don't tell ANYONE," Jess mouthed, waving, and Shivs nodded, licked her finger and held it up for answer.

That was partly what made it so bad that Shivs told on her, that she'd sworn. It seemed that she'd only held out for one night, because on Monday afternoon, Jess was sitting in the kitchen eating a ham and peanut butter sandwich, with TillyTilly idly dipping her finger into the jam, when the phone rang. As soon as it did, Tilly leapt up, her eyes meeting Jess's.

"McKenzie," she hissed. "Siobhan TOLD him about me! I told you that she wasn't a good friend, Jessy."

The phone rang for ages; finally, her mum picked it up.

Jess put down her sandwich and stared back at Tilly as they both tried to listen to what was being said.

"No way," Jess said forcefully, but when her mum came into the kitchen and tersely told her to grab her coat because Dr. McKenzie wanted to see them, she was forced to take it back.

"I hope Daniel's feeling a bit better," Dr. McKenzie said to Jess's mum when they got there. He said this over Jess's head, and she sneaked a glance upwards to see her mum shaking her head with the corners of her mouth tremblingly downturned.

"I'll talk to you about it later," Sarah told him, infuriating Jess, because what was this? She was acting as if Jess didn't know about being sick, as if there was something *left* to know beyond the constant, aching wish for the sickness to just go away. So she started off in a bad mood anyway.

Dr. McKenzie must have been able to tell, because he began tentatively.

"Jess. You know what I was talking about before, about things being real in different ways?"

Folding her arms, Jess let herself fill up to the very top with indignation at what Siobhan had done. Why couldn't she just *shut up*? If it had been Jess, she'd have kept the secret, she'd have kept it even if . . . even if she was shut in the basement for years and years. Shivs thought that her dad could fix anything, but Jess already knew and could have told her for free that parents fix nothing—they only pushed things to the bottom limits of *worse*. What was going to happen now?

Dr. McKenzie continued talking in spite of Jess's stubborn silence.

"Now I've been thinking about our last talk, about your friend Tilly, and I thought of something—"

(Oh, such a shameful lie, Dr. McKenzie, the truth shall set you free. We both know Shivs told you.)

"Sometimes the different types of being real can be the same thing with people. There are some things, people, that can *seem* very real, especially to you, Jess, because you have a big imagination. But sometimes they aren't real in the same way that I am, or your mother is. For example, if you had no one to play with, you might . . . meet a friend that's exactly the type of friend that you wanted in every way—"

"TillyTilly isn't imaginary, you know!"

"Why is she so shy, Jess? Why have neither of your parents met her even though she plays with you all the time?"

Jess gave him her foulest stare, waiting for him to finish making his point, acutely aware of her mother's own stern glare at her. She'd get told off later for being rude.

"TillyTilly isn't imaginary," she growled at him.

Dr. McKenzie didn't skip a beat.

"I know she's not imaginary. She's real because she's a part of you."

Jess threw her hands up in the air in frustration at his stupidity.

"She's NOT! What's the MATTER with you?"

"Jessamy, don't you shout at Dr. McKenzie," Sarah told Jess, pleasantly but with an undertone of steel running in her voice.

Jess folded her arms again and stared at her mother, then at Dr. McKenzie, who was picking up the little bowl of Jelly Babies.

"I'm not having one of those, either."

He put them down, not taking one himself this time. He began talking to her mother instead of her.

"Of course, I'd have to see if Jess will talk to me more about . . . TillyTilly before I diagnose anything, but it might be worth your taking a look at some of this material, Sarah."

Jess watched as he handed her mother a sheet of paper with some names and titles scribbled on it. Dr. McKenzie glanced at Jess to see if she was still in her sulk.

"It's possible that TillyTilly is an alter ego, although she could also be an internalised imaginary companion. It seems as if we have a situation where Jess has discovered a need of an outlet for emotions that she doesn't want to show. She may have kind of . . . created, for lack of a better word, a personality that is very markedly different from her own—"

Sarah interrupted him. She folded the piece of paper over and over, trying to understand what he was saying.

"So TillyTilly isn't real—I mean, objectively real," she added, looking at Jess, who was scowling massively.

"But . . . the way she used to talk about her! You should have heard her—they had a picnic, and they wrote a poem—"

She turned to Jess. "D'you still have that poem?"

Jess shook her head.

"Well, I feel silly. I should have, well, *known*." Sarah played with the fringed ends of her scarf and chewed thoughtfully at her lip as she looked at Jess.

But Jess was looking over Dr. McKenzie's shoulder, at where TillyTilly was moving an egg-shaped glass paperweight around on his desk. When Jess caught her eye, Tilly shook her head sorrowfully, but said nothing.

"What's an alter ego?" Jess asked abruptly, her eyes still on Tilly.

"It's . . . a different side to you that you normally keep hidden because it only comes out when you're scared or angry," Dr. McKenzie told her.

"So you mean . . . when Jess screams, and when she breaks things, that's a side of her that she calls TillyTilly?" Sarah broke in.

Dr. McKenzie nodded briefly.

"My father would die laughing," Sarah added after a stunned silence.

TillyTilly was now sitting on the floor beside Dr. McKenzie's chair, pulling a Jelly Baby apart and rolling the bits into little balls between her fingers.

(TillyTilly, don't, you'll make a mess.)

"You know you're wrong, don't you?" Jess informed Dr. McKenzie, as grandly as she could. But her knees were jiggling up and down with fear. Oh God, what if he was right and she was just this mad, mad girl who did things that she couldn't control?

"Sometimes we do things that we don't like and that we can't understand, Jess. It's possible that all TillyTilly means is that part of your mind, say, the part of you that can show you're angry in a reasonable way, hasn't developed as quickly as other parts, like the part of you that likes reading lots of books—"

He paused and his brow puckered as he looked at the little green balls of dismembered Jelly Baby at his feet before scooping them up.

"Listen, Jess, we can talk about this more later, but I just wanted you to know this so that next time you see TillyTilly coming, you can remember that she doesn't have to be there."

She doesn't have to be there. That's what Shivs had said, too. What was wrong with everybody?

TillyTilly threw her arms around Jess's shoulders, hugging her close.

"I do have to be here, you need me," she whispered in Jess's ear, and Jess was aware of trying not to shrink from Tilly's touch so as not to make her angry and she wished that sound
(hmmmmmmmmzzzzzzzz)
wasn't rocking through her and making her feel faint. Dr. McKenzie thought that he knew what TillyTilly meant, but he was wrong. Nobody knew what Tilly meant, and nobody knew what Jess meant either, though with Jess, they could if they really wanted to.

"Please don't talk to TillyTilly again," Sarah begged, as they got on the bus to go home. She was flustered paying the bus driver, and dropped her gloves, floundering to pick them up until Jess snatched them up for her. On rising, Jess was surprised to see that Sarah's eyes were filled with tears. Not knowing what to say, Jess took a seat by the window and stared out, unseeing, at the houses and shops and cars moving past.

Sarah sat down beside her and squeezed her hand.

"Think of it like not speaking to a normal friend. She can't make you play with her."

Jess began to drum her feet lightly on the bus floor as she tried not to listen to the pleading in her mother's voice. She tried, instead, to imagine how she really could have done these things herself. She saw herself kicking the computer, pushing it off the table, making sure it was broken beyond repair because she hated her mother.

And the mirror. Could she *really* have taken it off the wall and flung it to the floor so that the glass sprayed out in jigsaw-puzzle pieces, then calmly put the empty frame back on the wall, at an angle?

And not *remember*?

The trouble was that, with TillyTilly, it was possible.

Possible, but not true, she decided.

"Jess. Promise me?"

Silence.

"Jess? Please. It's already hard with your father being poorly—" Sarah's voice was rising out of her control, and Jess flinched a little bit, embarrassed.

"Yeah. OK," she mumbled, noncommittally. Everyone acting as if she had a choice. But she wasn't the fairy; she wasn't.

"OK what?"

"OK I won't talk to her."

Oh, Shivs, why did you have to tell? You are a bad friend. Good friends don't tell secrets like that. Why is TillyTilly always right?

TWENTY-TWO

———

Jess would be nine on July the twenty-fifth, during the school holidays.

"We were wondering if you'd like to spend your birthday in Nigeria," her mother said brightly as Jess chopped the crust of her toast up into little, little pieces at the kitchen table.

We?

Jess looked at her father, who was wearing a T-shirt, pyjama bottoms and a belted dressing gown and propping himself up at the table with his elbow. His cornflakes had descended into a pool of mush before him, and he seemed to have been reading the same two lines of the morning newspaper over and over again, his lips moving slowly as his finger traced the lines of print. His chin was covered with thick stubble that was spreading up his cheeks.

His hair looked a mess. Jess didn't think he'd brushed it for ages.

She worried about things like this—him not drinking or disposing of his own coffee, him not smiling, him looking so tired all the time but not sounding like he meant it when he said so, him not brushing his hair. He didn't look like part of the "we."

What would he be like in Nigeria?

What would her grandfather say?

He'd probably look straight at her with those keen, sparkling eyes and know that it was Jess's friend who had done it, and therefore Jess's fault.

She wouldn't be gold anymore, because he'd know the truth.

She tried to think of what the Yoruba for "mud" would sound like.

"So what d'you think?"

Her mum put another piece of toast on Jess's plate. Jess was annoyed. She didn't want any more toast. She stabbed at it with her table knife.

"I don't know."

"Don't you want to see your grandfather again? I thought you missed him."

Jess carried on stabbing.

"If you didn't want it, you should have said so," Jess's mum told her, yanking the toast out from under Jess's knife in one deft move.

"I don't want to go," Daniel said quietly, from opposite Jess.

Sarah and Jess both looked at him in surprise.

"But I thought we agreed—" said Sarah.

"I don't want to go. I didn't really want to go the last time either," he informed her languidly.

Sarah didn't reply, but quickly began buttering her toast and spreading it with jam. Jess risked a look at her to see if she was going to explode and start an argument, but she seemed pretty calm.

"It's nothing personal," Daniel added abruptly, as if Sarah had protested (was a different version of the "conversation" running in his head?). He rubbed his eyes. "I just don't want to go anywhere."

"Yes, OK," Sarah said testily. Then, in order to end this exchange, she turned to Jess while Daniel went back to the crucial two lines of black print on his paper.

"Just let me know when you make up your mind, OK?"

Jess nodded, then caught a flash of TillyTilly lurking in the passageway between the sitting room and the kitchen—the pockets of her school dress seemed to be stuffed full of paper—but she had disappeared again in a second.

"Can I have another piece of toast?" she asked, to her mother's clear exasperation. Jess didn't care; she wasn't going to go out there by herself so that TillyTilly could invisibly pull her hair and push and pull at her when she refused to speak. It was hard not being able to talk to Tilly and not being able to talk *about* her either. Dr. McKenzie and her mother were wrong: TillyTilly's presence was no longer a matter of Jess's choice, if indeed it had ever been.

(I wasn't pretending to be someone else; it was TillyTilly dragging secret things out of me like she sometimes does. I didn't choose TillyTilly, I just couldn't say Titiola right. Really, truly, please believe me.)

Her father was passive and uninvolved, apparently unaware of TillyTilly's now imaginary status in the household. Taking the opportunity of having him as a captive audience in the sitting room as he watched television—always the adverts; occasionally he smiled at some unknown or hidden element of them—Jess had told him of the problem of TillyTilly. She bit down her fear and risked her secret; she told her father that Tilly was real, and, barely even acknowledging it with a nod, he had told her in exchange that there was a very small person trapped in a space like this. (He held up his hands to describe a narrow box shape.)

The person was fast asleep.

Everything was colourless and slow because this small person was asleep, and nobody knew how to wake them up. They wouldn't wake up because they didn't really want to—it was too hard being awake. He asked her if she understood, but she had stared at his face, which was wet with tears even though his voice remained steady and low, and then she'd looked around the sitting room at all the colours and told him yes, she understood, because she wasn't sure if he knew that it was Jess he was talking to, and anyway it was her fault, so she had to understand. The doctor had given him some special pills, but she never saw him take them. Once, when Jess was on the stairs and her parents were in the sitting room, she had heard her mum ask, "Please tell me what's the matter, please. Is it work? Is it me?" but he only said, "No and no and no, no, no. I'm just tired. So tired. That's all."

It had been hardest not to talk to TillyTilly the previous night, when Tilly had said to her, "You're angry, Jessy. You're angry with Siobhan, she's made it all worse and now you're not allowed to speak to me in case I do something. But I'll be good! I won't do anything you don't want me to!" The candles had been placed all around Jess's bed, and TillyTilly had been talking from behind the big wooden board with the long-armed woman on it. Jess couldn't see Tilly's face, but she could see her arms supporting the board, and the fraying blue-and-turquoise friendship bracelet on her wrist.

"You understand that I've got to *get* Siobhan, don't you?" TillyTilly said. " 'Cause you won't really forgive her until she's been *got*. You're really angry with her, Jessy, and I know it's because you never had a proper, really really here friend, and now she thinks you're mad. It scares you for people to be scared of you and think you're weird, remember?"

It was no use; Jess could still hear her from the safe place, and it took every bit of strength she had not to reply. She couldn't let TillyTilly say this; she couldn't let Shivs, who was brisk and bright and strong, be taken away and replaced with . . . she didn't know. Just . . . someone else who didn't know why they had to be there, who slept most of the day and had a flat dullness in their eyes for the rest of it. Being *got* was supposed to be like being beaten up, bruised, bleeding, crying, but this was stranger and worse.

It was as if TillyTilly had a special sharp knife that cut people on the inside so that they collapsed into themselves and couldn't ever get back out. No colours, her father had said. No colours! She wasn't angry at Shivs, although she had been. They'd made up, they'd spoken on the phone, and Shivs had apologised ramblingly before explaining that she'd been scared, not for herself, of course—you wouldn't catch Siobhan McKenzie being a scaredy-cat—but for Jessamy.

"I felt as if she didn't really . . . well, *like* you much," Shivs had said lamely.

(That's not the problem, she likes me too much.)

Jess kept all of this in her mind, trying to think of other things as well, while TillyTilly reminded her that Shivs had sworn

(see this wet, see this dry, stick a needle in my eye . . .)

not to tell.

Tiny flames were leaping all around her, and Jess peeped at them through her half-closed eyes, trying not to feel as if the charcoal woman was staring at her. She wasn't going to let TillyTilly *get* Shivs, she wasn't, she wasn't, she wasn't.

"I told you that this McKenzie would only bring trouble," TillyTilly had said finally, before emptying the room of herself, the candles, and, last of all, the tall, inexplicably reproving board.

"Jess, do you know what happened to my tea lights?" her mother asked, now, at the breakfast table.

Jess shook her head and eyed her father as he rose and wandered out of the kitchen. He looked at TillyTilly, who had come back again, as she sat waiting on the staircase. He looked *straight* at her, as if he saw her but didn't fully register what he saw, and Jess saw TillyTilly shrink up small against the wall as if something in his gaze frightened her. But neither Jess's father nor TillyTilly said anything, and after that split-second pause, Daniel padded into the sitting room.

"It's really quite strange because I had three packs of them: all gone." Her mother seemed about to continue, but was interrupted by the trilling of the telephone, which she rose to answer. After a second, "Jess, the bell tolls for thee," she announced from the hallway, beckoning Jess.

It was Siobhan, who was reminding her that she was coming over at five to spend the night.

"Oi," Shivs said, lowering her voice to a static crackle, "my dad doesn't really want me to come. He thinks . . . I dunno."
(I don't want you to come either, Shivs, but I do, but I don't.)

Jess had no time to force her voice over the drowning of her heart, because Shivs quickly filled in. "But then my mum told him not to worry, and that you're this really nice girl and properly brought up, and you're really good for me because you're all intelligent and stuff. So I'm still coming!"

"Oh," Jess managed to say.

"I dunno. I just thought I'd tell you. Um." The turn of Shivs's voice was tinted with remorse. "All right, see you then, yeah?"

"Yeah," Jess croaked, ignoring TillyTilly, who was stretched out over the ceiling like a grinning sheet.

Shivs shouted "BYE!" at the top of her voice and swiftly hung up.

Perturbed, Jess went and sat back down in the kitchen while her mum washed up and muttered aloud a brief list of things that needed to be fetched. She supposed that she shouldn't be surprised that TillyTilly knew how to use the phone: she knew how to do everything.

"I want to go to Nigeria for my birthday," she announced to her mother, who cheered her decision. It didn't matter if her grandfather did know the truth about what had happened to her father—though he hadn't mentioned her "thief friend" again—Jess had a feeling that he would also know how to make TillyTilly stop.

"We might have to leave your father behind in England, though," her mother told her.

"Want me to tell a ghost story?" Shivs said in a loud whisper, turning her torchlight into Jess's face.

Jess blinked furiously and only just managed not to fall out of the bed. It was a slightly uncomfortable squeeze with both of them on the single bed under two sets of covers, but she'd ignored the blow-up mattress that her mum had set up on the floor and insisted that they both sleep on her bed. She'd also reopened the bedroom door after Shivs had kicked it shut in her customary way, because she wasn't taking any risks whatsoever.

"No . . . no ghost stories," Jess told her, trying not to sneeze as a strand of Siobhan's hair encountered her cheek.

Shivs twisted restlessly around for a little while, then scratched her head.

"Why can't I sleep on the floor, anyway? You got mice or something?"

"Ewwww, no. I just . . . don't want you to pull my leg or anything in the night. I get scared."

"Awww, I won't, though! Let me sleep on the floor, please please please! I need room! I put my arms out and everything— I'd make you fall out!"

"No!"

"Awwww but I'm sleepy, Jess," Shivs complained. "And you won't even let me tell a ghost story to keep myself awake."

"If you complain any more," Jess said quietly, in a spooky voice, "I'm going to make you go downstairs and eat some more of those spicy prawns—I know there's some left . . ."

"Aargh," Shivs said, "shabby." She hadn't liked the spicy prawns at all, and Jess giggled aloud just thinking about Shivs's pop-eyed expression when she'd shovelled a forkful of prawns, mushrooms and rice in her mouth in defiance of Sarah's warning to "go slowly."

"Hah, you can't take your pepper," Jess's mum had said, shaking her head while Shivs jogged silently around the room gasping for air until she was taken upstairs to brush her teeth and tongue with Aquafresh. She'd had to have a burger and chips instead.

Shivs stopped wriggling and turned over so that her face was jammed into the pillow.

"G'night, then," she murmured. "S'not my fault if you end up on the floor."

Jess sat up a little bit and watched, grinning, as Shivs snuggled down farther, slipping her thumb into her mouth. It was OK, it would be OK. She only had to make sure that she watched Shivs all night. She couldn't sleep at all, she wouldn't sleep, she would fight TillyTilly to the last about this—

But, of course, she did eventually fall asleep, with her arm flung protectively over Siobhan's shoulder.

"Pssst! Wake up, Siobhan!"

Jess was calling her, she had to get up, and she had to go somewhere, didn't she? Yes, and quietly. Or was that the dream? Siobhan stretched, cracked her eyes open and peered about her.

Jess was nowhere to be seen; she had been calling from outside the room, but now she had gone.

"Siobhan, wake up!"

"Uhhhh—" Shivs wondered who had groaned, then realised that it was her. It was cold, her hands were cold; she didn't want to get out of bed, she wanted to go back to sleep, but she was worried about Jess, who wanted her to go somewhere. She half climbed, half fell out of bed, not feeling the roughness of the rug under her bare, numbed feet, and stumbled out of the bedroom door. There were no lights on anywhere, and her squinted eyes were taking an incredibly long time to become accustomed to the darkness.

"Jess?" she called softly, then waited. From somewhere downstairs, Jess giggled. Were they playing hide-and-seek? Shivs blinked and shook her head, feeling more wide awake. She started down the stairs, deciding not to call out any longer. Two could be cunning. Hesitating halfway down, she peered into the dark and tried to decide whether Jess would be in the sitting room or the kitchen. The sitting room—she would be hiding behind a chair. Putting a hand over her mouth so that she didn't laugh aloud, she began to tiptoe into the sitting room. Shivs was a little bit frightened in there, almost not quite daring to crawl around the sofa to find Jess. Jess wasn't there; the room was dark and felt like an open mouth—some sort of mist was moving through it, a pervading warmth, and the carpet seemed to ripple slightly under Shivs's feet, like a tongue.

All right, so now she was being silly, she told herself.

Her eyes had still not adjusted, and the shoulder of her loose nightie was slipping down her arm. Nervously, she tugged it up again.

"Shivs—" It was Jess again, and her voice was louder and more urgent. Now it sounded as if it was coming from *up*stairs.

How would she have done that, got upstairs again already?

Backing out of the sitting room, Shivs looked up the stairs to see Jess standing at the top, framed by a faintly incandescent brightness against the pitch black. It was strange, the way she looked, her features sharp and beautiful, as if there were a lantern burning under her skin. But she wasn't holding anything—no torch, no candle, nothing. This was a dream, it must be.

A strange expression crossed Jess's face and she looked over her shoulder at something behind her, her hand going up over her face before she turned back to Shivs. "Shivs, don't—"

There was a lifting, a jolting and a falling back into place as something *swung* in Siobhan's sight, and she immediately saw that Jess was not standing on the top step after all; there was another girl behind her. Only the shape, only the shape of another girl, but she didn't want to see her come into Jess's fierce light.

She had seen, but not quite seen. For a second, she thought that she wouldn't be able to move, that she'd never move again, but then her knees gave way, and, dropping down with her hands over her face, Siobhan tremblingly waited for everything to stop happening.

Someone came, and the someone touched her.

"It isn't really happening," Jess quavered from the staircase, watching Tilly Tilly and Siobhan running together, screaming without sound as they

(*or was it only Siobhan? or only Tilly?*)

threw Siobhan against the front door, against the walls, on the floor. Siobhan's body was twisting, her face shaped into a grimacing smile as she pranced jerkily into the sitting room with her nightie swirling out around her thin frame, then leapt back out as Jess breathlessly ran a little way down the stairs, and gripped the banister so tightly that it hurt her fingers. She didn't quite dare to try and stop Tilly now. It was some fearsome, grotesque dance: Siobhan tiptoeing and then dragging across the floor, her red hair falling out of its loose knot and over her shoulders as she spun into the kitchen, while TillyTilly, partially elevated in the dim light, was somehow *operating* her, although Jess couldn't see quite how: her hands were at Siobhan's back

(in her? above her? Oh, don't be in her, don't let TillyTilly have her hands jammed into my friend's body)

and Siobhan was gasping and laughing, and they all went into the kitchen and Siobhan/Tilly knew where the knife drawer was

(of course! of course!)

and Jess knew that she hated both of them when Siobhan started to hurt herself with the knife edge, because it was her fault and she was bleeding too and she couldn't stop.

Only apparently none of that happened. Because Siobhan had only fallen all the way down the stairs and broken the skin of her neck quite badly on the pointy end of the banister when it had inexplicably broken off. Just how, they didn't know. It didn't matter that all the knives were in the knife drawer, clean and untouched, and it didn't matter that when Jess had stopped screaming Siobhan was all in a heap on the bottom step, but it mattered that TillyTilly hadn't liked Shivs from the start. Only now could Jess tell her that it was OK that she couldn't keep a secret; she was a good friend now that she was going to die.

"Did you push her?" Sarah asked Jess after Dr. McKenzie had arrived and the ambulance had taken Shivs to the hospital. She sat in the living room with her hand over her mouth and kept saying aloud that she was trying to understand how Siobhan had taken such a serious fall, and what pressure a four-inch piece of strong wooden banister end would have to undergo to break and leave a jagged, spiking thing. Jess was bundled up in her mother's arms, her eyes closed, her breathing erratic. Her lips were almost blue. Her mouth was framing a word over and over again, the same word, sometimes slow, sometimes fast: "Tilly, Tilly, Tilly, Tilly, Tilly."

"Why can't you stop being angry, Jessamy?" Jess felt Sarah mumble into the shoulder of her nightie.

Jess replied, "Tilly, Tilly, Tilly, Tilly, Tilly."

Upstairs, Jess's father had been woken up by the commotion, and when Jess opened her eyes, she saw him step over the piece of banister that had fallen away and walk into the kitchen as if he hadn't seen it.

"Just forget all about it. It's over," TillyTilly said, somewhat petulantly from Jess's bedside. Jess, with the covers pulled up over her face, tried to breathe quietly, but her heart was fluttering, letting her know that it was not after all OK to be scared. She had given up on her safe place. There was no safe place after last Saturday night; nowhere was safe when downstairs Shivs had been forced to dance that clumsy dance in her pyjamas, lifting her feet high, so high, colliding with every surface until she went to hospital and was all white and still and not getting better. Everyone thought that she, Jessamy, had pushed Siobhan, and in a way she was glad to be blamed at last; it had been bound to happen, she couldn't have three people *got* and just get away with it, no way. She knew why Shivs's being *got* had been different from her father's—TillyTilly had not liked Shivs from the start, and Shivs had said that she wasn't scared of anything, but she should have been scared, trying to tell Jessamy that her own twin sister didn't like her. That's what TillyTilly was telling her now.

"You're not really allowed to go and see Siobhan in hospital," Jess's mum had told her, even though Jess hadn't asked. She knew that Dr. and Mrs. McKenzie wouldn't let her; they didn't think she was a *bad* girl, TillyTilly had told Jess during the fever-days following Shivs's being *got*. They just thought that Jess was very troubled, and she needed to see a new doctor. But that wasn't going to happen, because this time TillyTilly was going to look after her and make sure that she didn't have to see a new doctor and get in trouble all over again. Jess had accepted that while she was sick, but now she was better.

"You're a ghost," Jess whispered to TillyTilly from under the covers.

TillyTilly began to get angry.

"I'm not," she insisted. "I'm not a ghost! That's a dumb thing to say!"

"You are," Jess insisted, fainter now as she grew less certain.

"Jessy, I'm not a ghost! I am NOT a ghost."

Jess turned over, teeth gritted.

"What happened to your twin then?" she asked.

She heard TillyTilly breathing quietly, but no reply. Jess recalled Shivs's screaming and the stream of red-black.

"I don't know," TillyTilly said, her voice pressing soft into the dark.

"What?"

"I can't remember. All gone. Only my name—"

Oh, God. Only Titiola's name was left, and Jess had taken even that. It couldn't be, it couldn't be. How could you forget being ripped away from your twin?

"Ah, Jess, but you did," TillyTilly said aloud. "It's the ripping part that you forget first. It never comes back."

"TillyTilly, but you *are* dead, aren't you?" Jess pleaded, turning back towards the now indistinct form of her friend kneeling at the bedside. She timidly touched Tilly's hand. "I don't understand."

"No. Now forget, forget," TillyTilly said, pulling down the covers and touching Jess's forehead with her soft, brown hand. She was the long-armed woman now, and she smelt of coconuts.

Jess had her eyes closed and didn't open them, because then she fell deeply asleep and dreamt that she was flying, flying high above all the land, onward and onward, disappearing like a pin thrown into the blue. The rushing wind stung her eyes into slits, and her fluffy hair rippled out in sheets behind her, sometimes whipping in her eyes and lashing across her cheek. She would never fall, because her friend was flying with her and would catch her.

It was a blessing, even if she didn't know it—the remembering of so many things that were her fault being drained away from her by her sister, who had promised to take care of her. Memories were burdens that took Jessamy through three worlds of hurt, the three worlds that only twins inhabit, and she was only half a twin.

Yet even as she fell asleep, Jess was aware on some level that her memories were being moulded so that they were all different, and that Siobhan had not been dancing, but rolling, *bump bump bump*, from upstairs to down, terrible, she shouldn't have pushed her, why had she pushed her?

It was a hot day in June when Jess returned from the park through the back door into the kitchen, and noticed that there was an empty coffee cup in the sink.

It was her father's.

Puzzled but happy, she smiled, feeling as if this was somehow a gift. She dropped her mother's hand and ran through the kitchen and into the passageway, shouting, "Daddy?"

He was in bed, but that was OK. She wanted to tell Tilly, but she was nowhere to be found.

III

ONE

———

"Daddy, there were, like, ten people in that car!" Jess risked the gusty whirring of the air-conditioning on her face as she knelt up on the seat and gesticulated wildly at the battered light-blue Ford that had just pulled ahead of them on the road. The people were crammed inside the car so tight that from the back they looked like one dark mass, as if they had been mixed together and spread across the car windows. You could differentiate backs of heads and necks, but only eventually.

"Um, I think that's another cab," her father said doubtfully, fanning himself with a newspaper as he looked at her mother for verification.

"Yup! The police don't really care about that sort of stuff round here," Sarah told Jessamy, who was gaping as she tried to imagine being in the backseat with six or seven other people, all in a ball of sweat, elbows, knees and rough hair.

They were back in Lagos, two days before Jess's ninth birthday.

"The buses are worse," Sarah smiled, to loud guffaws from their cabdriver.

Daniel playfully dragged Jess back down into a sitting position on the seat and threw his arms around her. She briefly rested her head on his shoulder and twisted a few strands of his hair around her finger, delighting in his laughing "ouch," glad that he was here and real, and that his eyes and hands and movements were his own again. Then they were both laughing as Sarah told them (and the driver) a new story that her friend Yemi, who lived at Ojoo, had told in a letter she had written her. The roads entering and leaving the immediate vicinity of Ojoo were extremely bumpy and filled with potholes, and Yemi had written that a truck loaded with petrol had crashed just outside the town. The driver had managed to escape the entanglement relatively uninjured and flee the scene for assistance, the immediate result of which had been about thirty people ignoring imminent danger and running out with buckets to fill up on diesel for their electricity generators. If you could afford a generator in the first place, you could never have enough fuel for it, since NEPA was always in the throes of some system failure that meant no light, and petrol was very expensive. It was an irony, said the driver, nodding sagely, that in a country where the chief source of wealth was petrol, people were behaving as if they'd never seen it before. Sarah bitterly suggested government corruption and Daniel tentatively agreed, but with a pull in his voice as if he suspected that he might be laughed at for offering his opinion. The driver, sent from Bodija by Sarah's father, who had airily ignored her insistence that she could get a cab herself, laughed at both of them.

"Ah, no, that cannot be the reason," he said, casually checking the rearview mirror. "Our military boys are too honest for all of that now!"

Then all three adults sniggered in some mysterious solidarity that left Jess to wonder instead at the curious thought of a small crowd running out in flip-flop sandals to take what they needed, even if the taking might kill them.

The first person that she saw when the car had come in through the gates was Uncle Kunle, but his shouts of welcome as he helped Gateman to unload the suitcases were mainly for Jess's mother. It was Aunty Funke, in a dazzling blue-and-silver *boubou*, who, after greeting Daniel and Sarah, swooped on Jess, enfolding her in a big, soft embrace.

"Ah-ah! What is this, now? Are you sure this is Jessamy?" she teased, taking the by now diffidently smiling Jess by the hand and leading her into the house, where it was cooler. "Did someone come from the sky and just stretch you upwards and upwards?" Funke continued, making Jess laugh.

Inside, Ebun was as cool-faced as ever. Her hair, wrapped around and around in black thread, looped stiffly outwards from her scalp. She sat on a chair in the hallway, talking in unhurried Yoruba to the new houseboy, Kola, who stood at the ironing board set up against the wall, neatly sprinkling water from a small bowl onto a rumpled white shirt before setting about it with the hot iron. When Ebun saw them, she approached, smiling vaguely, hugged Jess and told her that she was welcome. Jess greeted all her cousins, even deigning to drop a kiss on the deferential Bose's cheek as the six-year-old stood before her with downturned eyes.

Then, impatient to find her grandfather, she ran out of the back of the house and up the outside stairs that led to the upper level, where the sleeping rooms, the kitchen and her grandfather's study were. In her haste she ran straight into the man that she was seeking, and she hissed with the pain of her nose bumping his arm as he stretched out to catch her.

"Wuraola! My own Wura-Wura! You are too much in a

hurry!" her grandfather laughed, picking her right up off the ground and patting clumsily at her nose. Jess shrieked exultantly as her grandfather spun her around, letting her go for a split-second before catching her again and putting her down.

"Daddy, she's too big for that," Sarah said half-heartedly, putting her head out from the parlour where she, Daniel and Biola were loudly catching up. She watched, smiling, as Gbenga beckoned to Jess and told her, "Wura! I have something to show you!" Jess took his hand and he walked her to his study, pausing to shout out, "Ebun and Tope! I trust that you are bringing minerals to the sitting room for everyone—" There was a rippling cheer from downstairs, and then Jess, smiling up at her grandfather, was led into the high-shelved, cream-and-brown-wallpapered study.

Jess had to reach out and steady herself on a shelf as the memory of TillyTilly impishly grinning in the chair by the big desk hit her with some force.

"See! It's a birthday present for you and your sister!" Her grandfather pushed her up towards the desk, where a small wooden statue sat. Jess tried to halt and snatched at her grandfather's big hand, because she didn't want to go near it. If Fern was supposed to look like her, then this statue didn't look anything like Fern. She couldn't imagine anyone being at peace because of this carving, with its long, heavy features and clasped hands. It looked too bulky and too light a brown, with some deeper brown blotches, as if it were covered in previously dark skin that had been bleached. The head seemed unnaturally pointy, and the sloping cheekbones and stylised, pupil-less eyes not glossy-book beautiful, but real and here before her, supposed to represent Fern but not. The only beautiful thing was the hair: the intricately chiselled pattern of braids pouring down over the shoulders. But even as a woman, neither she nor Fern could look like this, ever, ever, amen. Overflowing with a fear that now some could-have-been-would-have-been Fern would dog her thoughts and dreams, Jess turned quickly away from the statue and threw her arms around her startled grandfather's belted waist.

"Why didn't YOU tell me about Fern?" she whispered into his shirt.

Her grandfather put his hands on her shoulders. He sounded troubled.

"We don't do things that way, Wuraola. When someone dies, it's a special thing, almost secret. If someone dies badly or too young, we say that their enemy has died. There is no way to say these things directly in English. It's a bad thing for you to have lost your sister. She's half of yourself. That's why . . . you needed to be older to understand what it meant."

There was more to understand? Jess was tired of it all.

Her grandfather tipped her chin up so that she was looking at him.

"Wuraola," he said sternly, as if he was about to tell her off. Then he stopped.

"Yeah?"

"Wuraola."

He looked so serious that she grew worried.

"Yes, grandfather?" she tried, tightening her arms around him.

He shook his head and said again, slowly, deliberately, "Wuraola."

"Yes?"

"How many times did I call you?" he asked gravely.

"Three?"

"Three. Now tell me this truth: Who told you about Fern?"

Jess pulled away from him, stumbling out of the study and outside. He followed her, silent—did he have to follow her, holding her intently in his sights like some wise and stalking creature?

"I—I don't know. I can't remember," she stammered. It was almost true: she was forgetting so many things about TillyTilly, but she couldn't forget the baby that Tilly had taken from her arms, the baby who had been crying for such a long time until it was quiet and solemn, gazing with its tiny, crumpled face. To be remembered. Tilly didn't *need* to be remembered, but she wanted to be. Why? It was the same with Fern. But people forgot, they forgot, and it wasn't her fault. Jess's grandfather caught her up in his arms again when she tried to escape him and slide across the wall, wailing, with tears slipping from her as if they would never stop.

Later Jess could never remember the actual day of her ninth birthday.

Not even the morning part of it, when she woke up to Aunty Funke's yam and special egg

("Many, many, many happy returns of the day, Jessamy!")

and then helped her mum to put things outside, around the back of her grandfather's house, under a specially set out green-and-white canopy by the outside stairs. They had decided to do things Hobbit-style, and Jess and her mother had picked out presents for each of her cousins and for Uncle Kunle, Aunty Biola and Aunty Funke, and a big, hardback secondhand anthology of African poets for her grandfather that her mother had found in a small bookshop. The night before, her cousins Akin and Taiye had been bullied into bringing out a table from each of the sitting rooms to join the ones that the canopy people had provided, even though they'd protested that someone might steal the tables, and that it would have been better to put them out the next morning.

"Let me see the face of the man who would steal my tables," her grandfather had said scornfully.

Jess didn't feel nine. She didn't feel any age; she never had. The joined tables were facing the Boys' Quarters, and every now and then Jess glanced at them, squinting at the windows, trying to see if she could see someone moving. No one was. She wasn't sure if even TillyTilly would dare to risk her grandfather's wrath now that her hiding place (and her candle-stealing antics) had been discovered. Jess had to bend and slap at her ankle as a fly attempted to nestle in the mosquito bite on her leg, and Sarah turned to Daniel, who had just brought out a stack of the rented white plastic chairs, and said, "We need to get something to keep these flies away—"

"Don't ask me, it's your country . . ."

"Ha ha!"

Jess peered at the array of chairs that her mother and father were putting out.

"Why are there so many chairs?" she wondered aloud, crouching down on the sandy ground. That was when she realised that TillyTilly was there, actually there, kneeling under the end table, gazing at her seriously. She was barefoot and wearing her net-curtain dress again, but her hair was loose, fanning dark and blowsy over her shoulders and back. She looked like some sort of shantytown princess.

But Tilly couldn't really be here; there was something in the dimensions of her that made her look like one of the paper cutouts that Jess had snipped from the books in Year Five— creasable and thin at the edges. Jess didn't hear her mother's cheery reply.

"There are loads of people coming to see us, Jess—people who just missed us last time. You know . . . cousins and sub-cousins and random friends and whatnot . . ."

"Surprise!" TillyTilly mouthed, beginning to crawl towards Jess.

Jess didn't like her eyes, they were wide and glaring, as if the gap between eyelid and eyelid had been pushed so far that it would never close, and they would never fully meet. Why did she look like this? Jess began to hurry out from under the table as she recalled the last thing that she had heard her mother say. It seemed (wrongly) as if she'd only just finished saying it, only just said, "I'm just going to go and give Aunty Funke's *jollof* rice a stir so I can say I helped to make it—"

Oh, TillyTilly and time.

"Happy birthday!" Tilly's voice sounded manically bright as she came out from under the table and dusted down her dress, her eyes fixed on Jess. "Happy birthday to you, Jess, and to Fern."

Jess turned and began scrambling up the stone stairs.

"Time to swap!" Tilly cried. "I did my share, I *got* everyone you wanted me to! I want to be alive, too!"

"Mummy. Mummy—"

"I said HAPPY BIRTHDAY," TillyTilly yelled, dragging at Jess's ankles.

Jess let out a piercing scream and struggled against the hands that seemed made of steel as she tumbled down step by step, hard stone grazing her knees into ridged flaps of skin. A balloon came loose from the canopy and drifted past Jess's desperately flailing hands. It was a stinging yellow, Jess's least favourite colour. It spun in her vision, that yellow balloon.

"You shouldn't have come back here," TillyTilly told her, before Jess fell
(down far, as her father might have said before he got better)
so sudden, so sudden . . . she hadn't known it could get this BLACK, and both she and TillyTilly were screeching "Happy Birthday!" as they fell and fell, but this time they didn't crash

against the earth as they had before—TillyTilly landed safely somewhere, and Jess just kept on flying. She'd shed her body as if it was some shell that the sea roars through, and yes, she'd said she wanted to fly, but she hadn't meant it, not like this, not when she was soaring *through* things.

Her grandfather was shouting "*Wuraola! Wuraola!*" But the sound was warped and all wrong. It was a distorted voice down a long-distance line, soon to be cut off by flat beeping.

Sarah propped Jessamy up on a chair, tutting.

"What's the matter with you? All this screaming again?"

Jessamy's grandfather was hovering around in the background behind her, having come running down the stairs, slipperless and shouting his head off, and they both breathed a sigh of relief as Jess rubbed her poor ankle (the same one that had the open mosquito bite on it) and whined, "I fell down the stairs. It huu-uuurts!"

Her cheeks were deeply flushed and her eyes startlingly lightened by the sun's beams so that they looked more golden than hazel. And the end of her fluffy ponytail was dishevelled, but that was all, that was all. She was even trying to smile, though her mouth seemed loosened and was shaking.

"Well, there was no need to scream like that! I mean, Jesus on toast, Jess, it frightened me! *Happy Birthday, Happy Birthday*," Sarah mimicked, in a high, girlish voice, forgetting that this had sent spikes of unease shooting down her back when she'd first heard it.

"Sorry," Jess said, then scrambled off Sarah's lap as Aunty Biola came down the stairs carrying the enormous birthday cake.

"Cake! Cake!" she said, merrily, bouncing around in Aunty Biola's path as her aunt smilingly tried to outmanoeuvre her so that she could get safely to the table. It was like a frenzy in her; Jess was jumping as high as she could manage, gleefully attempting to poke the cake, which Biola was holding higher and higher until the cake was in danger of toppling off its silver platter.

"*O ya*, stop that, now," Jess heard her grandfather bark out from behind her. Sarah looked on in bafflement as Jess and her grandfather levelly met each other's eyes, Jess's expression suddenly sullen as she moved out of the relieved Biola's way. Her father may have sternly told her off many times, but Sarah had never heard him speak this way to his Wuraola. She shrugged, reminding herself that Jess needed antiseptic for her knees, then began following Biola up to the kitchen, followed by Jess, who skipped up the stairs after them. She passed her grandfather without a glance, even though he frowned at her all the way up the stairs.

And as evening fell and Jess stood on her chair so that she was better able to blow out the candles on the enormous pink-and-white cake that Aunty Funke had made, Sarah leaned back into Daniel's arms and watched thoughtfully as Jess, surrounded by a blur of smiling faces, cheers and clapping (and the soft smacking of balloons together as Bose and Femi attacked each other), blew out all the candles in one gusty puff and clapped her hands delightedly as she sang loudly along,
(HAPPY BIRTHDAY TO YOOOO)
finally smiling contentedly, because even if Jess's voice did seem a little nasal (did she have some kind of fever coming on? it couldn't possibly be malaria already), she was happy, at last.

Reclining on a sofa in the downstairs living room, Daniel was watching Sarah, Bose and Femi munch contentedly on the firm sweetness of sugarcane, plucking back the green with their fingers to reveal the creamy yellow-white that left gluey juices on their hands and clothes. Sarah's father had sent for the sugarcane, but aside from Daniel, he was the only person in the room not eating it. Instead, half lying on the opposite sofa with his eyes closed, he was nodding occasionally in response to what Sarah was saying. A newspaper was on his lap as he ruminatively chewed on half a bitter kola nut, which he occasionally dipped into a small bowl of yellow salt that was set beside him. Bose and Femi were pushing trucks around on the floor in between their sugarcane eating activities, hers yellow and with a broken windscreen, his blue with the PepsiCo logo on the side.

Sarah changed to English. Daniel drooped for a few minutes longer under the unrelenting sun flowing in through the open, uncurtained window, then got up and put the setting on the fan to high. To his amazement, Sarah, who had been in the middle of explaining the plotline of her children's story to her father, stopped, complaining to him, "Aw, why? It's all cold now!"

"What?!"

Sarah began an exchange which they both knew would inevitably end in Daniel's switching the fan power back to medium, but was interrupted by her father suddenly opening his eyes and saying, "Bisi-mi. When was the last time that you prayed?"

Discomfited, Sarah glanced at Daniel, who put his hands up to show that it wasn't his situation.

"I can't remember," she said at last. "It was probably recently, though," she added hopefully.

Gbenga Oyegbebi shook his head and closed his eyes again.

"Eh heh, so I see that you are now too big a writer to say any prayers. There's nothing God can do for you."

Daniel began to feel alarmed, hoping that there wasn't going to be an argument right before his eyes. Where had this come from, anyway? Hopefully, he waited for the discussion to slip into Yoruba, but it didn't. Evidently his father-in-law wanted him to hear this.

"Daddy, you know that's not true," Sarah said, calmly

enough, wrapping the remains of her sugarcane in some news-paper that she had gestured to Bose to bring from Gbenga's lap. Gbenga laughed quietly and dipped another corner of the kola nut into the salt, still without opening his eyes.

"Bisi, I am your father. You think I don't know why you don't want to pray, but I'm telling you now that you're wrong. Think on Jesus! Think on him so that you don't start thinking only of yourself, going inwards and inwards until there is no life outside of Bisi—"

Daniel heard the strained tone in his wife's voice; she was checking herself so that she didn't disrespect her father, much in the same way that she restrained her quick anger when she spoke to anyone important.

"Daddy. I don't think only of myself, I assure you. How much does it matter whether I pray or not?"

Sarah's father shook his head and clicked his tongue. "Bisi, how could you, now? You know that when you pray, you are heard, if not by God, then by yourself. When you pray, you tell yourself what you truly want, what you really need. And once you know these things, you can do nothing but go after them. *Sae* you understand?"

Sarah flicked an embarrassed gaze at Daniel as Bose and Femi, apparently not liking the seriousness of the conversation, crawled out of the room in a spectacular truck chase, making growling motor noises under their breath.

"Daddy, I'll try and pray."

"Try, oh! Believe in curses, believe in miracles, believe, be-lieve, believe in these things even if you don't see them happen. Remember, I am your father. And I tell you, forget about the face of Jesus."

The face of Jesus?

Daniel looked at Sarah for clarification, but she was reeling with surprise.

She opened her mouth, then closed it, opened it again.

"How—?"

"Where is your daughter?" Sarah's father interrupted her.

The whirring of the fan came to an unexpected halt, accompanied by Funke's shout from the kitchen: "Up, up, Jesus! Down, down, NEPA!"

And all three of them laughed, curses, miracles and the face of Jesus carried away on the humid air.

The next day Sarah was sitting in the kitchen with Funke and Biola, deliberating the merits of bread and butter over the "arduous" efforts of *akara*.

"Hah! Arduous! Big writer word! *Akara* is only arduous to you, Bisi," Funke snorted, with the supreme confidence of a woman who has no fear of her kitchen. "I already soaked and grated plenty of beans and put them in the freezer. I can take them out and blend them and make *akara* whenever I want."

"Well, good for you," Sarah told her. "I just hope that one day you don't run out of oil for the generator, because when those NEPA devils cut off the electricity again, what would happen to your precious beans then?"

Bose skidded into the kitchen, the sleeves of the blue shirt of Akin's that she'd decided to wear floating out around her arms. "Aunty Bisi, Aunty Bisi, Jessamy can speak Yoruba!"

Conversation came to a surprised halt as Sarah laughed aloud and Biola reached out and grabbed Bose, tickling her until she screamed.

"Ha, Bose, no! Jessamy is our very own *Iya Oyinbo!*"

"*Irọ, irọ,*" Bose chortled, before breaking away and pointing to the upstairs sitting room a few doors away. "Ebun is teaching her!"

She leapt excitedly in the air, in expectation that her statement would be verified when Jess, squealing with laughter, was jostled into the kitchen by Ebun and Tope, who attempted to cajole her into saying a few words in Yoruba. She would not.

Sarah leaned forward and caught Jess's hands, bringing her closer. "*Kilo de?*" she asked. "What's the matter?"

Jess tipped her head to the side and peeped shyly at Sarah from under her eyelids. The sun had struck her irises liquid gold again. She took a deep breath.

"*Ko si nkan-nkan,*" she replied at length, capturing the accent and even the lift in tone perfectly.

Ebun, Tope and Bose crowed in delight. "It's nothing! She said, 'It's nothing!' "

Sarah nearly fell off her chair in bewilderment. "That's wonderful!" she cried, once she'd taken a second to recover herself. "What else can you say? Go and say something to your father!"

She could just imagine Daniel's face; his nine-year-old daughter picking up a language in minutes. It was so strange, though! But maybe Jess had picked up more language than she had been aware of on the last visit. Jess nodded at her suggestion, but first moved across the kitchen and climbed onto Aunty Funke's lap.

"Aunty Funke, *ẹ jọọ, mo fẹ akara,*" Jess said to her aunt, who had a hand over her heart and was laughing fit to burst.

"Of course you can have *akara!*" Funke told Jessamy, before darting a triumphant look at Sarah and adding: "I have beans ready frozen!"

"Hah! But Jessamy, where is *Iya Oyinbo?*" Biola teased Jess, as Daniel came into the kitchen, sleepily rubbing the back of his head, to find out what all the commotion was about.

Before Sarah could explain properly, her father added his part to the enquiry.

"Ah-ah! Is there a party? Are musicians coming to town, or what is it?" Gbenga called grumpily from the kitchen doorway. No one had heard him coming. His steel-grey hair was flattened to his head, and he had a red-and-yellow towel wrapped with a thick loop around his waist, cutting off the rough shirt that he slept in so that it bulged outwards. Jessamy slid off Funke's lap and crawled quietly under the table as everyone in the room strove to be the first to tell him.

"I taught Jess Yoruba," Ebun said, proudly, pushing Tope when she disagreed, clamouring, "No, I did, I did!"

Jess's grandfather moved into the kitchen, and Biola vacated her chair, which was nearest to the door, so that he could sit down. He rubbed his chin thoughtfully.

"Eh-heh, so you taught Wuraola Yoruba. Let her come and talk to her grandfather then!"

"Good point. Where is she?" Daniel asked, leaning heavily on the back of Sarah's chair as he yawned.

The cousins looked at each other, nonplussed, but Sarah bent a little in her chair as her eyes swept the darkness under the table set against the wall; she could see Jess's bright eyes peering watchfully at her.

"Hmmm," she said, motioning to Funke to pull her daughter out from under there, which she did with difficulty due to Jess's subdued protestations and struggle.

"Ah-ah! What's wrong with you?" Funke asked, presenting Jess to her grandfather. He watched her calmly, his chin in his hands.

"*Fi mi sile, Baba Gbenga, fi mi le, e joo,*" Jess moaned faintly, still writhing in Funke's firm grip, before Gbenga had even said anything. She fell silent when he started back in his chair and then looked around the room at everyone—at Ebun, who was saying, "Ha! I hadn't even taught her that yet," and at Sarah, who was now mystified and slightly uneasy, and even at Daniel, who was gazing at Jess with mixed pride and concern. Then he stood up and shook a finger at Jess with an expression of anger crossing his face, one familiar to Sarah *(You this girl! I know what to do for you!)* and left the room, hastily retying his towel as it began to slip around his hips. Sarah had to hold herself down in her seat to prevent herself from running after him, propelled by her sudden, unjustifiable but implacable fear that he was going to fetch his belt *(Ah he wouldn't, he couldn't, not to his granddaughter?)* and when she looked around at Biola and Funke, she saw with part relief and part dismay that she wasn't the only one who was forcing herself to stay still.

"Why did you tell your grandfather to leave you alone, now?" Funke was asking Jess, holding on to her shoulders and looking keenly into her face.

"We never talk to our elders like that, Jessamy," Biola added, as Tope, Bose and Ebun fled, giggling, to spread the word to the other cousins. "It looks as if *Iya Oyinbo* has not gone *too* far away after all—"

Sarah couldn't restrain herself any longer and hurried out of the kitchen to knock on her father's bedroom door.

"Eh," he said, by way of an invitation for her to enter. She opened his door to find that he had speedily dressed, Western-style in brown, belted trousers and a white shirt and was now putting his shoes on. He grunted but didn't say anything when he saw her, instead picking up his wallet from the dresser and putting it into the pocket of his trousers. She spoke to him in English, trying to calm him down. He looked impassive, but his movements told her that he was agitated. Why?

"Daddy. Where are you going?"

"Nowhere."

"Daddy—"

"Why are you asking me where I am going? Are you now my parent, or what is it?"

"I just—"

"I am not old enough for those roles to change, Bisi. *O ya,* move aside."

She trembled, but stayed where she was, and he drew back in disbelief.

"I don't want you to be angry with my daughter. I don't know what's the matter with her, but . . ."

"Bisi."

"Daddy!"

"Where is your daughter?"

"Daddy, what do you mean?"

"Bisi."

"Daddy?"

"I said, where is your daughter?"

She knew better than to answer "in the kitchen"—his temper was beginning to sound clear in his voice. She hovered in front of him, buying time.

"I'm going to find Iya Adahunse," he said

"Iya Adahunse! Why?" Disbelief rang high and loud in Sarah's voice.

"For Wuraola."

"For—?"

"Who's Iya Adahunse?" Daniel said from behind Sarah, stumbling awkwardly over the name. Sarah didn't look at him, maintaining fierce and steady eye contact with her father as she tried to understand his concern.

"She's . . . kind of . . . traditional . . . like a sort of medicine woman."

Daniel paused.

"What d'you mean, traditional? D'you mean a witch doctor?" he asked, turning Sarah around to face him. His expression was incredulous, his eyes thinning to blue-green slits as he looked at her askance.

Sarah didn't reply but tried to twist out of his grip as she reached out to her father, who had by now strode out of his room and was heading purposefully down the stairs. She was conscious of Biola and Funke standing in the kitchen, unsure whether or not to intervene.

"A witch doctor? My daughter isn't having anything to do with a witch doctor," Daniel insisted, now letting go of Sarah and starting after Gbenga. "Jesus, what's going on? She learns a bit of Yoruba and now she needs to see a witch doctor?" he shouted after Sarah's father.

"Don't follow me!" Gbenga warned him loudly.

"Don't make the mistake of thinking that this is something that you know anything about. Bisi, warn your husband, oh! Warn him not to follow me!"

"Don't you warn me! I'm warning you! You're insane! INSANE! One minute you're telling her to think on Jesus and the next you're calling a witch doctor!"

"INSANE?!" Sarah's father roared.

Desperately, Sarah ran into the kitchen with her heartbeat thumping loudly in her ears. Pushing Funke aside, she scooped Jess up into her arms before running to the top of the stairs so that both men could see her. Jess was heavy, and it was awkward to get a hold on her.

"I'm going away," she shouted, clutching Jess's soft, quivering body to her own. "I'm taking Jess away. I'm not having her around the two of you, fighting with each other!" She didn't even know what she was saying. Jess tightened her arms around

Sarah's neck, snuffling with terror, and Sarah found the impetus to keep shouting into the dumbfounded silence that she had created.

"Daddy, Jess isn't seeing Iya Adahunse, she isn't! Yes, you're my father, but I'm her mother, and nothing's the matter with her! Daniel, my father isn't insane! I've had enough of both of you— I'm going to my room, with Jess, and tomorrow morning, we're going to stay with Toyin in Lagos. Biola, call Toyin and tell her to expect me," she said recklessly, spinning around and half running to her and Daniel's bedroom before depositing Jess on the bed and slamming the door shut.

Sitting up on the bed, Jess reached out her arms to her mother, her entire body racked with the shudders of impending tears.

"Mummy—"

Sarah went to her, cuddled her, stroked her hair, trying to think clearly, trying not to become upset herself.

"I won't speak Yoruba again if you don't want," Jess offered quietly, mumbling into Sarah's hair.

Sarah stroked her back and managed a laugh.

"It's not your fault, Jess, don't worry. We'll just . . . go to Lagos for a couple of days and come back when your father and your grandfather have cleared up their silly fight."

The men were still shouting at each other. Gbenga sounded amazed that Daniel had dared to challenge him.

"I love you," Jess whispered, patting gently at Sarah's hair, and Sarah, surprised, pulled Jessamy down a little so that she could look at her properly, at the tears that were drying on her face. Big eyes, so light a hazel.

"Don't cry anymore, Jess," she said faintly.

TWO

———

In the morning, a hot morning, like any other in this place, news was brought to the Oyedele compound at Bodija.

There had been a car crash on the road to Lagos. A brown sedan, swerving near Mowe with its fender half falling off, eventually collided with jarring force with another car, Toyin's husband's car, in which Jessamy and Sarah were riding. There had been a car crash. On the road. To Lagos. Jessamy, stubbornly unseatbelted in the backseat, flung madly around as the car soared off the road and spun into the bushes, like a bumper car gone wrong and mad and dangerous. The pileup of cars, furiously beeping, the shouting on the tarmac as the occupants of the sedan leapt out and ran around frantically in the middle of the road, clutching the backs of their heads. Even in small pieces, it was hard for Daniel to assimilate. He sat in the backseat of the car, staring at the small, square hat perched on the head of his father-in-law's driver, trying not to think of Jessamy knocked unconscious, blood trickling everywhere, blood on glass, glassy blood, Sarah screaming . . . No, no, Sarah wouldn't scream, she wasn't a screamer. But Jessamy was. Jessamy was a screamer, wasn't she? He wished that he could focus on the hat. Gbenga sat silent beside him, smelling sourly and faintly of camphor and sweat, holding a large, dark-blue drawstring bag on his lap. Daniel had no idea what was in it (didn't care), but it leapt on Gbenga's lap every time the car bumped on the road. Jess's grandfather was looking straight ahead, thoughtful, as if he was daydreaming. *(Don't you daydream when my daughter's hurt, you crazy bastard.)* The driver's hat had wavy green thread patterns woven into it, but Daniel couldn't follow the waves, he couldn't concentrate on the hat. Oh, and how *appropriate* was it that there was now even more traffic than usual on the long, long, endless, strange drive from Ibadan to Lagos, to St. Mary's Hospital. He didn't want those roadside vendors to approach the car, because he didn't want to have to cope with the joy of crushing their questing fingers in the inexorable rolling up of the car windows. Car crashes happened everywhere, but if his daughter was dead he would hold this country responsible.

At the hospital, Sarah clung to Daniel, refusing to let him go into the private room where Jessamy lay, a motionless mass of tubes and brown flesh and sad green hospital gown, not a girl at all, rather a congruence of pain. She had to apologise to him first: it was all her fault; her stupid way of handling conflict had made this happen. She had thought that either he wouldn't listen to her, or that he would agree, but to her surprise, he did neither. He listened sprawled in a chair up against the wall, nodding distractedly as behind his glasses his eyes took in the rest of the people moving around the building: doctors and nurses in dusty white coats; a squat, severe looking woman in green *iro ati buba* arriving with a bowl of home-cooked food. He told her that it didn't matter about blame. She didn't know that Daniel didn't want to go in anyway; he was delaying the dreaded entry for as long as possible. Jess might be OK, Sarah told him, Dr. Adenuga had said that she might be OK. Daniel asked if Jess had regained consciousness since they'd taken her out of the car, and Sarah was forced to tell him no. "Might, might be OK," Daniel repeated in an expressionless voice that mocked all her hopes. They were talking about fractures and damage and things, but it wasn't a thing that she could comprehend because it didn't sound like anything that could happen to a child. Children weren't hurt like that.

Jess's grandfather seemed to be dealing with it in his way, though; he had hardly greeted Sarah, instead pushing past her and insisting on seeing the doctor treating Jessamy, who was a friend of his, battling to be allowed into Jess's room. Once there, unknown to both Sarah and Daniel, after ignoring the stare of the nurse by the bed and looking blankly at this unrecognisable granddaughter with her face silhouetted over a metallic neck brace, Jess's grandfather took Fern's heavy *ibeji* statue out of the drawstring bag he had brought with him and, confident that Dr. Adenuga's instructions for it not to be moved would be obeyed, put it in the far corner where it could watch.
And when he'd gone, the *ibeji* statue
(dull, unbelieved-in wood)
guarded the corner for the little twin who needed its help
needed the forgiveness it brought
needed to *win*
more than ever.

The Bush. A wilderness. A wilderness for the mind.

She had expected this place that Tilly and her mother had told her about
(sometime when she had been real . . . long time ago)
to be dry and arid, and for a little while it was—dried out, crackling vegetation moving past her while she stood still, some wild

animal calling to her in its own pulsating tongue *hmmmm-mzzzzzzeeeeeeee*, that Jessamy Harrison was a little girl who was going to die.

Why? she had asked, crying out and out and out until her voice became scratched and hoarse and she thought it would dry up and die too. There had been no reply. Why did anyone ever die? Punishment or gift?

It was a wilderness here and Jess had been getting lost and beginning to despair that she'd ever find her way out until *someone* came and bore her away on their back, away, but still not home. Not home, never home, no. She had stopped flying and had fallen a long time ago, and didn't know the way. Sometimes the person carrying her was Siobhan, red hair brilliant against the delicate white of her naked skin; only she knew it wasn't Siobhan really. Siobhan was still dancing somewhere, unable to stop until the bad fairy said so.

"We're nearly there," Siobhan-who-wasn't had kept saying to her, but they never were. Sometimes it was TillyTilly, but not very often, because TillyTilly could only come when she was asleep in Jess's body; she could only come in the dreamtime.

"You have to stay here for a long time, Jessy," TillyTilly would say when she came, and then Jess would try and fight her, scratch her, beat at her, crying that she had to let Jess swap back. But TillyTilly would laugh and throw Jess off, cartwheeling away into the sandstorm that whipped Jess's lips and made her eyes small pools of hopeless, grainy yellow. Whoever it was that really came and helped her, they didn't have a proper name. They wouldn't speak to her, or let her see their face, and Jess learnt to be carried in silence. Oh, Tilly and time. Tilly and space, too.

There had been a jolt, some kind of slamming both inside and out, and Jess now began to see a way to return.

Jess's vision blurred as she and the silent girl stumbled into the mouth of a leafy green clearing. Things were growing, different from the dead land before. Wheezing, holding her side at the sudden change of air, Jess was tempted just to let herself fall, but the thick, wet, brown sludge that was underfoot repulsed her, and instead she peered cautiously about her. Away from the unchanging russet tones that she had become accustomed to, it was difficult to see, and the trees ahead seemed to catch the light coming from where she stood, yet without throwing it up before her so that she could see farther. The way was dim, and she could hear a distant noise, like water running, but then again maybe like a bird calling through the spaces between the trees, the sound changing until it was deep and liquid.

She heard her name.

"Wuraola!"

Above the faint but insistent dripping, she heard her name, a resonant whisper, the word so transformed that she stood for a second transfixed before realising that somebody there really was calling her.

She listened again, thinking herself mistaken, but there was no repeat.

She paused for a second, thinking fast, moistening her lips, which had dried again with fear.

SHOULD she? Go?

Should she go?

Her head felt heavy, as if it was wobbling with ungainly weight at the top of her neck, which had become slender, like a flower stem, in proportion to her skull. She could feel the air cycling out through her nostrils as if it, the air, was alive, and her body was doing nothing to help her breathe. She tried to retain her fear, but could not even hold on to that. Everything seemed fuzzy. If she did not go forward, the sludge underfoot would claim her for sure. Soooo tired. And the way not to be tired was ahead, where somewhere, the sound of her name still lingered like the memory of light at the base of a glass lantern.

"Can I go?" she asked the girl on whose back she had come this far.

The girl bowed her head but didn't reply. Her hair was dark and matted, tangled with leaves and small, broken branches. Jess climbed off her back and tottered before she placed a hand on a tree trunk to steady herself and thanked the girl. The girl didn't answer her, but shook her head sorrowfully and drew Jess close so that she was gazing silently into her face.

Jess realised with a feeble, drowsy awe that she was looking at herself. Face, unsmiling lips, eyes full of the dark that she'd found in the midst of the wilderness. And small, tiny: the beautiful details of baby hair growing in as fuzz at the start of the forehead, away from the knotted hair.

She was wrong, the silent girl told her with a slow shake of the head. Not . . . herself.

It's . . . her.

Jess had to adjust her thanks. The feeling of having to do this was precious and easily bruised, like a tender, budding thing that could grow or fail and die, depending on the whim of the earth. It couldn't die, it mustn't, not after all this, how could it?

She believed in the fatal flaw.

"You can share my name," she promised, not even knowing now if she was speaking aloud, if she could or should to this girl, who had held her without hands.

Ah, and the girl was gone . . . she had dissolved and dissipated as if she had been taken away into the sky in a stream of light, sprinkled brown. Upwards. There was a mist spiralling into clear blue light, breaking away into smaller puffs the higher it went. Jess gazed and gazed at the sapphire lid of this place, dreaming of what it meant . . .

Wuraola . . .

Jess moved forwards, slowly, feeling as if she was wading through treacle, or honey, maybe, thick and clouded. She was going to *get* TillyTilly, and Tilly was big, and strong, and more than just a little girl whose twin had died. Tilly was the sun, and the storm cloud that blotted it out. But there was a sister-girl now, one who could now call herself Wuraola where true names were asked for. Jess charged onwards, stamping on leaves both brittle and wet, feeling them crack in her spine, but smiling ferociously, smiling transfigured, overstepping big, gnarled tree roots and not falling down, oh, not now.

It was TillyTilly who had been calling her, thinking that she could win again, but when Jess faced the girl who was at once too tall and too short, blotting out the trees, her long arms reaching out hungrily, her thick black hair flying out in all directions, she wasn't afraid. And because Jess wasn't afraid, Tilly was. The glue in the air dried and cracked.

"Don't, Jessy, please," TillyTilly pleaded in a scream that rang in Jess's ears, but Jess ran at her with the wind, an invisible current of fast-moving air behind her, taking her feet nearly off the slippery ground (she didn't hear the silent sister-girl telling her that it wasn't the right way, not
the right way at all)
and
hopped,
skipped,
jumped
into Tilly's unyielding flesh as she clawed at Jess's presence
(it hurt them both burningly)
back into herself.

Jessamy Harrison woke up and up and up and up.

PRAISE OF THE LEOPARD *(Yoruba)*

Gentle hunter
his tail plays on the ground
while he crushes the skull.
Beautiful death
who puts on a spotted robe
when he goes to his victim.
Playful killer
whose loving embrace
splits the antelope's heart.

ACKNOWLEDGEMENTS

DAH (DAVID GIBBONS) because this novel wouldn't have happened, none of it, if it wasn't for you.

FIFI (RAFIF AL-RUHAIMI), my first girlina-fan, partly because you missed your stop on the Tube whilst reading a story of mine (how cool!), and partly because you charmed/bullied me into writing more.

KITTY (CATHERINE UMEH), that Ibo girl, and **LEE-LEE (LIDIA DE FREITAS)** of the CVMS Paperclip Klan—you've both been amazingly encouraging, and because you put up with my bitter tirades against everyone who dared to be having a life whilst I wrote *The Icarus Girl*.

JON-O-FUN (JONATHAN JAMES) for the same, and also 'cause you're, like, a total dude. Plus . . . you joined in my rants against peanut butter.

JENNY WILLIAMS because you're kind to everyone, including me, when they need it most.

ROBIN WADE for your friendship, and also because you're a wicked literary agent.

ALEXANDRA PRINGLE because I'm so glad my first novel was edited by someone who is sensitive to what I'm trying to say. Also, you are so much fun! (Hey, thanks for taking me to that educational reading, Alexandra . . .)

LORNA OWEN and ANTONIA TILL, that fierce Helen-critic (haha), who both engaged so startlingly with Jess's world.

A NOTE ON THE AUTHOR

HELEN OYEYEMI was born in Nigeria in 1984 and moved to London when she was four. She is a student of social and political sciences at Corpus Christi College, Cambridge. Her first play, *Juniper's Whitening*, was staged at Cambridge in May 2004 and recently published by Methuen in the U.K.; *The Icarus Girl* is her first novel.

A NOTE ON THE TYPE

This book was set in a digital revival of Bembo. It was originally designed by the Bolognese type cutter Francesco Griffo (1450–1518), who worked for the celebrated Italian Renaissance printer and publisher Aldus Manutius. Manutius had commissioned Griffo to design a new typeface for the 1495 publication of a small treatise, *De Aetna*, by classicist Pietro Cardinal Bembo about his visit to Mount Etna. The typeface is named in his honor. Griffo also cut early italics, music types, and is attributed with cutting the first roman types with which we are now familiar. Along with Garamond, Bembo is considered one of the first "old-style" typefaces. During the early sixteenth century the French type founder Claude Garamond used Bembo as his model for his own widely popular typefaces. For this reason Bembo is generally acknowledged to be the foundation and standard for old-style typefaces. The modern version of Bembo was redesigned in 1929, under the supervision of the British typographer and printing historian Stanley Morison for the Monotype Corporation. Highly regarded as one of the most readable text faces, each stroke of Bembo's letterforms are characterized by moderation, clarity, and balance of proportion, enduring as a classic until today.